Weed War.

Tony Sharples

US English Edition

Contact email: sharples.writer@gmail.com

www.tonysharples.com

ISBN: 978-1-7636554-0-9

DISCLAIMER

This is a work of fiction. Unless otherwise indicated, all the names, characters, businesses, places, events and incidents in this book are either the product of the author's imagination or used in a fictitious manner. Any resemblance to actual persons, living or dead, or actual events is purely coincidental.

References to some locations, botanical references, military references, references to the drug trade and some events are real, but are not intended to be accurate depictions of reality.

One day I found myself pondering a strange thought.

*What would happen if we all woke up one day
and weed had disappeared from the face of the earth?*

The result is this story.
I've had massive fun writing it,
and hope you have just as much fun reading it.

This book is dedicated to my wife Nellie
for putting up with my constant creative tangents over the years.
More to come!

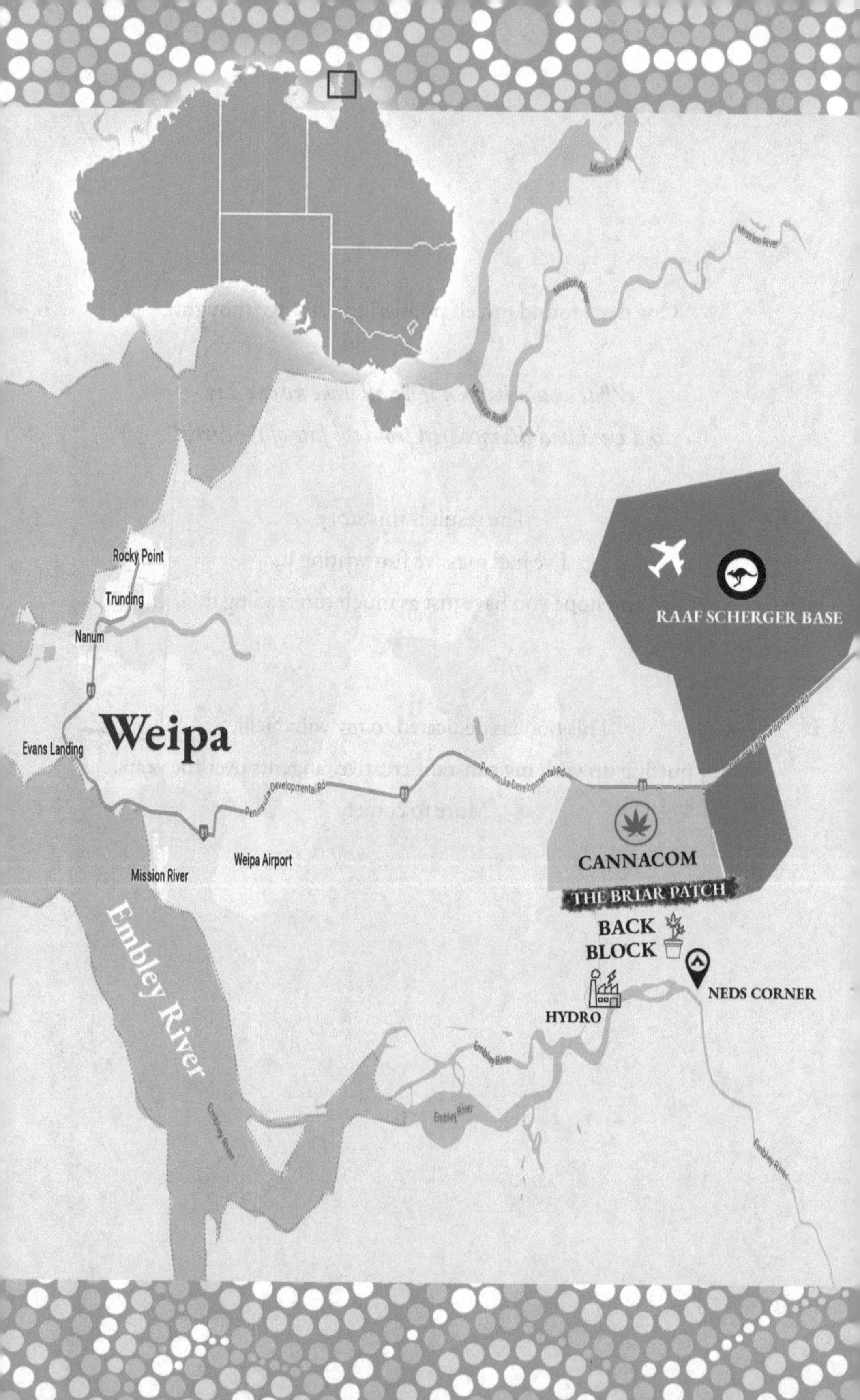

Mission River
Mission River
Mission River
Mission Rd
RAAF SCHERGER BASE
Rocky Point
Trunding
Nanum
Weipa
Evans Landing
Peninsula Developmental Rd
Peninsula Developmental Rd
Developmental Rd
Mission River
Weipa Airport
CANNACOM
THE BRIAR PATCH
BACK BLOCK
NEDS CORNER
HYDRO
Embley River
Embley River
Embley River
Embley River

TAKE THE HEAD SHOT.

"**I**'ve got her in my scope," the Chinese sniper said.

"She looks like Willow Barrant, the Aboriginal woman in my target package. I could take an easy head-shot from here."

Tong Lo had spent hundreds of hours training with China's elite Snow Leopard Commando Unit to take a shot just like this. He peered through the massive scope on his McMillan TAC-50 rifle, thankful that privately funded mercenary operations like this supplied the world's best gear.

He lifted his view away from the scope, trying to assess the wind moving across the valley.

"Should I proceed?" he repeated. No answer.

Today was, in the Aussie vernacular, a 'stinker'. The blazing afternoon sun was beating down, and the humidity was through the roof.

About 500 feet below the sniper's firing position, two sweaty Australian men and an Aboriginal woman were carrying small potted seedlings from the edge of a cannabis crop. They placed them on the rear tray of a large farm quad bike. A young Chinese woman nearby dug some fully grown cannabis plants out of the ground.

They all looked nervous.

Tong Lo whispered into his satellite phone, "This crop is small compared to the one up at the main farm –but it's alive. A few thousand plants. All the cannabis plants back up at the main farm are dead. Just like everywhere else."

He looked back through the scope of his sniper rifle. Its crosshairs fixed squarely on the black girl's chest.

Tong Lo whispered, "I think I could drop two of them from my position up here. Then the others in your team can go down and clean up the other two. They look like they won't put up much of a fight."

Bo Aung Win Zin, ('Win' to his friends) a young Burmese national, sat on a hilltop nearby. A sleek new Iridium Extreme 9575 satellite phone in his hand.

Win liked to show off. He dressed himself from head to toe in the most expensive tactical military gear money could buy. As the leader of Asia's Sam Gor Golden Triangle drug cartel, he could easily afford the very best.

"Take the shot," Win said.

Another voice suddenly cut into the call on the satellite phone.
U-Chin, his aging grandfather, shouted angrily,

"Absolutely not. We promised the others. A quiet and quick extraction. We want them alive. With as many seedling samples as you can fit on the trawler back to Papua. Let me know when the mission is over."

Tong Lo asked again, "Orders?"

Win reluctantly said, "Stand down."

Win sneered down at the cannabis crop in the valley below. Pissed off.

"Send the team down to take them alive," Win ordered.

"Then get the plant samples ready to take to the boat. Try to avoid gunfire. We're still close to the Air Force base."

Win angrily threw his satellite phone. It smashed on a nearby rock.

***

Inside the CIA Headquarters at Langley in Virginia, a computer server silently logged the completion of Win's phone call. It automatically forwarded an encrypted audio file of his conversation to Major Thomas Crensch.

The war for Willow's crop was about to begin.

CHAPTER 2

TO THE BOTANIST BORN.

Twenty years earlier. Clermont. North Queensland.

Constable Pete Davidson wasn't a happy camper as he drove his police car past Willy Barrant's place. It was 5am, and the thermometer was just above zero.

The cop had driven twenty miles out the Dingle Road after getting a report about a car accident, only to find a parked car with a sleeping driver inside. He was heading back into town and his stomach was rumbling. Harvey's Truckstop would be open when he got back to town. He could almost smell the coffee as he traversed the skinny farm roads.

As he drove past the Barrant place, he could see a Combine Harvester and a truck moving slowly across a field. Its lights were blazing in the pre-dawn light.

He thought for a moment about stopping in to say hello to Willy, but an enormous yawn killed that idea.

Pete flashed his headlights. The Combine Harvester flashed back at him.

He smiled and kept on driving.

Willy Barrant was a Moisture Magician. He had to be. He'd established his small wheat farm in a place where drought was a constant adversary.

Willy shifted his ass uncomfortably. The straw from a rough bale of oaten hay he was sitting on dug into his skin through the holes in his pants. He needed new pants, but that would have to wait until the new wheat crop was in. He took a sip of tea from an enamel mug as he spoke to a farm worker seated on another bale nearby.

"I was born on an Aboriginal reserve. Up north, near Weipa, on Cape York Peninsula. Napranum Land. Worked my guts out for twenty years," he reminisced. "Saved enough to buy this 100 acres of farmland. Got married. Started growing wheat and a family. Probably should have bought a lot further down south, but the land was cheap up here on account of the lack of rain. All we could afford."

He stubbed out his cigarette and added, "Everyone said we were crazy."

Willy looked out into the distance. The deep orange sun was now mostly above the horizon. He stood and emptied his mug onto the dry red ground.

"Better get moving," he said.

***

It was a good thing Constable Davidson hadn't stopped at the farm.

Willy's daughter, eight-year-old Willow Barrant, sat in the driver's seat of their Case IH Combine Harvester. She wore her school uniform. Her feet could barely reach the pedals. A row of powerful lights built into the roof illuminated an endless sea of wheat in the morning light.

Willow had been driving quad bikes, tractors and the family Combine Harvester since she was just six-years-old.

Willy stood in the middle of the field, running his fingers through the tall strands of golden brown wheat. He snapped off a head of seeds and rolled it between his palms.

He spoke into a walkie talkie, "Still way too much moisture in the air. Maybe another hour if these clouds clear."

Willow listened intently on a handset in the harvester's cabin.

"I'm going to check over the other side of the hill," Willy said. "I'll let you know when you can roll. Then I'll get the truck and come back to let you offload."

***

Willy grew wheat in winter, and, if the Moisture Gods permitted, he might get in a crop of sorghum for the summer. After years of droughts, often followed by floods, Willy had become a master of moisture. Water ruled every aspect of his life.

He loved the water for the life it gave his crops.

He hated it when the massive floods around 2000 took his wife and eleven-year-old son. Leaving him alone to raise Willow.

***

Willow put her feet up on the steering wheel of the harvester. She pulled out a large, dog-eared book titled 'Wheat Growing In Australia.' and started reading avidly.

She felt enthralled, like it was a copy of a gripping Secret Seven novel. After writing some notes on the pages, she carefully put the book away.

She popped the silver foil off the top of a small bottle of milk and slowly sipped the delicious top creamy layer from its neck.

Willow looked at the cheap plastic watch Auntie Jemma had given her for her last birthday. It was time!

She eagerly clicked on the AM radio in the cab and listened intently to the local crop reports broadcast on the ABC.

Forty-five minutes later, Willow's handset crackled to life.

"I think we're ready. Let's get a few runs in while I go over and fetch the truck." Willy said.

Willow reached down, turned the ignition key, and the 8.3-liter Cummins engine roared to life. She expertly jockeyed the steering wheel and the cutting blade controls for the header.

The massive dull red harvester lumbered down the field. Using just one finger, she made tiny adjustments to the steering wheel to keep the Header on the front of the beast in a perfectly straight line.

The smell of fresh cut wheat in the air filled the air as she traveled down the field. Fine wheat dust crept into every nook and cranny. After a few runs, she grabbed the hand-held and said, "I'm nearly full. Need to offload the grain tank."

She brought the harvester to a halt. Her father pulled alongside.

Willow engaged a lever to move the unloader pipe over to the truck and then engaged the elevator to pump out the grain tank.

Willy chatted to her on the hand-held. "Let's try to get four more runs in before I take you over to the gate to get the bus to school. Johnno should be here to take over by then."

With the grain tank now empty, Willow engaged the Header and slowly lumbered off down the field again.

Smiling. In her happy place.

CHAPTER 3

SQUARE MELONS, COCKTAIL TREES AND A COLLINGWOOD SHITBOX.

Ten years later, Willow had finished high school.

Eighteen-year-old Willow stepped nervously out of the taxi that had driven her from Melbourne Airport. It was 9:00 p.m, and the street was poorly lit. Willow's new student share house was a shitbox. In Collingwood. The bad part of Collingwood.

Her scholarship to Melbourne University included an allowance for somewhere to live, but this decrepit house, with four bedrooms and one shared bathroom, was all she could afford. She dragged her single large suitcase up the front steps and knocked on the door. There was no answer. A few minutes later, she knocked again. No answer.

"What?" Willow muttered to herself. "She definitely said she was going to be here after 7 o'clock."

She pushed her suitcase behind a shrub in the garden and had a quick look down the street to make sure that no one was around to steal it. Then she crept down the side of the house.

She took a peek in one of the side windows, but quickly pulled her head back when a thin red laser line arced across the windowpane. A red laser dot traveled along the side of the neighbor's house.

She leaned across to peek through the window again and could see that the room in the house was completely dark. A beam of light from a rifle-mounted torch entered through a doorway. It immediately moved across the room, then disappeared from view.

Shortly after, she heard a series of rapid-fire popping sounds, as another tight beam of torch light rushed across the dark room, followed by the sound of a body thumping against one of the inside walls.

Willow was seriously worried that there was a home invasion going on inside, so she started backing down towards the front of the house again. She stopped when she felt her body bump into a person standing in the darkness. She turned and screamed as she found herself face to face with a person wearing a full tactical army uniform, complete with night vision goggles and a rifle.

Willow turned to run for her life when the person suddenly flipped up their night vision goggles and said, "Hey babe, you must be Willow. The new girl. Right?" The green light coming from the night vision goggles revealed the smiling face of a geeky Chinese girl.

She said, "Hi, my name is Shu. Shu Chen. I'm guessing you are our new roomie." Shu pointed her rifle back towards the front of the house and added, "We'd better get inside." Willow just stared in shock at the rifle Shu was holding.

Sensing she was concerned, Shu aimed the rifle at the neighbor's side wall and fired off several shots. A cascade of small gel pellets splattered harmlessly against the bricks. Willow breathed an enormous sigh of relief.

Shu pressed a button on a throat mic that she was wearing, and said, "Hey guys, the new roomie is here."

The light flicked on in the room down the side of the house. The window slid up. Two young guys, also wearing full tactical army gear, poked their heads out the window.

The tallest guy said, "Hi, I'm Freddie Delgado." He was around twenty-years-old, with tanned Latino skin. The shorter guy was around the same age, but skinny and pasty. "Hi, I'm Castor Dimarkos, but everyone just calls me Caz." he said.

Shu walked towards the front of the house saying, "We'd better get inside, because these gel guns are not strictly legal for use outside in Victoria. It's a bit of a gray area." Willow, still a bit shocked, fell into step behind her. She retrieved her suitcase from the garden and followed Shu into the house.

With the lights now turned on, the house looked relatively normal. Willow breathed a sigh of relief as Shu lead her to her new bedroom in the share house.

"This is your room," said Shu. "Mine's just down the hall. Freddie and Caz have rooms at the front of the house, but we all share one bathroom. Freddie works at an electronic store in Fitzroy and Caz is a diesel mechanic." Willow parked her suitcase in the bedroom and they all sat down in the living room. Caz and Freddie had stripped off their tactical army helmets and vests and, thankfully, also now looked quite normal.

"Sorry about the fright," said Caz, "but Wednesday night is pizza and gun battle night in the house." Freddie fidgeted with a Ziploc bag full of weed. He pushed some of it into the bowl of a small bong, then passed the bong and a Bic lighter over to Willow and said, "Welcome aboard!"

***

They shared the bong and some pizza, and then Shu took her on a short house tour. There wasn't much to see.

Freddie and Caz's rooms at the front of the house were like she'd imagined. Black bedsheets that looked like they hadn't seen the inside of a washing machine for months. Small piles of clothes strewn across the floor. Empty cans of bourbon and cola filling wastepaper baskets.

The small bathroom was surprisingly clean and organized. Shu explained, "They both do Army Reserve, so they've had some discipline beaten into them. It means they are both out doing that most Tuesday nights, which is great if you want some quiet time."

As they headed towards the back of the house, Willow could hear a distinct whirring noise. It got much louder when Shu opened the door to her own bedroom. A long desk stretched the cross the entire length of the room. A gaming computer with three monitors sat at one end of the desk.

At the other end, a 3D printer rocked back and forth, as it printed a small grey WarHammer figurine from a reel of PLA filament. Spray-paint cans, cutting tools, paintbrushes, and masking tape covered the rest of the desk.

High on the wall above the desk was the biggest gun rack Willow had ever seen. In fact, Willow had never seen a gun rack before, but if she ever did, it would be nothing like the size of this. She gawped, "Jeeesus, what's that?"

Shu smiled and said, "Don't worry, they're all fake. None of them have moving parts. I printed them all up on the 3D printer and then painted them to look real. I make a small fortune selling them at the cosplay shows that come into town. Pays for most of my rent while I'm doing my course at uni."

She lifted a menacing AK-47 off the wall and handed it over to Willow. It felt as light as a feather, but it looked like the real deal.

Willow asked, "But what about the guns you use for the gun battle around the house?" Shu said, "Those are real, but they're gel blasters. They just fire soft pellets. Harmless. A weeny bit illegal, though. You can't use them or carry them outside."

***

An hour later, Shu and Willow had the munchies. They sat in the kitchen, drinking jasmine tea, while scoffing down chocolate ice-cream and chocolate biscuits.

Shu asked, "So how did an Aboriginal chick like you end upon a scholarship to a Uni in Melbourne? Doing fucking botany of all things!"

Willow looked up at the kitchen roof and thought for a moment, then she mused, "Funnily enough, I think my botany career started with square watermelons."

Shu looked confused. "Watermelons?" she asked.

"Square watermelons," Willow said. "When I was a kid, there wasn't a lot to play with on the farm. Just plants and sticks and rocks and dirt, mainly. I was always looking for something to do to keep me occupied. And one day I saw a picture in a magazine that showed how people in Japan were growing watermelons that were shaped like cubes. Instead of round."

Willow dipped a biscuit in her cup of tea.

"And I immediately thought, 'I could do that'. All I'd need is some watermelon seeds, some dirt and some wood to make the square box shape. So, a few months later, I had grown some square watermelons. But that wasn't enough. Just for fun, I made them in triangles, hexagons and other shapes. They were always a hit when I took them into school."

"Yum," said Shu. "One of those would go down a treat right now."

Willow refilled her teacup and continued,

"Then the science teacher at school told me about something she called a cocktail tree."

Shu exclaimed, "A what?"

Willow smiled and said, "No, it's not like margaritas and cosmopolitans growing on trees. It's a competition that people who graft plants are into. Technically speaking, you can graft just about anything onto a tree. So, I tried grafting an apple onto a peach tree. And that worked fine. Then I moved on to grafting different cherries and plums onto the same tree. I had quite a few failures, but then I learned how to make it work."

Shu stared at her intently, wondering what a tree like that would look like, as Willow continued,

"Did you know it's possible to graft up to ten different fruits onto one tree? So, I eventually ended up with my very own cocktail tree. People visited the farm from miles away just to see it. The local paper came and took some pictures, too."

Willow laughed and said, "I even wrote an essay about it in my science class at High School."

"Is it still alive?" Shu marveled.

Willow replied, "No. It lasted a few summers and then the drought got to it. The water tank on the farm was so low I had to stop watering it. Looking back, that hit me pretty hard. It was like being forced to kill a child. I'd put years into sustaining it. Like my dad, I grew a healthy respect for water as I watched it wither and die in the yard."

Willow pondered that thought for a moment, then continued, "But that cocktail tree kept on giving well after it was dead." Her eyes sparkled.

"I got called into the school Principal's office near the end of the year. I thought it was because I busted that boy's nose during a game of footy. He fucking deserved it! Dad was in the office when I got there. But it turns out the school had sent off the essay and pictures of the tree as part of a student competition. And bugger me, if that cocktail tree didn't win me this scholarship to go to Melbourne Uni to study botany."

Willow sucked on her ice-cream spoon, then she continued the story. "When we got back home, I told Dad I didn't want to go. I'd started doing some work trying to graft different strains of wheat together to make something that was a bit more drought resistant than the stuff we were growing. I thought that by hanging around, I could make a difference on the farm, but Dad was adamant that Uni was the place to be. He said it was like that old story about how you can give a man a fish and he can eat for a day, or you can teach him to fish, and he can eat for the rest of his life."

Shu nodded in agreement, then Willow continued,

"Dad thought Uni would teach me more about plant biology and that would be more useful for everyone trying to grow crops in dry places like our farm. We fought about it for a few weeks over Christmas, but eventually my dad packed me off on the plane to Melbourne.

The scholarship included an accommodation allowance, and the P&C at my school pooled some money together and bought me a second-hand mobile phone before I left. So, I could talk to Dad."

Caz disrupted their chat, shouting from another room. "Hey Willow, did you say you were doing botany at university?" Willow shouted back, "Yes, why do you ask?"

Caz walked into the room while holding an empty three liter Coke bottle that he had cut up to create a makeshift terrarium. Four small cannabis seedlings were growing from the soil in it.

He lowered it on the kitchen table in front of her and announced, "I think you are my new best friend! Two of these plants are growing great, but the others look like crap. I think I need the plant equivalent of a vet. I'm guessing that's what a botanist is."

CHAPTER 4

BOLIVIA. WE HAVE A PROBLEM.

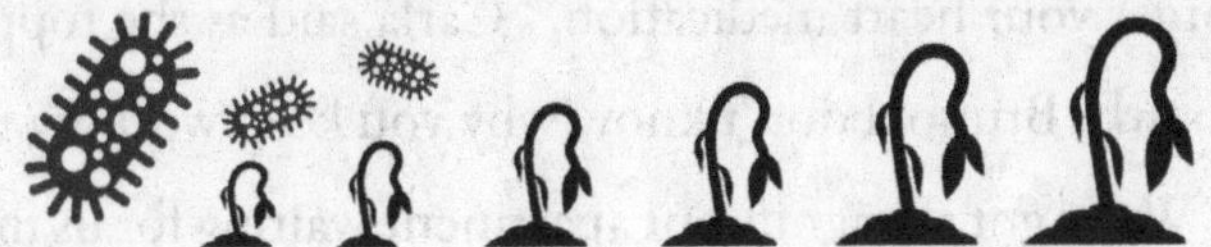

The Chapere Valley in Bolivia was a like a little piece of heaven on earth. Puffy white clouds hugged the lush farmland spread across its remote green hills. Millions of cannabis plants flourished in the hidden pockets of the valley. On a sunny day, you'd swear you could see the plants growing taller before your very eyes.

Bruno Gutierrez, a local cannabis farmer, looked like he stepped out of a coffee commercial. Approaching eighty, with a broad toothy smile, topped by a simple, brown farmer's straw hat.

Everyone in the valley loved 'Papa Bruno'. As much as you can love a cartel boss. If you got on the wrong side of the old man, you might find him standing behind you, with his trusty old Mosberg rifle, about to put a bullet into the back of your skull.

This morning, Bruno's thoughts were far from murder.

He was more interested in the plate of lightly steaming Saltenas pastries his wife Carla had lovingly prepared for breakfast.

"My love –you are indeed the perfect wife," he teased as he sipped his coffee. He eagerly dipped the golden savory treat into a bowl of peppery Llaju sauce. "Mmm," he moaned in appreciation.

"Don't forget your heart medication," Carla said as she topped up his coffee. "Honestly, Bruno, I don't know why you keep working this hard," she chided. "We've got a magnificent apartment waiting for us in Santiago. Right near Jimmi and the grandkids. You need to think about retirement."

"Retirement is easy for most." Bruno mused as he headed for the farmhouse door. "But when your 'jefe' is Money Munoz –and you are dealing with the Sinaloa Cartel it's not so easy."

Bruno stopped. He kissed Carla and said, "Money and I are talking –but nothing's resolved. All I want to do right now is get this crop harvested, processed and out the door –so I can cash it in."

Carla handed him a small wicker basket, lovingly draped with a red checked gingham cloth.

"Some warm Bunelos for the girls up at the sheds," Carla said.

Bruno took a deep sniff of the basket. He peeked inside. The flaky round pastries had a dusting of sugar.

"And for me?" he asked.

"You'll get Bunelos every morning when we are finally off the farm and living in Santiago," Carla chided.

Bruno smiled and walked out the kitchen door.

"I'll be back by 2 o'clock," he said. He walked past a sleeping armed guard on the veranda. Bruno grimaced and gave the sleeping man a hard kick as he passed.

Bruno jumped onto a muddy All-Terrain Vehicle (ATV). The off-road four-wheeler roared away from the farmhouse. He softly smiled as the old ATV bumped its way through dappled sunlight to the front gate of his farm.

Bruno waved as he passed three heavily armed guards at the fortified sentry post by the farm's main gate. They saluted back respectfully.

Ten minutes later, Bruno pulled up on the crest of a meandering green valley. He stepped off the ATV and stretched his weary bones. Time to get to work.

He walked past a large, open-sided shed. Thousands of large fronds of cannabis plants hung from drying racks bolted into the shed's roof. Outside the shed, a Latino worker threw cannabis flower heads over a large plastic tarpaulin laid out on the ground. Another worker used a long plank to spread the flowers out so they could dry in the baking sun.

A group of four other farm workers gathered around a second tarp. They shoveled dried cannabis into large pink-striped plastic storage bags.

Bruno, carrying the wicker basket of baked goodies, ambled into a large room at the back of the farm's main drying facility.

"Buenos," he announced to a group of ladies inside.

They were hard at work compressing the dried cannabis into tight bricks. Wrapping them in cling film and weighing them. Bruno put the wicker basket down on an old wooden table. The scent of sweet pastries mingled with the pungent smell of drying weed.

The women all immediately stopped work.

They gathered expectantly around the covered basket.

"From Carla," Bruno said, lifting the gingham cloth away.

The women tucked into the warm Bunelos. Smiling and chatting.

Bruno walked over and poured himself a thick brown liquid from an old beaten urn on a wood-burning stove.

Ernesto, a farm hand, appeared at the door. He looked scared.

"Err –problemo." Ernesto muttered.

Bruno smiled. "Ernesto, what could be a problem?" he asked.

Bruno grabbed a Bunelo from the basket and took a bite. He gave the ladies a playful wink that said 'don't tell my wife'.

"Bunelos? A beautiful day?" He looked at the ladies tucking into the pastries. "Beautiful ladies? There's no problem here?" The ladies giggled.

Ernesto beckoned for Bruno to come outside. He nervously repeated, "Papa Bruno. Problemo." Bruno walked to the door and out onto the old wooden farm veranda.

The long wooden verandah was Bruno's happy place. Most mornings, he would spend his time in a rocking chair drinking hot mate de coca herbal tea, overlooking the 100 acres of his pristine, green cannabis crop. It stretched to the horizon.

Except, this morning, the entire crop was wilted and brown.

Stone dead.

CHAPTER 5

THE BILLIONAIRE BUNKER.

Bruno's boss was Mateo (AKA "Money") Munoz, the patriarch of the Sinaloa drug cartel. Money lived on Miami's exclusive Indian Creek Island. The locals called the island the 'The Billionaire Bunker'.

The three hundred hectares of pristine island sat smack bang in the dress circle of Miami's Biscayne Bay. Home to Ivanka and Jared and Julio Iglesias. Old school money. The Internal Revenue Service always said The Bunker was the place you took your dirty money after you'd laundered it in London for a few years.

Money Munoz bought his plot on the island thirty years ago. Back when the Falcon Brothers and Sal Magluta were the big hitters in the South American cartels. Money Munoz was smart. He aligned himself with the Sinaloa Cartel early, and his fortunes had grown ever since.

Money chose the plot for his palatial home for a deeply personal reason. Every morning his mansion on the island gave the Versace-clad drug-lord a commanding view out over the skyline of Liberty City, Miami's most dangerous and drug-ridden shitbox of a suburb.

It gave him a view right back to where he first came from as a boy.

Nothing pleased Money, and his busty younger wife Mariana, more than giving new guests a grand house tour. Money always considered Mariana herself as part of the tour. She was a true Buchona. Well north of fifty, but with the tits, ass and waist that only a talented surgeon could build.

The massive deep blue swimming pool, the purple crushed-velvet home cinema complex and the gaudy disco bar and had already wowed this morning's guests.

Now it was time for the pièce de résistance of the tour.

After a brief elevator ride, they exited into a massive underground complex. It was the home's underground Olympic-grade shooting range, with a gym and military-grade parkour training course.

Money walked over to a modern rubberized table. He picked up a set of Honeywell Impact-Sport ear-covers. Then he handed a set to each guest.

"It can get noisy down here," he shouted.

"My daughter Valeria is usually training down here at this time of day."

The acrid smell of burnt gunpowder filled the large room. Spent bullet casings covered the floor.

BOOM. BOOM.

Loud pistol shots rang out from the far end of the room. Followed by a TINK. TINK. sound, as the Aguila Super Extra 38 Grain bullets from Valeria's gun smashed into pop-up metal targets around the hi-tech obstacle course.

Valeria Munoz bounded like a gazelle along a high metal walkway above them. She side stepped quickly across some rubber angled floor bolsters. Never missing a step.

To her left, a human-shaped metal target popped up. She steadied her footing as she pulled a gold-plated Dan Wesson DWX pistol from her hip holster. She emptied three 9mm rounds into the dead centre of the plate steel target. TINK. TINK. TINK.

Valeria, wearing a khaki Lycra leotard and pink rock-climbing shoes, strode over to the visitors, catching her breath.

She removed her Oakley Radar EV Path sunglasses and ear-wear. Then placed the distinctive, red-handled Wesson DWX pistol on a low stone and rubber table. A random assortment of expensive handguns and rifles littered the table.

"Marcelo –Fayana –meet my daughter Valeria." Money said, proudly introducing her. "She runs the day-to-day aspects of all my business operations."

Marcelo walked over and pointed to Valeria's red pistol. Impressed.

"May I?" he asked.

"Yes, of course," she responded. "I've only had it for a week."

He gripped the gun in his palm, getting a feel for it.

"The DWX. So light. All-aluminum." he marveled.

"I've heard it called the 'F1 car' of handguns. Do you agree?"

Valeria wasn't so sure.

"I've shot better." She said demurely.

She pointed to the $2,000 weapon and said, "Take it, if you like it. I have many more just like it."

Valeria looked at her Apple watch.

"Sorry, I'm on a timer for my run this morning," she said. "I'll meet you upstairs for a drink."

She randomly grabbed another pistol off the table, checked the magazine, then bounded off down the parkour course again. Her movements followed by the sound of grunts and more gunshots.

Forty-five minutes later, Money's house tour was over.

Money's guests lounged on plush sun-beds. They sipped on blood-red Miami Whammy's in fruit-filled poco-grande glasses.

Mariana and Fayana sat in the corner of the pool deck, under the cool shade of a large pink umbrella. They were busy comparing Birkins. Mariana proudly showed off her mint-condition vintage lime-green Kelly Doll. Circa 2002.

Marcelo and Money lay on white loungers at the other end of the pool, reminiscing about the old days.

"I think it's time to retire," said Money.

"I'm not getting any younger, you know —and Valeria really runs the show for me, anyway."

Marcelo looked out at the Miami skyline.

"And Miami ain't what it used to be," Marcelo added, "with the Trumps –and the freaking Russian mafia –buying the place out. The business sucks too. Now the trade is all chemicals. Addys and Blue Silk, Yayo, Special K, Dexies, Dollies and Roxies. Fuck me –I can't even remember half the names anymore."

Marcelo finished his drink.

"How's your boy, Manny, doing out on the West Coast?" he asked.

Money said, "Typical son. His balls are often bigger than his brains."

They both laughed out loud.

"You know they call him the 'Big M' over in Juarez now. He's had to calm down a bit. He had a big blowup with the Feds on the El Paso side of the border. It's brought him a lot of unwanted attention. He's got a lot to learn. Val is far more level-headed."

Money waved to a butler. He wanted another two cocktails.

"And what about the fucking Venezuelans?" Money laughed, shaking his head.

"Oil money. They think they own the place."

Marcelo smiled and nodded his head.

"Fucking Venezuelans!" he said.

They both laughed out loud again.

A lift door near the far end of the pool deck chimed.

The stainless-steel door slid open.

Valeria stepped out onto the pool deck, now wearing a fluorescent orange Dior bikini.

She plunged into the pool beside the sun-beds and started swimming some lazy laps.

Her taut, athletic body glistened in the Miami sun.

The chit-chat between Money and Marcelo came to an abrupt end when a butler emerged onto the pool deck and walked over to Money.

"I'm sorry Mr. Munoz –," he whispered, "But you have a business call."

"Mr. Bruno is on a video call in the Comms Room. Urgente."

Money stood reluctantly.

"Business," he said.

He wrapped a white embroidered Versace towel around his overflowing tanned waist, then he called out to Valeria, "Hey Valo, keep Marcelo company while I take a quick call."

Money turned to head into the house, but then he paused and turned back to Marcelo.

"Fucking Venezuelans!" he mused.

They both burst out laughing again.

The mansion's Comms Room was a complete contrast to the gaudy Versace-style of the rest of the Munoz household. No Swarovski chandeliers, Gucci wallpaper or gold leaf balustrades. The room had a sleek Nordic-look. Minimalist white furniture, a couple of simple pink and white Keith Haring originals, and automatic shading glass walls.

This part of the house was Valeria's domain.

The butler flipped a switch. The windows and door glass turn opaque. Then he left his boss alone.

A large TV screen slowly lowered from a slit in the ceiling. It flickered to life to reveal an anxious Bruno Gutierrez on a Facetime call.

"Bruno, my old friend. You look like you've seen a ghost," said Money. "How can I help you?"

On the video screen, Bruno shook his head in disbelief.

"The cannabis crop. It's gone," Bruno stammered.

Money looked puzzled and said, "Mierda —A fire? A flood?"

"None of those," said Bruno.

"It's just died. It withered over the last few days. Estar muerto."

Money looked shocked.

"So, part of the crop has died? He asked, "How could that happen? Poison? DEA?"

Bruno looked aghast. "No. EVERY last plant is dead," he said slowly,

"I've heard the same thing has happened over at the Ganzanello place, too. That's two valleys over. Twenty miles away. It makes no sense to me."

Money looked disturbed and said, "Give me some time, my friend. I'll make some calls. Tell your beautiful Carla not to worry. I miss you, my friend. Keep close."

The video call shut down.

Money walked over to a wall and pressed a button.

A white panel slid up to reveal a large printed cork-board map of Mexico and South America.

Money grabbed a red pin from a tray.

He stuck it into Bruno's farm location in Bolivia. Then he grimaced.

There were a lot of other red pins on the map.

CHAPTER 6

GRADUATION DAY.

Royal Exhibition Building, Melbourne, Australia.

Twenty-one-year-old Willow Barrant sat at the back of a large group of science graduates, trying to maintain her composure. The sun streamed through the large semi-circular stained glass window at the end of the hall. Emily Wurramara's song 'Blue Moon. Black Sea' lilted calmingly in her ears through a set of AirPods. The main hall was buzzing with excitement for Melbourne University's 2017 Graduation Day.

Her dad, Willy, sat a few rows back in the family section, with Willow's roomie Shu Chen keeping him company. He hadn't looked this happy since the Weipa Raiders last beat the Napranum Bulldogs on the local rugby paddock. He gleefully thumbed through the booklet the university had printed for the occasion.

He beamed and said, "My little girl. My little girl! Her mum would be so proud of her." A tear rolled down Willy's weather-worn cheek.

Willow wasn't worried about the graduation ceremony.

She only had one thing on her mind.

Beth Gott.

Willow held an old photo of Beth Gott, the renowned Australian botanist, and rubbed it nervously between her fingertips. In her lap she had a dog-eared copy of the book 'Koorie Plants. Koorie people.', co-authored by Gott years earlier. It was the seminal book on the topic of plants as traditional aboriginal food. Today, the university would announce the winner of the prestigious Gott Prize.

The winner received $2,000. A paltry sum, but enough to buy an air ticket overseas. More importantly, the prize also came with a two-year Fellowship at the world-renowned Department of Systematic and Evolutionary Botany at the prestigious Zurich University in Switzerland. The 'Top Gun' of the worldwide Botanist fraternity. Willow had her eye firmly on that prize.

The student graduation ceremony went off without a hitch. If you don't count Willy standing up and cheering out loud when Willow's name was called out to go up to the stage.

He shouted, "That's my little girl," at the top of his voice.

The crowd broke out in nervous laughter. Shu was too busy blubbering to stop him.

An hour later, the freshly minted graduates and their families gathered in an anteroom, eating scones and thick chicken, aioli and cucumber sandwiches. Willy was mingling. He was on a mission to tell just about anyone that would listen that his daughter was one of the graduates. Willow and Shu huddled near a bar and drank Coronas. They clinked bottles.

"So Shuey, what are your plans?" said Willow.

Shu took a long sip of her beer and said, "I'm planning to get very pissed here while the beers are free and then head out on the town."

They clinked bottles again and Willow said, "Not today. I mean, what are you going to do career-wise. What's next for my little Shu?"

Shu thought for a moment and said, "You know what? I don't think corporate is for me. I'm thinking of signing up for the Defense Graduate Program Intelligence Pathway. With the Army. Signal Corps. Maybe Engineering and Technical."

Willow threw her a quizzical look. Shu continued, "I graduated with Honors, so I think I've got a shot at a Signals Directorate Scholarship at ANU in Canberra. The starting pay is OK, and I'll get to play with some really advanced technical shit down the track."

Willow said, "Canberra? You'll freeze your ass off. And you won't know anyone there."

"Not really," said Shu. "Freddie and Caz are thinking about heading that way, too. Not to Canberra. But joining the ADF. They'd be doing Basic Training down below Canberra at Kapooka. Near Wagga."

Willow shook her head and lamented, "Jesus Shu –god help us all if those two ever get their hands on some real weapons."

They were interrupted by the entrance of a guy in a long black dress-coat. He was holding a big brass bell.

He rang the bell to grab everyone's attention and shouted,

"Here Ye! Here Ye! Can everyone return to the hall for the announcement of this year's Gott Prize."

A hush went over the room.

Game On.

After a short video about Beth Gott's life and achievements, the Dean and the Head of the School of BioSciences walked up to the lectern.

The Head of School made a brief speech about the prize - even cracking a joke from the movie Top Gun. She finished her speech with the line, "*I gotta send somebody from this squadron to Miramar. I gotta do something here. I still can't believe it. I gotta give you your dream shot! I'm gonna send you up against the best.*" The geekster crowd of Uni Botanists cracked up.

The Dean took to the lectern and said, "I won't keep you in suspense."

He pulled out a beige envelope.

"I'm sure most of you have already planned how you'd spend the $2000 prize money. Most likely on beer at The Provincial Hotel, I'd guess."

There was more laughing – then a nervous hush as the Dean ripped open the envelope and announced,

"The winner of this year's Beth Gott Prize is – Willow Barrant. For her outstanding work in plant micro-propagation and the cloning of new species for arid areas."

Willow took a deep breath.

A few rows back, Willy rose to his feet, but Shu grabbed his shoulder before he could fully stand. She thought about it for a nano-second, then decided, 'Fuck the pomp and ceremony'. They both stood up and started cheering.

Willow was on her way to Botany's Top Gun.

CHAPTER 7

Settling Into The Chocolate Box.

Forty rushed days later. Zürich. Switzerland.

On a scale of one-to-ten, Zürich's shitty weather in mid-January rated a hard 'zero'. The 'deck the halls with boughs of holly' charm of Christmas was a long, distant memory for the Swiss. In January you were lucky if the thermometer nudged above freezing.

A good coat and a suitable set of boots were essential. Willow had neither as she stepped out onto the icy taxi rank at Zürich Airport.

Her Fellowship at the university gave her special permission to start in the January semester rather than having to wait until August. So, she'd left Weipa in a god-almighty rush. It also meant that she missed all the orientation a typical student would get. Classes would begin the day after she touched down.

As she jumped into the warmth of her taxi, she squealed, "Fuck it's cold out there."

The young Swiss taxi driver looked at the t-shirt and jeans she was wearing and said, "I'm not surprised. Why are you dressed for the beach?"

"Queensland isn't the best place in the world to buy puffer jackets and snow boots in January," she replied. "I'm going to a place called Hammerstrasse. Number 61."

She read from a slip of paper in her hand.

"It says here to tell you it's near the Tropenhäuser im Botanischen Garten der Universität Zürich. But I need boots and a jacket first. Where can I go for that?"

The driver thought for a moment and suggested, "There are a bunch of clothes shop near there. Near Forschstrasse. You could drop your bag first and then I could take you there." A quick trip to a local Manor store sorted her with some waterproof Muck rubber boots and a couple of Jack & Jones puffer jackets in a suitable 'Botanist green'. The university had massive greenhouses under clear protective domes, so she knew she would get wet and dirty most days.

Her Fellowship included rent for a tiny apartment on Hammerstrasse, a quick squelch through the snowy slush from the campus.

As probably the only aboriginal woman in Switzerland, Willow was an exotic campus oddity, but she made friends fast and picked up the local language quickly.

Most people she met assumed she was Nigerian –until she released her thick Aussie drawl.

As winter became summer, her life and learning flowered.

By June, Zurich was looking like a postcard of green valleys, beer steins and snow-capped mountains. You could almost hear the faint sound of yodeling lilting in the air. Willow was in her kitchen, lapping up a coffee and the sun streaming in the window, when her doorbell chimed.

"What the –," she muttered. It was only 6am.

She rubbed the sleep from her eyes, tidied her hair as best she could, as edged toward the front door.

Two shadows were lurking outside in the pre-dawn light.

She took a tentative look through the peephole in the door and moaned, "Jesus, guys. It's not even morning yet."

She swung the door open. Trying her best to look happy.

Standing outside were Caz and Freddie.

They were dressed in Australian Army greens and carried massive army-issue backpacks. Both were still well and truly drunk from an evening of partying that hadn't quite ended yet.

"Wills!" Freddie said, planting a big bear hug on her.

"Willo's – how are ya?" Caz slurred, desperately trying to stay vertical.

She shuffled them inside, so they didn't wake the neighbors. Caz stopped and added, "and we have a surprise guest."

He stepped aside to reveal Shu standing behind them.

Shu, perfectly sober, gave Willow a hug and said, "Someone had to do the driving."

Three hours later, after a good sleep on the sofa and floor, Caz and Freddie sat down in Willow's kitchen and quickly devoured carbs. Coffee, toast, marmalade and cheese. Willow and Shu, less in need of a hangover cure, were having some birchermüesli.

"You said you might visit in summer. Even a little notice would have been nice," said Willow.

Caz shook his throbbing head and said, "Sorry Wills, they sent both of us out to Ramstein in Germany for some R&R. We were based outside of Dubai. Fuck, it's hot there. Dry as a dead dingo's donger. We would have gone anywhere to get out of the heat."

He looked out of Willow's window to the leafy park below and said,

"Haven't seen a tree for months. –Sand. –Sand. –And more fucking sand. When we got to the base in Germany, we figured we could drive the 250-or-so miles to Zurich to pop in for a visit. Then we ran into Shu."

Shu said, "A team from my RAAF squadron has been training at Rammstein for the last three weeks."

Caz popped a Panadol in his mouth and washed it down with some water, then settled into a chair in the sun.

"We only decided at about 6 o'clock last night," he said.

"We ran into some friendly Dutch girlies getting gas in Basel. They were heading to Zurich too, so we've been doing a weeny bit of partying at their place until they chucked us out," Caz concluded.

"And here we are."

Shu shook her head in dismay.

Willow stood and took a good long look at them and said,

"The Army? And the Air Force? You three?"

She pointed at Caz and Freddie, and said, "Last time I saw you two in Melbourne, you were at Comic-Con dressed as Master Chief and Jacob Keyes from Halo. And here you are now. The real deal. What gives?"

Caz poured himself another coffee and said, "We were looking for a bit of adventure. And the money was good. So we signed up. Training in Wagga for a few months, and then deployment to the sunny UAE not long after."

Caz let out a long belch and added, "Operation Accordion, they call it. Mostly medical and maintenance support. Pretty breezy life. So we aren't complaining. We'll be deploying to Afghanistan after this. But looking forward to that. Boring as bat-shit holed up on the base in the UAE."

Over in the chair, Freddie's eyes slowly rolled shut, then he snorted himself awake.

"So Willo's, how's your dad these days?" he asked.

Willow leaned against the kitchen bench and said,

"It was tough when I left. There was barely any time between the end of the Uni year in Melbourne and heading to the fellowship at the Uni here. I got up to Weipa to see him for a few days."

Freddie looked a bit confused and said, "Weipa? Way up north? I thought he was on a farm."

Willow looked forlorn, and said, "He had to move off the farm last year. His heart's a bit weak, so he sold up and moved up to where most of his relatives are. He grew up on the Cape. There are only a few thousand people in town, but he knows a lot of the locals already. I get to Facetime him every few days. He seems happy."

Wills looked at her watch, unplugged her laptop and put it in her day-pack. "So, how long are you three planning to stay?" Willow asked.

Freddie answered, "We must be back on The Ram in three days. So we have a couple of days, allowing for the drive back."

Willow thought for a moment and then said, "OK. It looks like you three need some more sleep. So get that. There are some good places for lunch nearby." She slid a key across the table and said, "I'll be at work at the Uni until 6pm. Then let's head out on the town. OK? I'll try to rustle some friends together."

Freddie nodded back as she opened the door to leave, but Caz was already fast asleep in his seat at the kitchen table.

Willow turned to Shu and said, "Your responsibility, right? If there's vomit involved when they get sober, you guys are cleaning it up."

CHAPTER 8

MEREDITH AND MCDREAMY.

Zurich University staff never fail to mention Einstein's time as a student there. With over 150 departments, the campus was massive. The Department of Plant and Microbial Biology stood out like a tall poppy. Botanical Sciences Departments worldwide regarded the faculty as the 'Miramar' or 'Fighter-Town'. It was for the best-of-the-best.

The local Swiss bartenders liked to call it 'Pot Gun'.

In a beautiful botanical garden, the Department was renowned for its work in plant genetics, epigenetics and molecular plant physiology. The small team Willow had joined focused on epigenetics, studying microbial and genetic processes to build plant 'fitness'.

The curriculum guide described it as; *Epigenetic regulatory mechanisms facilitating metastable changes in gene activity and the fine-tuning of gene expression patterns, thus enabling plants to survive and reproduce successfully in unpredictable environments*'.

Willow described it as '*building plants that can kick-ass in any climate*'.

This morning, because of the surprise visit by Freddie and Caz, Willow was running late. She was also keen to see how her current experiment at Project H-17 was progressing.

Project H-17 was a laboratory in an ultra-modern geodesic dome located well away from the rest of the campus. Its purpose was to study Hop Latent Viroids - or HLVs. The running joke on campus was that the facility had unlimited funding and free beer, because of the sponsorship it received from The Carlsberg Group. Beer was a big business in Europe. HLVs caused poor growth, brittle stems, and reduced foliage on hops plants. The leaves first turned yellow, then quickly turned brown and died. Not good news for Europe's beer drinking public. Students at the University referred to the tall, round geodesic domed H-17 laboratory as the 'Beer Tent'.

Willow, dressed in a white lab-coat, stood in a campus classroom. She was at the end of a long table covered in seedlings and mature plants. She turned to a nervous group of interns shadowing her and said, "My primary interest is the Trema. It's a tree that's part of the Cannabaceae family."

She handed a tray of seedlings to one intern.

"Here in the lab we look at a range of plants from Humulus, or beer hops, all the way to Cannabis. All part of the same family. The Terpenes in hops give the buds their crisp, bitter taste. In cannabis, the Terpenes give you a buzz."

She hefted a large plant in a pot onto the bench, and said, "Over in the dome I'm gene sequencing Trema trees like this against hops and cannabis. It's got an extensive root system, which makes the Trema tree incredibly drought resistant. I'm hoping to migrate the benefits of the root system to other plants in the family."

She hefted a different plant onto the bench and added, "And I'm doing a bit of side work on the Aphananthe tree. Aphananthe aspera was used to make rope by my indigenous ancestors back in Australia."

Willow handed an intern a petri dish filled with a white creamy substance.

"This is a tonic from the tree bark of Aphanathe Cuspidata. It's great as a moisturizer. Give it a try."

The intern nervously dabbed some on her nose and rubbed it in.

Willow wrapped up the intern presentation and the students obediently filed out of the classroom.

"Tomorrow we'll be looking at how Parasponia can neutralize nitrogen levels in the soil. See you all here, bright and early."

***

The Botany Laboratory in the 'Beer Tent' had carefully controlled access. It was a bio-secure lock-down site. The staff wore white lab coats and blue PPEs, they were often mistaken for doctors and nurses around the campus.

Entry was only available with a secure swipe card, followed by a head-to-toe wash-down in a decontamination shower room. Then a change of clothing into a fresh set of sterile PPEs to wear on the other side. Same again on the way out.

As Willow entered the main reception room, Terrence Aguilar, a fellow student, was scanning his security card. He was a mid-20's American.

Latino-born, he grew up in El Paso, Texas. The female staff found him cute as hell. He was an annoying prankster most of the time.

'Tezz' was one of the many foreign fellowship students on the campus. He was taking part in a two-year botany program similar to Willows. The US Government sponsored him.

Tezz and Willow were very close. He lived just a few doors down from her on Hammerstrasse. They often strolled to and from the campus together. She loved his company and his charming drawl, but the pranks often wore thin.

After going through the main reception office, a long hallway forked to reveal the two doors to the showers. Males to the left. Females to the right. Staff followed the same process each time they entered; Get naked in the male or female change-room. Walk through the overhead shower system. Then get dried and dressed in new PPEs in a private curtained room at the end.

Terrence, dressed in his usual white lab coat, was about to step through the doors into the Male change room. He took off the lab coat and hung it on a coat rack.

"Morning, Miss Grey," he said in his cutest Southern Texan drawl. It was a temperate 25 degrees inside the facility, so he was now only wearing running shorts and a leaf-green singlet. He stepped inside the Male change-room.

Willow entered the female side. Beyond the shower, at the far end of the room, was a set of curtains leading to the change-room inside the lab. She flicked on the shower.

Terrence had also stepped into the shower on the male side. Water gushed from showerheads in the ceiling above.

"Morning, McDreamy," Willow shouted above the sound of the water.

Willow had a running joke that Tezz looked a little too much like 'McDreamy'; Dr Derek Shepherd from Grey's Anatomy on TV. Particularly when he donned his white lab-coat. Once inside the lab, he often called her 'Meredith' or 'Miss Grey', confusing the hell out of the other faculty members.

As Willow stepped into the female shower area, she could hear McDreamy singing on the other side of the tall rubberized walls dividing the room.

"I see a little silhouetto of a man. Scaramouche, Scaramouche, will you do the Fandango? Thunderbolts and lightning, very, very frightening me." he bellowed, as the warm shower gushed from above.

The overhead shower array on her side of the wall kicked-in automatically as Willow approached. She gingerly reached out and tested the water temperature before walking through. One her first day in the lab, the other students had pulled the time-honored prank of turning the shower temperature down to icy-cold. Screams usually followed.

Willow toweled off on the other side of the shower. She pulled the long curtain to the change-room aside. Then she screamed.

In the middle of the room was a skeleton, borrowed from the Biology lab. It was kneeling down on one bended-knee. The skeleton was wearing a white lab coat. It was holding a tiny three-leafed cannabis seedling in a red velvet-lined ring box, held in an outstretched hand.

On the other side of the wall, Tezz burst out laughing and called out, "Will you marry me, Miss Grey?"

"Meredith?"

"Miss Grey?"

CHAPTER 9

DRUG CARTELS AND AFRICAN METEORITES.

Freddie, Caz and Shu had stumbled into Zurich on the day before the Bulach Beer Festival. It was perfect timing.

Willow arrived home to find that they had changed into their civvies and had force-fed their army uniforms into her tiny washing machine. Showered and dressed, they were ready to party again.

Willow had brought home some friends. Chloe and Lena, two cute Swiss students, plus the Yank contingent of Tezz and his Latino Geologist buddy Marco.

After a brief introduction, they took the train north to Lindenhof.

Two hours later, they were wading through a plaza of stalls offering craft beers and street food. Marco arrived at their alfresco table with a round of precariously balanced steins and said, "OK. Bierlab Royals for the Aussies." He deposited some beer steins on the table.

"Schlachthuus Pale Ales for the locals, and two frosty LagereBrau's for me and Tezz."

He handed Tezz the last frosty stein.

At one end of the long table, Marco and Caz were doing their best to impress Chloe and Lena with drunken chit-chat. Chloe playfully poked Caz in the chest and said, "We have a saying in Switzerland. 'Nöd all Tassli im Schrank'. It means; you don't have have all your cups in the cupboard."

She flirted with Caz, saying, "I think your Caz is definitely missing some cups."

Willow and Shu burst out laughing. Lena and Marco nervously sized each other up.

Freddie and Tezz, at the other end of the table, were engrossed in a deep, drunken conversation.

Freddie said, "Fuck man. You grew up just across the road from Ciudad Juarez? El Paso must be nuts. It sounds like murder-central across the border in Mexico."

"It's not as wild as you think. The crime rate is relatively low on the US side," said Tezz, "But, yes, the Mexican side of the border is a different ballgame. When I was growing up, the original Juarez drug gangs were pushed out. The Sinaloa cartel now runs the show there."

Tezz took a long drink from his stein.

"Now the gangs in the city are under the control of a young guy called Manny Munoz. The locals nicknamed him 'Big M'. He's the son of the head of the Sinaloa cartel. A guy in Miami called Money Munoz. Manny runs the cartel's West Coast operations for the family. His sister, Valeria, runs everything else."

Freddie was impressed. Tezz seemed to know a lot about the Sinaloa cartel. He took another big chug of his beer and said, "I heard about those cartel motherfuckers. Don't they cut people's heads off? Hang them in the street?"

"Yes – and now they blow things up," said Tezz. "In 2010, the Sinaloa Cartel went to a whole new level. It was around the same time Big M first arrived. They planted a huge car bomb to target the US Federal Police Force in El Paso. My father was one of the police officers the explosion killed, –I was just fifteen."

Freddie leaned over, patted Tezz on the shoulder, and said, "Fuck man. I'm sorry to hear that."

Tezz said, "My father was a key operative in a drug task-force. The investigators found that the orders for the bombing came directly from Big M. He targeted the task-force members to send a message to the US authorities. He was only in his twenties back then. Now he runs cartels' operations for the entire west coast."

Tezz finished his beer and said,

"One day, I'm going to bring that motherfucker down for what he did to my family."

Willow suddenly yelled down the table above the noisy room, "Hey! McDreamy! Care to rejoin the party?"

Tezz smiled and yelled back, "Hey Meredith! Did you tell them about the trip to Africa yet?"

Freddie and Tezz slid down the long table to join the others.

Chloe and Lena suddenly look very excited.

Lena blurted out, "Oum Dreyga?"

Chloe added, "Noooo. Did you? You guys got the UN field trip to Western Sahara? Gopfertammi. Erm –Holy shit. I thought they hadn't announced that trip yet."

Willow said, "We got a text this morning."

She turned to Caz, Shu and Freddie to explain, "The UN has invited our university to send two people to visit its research site at Oum Dreyga. The whole Botany Department applied. It's in Western Sahara. Tezz and I just found out that we were the two chosen to go."

"It's the site of the H3-5 Chondrite Meteorite strike." Chloe added. "It blew a massive crater in the Earth near the Mauritanian border. The place is mostly as dry as a bone, but there are several plant species there that have adapted to live in almost zero moisture environments. There's been a lot of local militia activity there in the past, so access is rarely allowed there these days."

Tezz whispered down the table, "We will also be part of a special military Survival Training program they will embed us into."

Caz said, "That sounds like it would be freakin' awesome."

Tezz said, "They invited both of us to embed for the duration of the Survival course. As observers. To provide input on plant chemistry and potential water sources."

Willow added, "We're leaving in two weeks. We fly into Dakhla airport and then get a Moroccan Air Force chopper over to a UN facility near the crater. Apparently, the drive across the desert is too risky."

Freddie raised his empty stein and toasted,

"Well, congrats to the two of you. We'll make soldiers out of both of you one day."

"Who's up for another beer?"

***

Two days, and many beer steins, later Freddie, Caz and Shu drove back to Rammstein.

Willow and Tezz received an extensive briefing on the dangers involved in the excursion to Oum Dreyga. They would stay at a secure UN base nearby. They were busting with excitement as they packed for the long flight to western Africa.

CHAPTER 10

HELLHOLE. (NOUN) DUMP. SHAMBLES.

The town of Dakhla in Western Sahara was a hellhole.

The beach north of the town was stunning. It was a mecca for kite-surfers. The rest of the town was pig ugly. Boring yellow sand, filled with really boring sand-coloured buildings.

Willow turned to Tezz and pointed out the airplane window. She yelled over the engine noise, "Check that out!"

As the plane descended, she could see why the desert between Dakhla and Oum Dreyga was literally called 'No Man's Land'. There were no proper roads, just ruts in the ground showing that traffic had passed. It looked post-apocalyptic.

After landing, they got an ancient taxi over to the local helicopter base. The driver had wired a noisy computer fan into the cigarette lighter to provide a tiny amount of air movement in the car.

The desert around Dakhla was 'interesting'. Filled with PET bottles, rubbish, and thousands of rusted old car wrecks, which had been stripped of parts for resale in neighboring Mauritania. The landscape, between the car wrecks, was dotted inextricably with hundreds of old, boxy sand-covered televisions.

The taxi driver smelled like tobacco and sweat. The car smelled worse. One of his legs was just a stump.

When they got out of the car at the Moroccan Air Force helipad, the driver opened his door to let some air into the car. He warned them, "Don't wander too far here in town –or out at the crater site. There are old land mines everywhere." He rubbed his stump to make his point, then pulled his door shut and drove off, leaving them just standing there on the open tarmac in the blazing heat.

***

After twenty minutes, they heard the dull 'whump' of the sound of a large Morrocan military helicopter approaching. Half an hour later, they were on their way to the Oum Dreyga crater location.

As the helicopter approached the remote UN base, the pilot made a quick diversion to allow them to enjoy an aerial view of the crater site. After flying over an endless sea of dead flat yellow and red sand, it was a relief to see something resembling a real 'landscape' below them.

The pilot spoke over their headsets as they flew in a high arc.

"If you follow the line of that ridge to the left, you can make out the shape of the original meteorite impact site."

"We'll stay above 1500 feet, and swing around to the north before coming in to land. To make sure we're high enough to avoid any trigger-happy Bedouins with AK-47s near the town. Sorry, folks. The landing will be touch and go. No-one stays out here unless they really have to. The locals get fired up when there's a military chopper like this around."

Willow looked at the pilot with some concern, and asked,

"Just how dangerous is it down there?"

He smiled back and said, "It's a bit of a Mexican stand-off. The locals like the money and work at the UN base, but every-so-often there's a flare up, and it can get ugly real quick. Some scientists once got kidnapped by the militia. They'd driven overland from over near the border instead of using a chopper. They took the hostages back over to Mauritania –but the locals sorted out their release after a few weeks."

Willow looked surprised and said, "They didn't mention that in our briefing. So, they had to spend a few weeks over there?"

The pilot joked back, "The kidnapping would have been the least of the scientist's problems. Mauritania is hard-Muslim. No drinking. No fun. I wouldn't go there for a million bucks. It must have been boring as bat-shit for them."

As the pilot adjusted the flight-path he added, "The locals have been a bit riled up for the last few weeks. We've had quite a few people come through wearing NATO and US military uniforms for this exercise. They're not too happy about that."

Tezz figured it must be the Army's SERE (Survival, Evasion, Resistance, and Escape) training group they were going to be joining for a few days.

"Just watch your backs," the pilot said with a shrug. "The Sunnis don't take nicely to NATO and the CIA meddling in their local affairs. The Mauritanians take an even dimmer view of it."

Willow looked surprised and said, "The CIA? Out here? I thought this was a UN mission."

The pilot shrugged again and said, "The CIA has their fingers into everything out here. It's been that way since countries from Morocco down to Liberia started discovering deposits of copper, cobalt and manganese. Everyone wants to control Africa's new black gold."

Willow and Tezz choked on a cloud of swirling sand as their helicopter did an entry, and then a quick exit, of the UN facility. The blue-helmeted co-pilot literally threw their bags out of the cargo hold and slammed the door shut.

"Good luck!" he yelled, then he bolted back into the chopper.

***

A young Arab guy with a big, toothy smile was waiting to greet them. He ushered them into a demountable building to escape the oppressive heat and billowing sand.

He pointed to his name tag, which read 'KHOUNIS', then he garbled something in the local Hassaniya language.

No luck. He then switched to French. "Ca va?" As he offered them a seat, he tried, "Bienvenu?" Still no luck, so he switched to perfect Spanish, "Bienvenidos?"

Terrence gave him a big smile and said, "Muchas gracias".

Sigh of relief. Communications established.

The UN facility at Oum Dreyga looked more like a military Forward Operating Base than a peacekeeping or scientific mission. They'd strategically chosen the location, with miles of flat sand on all sides, enabling the visibility of attackers from any direction. Tall, thick, reinforced walls surrounded the whole place. Only one entry point, with heavy steel double gates, leading into a kill-box with machine gun sentry positions.

The base also had a secondary set of steel gates, in case attackers ever breached the main gate. The helipad was in one corner of the main living zone. White UN Toyota Land Cruisers baked in the heat, next to demountable buildings, solar panel arrays, and haphazardly placed shipping containers.

The facility had just three trees. Shade was a luxury.

They walked over to a converted shipping container. It had US Army safety posters stuck all over its walls.

Once inside, Khounis gave them a totally confusing safety briefing, and a short induction on local customs. This mostly involved pointing at posters and reciting a well-rehearsed bunch of talking points, in Spanish, and then in broken English.

There were lots of posters that referred to land mines.

After the briefing, Khounis led them through the sand toward a large demountable with a dirty curved roof in the center of the complex. A sign above the door read 'CHOW HALL'.

"We'll take you out to the valley in the crater tomorrow," Khounis said in broken Spanish. Terrence translated for Willow as they walked.

"Dr Stewart will give you a briefing on the scientific elements of the trip. He's one of the few civilians here."

Willow was excited. She asked, "Do you mean THE Dr Stewart –from Cornell?" Khounis just gave her a blank look and kept walking.

They entered a reception room at the front of the Chow Hall. It acted like a small air-lock, and hummed with the sound of industrial scale air conditioning. A guy in full US military tactical gear, holding an assault rifle, bustled past them.

"Morning." the soldier said. He looked very drunk.

Khounis continued his briefing. "Most of the US Army team that are doing the Advanced SERE training arrived last night. That exercise starts tomorrow. Major Crensch will brief you on that tonight."

As they entered the main Chow Hall room, The Beastie Boys' song 'Make some noise' greeted them with a deafening roar.

CHAPTER II

MOMENT LOST.

The big Chow-Hall building at the center of the Oum Dreyga UN compound looked like a nightclub or frat house on the inside. Drunk male and female soldiers danced wildly to the pounding beat of the Beastie Boys. Ice chests overflowed with bottles of vodka and beers from around the planet.

Every surface was strewn with red plastic cups. A smoker and a grill stood in the corner, barbecuing slabs of beef, below a set of stainless-steel extractor fans. The air was heavy with the smell of weed and sweat. A couple of soldiers were locking lips in a corner.

A rowdy game of beer-pong was in progress on the opposite side of the room. Not exactly the white-coated environment science-geeks Willow and Terrence were expecting. Over at the beer-pong table, the crowd roared as a young female soldier downed a red cup full of beer.

They walked over to the soldiers and Terrence nervously asked, "We are looking for Dr. Stewart. Where can we find him?" The crowd burst out laughing and pointed over to the far corner of the room.

One of the beer-pongers said, "We lost him about an hour ago."

Dr. Stewart, a sixty-something man with greying hair and spectacles, lay sprawled on a line of plastic chairs, fast asleep. Still holding a half-empty cup of beer.

They walked over, and Willow prodded him on the shoulder. He roused and slowly opened his eyes. Straining to focus in a beer haze. He rubbed his eyes and sat up.

Willow said, "I'm Willow, and this is Terrence."

Dr Stewart rubbed his throbbing temples and thought for a moment, then he said, "Ah – Yes –Our guests from the University in Zurich. A pleasure to meet you."

He looked around the room, then said, "Let's try to find somewhere a little quieter. These Army boys party a bit hard for my liking."

They trudged across the boiling sand to another demountable building. A sign above the door read 'BOTANICALS'. They stepped inside and discovered that it was a basic laboratory setup. Long tables with petri dishes filled with dirt. Rows of seedlings in pots. A bench with microscopes and chemical sample analysis machines stationed along it. Above that stood a wall unit with plant samples stored in tall glass jars. There were several computer desks.

Dr Stewart apologized, "Sorry, it's just us for the next few days. Most of the regular scientific staffers took off to Morocco a few days ago. For a bit of R&R. And to make room in the sleeping quarters for the soldiers."

They took seats around Dr Stewart's desk in a corner of the room. He poured and drank a large glass of water.

"For my inevitable headache," he said, smiling.

Then poured a glass for each of them.

"Now –let's talk about your trip to The Khadra first," Dr Stewart said.

The Khadra Valley was a freakish valley oasis on the edge of the Oum Dreyga escarpment. It was the real reason Terrence and Willow were so excited to visit. They'd both talked incessantly about it for weeks.

When a meteorite smashed into the Gour Lafkah Mountains in 2003, it ripped the deep valley from the earth. The Khadra valley was fed by a series of small mineral springs, which meant it was now crammed with strange and unique vegetation, rising like Lazarus out of the earth. Enterprising locals had scavenged and sold the larger chondrite meteor fragments soon after 2003, but they now tended to avoid the place, as they believed it to be haunted. Researchers established a specialist lab at the UN base to investigate the plants in the valley and their ability to thrive in such harsh desert conditions.

Dr. Stewart ushered them over to a laboratory workstation. It was covered in plant samples in tall glass jars.

"You can use this station while you're here," he said. "The two colleagues that work here are also studying plant genetics related to arid environments. They laid out a lot of their notes on the Khadra for you before they left."

"Thanks," said Willow. "they emailed us a lot of information before we left Zurich too."

Dr Stewart, still a little unsteady from the earlier rounds of beer-pong, took a seat back at his desk and said, "Major Crensch has asked for you to meet with him tomorrow at 8pm –to brief you on the embed for the Army SERE exercise."

"Who's he?" asked Willow.

Dr Stewart replied, "Major Thomas Crensch. He runs the military side of things here."

Willow and Terrence busied themselves looking at the plant samples and reading the briefing notes. Terrence turned to ask Dr. Stewart a question, but found he was slumped over his desk, snoring.

***

The next morning, Willow and Tezz choppered out to the Khadra site. They spent the day rock-hopping, taking photos and collecting soil and plant samples. Like Botanists in a candy store.

The sun set over the idyllic Khadra valley at about 6-30pm. It bathed the verdant valley in a magic golden light. The temperature had dropped to a pleasant twenty-five degrees, and the heady perfume of wild Beebrush and Dwarf Lomandra wafted up the lush valley. The view looked like something from the pages of a website about a romantic resort.

Willow and Terrence sat beside a clifftop rock-pool at the edge of the valley, bare feet playfully dangling in the cool water burbling from a tiny spring spilling into it. They'd opened a bottle of wine earlier and thirstily drank it straight from the bottle.

Willow stood to take in the breath-taking valley view below them.

"It's –it's wonderful. Better than I'd ever imagined," she mused, "To think that a meteor, and some spring water, could create this in such a short time. Amazing. It's like Shangri La."

Terrence stood and joined her at the edge of the cliff. Standing close.

Willow turned to look at him. They held each other's gaze in the golden light. Terrence looked deep into her eyes.

"Yes. Wonderful," he said.

She looked back at him, holding his gaze. Tezz moved closer. He slipped his hand around her waist as Willow reached up and lightly caressed his shoulder. He leaned in to kiss her.

Suddenly, the thump –thump –thump of a fast-approaching military chopper shattered the golden tranquility. It's urgent red lights flashing in the early summer evening. The sand quickly started whipping up around them, and then became a full-blown sandstorm as the chopper landed nearby. Khounis leapt out.

"Hurry! They can't wait," he shouted.

Willow and Tezz ran toward it.

Moment lost.

***

At 8pm sharp, Khounis banged loudly on the door of the botanicals' lab back at the UN Base.

"Quickly," he said, "Major Crensch is waiting."

He ushered them toward a sandy, camo-net covered building over near one of the gun towers at the entry gates.

As they walked, Khounis joked in broken Spanish, "Good to see you kept away from the land mines –are still walking on the two legs!"

Willow looked at Terrence for a translation, but he just said, "You really don't want to know."

Most of the buildings at the Oum Dreyga Base carried some sort of pale blue color theme to reflect the independence of the UN's operations. The building Major Crensch was in bore no markings at all. They entered the room and found a plain office, but with a picture of the President and the Presidential Seal on the wall. They saw an American flag hanging from a short pole. The Major sat at his desk perusing two green personnel files.

"Welcome," he said. "Please take a seat. How was your day out in the valley today?"

"Fine," said Tezz, trying not to gush about it.

"More like fucking amazing," blurted Willow enthusiastically.

Crensch smiled and said, "Ground temperature wasn't bad today because of the cloud cover. It's going to be much hotter when we are out on the other side of the crater tomorrow for the SERE exercise."

He pointed to a coffee urn on a workbench and said, "Grab a cup if you like. I bought the beans from my favourite store near my home in DC."

They both declined. A good night's sleep would be important tonight.

Crensch parked the personnel files at the corner of his desk.

He said, "Miss Barrant. Very impressive credentials. I've read your study on plant genetics and survival in arid environments. Impressive indeed."

Willow replied, "I'm glad to see that anyone at all has taken the time to read it. Sometimes I think we do all this work at the lab –and no-one ever looks at it."

"I've also read some of your early papers on native plants as food and medicine. The ones you wrote back in Australia." Crensch added.

Willow felt impressed.

Crensch laughed and added, "We even got a copy of that little university paper you wrote on the use of traditional use of native plants as weapons. Interesting!"

Willow looked surprised and said, "But I didn't even publish that paper. How?"

The Major looked a little smug and said, "We have our ways."

Crensch turned to Tezz and said, "Mr. Aguilar. We've heard a lot about you, too."

The Major took a sip of coffee and said, "Sorry to hear about your father in the car bombing back home in El Paso. We interact very closely with the DEA on the LATAM cartels. I met your dad once –down in Costa Rica. He was a fine police officer."

Willow furrowed her brow, then turned to Crensch and asked, "And who would 'we' be?"

She looked around the room. "I thought this base was a UN site. Some sort of peacekeeping zone."

Crensch smiled back at her and said, "Well –let's just say 'we' work closely with the UN as well. Particularly when it comes to advancing our SERE training program. Lets just call us 'Special Operations'."

He changed the topic by pointing to a topographical map of the crater on the wall, and said, "As you know from your briefing papers, the 'S' in SERE training stands for Survival. And that's why you'll be embedding with us for the next few days." He handed each of them a briefing document for the exercise.

Crensch continued, "Most of the trainees doing this exercise will never have seen the sort of plant life that they'll find down at the crater. It's unique. Your aim is to help them identify, and make use of, what they find down there. Hopefully without making themselves sick –or dead."

Crensch took a slow sip of coffee while Willow and Tezz thumbed through the documents.

He said, "Sorry if the team was rowdy last night. They've all been out in the low-desert living on dry biscuits, dates and desert gourds for the past two weeks. They were all ornery when we got back here."

He leaned back in his chair.

"Khounis and the QM will sort you out tonight. We will perform the exercise in full tactical uniform. You're both included. So, welcome to the US Army –at least for the next day or so. Get some sleep. You'll need it."

***

64

After a short walk across the compound, they were both standing in the Quarter Master's store.

Racks containing army uniforms and tactical gear lined the room. Across from the clothing was a locked caged with LOTS of guns. More than Willow had ever seen in her entire life. Sgt. Kerry Stokehouse, the QM for the exercise, ticked items off a checklist.

Tezz was killing time, waiting for Willow to get kitted out. He rummaged around the room, then picked up a miniature flame thrower from a shelf.

"Camp fire starter?" he joked. Stokehouse was unimpressed.

Willow stepped out of a changing room wearing a full US Army desert camo combat uniform. Heavy pants and jacket over boots and a plate carrier vest, plus webbing and a tactical helmet with full Comms. She looked very uncomfortable.

"Woo –GI Jane!" hooted Tezz. Willow frowned.

Sgt. Stokehouse checked items off Willow's checklist.

She handed Willow a patch that read 'BARRANT' and another that read 'EMBED'. Stokehouse said, "These two Velcro patches go on your chest pad".

She passed Willow a third Velcro patch in the shape of a large band-aid. It had the word 'A+ POS' hand-written on it.

"This blood group patch goes on your upper arm. Keep it visible." Stokehouse said.

Willow studied the blood group patch and asked, "Why would someone need to know my blood type?" Then the realization dawned on her.

Stokehouse simply nodded and said, "Yes."

Shortly after, Tezz walked in from another changing room wearing the same type of camo uniform. Willow was becoming wary. She found it odd that Tezz looked very comfortable in his military gear. He expertly adjusted some webbing and his helmet Comms gear. It looked like this wasn't his first rodeo.

Tezz asked Stokehouse, "Doesn't this normally come with a holster for a pistol?" She gave him a wry smile, but dutifully checked her list, anyway.

"Sorry, no guns for you two," she said, "not standard issue for Botanists. I could give you a spade?"

Tezz looked at Stokehouse and joked, "Maybe I could get some NODs? Night vision?"

She shook her head and said, "Nup".

Tezz looked disappointed, like a child who'd discovered the Lego store didn't have the model he was looking for in stock.

Fifteen minutes later, Willow and Tezz stood outside the QM store, dressed head to toe in full US Army combat kit. A world away from their usual white lab coats and PPE.

Willow turned to Tezz and gave him a wary look.

"OK soldier-boy, can you tell me what the fuck is REALLY going on here?" she demanded.

Tezz shrugged and said, "It's just for safety, Wills. Standard Operating Procedure. Just in case we meet some locals out at the crater who aren't so –erm –friendly."

Willow grabbed him hard on by shoulder and said, "You know that isn't what I mean. Who are these guys? Crensch –Huh? This doesn't feel like a peace-keeping force to me. These guys are hardcore."

Willow stared at Tezz slowly, from head to toe, and said, "And why do I get a feeling that you feel quite at home here?"

Terrence lowered his voice to a whisper.

"OK –The SERE program that runs out of here. It's not just for the UN." Tezz answered. "It's what they call a Secret Squirrel. An undercover operation."

They started walking back toward their sleeping quarters.

"It's funded jointly by the CIA and DEA." Tezz said, "With the permission of the UN to use the base, of course. Everyone trains here. Interpol. Special Ops. The SAS. The EU."

Tezz stopped for a moment. He smiled, as he tried to break the tension in the air, "And sometimes, even the UN." he joked.

"I've worn tactical uniforms like this before," he said. "You have to remember that my father was dealing with the cartels, and he often got involved in operations with the local SWAT teams. It was his day job. So when I grew up, my play toys were things like plate carriers and tactical helmets. Just like these. Like any kid, I wanted to be just like my dad."

Willow furrowed her brow again. "So that's how Crensch knows your father?" she asked.

Tezz continued, "While he was working with the DEA, my father also lead similar survival training exercises, but he did it down south in the jungle in Costa Rica."

"And it goes deeper than that," Tezz replied awkwardly.

"Just like your study at the university in Zurich is funded by your Australian University Fellowship award –mine is funded by Uncle Sam." Tezz said, "–the DEA specifically. And, I'd guess, it's not exactly a coincidence that I'm doing work on the Cannabaceae plant family while I'm on their payroll in Zurich. That's probably why they chose us to come here and embed on Crensch's exercise."

They both took a seat on some deck chairs near their sleeping quarters. Willow listened intently as Tezz told her more about his father.

Between the intimate moment overlooking the Khadra, and the revelations about his past, she was seeing Tezz, the Botanist, in a new light.

CHAPTER 12

RUN FOR YOUR LIFE.

As much as the mandatory army uniform freaked her out, Willow was smart enough to realise that the advanced SERE exercise at Oum Dreyga was an opportunity that couldn't be resisted.

In the morning, she pulled on her uniform to join the army crew for breakfast. On the way over, Tezz expertly re-adjusted her gear.

***

After breakfast, they found a convoy of troop carriers and white UN-branded SUVs waiting outside. Ready for the drive out to the crater. Behind to them stood two vehicles that Willow could only describe as 'Tanks'.

"Whoa Up!" she said to Tezz. "We're going to need a tank for protection where we are going?"

Terrence explained, "It's not a tank. It's a Bradley. It carries six people. The gun is really just to scare the crap out of anyone in a car or truck nearby."

Everyone piled into the vehicles and they headed off into the desert.

The Bradley drivers appeared to be on edge as they passed by the small local town on the way to the crater. Goats scattered as they roared by. Locals, holding AK-47's, scowled as they stepped out of their sand-colored homes.

*****

The group set up the base for the exercise atop a sheer sandstone cliff that dropped into the valley below.

Willow and Tezz set up a large tent, while the soldiers went away to learn how to purify drinking water. When the soldiers arrived back, they were waiting for them at the end of a long table.

Tall glass lab jars, each filled with plant specimens, covered the table. The soldiers had gathered next to it. Tezz and Willow were talking about the botanical properties of each plant. The specimens had been specially chosen to represent the types of plants that would be typically found in a desert area.

Everything was going well until the glass jars started exploding.

BOOM. BOOM. BOOM.

Three glass plant specimen jars on the table exploded. Followed microseconds later by the echoing retort of gunfire from the far away in the valley below. After quickly hitting the sand, three soldiers crawled to the edge of the escarpment. They pulled out binoculars and peered into the valley below.

Suddenly, everyone's Comms headsets came alive. One observer shouted, "Around fifteen enemy combatants on foot coming up through the rocks below! Armed. AK's. Three Technicals with 50 caliber guns mounted –coming up the main track toward us. My guess is the Mauritanian militia. Must have driven over from the border last night."

Willow gulped and slid closer to Terence, clutching his arm.

Major Crensch sprang into action, yelling, "That probably gives us five minutes clear. No use all of us holing up here and causing an international incident. Let's move."

Crensch waved toward the Bradleys.

"Everyone back to the vehicles. We'll see if we can outrun them back to the base."

He walked over to a group of soldiers.

"I want the two fastest vehicles to hang back. To lay down some suppressive fire to slow them down when they top that rise. Then rejoin asap. Buy us some distance. No heroics, please."

Crensch grabbed a field radio and barked, "Let's call in a helicopter in advance." He pointed to Willow and Tezz. "To get these civilian embeds off the base as soon as we get back. In case it gets ugly. Oscar Mike."

The personnel carriers took off down the sand track toward the base. The two Bradleys, each with a soldier manning its gun, took the rear. This would help with rear defense, but it slowed the column of 4WDs down to about fifty miles an hour. They dropped back into the cloud of dust coming from the lead vehicles.

Minutes later, Willow could hear rapid gunfire behind them.

After ten minutes, the convoy ripped through the small township at top speed, enveloping it in a thick, choking cloud of dust. As they left the town, the two vehicles that had stayed back rejoined the column. The convoy sped up along the flat, open plain leading to their home base. Willow could see that the two straggler vehicles had their rear windows blown out and bullet holes sprayed across their rear doors.

One of the militia Technicals suddenly appeared from the cloud of dust billowing out behind the convoy. It fired on the last Bradley. Most shots missed as it bumped and lurched across the rutted ground. The turret of the Bradley rotated, and a spray of bullet fire strafed the Technical. It exploded in a fireball and rolled several times.

The gates of the UN compound loomed into view. They swung open.

Another Technical appeared on the other side of the dust column. Willow saw it careening toward their vehicle. She grabbed Terrence by his collar and pulled him to the floor, as a bunch of heavy rounds shredded the rear of their vehicle. She moaned as a large metal shard ripped into her leg. Terrence's face was bleeding from the blown out window glass.

The Technical sped up and pulled right alongside, as the militia gunner swung his gun around toward them. Willow braced and hunkered down low. The militia shooter suddenly exploded in a pink mist and rolled off the back of the vehicle, as he took a direct hit from a spray of bullets from a Bradley nearby.

The rear of the Technical lit up in a ball of fire, as it screeched to a halt, and then slowly tilted sideways.

The convoy of vehicles drove through the gates of the UN compound to safety. The gates swung shut, then the gun towers opened up their weapons on the militia pursuers. The marauders circled the compound to avoid the gunfire. Soon after, several other beaten-up vehicles joined the militia fray. Masked militia men stood behind their vehicles and took potshots at the gun towers.

Inside the far corner of the compound, a helicopter was waiting with its rotors whirring. Ready to evac.

Crensch ran over to one of the SUVs. Willow and Terrence were inside, lying on the floor.

"You two, OK?" he shouted. "We need to get you out now, before more come from the town."

Willow's camo pants had a large patch torn away. Blood trickled out. The glass had cut Terrence's face, leaving bleeding pock-marks.

"You OK to get out and walk?" Terence yelled to Willow.

She shouted back, "I'm certainly not fucking staying in here!"

She grimaced in pain as she took the weight on her leg, then she started limping toward the helicopter.

Tezz put his arm around her and helped her along.

He yelled back to Crensch, "We're good. Give em hell!"

They jumped into the chopper and buckled in.

The helo lifted into the sky.

Inside the chopper, Tezz tore open a small medical kit from a pouch in his chest webbing. He cleaned Willow's leg wound.

He offered his bicep to her and said, "Grab this as tight as you can."

Willow said, "Huh?"

Terrence said, "Just trust me. Grab onto my arm, absolutely as hard as you can."

As she gripped his arm, he yanked out a large sliver of metal protruding from her thigh.

She screamed and released her grip.

Terrence shouted, "Don't let go yet! We aren't out of the woods."

She grabbed his arm and squeezed again as he tore open a sachet of antiseptic powder. He poured it into the wound. Pain ripped through her, and she screamed again.

Willow released her grip on his arm as he gently placed some gauze and a compression bandage on her leg. She started sobbing deeply into his chest.

"It'll be right. It'll be right," he whispered, as he lifted her head and stared into her eyes. She held his gaze for a moment.

Their lips were just inches apart.

He moved to hold her gaze again.

The helicopter bucked as it hit an updraft. Their faces lurched apart. Willow tried to sit upright, but a jolt of pain went through her.

Tezz held her steady. He looked deep into her eyes. He nuzzled her hair, then playfully grazed her cheek with his lips. She held his gaze, then moved closer and kissed his neck. They locked lips in a tender kiss. Willow slid her arm around his body to hold him close.

She halted when she felt a large sticky wet patch beneath his ribs.

"What the?" she exclaimed, as she lifted his arm. A dark red patch of blood was soaking the area around a large rip in his shirt.

He said, "I think a piece of shrapnel might have hit me too. It hurts a lot - but it doesn't feel too deep." Tezz winced as Willow carefully unbuttoned his shirt and then carefully pulled it off.

She cleaned the wound with some gauze and then sprinkled some of the remaining antiseptic powder on it. As Willow wrapped a bandage around his torso, she said, "There you go. It looks more like a scrape than a cut. Bleeding a lot, though."

Fighting the pain in her leg, she moved her body to press closer to him. Another shot of pain jolted through her.

With her cut thigh, and Tezz's bleeding chest, kissing time was well and truly over.

Tezz pushed her back into the seat, peeled off another strip of gauze.

"We need to get your wound wrapped up. It's deep," he said.

"Sorry, but I'm going to have to cut those pants off you so I can clean and wrap the wound properly."

Willow laughed out loud and said, "Now that's a pickup line if I ever heard one."

He smirked, raised one eyebrow, and teased, "Just wait until Dr McDreamy gets you high on a morphine shot."

As the chopper roared back toward the safety of Dakhla, Tezz administered a shot of painkiller using an auto-injector from the chopper's medical kit. Then he started cutting away the bloody leg of her pants.

Terrence turned to her, then laughed.

"Jesus. This is going to be a story to tell the grandchildren," he said.

Willow looked at him lovingly as he gently bound her blood-soaked bare thigh with a bandage and gauze.

Was it the morphine, or was something else kicking in?

CHAPTER 13

TIME TO TALK.

The trip home to Zurich involved two military plane rides and several painful stitches in Willow's leg at a medical centre in Barcelona.

They'd scanned the news for mentions of the conflict in Western Sahara, but there was not a single word. It looked like the local press were as compliant as the government officials.

At Barcelona airport, Terrence got a text from Major Crensch suggesting is would probably be career-limiting if they mentioned the incident with the local militia at the UN base. Willow and Terrence were smart enough not to put their fully funded fellowships at risk.

'Mum's the word', he texted back.

A day later, Willow and Tezz were back in Zurich. They put the drama at Oum Dreyga behind them. Willow was given a couple of weeks off work. Her leg wound prohibited her from entering the shower decontamination system at the lab in the Beir Tent. They'd told everyone she'd had a fall at The Khadra.

Tezz spent most of his days at her apartment helping her recover. It felt good. After three weeks, he put his flat on the market and moved in with her. Willow's leg was healing fast, but sex with Terrence usually involved an awkward game of 'Twister', with slow moves to avoid splitting her stitches.

A few weeks later, life had returned to normal, and Willow was back on campus.

***

"Check out the cute guy in the lab-coat," said the leggy Russian student. "He could examine me all night long."

Willow was sitting with a group of students in the university cafeteria when 'McDreamy' walked past outside, carrying a box filled with plant samples. He was looking very smart in his white lab-coat. Willow leaned over to the Russian student.

"Keep away from that one," she confided. "I've heard those Botanists end up with all sorts of icky skin diseases from the samples they handle. Ukkk." Willow stood up, then steadied herself on a walking stick.

"But the Geologists are worse."

She hobbled away, smiling.

***

It was late February in Zurich, so winter was still in full force. The city was slushy, but the snowy mountains around the city look like a fairytale. Life was about as good as it gets.

Willow tidied up the kitchen in the apartment as Tezz snored in bed. She was talking to her father on an iPad video call.

She looked at the academic calendar on the fridge and said, "Dad, can you believe it's February? I can't believe how the days are flying by." She sat down in front of the iPad.

"We'll finish both of our fellowships here in a few months."

Her father asked, "Have you talked to Terrence about it yet? What are his plans?"

Willow poured herself a strong coffee and thought about it as she stirred the cup.

"We didn't really talk about it over Christmas," she said.

"He was going to stay here with me –but jumped a cheap flight back to El Paso at the last minute. I wanted to go, but we are both pretty broke right now."

She buttered some toast.

"I think his mum has been having a hard time coping since his father was killed. He was over there for a couple of weeks. He never seems keen to talk about it, so I avoid the topic."

She rotated the iPad on the table so she could walk over to the stove.

"Tezz has been really quiet since he got off a call from here last week. They were arguing," she said.

"I don't think the authorities are having any luck finding the people who did the bombing. He's frustrated more than anything. And angry. He's been having late night calls with the local police. But nada."

She jiggled a hot pan on the stove, then slid a golden Swiss Cholermues, a rather thick, fluffy alpine pancake, onto a plate.

"Hmmm. I can smell those pancakes all the way over here on the Cape," her father said. "Save some for me."

She proudly displayed her breakfast to the iPad camera.

Willy said, "I don't care what the Swiss call it, it still looks a bit like an omelet to me."

Willow shifted the iPad so she could sit at the table and eat.

"So, we are both playing it slow for now," she continued.

"I don't want to push him too hard. But it's going to come to a head in the next couple of months. Zurich must be the most expensive place to live on the planet. So, we'll have to get out of here mid-year when our University funding ends."

She finished her Cholermues.

"Gotta go now," she said. "I'm due in the lab. Let's talk next week. Love you, dad."

She hung up the call, grabbed her coat, and headed to the door.

***

February rolled into March and April.

Life was wonderful for Willow and Tezz. Spring was bursting in Europe, but the decision about what to do after July hung heavily in the surrounding air. Willow had prodded Tezz a couple of times about it, but he wasn't keen to talk.

In early springtime, Willow received an unexpected email from Melbourne University.

It was an offer of a position in the Department of Plant Sciences after her fellowship ended. The salary was pretty good too.

They were setting up a new lab project that could use her expertise in Hop Viruses. Fully funded by a donor organization called The Cann Group. A large ASX-listed medicinal cannabis company.

The email was asking her to set up a date for an interview,

It was time for her and Tezz to talk.

CHAPTER 14

Tezz Drops A Bomb.

Date night was different this week. Usually, Willow and Tezz ended up out at a Zurich nightclub, or the noisy Rheinfelder Bierhalle, with friends, drinking and dancing off the stresses of the week and shouting above the bump and grind. Happy go lucky.

This time, Willow had chosen an intimate local restaurant in Alte Chasi instead. Way across town. Nice and quiet, and far enough away to avoid chance encounters with friends.

It was time for 'the talk'.

As the taxi pulled away, they stood on the curb, looking at the restaurant's menu in the window. It was freezing outside, but it felt positively balmy compared to the icebox conditions since Christmas.

Tezz was excited.

"I'm starving," he said.

They stepped inside and took a seat in a corner next to an ancient stone wall. The smell of grilled cheese and smoky steak filled the air.

Tezz licked his lips and said, "I'm starting with the Raclette and Gschwellti. God, I love drippy cheese."

Tezz scanned further down the menu and mused, "And maybe Rosti too? Do you think that's overdoing it on the potato?"

They ordered a small fondue and a couple of glasses of their favorite Vino Rosato to start.

Willow felt awful inside, like she was luring an animal into a trap.

After sharing the delicious fondue, then a cheese overdose of Raclette paired with a nice Merlot from Valais, she popped the a copy of the email from Melbourne University on the table.

Willow stammered, "I got this last week. So, I figured we needed to talk."

Tezz scanned the copy of the email and grimaced. Not the response she was hoping for. A bit like announcing you were pregnant, and your guy just says, "Ohhhh."

In an instant, he could sense her disappointment.

He reached out and took her hand. Looked her straight in the eye.

Tezz said, "You're right. We need to talk."

He slowly put the email printout back on the table.

"I've got some stuff going on too," he said. "Family stuff."

Tezz looked her straight in the eye.

"Big M's Sinaloa cartel in Juarez is going after Gabriela. My mother. They tried to kill her."

Chapter 15

Big M's El Paso Shuffle.

EL Paso, Texas. Three weeks earlier.

Gabriela Aguilar had just finished her weekly video call with her son Terrence when the bullets ripped her house apart.

***

Number 1135 Tula Avenue El Paso looked like a typical El Paso matron's home. Small. Neat. Single story to avoid stairs. Pale blue window shutters to block out the summer heat. On a small block, with no fence, a curved pebble footpath path, and an immaculately maintained garden. Gabriella had a single large Texas Mountain Laurel that smelled just heavenly in spring. Her Christmas lights had lit up a few minutes earlier, as the sun finally faded from the sky. They twinkled like fireflies in her low, manicured garden hedges.

Picturesque houses like Gabriela's, in tree-lined streets, made it easy to forget that El Paso was the epicentre of the war on drugs; 'Cartel Central'.

On the one hand, the cartel was rife over the border, just a few miles away. On the other hand, various discreet locations across the city headquartered places like Division 7 of the Drug Enforcement Administration, Joint Task Force North, the United States Border Patrol Sector, and the U.S. Border Patrol Special Operations Group. Strange bed-fellows.

***

Four gangbangers from Big M's Sinaloa cartel gang had slowly driven past Gabriela's home three times before they lit her house up with bullets from the street.

A cartel member stepped out of the rear of the car holding a large machine gun. A steady spray of .224 cal Valkyrie rounds blasted out of it. Gabriella's stucco walls shattered. After a minute of chaos, the gunner casually handed the empty machine gun back into the car and retrieved another one. He emptied that one into the house as well. Then he casually stepped back into the car and they just cruised slowly away into the night.

No great rush for the hitman. Just an El Paso shuffle between the cartel's round of nightly hits.

By the time Gabriellas neighbors carefully edged out their front doors, her home had smoke and flames rising from the roof. Forensics later concluded that someone had fired four hundred high ballistic rounds into the house. Emergency service sirens started wailing in the distance.

When the police cars and firetrucks arrived, Gabriela was still seated in an old leather couch beside a large stone fireplace in the middle of the smoking wreckage.

She'd been leaning down beside the chair to plug her iPad into a charger when the house exploded into a million pieces. It saved her life. She'd just stayed low, clasped her rosary, and prayed. The cops said her stone fireplace had stopped most of the bullets.

As more cops arrived, a murmur went through their ranks.

The police officers gradually realized that this was the family home of Detective Franco Aguilar, the lead cop the Sinaloa Cartel had killed in the city's notorious drug war bombing.

The hit on Gabriella's home had 'Big M' written all over it.

CHAPTER 16

THE BULGARIAN SECRET SQUIRREL.

Back at the restaurant in Zurich's Alte Chasi, Willow mostly just stared in shock as Tezz recounted the story of the hit on his mother's house by Big M's goons.

Tezz whispered, "The reason I rushed home for Christmas wasn't just because my mother was upset. It was because they were considering putting her into a witness protection program. And she was resisting."

Willow gasped. She took his hand and said, "Fuck, babe. Why didn't you tell me before?"

Tezz took a slow sip of his Merlot.

"The whole thing's a mess," Terrence said. "The Sinaloa cartel has been on a rampage since the El Paso car bombing that killed my dad. It was the first time they'd done anything that big on the US side of the border. There's been a big shift in the balance of power since Manny Munoz came into the scene. Big M thinks he's a big swinging dick."

Tezz took another drink and continued, "So, the US government –true to form –over-reacted big-time."

Willow asked, "How?"

"The Feds, the CIA and the DEA are all trying to hunt down Big M." said Tezz.

"But the Feds don't have jurisdiction across the border in Juarez. Everything they do has to be 'off-the-books'. The CIA is only involved because of the scale of the bombing. The US media are howling for arrests. But it's technically a DEA operation. So –it's a complete fucking mess."

A waitress approached the table. Willow smiled and shooed her away.

Willow said, "So, what has this all got to do with your mum? Why would they target her?"

Tezz looked around to make sure no-one was listening.

"Big M was becoming worried about getting caught –and eventually facing a trial in the US. So, to hedge his bets, he put out orders to shake down the families of the bombing victims. To send a 'message' that helping with the investigations was not a good idea."

Tezz paused, choking up a bit, and said, "She didn't even tell me. Can you believe it? We were having normal chats all the way up to Christmas. And then nothing from her. Later a friend rang to see if I was planning on coming home to stay with her *–with the shooting and all*."

Tezz moved closer to Willow.

"I was on the next plane out of here," he whispered. "I didn't want to worry you about it. Too many unknowns. Mum just kept begging me not to come home. Telling me she could handle it. I got her out of a neighbor's house she was staying at —and into a motel out of town as soon as I arrived."

Tezz fidgeted nervously with his glass and continued,

"My mother's house looked like a bomb had ripped it apart. I used some of dad's old connections to get information from the FBI and the DEA. I was trying to work out a deal with anyone who'd listen to get her some protection. But everyone was just passing the buck."

The waitress hovered again.

Willow said, "We'll need fifteen minutes. I think we'll need another bottle of the Merlot though." The waitress left with the order.

Tezz fingered his napkin nervously and said, "Then Crensch stepped into the picture."

Willow's eyes widened.

"Whaaa? Major Crensch? she gasped, "The CIA guy from Oum Dreyga?"

Terrence gave her a look that suggested, 'lower your voice'.

"One and the same," he said. "When he got back to the US, he got dragged into the joint CIA/FBI operation to hunt down Big M and the bombers.

He's been based down in El Paso for the last few months. He's as hamstrung as the rest of the agencies down there. I think they enlisted him to bend the rules a bit, so they can make some progress. He's in a warehouse near the airport with a small Special Ops team. They've started putting people undercover in the drug trade in Juarez."

Willow bit her tongue when the waitress arrived with a fresh bottle of red. She opened it and left.

Terrence continued, "But, after some arm-twisting with the Police Chief, Crensch pulled strings for me to make mum disappear off the El Paso radar. Crensch said he owed us for keeping the Sahara screw-up out of the media."

Willow looked relieved.

"Well, at least your mum's safe now."

Terrence shook his head and said,

"Not really. Big M and the cartel have informers on the payroll everywhere –on the streets –in the DEA. I need to work out a more permanent solution. Eventually, they'll find her again. And, if they don't, they'll just move on to hunting down my cousins to send their message."

Tezz pulled out to his mobile phone. He clicked and scrolled to a document attached to an email, then he handed Willow the phone and said, "So –I've been meaning to show you this."

Willow slowly read the document.

It was a letter of offer from the Central Intelligence Agency. They were asking Tezz to join a Secret Squirrel training operation. It was 1,000 miles away at NATO's Novo Selo Army Base in Bulgaria. He would start straight after he finished his Zürich Fellowship, a few months from now.

"Crensch knows I'm a local in El Paso, and I've spent time in Juarez growing up," said Tezz. "And that has value for his operation down there.

He wants me to spend twelve months doing Basic Training in Bulgaria. Outside of the USA. Then head back to the States to help them."

He took hold of Willow's hand and said, "I think I want to do it."

Willow shook her head in disbelief and said, "But why? It's a fucking drug cartel. It's dangerous. They could kill you."

Tezz took a slow sip of wine to give her some time to cool down.

"OK. –so –I could forget about it," said Tezz. "I could take some cushy job in the agricultural or bio-tech sectors. But my whole family will always be in danger until this ends. It's bigger than just me. And I'm worried it might eventually include you."

Willow pondered that thought.

Tezz said, "If we ever –err –became a –couple –you would get drawn into this mess too. I would NEVER risk that."

After the dinner and the talk, Terrence decided the least he could do was express and interest in Crensch's offer. To find out more. Willow begrudgingly agreed. Tezz replied to the text when they got home. He just asked for more information about the operation.

Date night was over. The Bulgarian Secret-Squirrel was calling.

Chapter 17

A Big Red Box Arrives.

Willow stumbled out of bed to the front door. She saw a man outside wearing a pressed black suit and tie.

"Courier maam," he said. He was carrying a large, heavy red box. After scanning the bar-code on the box, he handed it to her and left without another word. Willow took it and lugged it to the kitchen table.

She read the label and yelled out to Tezz, "A package just arrived for you!" She looked at the address label. "The address label says it's from Langley, Virginia." A large yellow warning label on the box read: *'RED BAG. Stop. Do not open. Diplomatic pouch. USFA-6513.'*

Tezz stumbled into the kitchen.

They opened the red mystery box together. Inside was a stack of classified documents. Most were stamped; 'D.E.A.'.

The box also contained a brand-new regulation US Army uniform; a multi-camo Crye G3 uniform, Solomon boots and tan ECH light-weight helmet. There was also a new phone and several SIM cards, plus a heavy duty Ziploc bag containing cash in several currencies.

Terence emptied the box onto the table and said, "Shit's getting serious."

He picked up the largest document.

The cover read; *'NATO Advanced SERE Training Program: RESTRICTED.'*

Willow took the document from him and thumbed through several pages. She closed the document, looked at the cover again, and asked,

"This says *'Advanced SERE'*. What does that mean?".

Tezz said, "It's my cover –while I'm doing Basic Training –according to Crensch." He tried on the tan-coloured helmet.

"To the world-at-large I'm a specialist Botanist at the NATO Base at Novo Selo in Bulgaria. Advising the program on botanical aspects of the training. How to find food. What not to eat. Using hallucinogens to extract confessions. Stuff like that."

Tezz unfolded the camo pants. Checked the size label.

"But what I'm really doing is a compressed Basic Training program with a focus on cartels, urban combat situations and counterterrorism. The Base at Novo Selo is one of the CIA's Secret Squirrel offshore training operations. They can't risk doing training like this onshore in the US. Big M and the cartel have too many eyes and ears."

He put the pants back in the box and added,

"When I eventually get back to El Paso, the world will just think I'm an average joe returning home after a few years at university. My records will show nothing to indicate my military training."

There was a personal note from Crensch at the bottom of the box.

Tezz picked it up and read it out loud.

"Terrence. Here is all the information you'll need to make your decision. Plenty more to find out in Bulgaria if you decide to go ahead. After you read everything in the package, please burn the box and contents immediately, no matter what you decide. The uniform is there if you decide to report for duty. Travel overland from Zurich to Bulgaria by train. Pay cash for the ticket. Do not fly. Major Crensch."

Willow and Terrence spent the rest of the afternoon reading all the documentation.

Willow tried the army uniform on as a joke. She paraded and danced around the house, which resulted in a sordid lap-dance at the kitchen table, followed by a "sexy dancing soldier" episode in the bedroom.

Willow read the backgrounders on Big M, the Sinaloa cartel, and the SERE Training Course. She found it all strangely enticing. The contributors and references in the Survival part of the SERE training manual read like a 'Who's Who' of the botanical and science world. Bio-Geneticists. Metabolic Experts. Traditional Medicine Gurus. Toxicologists. Animal Behaviorists. Hunters. Herbalists. Survivalists. Even weapon-makers. All the best-of-the-best in their fields.

The Advanced SERE Program made Bear Grylls look like a pussy.

She turned to Tezz and said, "You know, I think I could be pretty good at this."

They burned all the documentation in the fireplace that evening.

The next day was crunch time.

Tezz and Willow had a life-changing decision to make.

CHAPTER 18

SKINNING A CAT.

Willow enjoyed making lists.

With a lukewarm coffee and bowl of muesli perched on her bedside table, she'd created a list of reasons she should, and shouldn't, return to Australia after her Zurich Fellowship ended.

A long list of points were written on the left side of the page; 'Career. Money. Budget. Status. Dad. Summer. Tim Tams.'

On the right-hand side of the page was just a roughly doodled heart.

She looked at the list and sighed, "Fuck–."

Tezz was snoring blissfully in bed beside her. Sun filled the room with golden morning light. She didn't have the heart, or courage, to wake him yet. Waking Tezz meant the discussion about 'the decision' would start. Waking him might mean the beginning of the end.

Willow quietly sidled out of the warm bed. She put some fresh coffee on in the kitchen, then she looked at her list. She sighed again, "Fuuuuck."

Willow rolled out a yoga mat in the living room and sat in a meditation pose. She held the position, quiet and contemplative, for a minute as the sunlight warmed her dark skin, then she slowly opened one eye and said, "Fuuuuuck." There was no escaping it.

She sat alone at the kitchen table, sipping coffee. Deep in thought, staring absent-mindedly at the kitchen wall.

Up on a shelf she spied a small ceramic moggy cat. She'd bought it at a weekend market in Basel. The cat was holding a large butcher's knife, dripping in blood. A small plaque at the base of the comical ceramic cat read, '*There's more than one way to skin a cat*'.

She remembered bursting out laughing when she saw it at the market and had snapped it up for just one Swiss Franc.

She read the line again –and a thought slowly hit her; *There was another way to skin this cat.*

She raced into the bedroom and shook Terrence awake.

He looked at her through sleepy eyes.

Willow said, "I've got it!" She pounced on the bed next to him.

"I'm going to Novo Selo –with you."

Tezz looked confused.

Willow said, "They've got a Survivalist program, and I spent most of my life living in the middle of nowhere. I'm a fucking expert in native plants and surviving in unforgiving environments."

"Fuck Bear Grylls, I'm a natural for this," Willow announced.

Terrence, finally awake, said, "Wills. It's a military base. Not a commercial operation."

He sat up in bed and said, "Anyone going there must complete full US Army Military Basic Training. Most people there have probably done a deployment –or two. It's not a Scout camp.

The only reason I'm exempt is because they don't want me on US soil until I'm ready to go back home. Not to mention that you are totally ineligible for the US Army. You don't even have a green card."

Willow was persistent.

***

A few hours later, they were on a video call to Crensch.

Willow explained her plan enthusiastically. They could both do the SERE training. To his credit, Crensch listened and was careful not to pour water on her fire.

When she finished, he said, "I hear you, Willow, but Basic Combat Training would not be easy at Novo Selo. It will be the Bulgarian version."

Willow said, "I'm sure I could handle it."

Crensch continued, "In the US, our BCT course is ten weeks, then it finishes with an end-of-cycle test. At Novo Selo the standard combat training schedule is harder. It's tough, and I've heard the Bulgarians don't really have a Health and Safety Department."

Willow didn't look phased by that.

Crensch continued, "And they are tough-as-nails on any personnel from the US, because they think we are all a bunch of pussies."

He considered his next words.

"God only knows what they'll think of you," he said, "A woman. A Botanist. A fucking Aussie. And black to boot. Talk about a mountain to climb. The Bulgarians would have a field day trying to get you to break."

Willow crossed her arms angrily and said, "I'm tough enough. Not that easy growing up in outback Queensland. I've broken my fair share of people's noses and teeth in our local school footy matches. I can give pretty hard when the shit hits the fan."

Crensch laughed out loud and said, "Leave it with me for a few days. I'll ask my contacts some questions."

***

Four days later, they were on a follow-up video call with the Major.

"I have news," Crensch said. "The Novo Selo Training Area has a research facility on site that deals with 'CBRN'. That means Chemical, Biological, Radiological and Nuclear research and training. There's a group of scientists who do survival training and general research work. So, there's a lab and a scientific fraternity already on the base. They think they might have a use for someone with your skills."

He paused for a moment and added, "They're keen to upgrade the skill-set of the Survival Trainers on the base. Langley is happy to fund you there –but you'll have to get through Basic Combat Training, and a few months of Advanced Individual Training –plus some special forces selection processes, before we'd consider it a permanent position."

Crensch smiled. "Happy?" he asked.

Willow said, "Hell yes."

Crensch said, "You'll receive a draft contract in the next two days. You need to get back to me straight after you get it."

They hung off the call.

Willow was jumping off the walls with excitement.

***

Crensch had not mentioned that Langley had jumped at the opportunity of getting someone with her scientific skills into the scientific team at Novo Selo.

Turnover of survival trainers at the base was notoriously high because of the tough conditions and the continuous need to spend time on harsh training bivouacs in the freezing Bulgarian winters.

It was definitely not going to be a scout camp.

Chapter 19

Meredith Has Left The Building.

Willow was preparing herself for life as a trainee soldier. When they approved her paperwork, Crensch again reminded her how tough it was going to be.

She'd been hitting a local gym hard. Work on her fellowship in Zurich was winding down, so she spent hours every week on core training, boxing and MMA. She wasn't just aiming to get fit, she was aiming to get mean. She searched the city for the worst-looking gym she could find. Finding a gym like that wasn't a simple task in the 'world's safest city'.

She found it in an old industrial area. It was a rough neighbourhood where she knew the gym members would be tough and unforgiving.

After months of grinding workouts in the gym, her body had become sinewy and hard. She'd discovered a love of boxing. She'd also taken a lot of shit from the other members, but she saw that as just part of the training. A week before they left for The NSTA she topped her new look off with a severe military buzz cut.

Willow had transformed herself into a lean, mean fighting machine. No-one was fucking with her! She was ready for the rucks and runs of Basic Training.

A few nights before they left town, a guy had tried to mug her near the gym. She left him moaning on the dark cobblestones with three broken fingers and a smashed nose.

At home, and in the lab, Tezz had stopped calling her 'Meredith'.

The Meredith that McDreamy loved to tease had left the building. Way before they'd left for Bulgaria.

A ripped Aboriginal 'GI Jane' had taken her place.

***

When their fellowships in Zurich were complete, they sold everything in their apartment and boarded a train west for Sofia in Bulgaria.

They could have flown and bused from Zurich in about five hours. But Crensch was adamant. Public transport. Pay in cash. So they'd endured ten hours on a train to Bratislava, then a 12 hour bus ride to Sofia, followed by a five-hour train to Sliven.

A Bulgarian Army Jeep met them at the gaudy, mustard yellow Sliven railway station. They drove past beautiful valleys that looked straight out of 'The Sound of Music'. But many of the towns looked like soviet-era outposts. After a forty-mile drive, they arrived at the base.

The army servicemen based at Bulgaria's Novo Selo Training Area called it the 'The NSTA'. They also called it "The Nasty' if they were having a shit time.

The facility is a Forward Operating Site. It sits at the mouth of a remote 150 square kilometer valley. The valley often rumbled with the sound of army tanks and weapons fire. Most days, trainees in US Bradleys, M1 Abrams, and Canadian Strykers ranged over the valley, blowing up anything that moved. The sound of Javelin missiles firing, mortars being launched, and the whine of flying combat drones filled the air.

A remote corner of the valley contained the base's Chemical, Biological, Radiological and Nuclear training and research operations. The CBRN facility was ringed with a security fence. It was topped with razor-wire and plastered with threatening bio-hazard signs.

Trainees called it 'Godzilla Island'.

Over the years, they had daubed graffiti images of the mythical Japanese beast on some large rocks near the entry gate. It was the last place at the NSTA facility that any servicemen wanted to visit.

***

Once security cleared Willow and Tezz through the main gate, they issued them with ID cards. The driver dropped them at the central PX store. They did some shopping there. Willow bought a snow-globe with an Abrams tank inside. It was too cute.

After receiving a map, they spent the next hour doing a walking tour. Everything on the base seemed oversized, in case it ever had to scale-up its numbers if a conflict broke out.

To her delight, Willow discovered it had excellent gym facilities. There was a proper canvas-floored boxing ring set up in an unused warehouse that had once been used to store military tank shells.

She was told the boxing ring hosted an unofficial event on the last Sunday of the month. Trainees on the Base spent their paychecks betting on fights, usually between the Westerners and the Bulgarians.

Years of spilled blood stained the edges of the canvas and the corner pads.

WIN ZIN LIKES TO WIN.

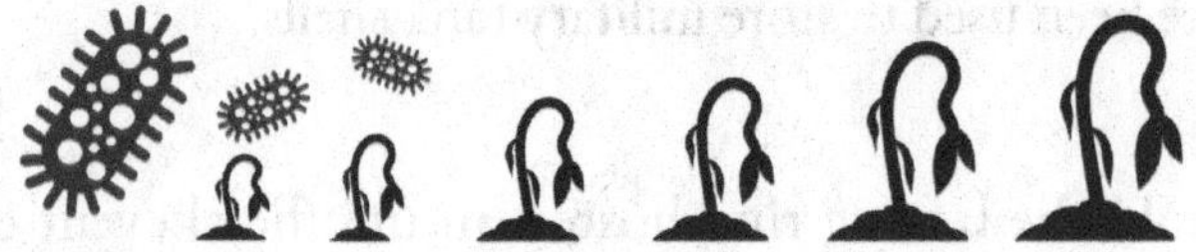

B o Aung Win Zin had a quirky tradition every time his private jet rolled out of his family's private hangar at Myanmar's Naypyidaw international airport.

He'd ask for a bottle of Louis Roederer Cristal champagne to be cracked open, then an extremely attractive air hostess would offer him a chilled glass. Nine times out of ten, the glass just sat in front of him as the plane took off. He wouldn't even taste it. The $500 bottle would usually end up down the galley sink by the end of the flight. It was his way of snubbing his birth country, declaring that he was a new age man of the world.

Win Zin was the heir-apparent to Sam Gor (aka The Company), the Golden Triangle's biggest drug cartel. He could afford shit like that.

"We are en route to Kunming. Flight time will be one hour and forty-five minutes," announced the pilot as the jet lifted off. The sleek plane lifted into the sky, over the impoverished Burmese farmers below.

Seated across from Win, The Company's accountant flipped through the cartel's monthly operations report. The short, balding man talked Win through the production and sales numbers for a cocktail of drug operations that delivered his family billions. Cocaine, GBH. Fentanyl. Benzos. Meth. Ketamine. Cannabis. The usual suspects. Even a booming trade in illegal tobacco. Their operations spread across Myanmar, Thailand, Laos, New Zealand, Australia, Japan, China and Taiwan.

Win stared out at the fields and shanty farmhouses below. A slight scowl appeared on his face. His family's global trade was split into two parts: The first was 'farmed product', like cannabis, opium and tobacco. The second, and fastest growing, was 'synthetics', drugs grown in drums and labs rather than soil and sun.

The accountant coughed nervously and said, "There's been a decline in our cannabis shipments. The weather in eastern India has been bad."

Win said, "I fucking hate the farm trade. It bores me to death. It's so –yesterday. I'd be out of it –if grandfather would let me."

The accountant grimaced and returned to his spreadsheets.

A hostess arrived with a gold-plated tray covered in an assortment of pills. Win selected two. Popped them in his mouth and closed his eyes. The accountant quietly closed his laptop and skulked to the back of the plane. Meeting over.

Win's private jet streaked across the sky, soon leaving Myanmar airspace and heading deep into China.

His family was heavily involved in a massive drug trade with China and had close ties to the government and the People's Liberation Army. Win traveled to China at least once a month. Mostly to meet customers. Sometimes he went to negotiate the sale of Chinese weaponry and its smuggling across the border to arm his local forces. Myanmar was a major source of revenue for the Chinese Army.

Win got his kicks from expensive military hardware.

***

When it came to drugs, the relationship between the Chinese and Myanmar governments was 'interesting'.

Historically, the relationship between Beijing and the Myanmar government operated at two levels. Positive and bilateral in public. Evil and duplicitous when it came to illicit drugs and the profitable armaments trade.

It started in the late 1940s when the Chinese nationalist Kuomintang (KMT) Party declared war on the drug trade. The Communists, under Mao Zedong, continued the push, but instead of coming up with a strategy to solve the problem, they just pushed it under the carpet instead. Tens of millions of Chinese addicts were persecuted. The severity of the war just forced the whole drug trade south. Across the Chinese border into neighbouring Thailand, Laos and Myanmar.

Problem solved!

***

The area down south, where the Mekong and Ruak rivers meet, became known as The Golden Triangle.

Win Zin's grandfather, Aung U-Chin, was the son of a humble rice and sugar-cane farmer, in the Shan region of Myanmar (Burma), when the push south happened. So he happily changed the family crops to opium and cannabis, and the rest is history.

The family became billionaires over the next few decades, mainly off the back of the opium and cannabis they grew. More recently, the dynasty branched into meth and other synthetics. Leading to a life of private jets, houses in Geneva and influence in all levels of the Government and military matters.

In Myanmar, Win Zin's grandfather was royalty.

Now in his eighties, U-Chin was slowly handing over the control of the Sam Gor cartel to his sons and grandsons.

***

His eldest son, Nay Chi, now in his forties, was the money man of the dynasty.

Educated at the London School of Economics, he now spent most of his time in Geneva and London juggling mansions and bank accounts, plus multiple wives and lady friends. The only time he'd set foot in Myanmar in the past decade was when U-Chin had a pneumonia scare.

He wasn't going to be inheriting the family business, nor did he want to.

Nay Chi's eldest son was Bo Aung Win Zin.

Now in his late twenties, he was being groomed to run the family production and logistics operations. U-Chin and Nay Chi paid millions for Win Zin to receive a sterling education at Harvard, but secretly, he mostly spent his time at nightclubs and strip joints, while paying people to write his papers and sit his exams.

What Win Zin really learned in the USA was the modern drug trade. Win Zin lived in a world filled with Coke and Meth, Addy's, GBH and Ket. Where precursor chemicals and synthetic drugs were king, and "cropper" drugs like cannabis were for yesterday's crowd.

Win sported trendy triad tattoos, wore a flashy Rolex and drove around the streets of the capital, Naypyidaw, in a Tesla Cybertruck he'd had stolen off the streets of L.A. and discreetly flown in on a military flight.

In his early twenties, he'd been shipped off for a year to train with the secretive Sea Dragon Commandos. China's knock-off of Delta Force. He'd learned how to be a soldier, but mostly he'd learned how to be a show-off. He graduated from the Dragons with the title of High Commander. In reality, they couldn't wait to see the end of him.

***

The military Junta in Myanmar happily turned a blind eye to the opioid and synthetics trade, but shunned the local cannabis growers and sellers. It was good Public Relations to be seen to be cracking down on 'something', and cannabis was an easy target.

Because of the crackdown, growing, possessing and exporting cannabis now attracted huge penalties. All the way up to death.

This had just pushed Myanmar's cannabis farms over the border, into places like Laos and India.

Along the Indian border, cannabis farms spread quickly. Across the districts of Ukhrul, Senapati, Tamenglong and Chandel. Places out of reach of the junta's draconian laws. Handy too. The billion-or-so Indians living nearby loved smoking weed.

Win. Win. As they say.

Chapter 21

Trouble On the Indian Border.

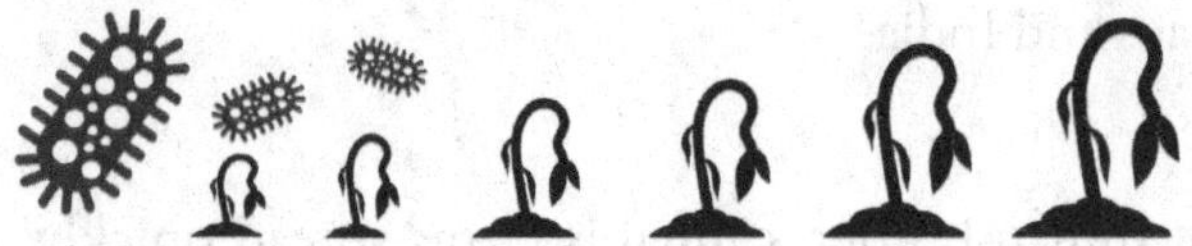

Burmese Kush is a hybrid strain of cannabis, known for its relaxation and mellowness. The plants are tall and graceful compared to the scrubby Thai varieties. It's slow to grow, and slow to take effect when smoked, but when it kicks in, it's potent and long-lasting.

'Mellow' was not a word that could describe the mood of the local Sam Gor cartel drug cadre, Saw Bo Thun, this morning.

The wild riot taking place on the street outside his razor-wire ringed mansion made sure of that. Shots rang out nearby.

After a length of iron pipe smashed through one of the front windows of the house, Thun's housekeeper panicked, shouting, "Mr Thun. What to do. What to do!"

***

The farming town of Chandel is technically in India, but many of the people who live there are Burmese nationals.

Most of the small farms around Chandel are subsistence cannabis croppers, employing laborers for pennies per hour. If the crop stops producing, the consequences are dire. Wages disappear. Food prices skyrocket.

In 2006, the Ministry of Panchayati Raj named Chandel as one of the country's 250 most backward districts. High praise. There had been an insurrection on the streets after the typhoon in 2009. Many had been killed in the ensuing riots.

***

Ten miles out of town, Mi Swe, a local cannabis farmer, stood on the verandah of her small wooden farmhouse. She was brandishing a Chinese-made Type 80 machine gun. It was smoking from continuous fire.

A line of blood ran down the side of her face from a running battle with her desperate farm workers earlier in the morning. A bunker of sandbags protected her, but empty bullet casings and the lingering smell of cordite surrounded her.

After a running battle with pickets and spades, there had been a quick stand-off between Mi Swe and her farm workers. Frustrated, they'd all jumped into trucks and onto motorbikes and headed into Chandel township to confront the authorities.

All was quiet now. But she wasn't taking any chances.

111

Mi Swe cried as she looked out over the rolling hills surrounding her farmhouse. The cannabis crop was her total livelihood. It had withered and was slowly turning brown, almost before her eyes.

She grabbed her mobile phone and punched in a number.

***

Ten miles away, Saw Bo Thun answered her call. He could barely hear her over the riot outside his own house.

Me Swe bellowed down the phone to make her point.

"Boss Thun. My crop is dead. It's the same all the way up the valley. My workers are in a state of panic. I think they are coming your way."

Trying to be as reassuring as possible, Thun spoke calmly. "I think they are here already. With the rest of the valley. The police have called in the military for support. I'll call when I have news."

Thun hung up and walked into the center of the house, trying to find a quieter room. His face was ashen.

He jabbed the keypad on his phone.

***

In the private boudoir of a Kunming nightclub, the muted sound of the Chinese dance music thumped against the crimson velour wallpapered walls. The jasmine and mint smell of Hermes Un Jardin filled the air.

Two pretty, young Chinese girls were busy showing Win Zin a good time, as he sat naked on a plush, golden throne in the center of the room. He took a swig from a bottle of Cristal champagne as he pushed one girl's

112

head deeper into his lap, smugly knowing that the bottle cost way more than both of the girls.

On a low golden table next to the throne, his phone came to life. He looked over to see the caller ID. It read Saw Bo Thun.

He ignored the call, leaning back further in the chair and arching his neck as the other girl traced her finger over the tattoos on his chest and started kissing his mouth.

The phone rang out.

The phone started shrilling again as the girl moved from his mouth, down to join the other girl in his lap.

He peeked across at the caller ID again. 'Saw Bo Thun'.

He exhaled sharply, then grabbed the phone. The girls looked up.

He motioned for them to keep up their good work as he took the call.

Win Zin barked down the phone. "Fuck, Thun. I'm in the middle of something important here. Call me tonight." He held the phone away from his mouth for a moment and uttered a deep moan. The girls were very, very good.

Then returned to the call.

"OK. OK. How can the crops in a whole valley die? Have you been up there to see for yourself?"

He tensed again in the chair. Barely controlling his lust as he listened to Thun talking.

He could hear the riot in the background.

"Yes. I'll speak to Hawk. See what the military can do. But you need to get up to the farms yourself. Send me some pictures of the crops. Get it done today."

He hung up. Leaned back, and moaned again.

An hour later, Win Zin swaggered through the empty nightclub, buttoning up his shirt. It was 10am. Only a few patrons remained, drinking and smoking in one dark corner. He walked up to the booth next to the stage and yelled to the DJ, "Turn this shit down! My head hurts."

The DJ immediately complied. A couple of thugs from the group in the corner stood up and glared across the room, but immediately retook their seats as they recognized him.

No-one messed with Win Zin.

Win walked through a gaudy red door into the manager's office at the back of the club. Piles of cash covered the desk. Win shook his head at the Manager and said, "That girl Gigi. Wow."

The Manager smiled, "My most popular girl. And my most expensive. You want her to come to your hotel tonight?" Win dismissed him and said, "I've got a drama over at Chandel to deal with. A problem at the farms. What was your take here at the club last week?"

The manager got down to business.

"A good week for Coke, as always. A lot of Ket. People still asking for China Girl and China White but most of the Fentanyl supply is going offshore since your father shut down the local trade in it. We could sell a ton of that. Trade in Ma is still small. Few are smoking stuff these days."

The conversation was cut short when Win's phone rang. He grabbed the handset and motioned for the Manager to leave the room. He scurried out.

Win answered the call and Bo Cetan, a young Myanmar Army Officer, appeared on the phone's video screen. His close friends knew Cetan as 'Hawk'. He was a member of the Myanmar armed forces, and a major enforcer for Sam Gor.

"Hawk. How's Army life treating you, my good friend?" said Win.

Hawk, dressed in army greens, standing inside a camo army tent, said, "Apologies for the noise, Bro. We're testing some new gear from the Chinese here. Check this out." Hawk turned the phone to show a soldier burning a mannequin in a paddock with a large flame thrower. The device stuttered and poured gasoline on the soldier's feet. It ignited, and he ran around with his lower legs on fire.

Hawk turned the phone around, smiled, and said, "Having a few technical issues with that one. What can I do for you, man?"

Win said, "We might have a problem on the cannabis farms up in Chandel. Reports of crops dying up there. Rioting on the farms and in the streets. Thun's house is surrounded. Looks ugly. Can you get someone to take a look? Get some pictures. I need to send something to my grandfather."

Hawk said, "I don't know why U-Chin still bothers with the crop trade. Weed is slow to sell in most places. And the margin is shit. Sure, the sales are good in places like the US and Australia, but it's not where the trade is heading."

Win agreed, "Preaching to the converted bro. U-Chin is concerned about the trade in synthetics. Says it's fucking people up too much. Drawing too much heat from Interpol and the DEA. But my day is coming soon, bro. And then we'll be getting out of the crop trade forever. Precursors, like meth, are where the money's at."

Win shifted the conversation.

"So, can you help in Chandel?"

Hawk said, "I'll send a team across the border. I've got a squad that needs some training. I'm sure we can give Thun some protection and get you some info to send to U-Chin."

Hawk looked at Win on the phone video and continued, "Bro you look like crap. Partying too hard?"

Win shook his head and said, "This local girl –Gigi. –and her friend. Who I think might be her sister. Fuuuck. Next time you are in The Ming bro! I need some sleep. Catch you when I get back."

Win hung up the video call, walked over, and thumped on the red door. The manager re-entered the room.

Win said, "I'm smashed. Let's pick this up tomorrow. Get me a car to go back to the hotel."

Win stood and walked toward the office door. Then he stopped, turned and said, "And Gigi. Book her for tonight. And her little friend, too."

CHAPTER 22

WELCOME TO GODZILLA ISLAND.

Willow and Tezz were driven over to 'Godzilla Island' in a Bulgarian army jeep. It was on an overgrown bend on Bulgaria's Marash River. Entry was via a bridge over a flood-plain that often reeked from the rotting carcasses of local livestock stuck in its mud.

At the far end of the bridge stood a set of tall soviet-era steel gates, ringed with razor wire. Last Halloween, one of the engineers had rigged some speakers that played the theme song to Jurassic Park as the gates opened. A rusty sign listed an extensive set of conditions of entry and displayed a prominent grid of dangerous goods and bio-hazard symbols. It may as well have read; "Abandon hope all ye who enter here."

The CIA liked it that way.

As their vehicle bounced through the gates, Tezz leaned over to Willow, laughing maniacally and jiggling a large rubber Godzilla he'd bought at the PX. He bellowed quotes from the movie.

"Let them fight!" he roared. "Only one will win! The mass extinction we feared has already begun —and we are the cause!"

The road ahead forked. To the right was the well-worn dirt track to the NATO Bio-Hazard training fields. To the left was a cobble-stoned road over to the main Bio-Research building.

They took the left fork.

The main Bio-Research building looked like something straight out of an old Movietone Dracula movie.

Imposing, with a foreboding Gothic feeling. After dropping them off, the nervous driver left immediately. No-one lingered at Godzilla Island.

A man in a white lab-coat walked out of the main building, past two gargoyles either side of the front stairs. Tezz stepped forward and bowed low before him.

"Dr. Serizawa, I assume?" he joked.

Tezz turned to Willow and added, "This is my colleague, Dr Emma Russell. Paleontologist."

The Godzilla jokes flew thick and fast at the facility.

The man in the lab-coat dryly responded, "I'm Dr Eamon Ghand. You must be Terrence Aguilar and Willow Barrant?"

He ushered them inside. They walked through the halls of the old dimly lit building, then they walked out a creaking wooden back door and down a skinny path through a thicket of tall close-knit hedges.

The other side of the hedge was the CIA's Secret Squirrel facility. It was like walking into another world.

Hidden from prying eyes was an ultra-modern Scandi-style laboratory building. Entry required a swipe card and a retinal scan. They entered a minimalist white reception area, accented with neutral shades of beige. It was bustling with lab-coated technicians.

Dr Ghand said, "Follow the blue line on the wall to the PX. The QM will kit you out with your gear. Then they'll take your bio-scans and give you your ID cards."

He pointed down a long, sun-filled hallway that was lined with floor-to-ceiling windows.

"Then follow the green line to the Induction Room. I'll see you there in about twenty minutes."

The QM issued lab coats and the usual lab PPE to Willow and Tezz. As they left, she handed each of them a small bag.

"A little welcome gift," she said, smiling.

Inside each bag, they found a camouflage baseball cap and a light gray t-shirt. The cap had the Japanese letters for 'Godzilla Island' (Gojira Airando) embroidered on it. Below the characters was the blue and yellow insignia of the US Army Chemical Corps. The t-shirt had a cartoon version of Godzilla on the back.

After changing into their lab PPE, they followed the green line to the induction room.

"Welcome." said Dr Ghand, standing in front of a large screen. "Technically speaking, when you take that left turn at the main gate, into this part of the CBRN facility, you are leaving The NSTA and entering –." He paused for effect. "Well –let's just say a gray area."

He paused again, searching for the right words, "Both diplomatically –and militarily speaking."

Ghand hit his keyboard to forward his PowerPoint presentation.

"Yes, there are areas here that conduct research into chemical and biological weapons. But we focus our efforts on how you can survive them, not make them." He smiled and added, "We leave that up to the Iranians and their terrorist friends."

A schematic map of the area appeared on the screen behind Dr Ghand.

"We run a significant 'Toxic Valley Exercise' for NATO every six months. We train the soldiers from many parts of the world on how to survive in a toxic or irradiated area. One in winter and one in summer."

Dr Ghand pointed to the right-hand side of the map. "Right now, you are in the main CBRN lab building. Most of the longer term staff live in villages off base. There are barracks on the base for fresh arrivals like you. We don't get many couples."

The slide changed, and he pointed to a group of buildings further down the valley and said, "In this set of buildings, we operate the world's most advanced military SERE training program. On behalf of groups like the CIA, DEA, Interpol and Mossad. The usual suspects. It's here that we train our most advanced Survivalist trainers, and it's also where we do specialist one-on-one training for 'off-the-books' Special Ops groups and Field Operatives."

The slide changed to show just the blue and yellow insignia of the US Army Chemical Corps.

"So, if you're going undercover in Colombia for the DEA –getting a covert posting to South Sudan from Langley –or running Embassy Security in somewhere like Liberia or Yemen, chances are you will do some specialist SERE training here first. We learned a lot after the attack in Benghazi."

Dr Ghand reached down to his laptop bag under the desk and pulled two personnel folders. He placed them on the table.

He opened them up and said, "And then there's you two."

He handed each of them a thick book titled 'Basic Combat Training'. "We operate this place like a military facility, and as per our agreement with the Bulgarians, we provide formal army training to everyone at the NSTA. That's not negotiable." He paused to let that thought sink in.

"So, while you both have very impressive skills in botanical sciences, I need both of you to complete the bog-standard US Basic Combat Training program and formally join the Army. That will earn you the legal right to be based here."

Dr Ghand handed a brand-new US passport over to Willow.

"Congratulations, Miss Barrant. You are now officially a US citizen. And the US Army has formally enlisted your brand new US identity as a recruit in their database. If anyone ever asks you to explain how you became a US citizen, don't answer. Just request that a military lawyer be present before you can talk."

He closed the personnel folders.

"Drill Sergeant Stephan Borelli and a small team over at the NSTA will help you complete your BCT –and then support you through Advanced Individual Training, where you will focus on your specific area of deployment."

He walked over to the window and looked outside.

"That means you will finish in the middle of the local winter. Not a pleasant proposition." Ghand said. "The Bulgarian winter breaks even the strongest of people."

Suddenly Ghand's phone chirped. He looked at the screen message.

"I have something to attend to. The Orderly will take you to your accommodation and get you settled in. I believe you have already received uniforms for your training."

Willow and Terrence both answered, "Yes".

As Ghand left the room, he turned and said, "Good luck. But remember, if either of you cherries get cut from either Basic or AIT –just like any other recruit –your days here will be over."

CHAPTER 23

BASIC COMBAT TRAINING BLUES.

Willow's alarm started bleating at 4-30am. It would continue doing that every morning during Bulgaria's Basic Combat Training (BCT) regime. The sun wouldn't rise for at least another hour.

Willow looked out the window of her Barrack's room as a set of jeep headlights arced across the training field outside. Drill Sergeant Borelli was right on time. In thirty minutes, Willow would need to be down at the company area forming-up with the others, before starting their morning PT session.

She shuddered at the thought of what this was going to be like mid-winter, when it would be snowing heavily outside.

Willow shared a room in the Barracks building with three other newbie female bunkies.

"I'm dying," moaned a voice from under a thick, warm blanket on the other side of the room.

"Coffee –I need coffee –." moaned Adrijana Marincovik. In the new batch of recruits, she was the sole local, from neighboring Serbia.

The girls named her 'Addy' because she was like a human shot of Adderall. Hyper 24/7. The guys called her the Energizer Bunny. The tall blonde, athletic recruit had fucked more than a few of them into a state of complete exhaustion.

Willow said, "Addy –you'd better make it fast. I can see them driving over to the training ground already."

Sandi Martin, a recruit from Atlanta, had already been up for fifteen minutes. She was scoffing down energy bars. For the first twelve weeks, the new recruits were constantly hungry.

Misaki Ito was slumped in a gaming chair in front of her curved computer screen across the room. She opened one eye. A battle was still raging on the Arma computer game, open on her screen. Misaki was a Field Agent for the Naichō, Japan's secretive Cabinet Intelligence and Research Office.

"Oh, fuck!" Misaki said, "What time is it?"

"Time to hit the deck," said Willow, pulling on her combat boots.

The bunkies had given Willow the nickname 'Nullah'. An Australian Aboriginal word for a fighting stick. In her first few weeks at the NSTA, she'd earned a reputation as a hard-hitter and devious fighter in the old boxing ring. Guys were having second thoughts about sparring with 'the angry black girl' during her intensive training sessions.

At 4-50 am, the platoon of twenty-five new male and female recruits filed down to the dark training field outside.

They formed a straight line. The BCT Guidebook called them 'active duty military members', everyone in the Army Corps called them 'grunts' or 'cherries'. Borrelli, in his Smokey Bear hat, walked along the line inspecting the recruits. They were all wearing their standard Army Combat Uniform and weighed down with heavy rucksacks.

"Your life is mine for the next twenty-two weeks." He bellowed.

"Twelve weeks of Basic followed by several more weeks Advanced Individual Training, or AIT, in your area of expertise. You will form-up at 05-00 daily. Rain, hail or shine. Lights-out is 21-00 sharp."

Borrelli walked down the line of recruits, stopped next to Willow and said, "By the end of the course, I expect that two-thirds of you will be gone. The winter is nasty on the NSTA and it's not even close to starting yet."

He eye-balled Addy and said, "And for the ladies here, it's not about your gender. That shit doesn't matter here. It's all about whether you can perform."

Borrelli walked further down the line, stopped by Tezz, and said, "Over on the main base, there would normally be around ninety in your group. Over here on the island, there are only twenty-five of you."

He lifted his hands and spread his ten fingers in the air and said,

"By Christmas, I'm expecting to count those of you remaining on these two hands."

He stared hard at Tezz and added, "Maybe one hand."

The day started with calisthenics.

Push-ups, sit-ups, squats, lunges, and burpees, then some strength training over in the gym. They wolfed down breakfast at 6am.

By 7-30am, they were on the firing range learning how to fire their shiny new M-16A2 Assault rifles. Then the instructors sent them out on a timed obstacle course before lunch, where they had to climb walls, crawl under wire, and navigate monkey bars.

The day ended with a two-mile foot march without their packs. This would quickly graduate to twelve mile ruck marches in full gear, plus training to simulate combat situations, like buddy carries, firefighter carries, and casualty drags.

By the end of the training, the raw recruits had become soldiers. They had the skills and endurance to perform on any battlefield.

***

Eleven cherries had given up or been cut from BCT.

The fourteen that remained were now split into smaller groups, to get ready for their twelve weeks of Advance Individual Training to learn the skills needed to perform their specific Army job.

Willow, and four others, were deployed to the Survivalist AIT Group. Tezz joined the Urban Combat Group (aka 'The Meat Eaters') specializing in room clearing, building entry, and urban movement.

Life was tough on the NSTA.

In November Tezz survived a fall from a second-story balcony of an Urban Operations Training Facility during a punishing building entry exercise. Nothing was broken, but his ego was severely bruised.

Three weeks later, Willow had almost called 'Quits' during the final day of a freezing twelve-day Level-C Survival Bivouac in the mountains out the back of the NSTA. Tezz had barely managed to talk her off the cliff.

Willow's AIT Survivalist sessions focused on the use of plant-based materials as food, a source of hydration, medication, anesthetic, and weaponry. They learned how to extract concoctions in the field that would enable them to blind a person, or maybe to poison an enemy or drug them into a stupor.

Misaki had bailed in Week 7 of AIT. Addy narrowly avoided getting kicked out when she broke a recruit's arm during a drunken fist-fight over on the main base.

By the end of AIT, Willow and Terrence were unrecognisable.
They'd both transformed into 'lean, mean fighting machines'.

***

Willow had added karate, kung-fu, and taekwondo to her boxing skills.
She'd become proficient in mountain-climbing, learned basic Spanish and French and could forage a meal in any environment. She could also

operate as a basic field medic and hold her breath underwater for many minutes. During her laboratory training sessions, Willow had boosted her skills in plant toxicology, plant chemistry, and she'd also furthered her genetic and cloning skills. She used her indigenous knowledge to expand the Lab's expertise in that area, pleasing Dr Chand immensely.

Tezz had become an expert in urban warfare tactics during his AIT.

***

In what seemed like just a heartbeat, Advanced Infantry Training was over.

They'd both survived.

Willow and Tezz rapidly advanced to the rank of Specialist E-4. They both wore golden eagle insignias to show their unique army status.

CHAPTER 24

BILLY BLAGG.

Winter had arrived. It was bitterly cold.

With every breath, Willow left a trail of white fog as she walked over to the lab on Godzilla Island. The outside temperature had barely risen above freezing-point since the start of the month.

In one corner of the lab, Willow had built a small makeshift greenhouse that was running the sort of temperature you would expect in the middle of the Mojave Desert in July. An array of strong heat lamps built into its roof kept it hot as hell. As always, one of her primary interests in life was to develop new genetic strains of plants that could survive in really arid situations.

She'd come up with a bullshit story to tell Dr. Chand, saying she was creating an environment to grow plants that soldiers would likely come across in hot desert conditions. Chand immediately saw through the lie she was telling him, but allowed her to proceed. Just to keep her happy while she did her other work.

Inside the hot box, she'd planted the same strain of hops and cannabis plants she'd been running experiments on back in Zürich. She wanted to see if she could develop a new plant that was massively drought resistant. After many failures, she had a small crop of mature plants and seedlings that were showing a little promise.

Willow had kicked off her snow-covered boots and put on a pair of runners. She slipped her white lab coat over the top of a thick woolly jumper. She walked over to the hot box. It glowed yellow from the heat lamps. She opened the door.

"What the fuck?" she exclaimed.

The tough little green plants and seedlings inside the hot box had somehow sprouted a mixture of enormous pink and purple flowers over the weekend. The sweet scent of Kalanchoe, Garden Cosmos and New Guinea Impatiens filled her nostrils. Willow stood there with her mouth gaping like a goldfish.

"Priceless!" a voice bellowed from the back of the hothouse.

A forty-something Australian Army Officer stepped forward from the shadows at the back of the room. Beaming a broad, friendly smirk. Tezz stepped out from behind a partition wall to join him.

"Plant problems?" joked Tezz.

Willow faced them, hands on hips. Pissed.

"What have you jokers done with my seedlings?" she asked angrily. They pointed to the far corner of the room.

"Do you mean those seedlings?" the officer said, in a broad, slow Australian accent. Her plants were safely stacked in the far corner of the room.

The officer walked over to her. His wry smile was infectious. Willow extended her hand, and he shook it.

"I'm Major William Blagg –Australian Defence Force," he said, "but everyone calls me Billy."

Willow frowned and said, "So, it now looks like I've got two jokers to contend with."

Terrence said, "He's just arrived on a secondment from the Australian Army. He'll be here for a couple of weeks to observe our next Toxic Valley training exercise. He's in the process of setting up a botany-based bio-tech warfare unit for the ADF. I think you both studied botany down at Melbourne University."

Billy smiled and said, "I'm building a team of Survivalists to specialise in the use of bacteria, viruses, and toxins. Edibles, Psychoactives and Medicinals too. And to develop new treatments for soldiers affected by biological agents. Needless to say. It's all a bit hush-hush."

He walked over to the hops and cannabis plants in the corner.

"I've heard that the Toxic Valley recruit training exercise you run here in Bulgaria is the best on the planet."

He picked up several of her seedlings and added,

"Maybe we should get these little guys back into the sauna before they freeze to death?"

Three hours later, Willow, Tezz and Billy sat around a small table chatting over lunch in the labs uber-cool cafe. Snow flurries whipped around the icy grounds outside the large windows.

Willow talked Blagg through the next Survival bivouac she'd be running at the NSTA. Billy was eager to be embedded in the training exercise.

"We start with a week of survival training up in the mountains. You'll learn to hunt and forage. Find medicinal plants, and understand poisons and psychotics. The usual stuff, but in a European context," she said.

Tezz grimaced and added, "Get ready to be colder than you've ever been in your life. It's evil up there. I've done it once and I'm never going back there."

Willow continued, "Then we run a large-scale chemical, biological, radiological, or nuclear (CBRN) threat exercise. We simulate survival in a contaminated battle environment down in one of the lower valleys. Recruits learn how to identify hazardous substances. PPE. Treating exposure to toxins. Communication chains. We get teams of NATO soldiers come in from the NSTA to play the enemy forces."

"It all sounds awesome," said Billy.

Willow said, "You won't be saying that when your ass is frozen to a rock up on the mountain in a few days."

Chapter 25

The Dreaming Tea Plant.

In winter, the valley behind the NSTA channeled an arctic airstream. It began in Finland, traversed over the Ukrainian flats and thundered into Eastern Bulgaria. The temperature fell below freezing, and the wind chill factor made it feel like Northern Siberia. It chilled you to your bones.

Billy huddled beside an old oil drum filled with burning logs. He was desperate for some warmth as he observed Willow at work.

Heavy snow was plastering everything at the Survival Training bivouac location, high in the mountains behind the NSTA. The wind had been howling every single day. His balls felt frozen solid.

"I think that will be the last of today's trainee dropouts," shouted Willow as she wiped some stubborn snowflakes away from her face.

She was helping a sobbing twenty-something Latvian soldier get into a jeep. He was wrapped in a foil blanket, ready to be taken back to the NSTA Medical Centre down the mountain. The soldier was shaking with uncontrollable shivers, a classic symptom of deep hypothermia.

Willow turned to Billy Blagg and shouted over the blizzard, "They've been dropping like flies the last two days. Thank God we end the training exercise tomorrow."

"You'll be bundling me into that jeep if this doesn't end tomorrow," said Blagg, barely able to talk through his chattering teeth.

Two days later, they were all safe and warm back at the lab.

***

Willow walked into the main genetics lab. She was taken aback, because it was usually bustling with activity.

Today it was deathly silent. As she walked around, she saw that all of her fellow lab technicians were fast asleep, slumped in chairs at their workbenches. Some snoring peacefully.

Billy stood beside one of them, using a thermometer to take their body temperature. He was also holding the person's wrist, taking a pulse reading. He added the details to a chart on a clipboard he had placed on their desk.

"Wha –?" said Willow as she gawked around the room full of peacefully sleeping scientists.

Billy held up a Ziploc bag full of dried green leaves. He was acting like a kid, excitedly showing off a new toy.

"OK Wills. You should be able to guess this one," Billy said enthusiastically. "I'll give you a clue. It's from back home in Australia."

"I mixed it into everyone's morning tea. They should all be out for about thirty minutes," he said with glee. "Can you guess what it is?"

Willow closely studied the leaves in the plastic bag and asked, "I'll need the State it comes from."

"Hmm," he said, "don't want to make it too easy." He rubbed his chin. Deep in thought.

"OK. My home state of Western Australia. Northern. From up near the Kimberley region."

Willow grabbed a teacup next to a sleeping lab technician. She took a deep whiff.

"Herbal, not fungal," she said.

"Earthy, with a weird Lemon Myrtle top-note, though."

She thought for a moment, her brain ticking over the options.

"I'm guessing Jilungin. My nan used to call it the Dreaming Tea plant. From the Nyul Nyul people. The elders there used to drink it all the time."

She looked around the lab at her sleeping colleagues, a bit perplexed.

"But at best, that's a mild sedative. How did you make it this strong?" Willow asked.

Billy beamed as he called her over to a bench. A dehydrator filled with dry leaves sat next to a small shrub with stubby olive brown leaves. He pointed at the plant and said,

"You are looking at the result of two years' hard work. I've been slowly splicing this plant with Dendrocnide Moroides. From the Urticaceae family. You'd know that as the Stinging Tree."

"Up my way, we also call it gympie-gympie, or the suicide plant. It's as poisonous as hell." Willow reminded him sternly. "The Lab Manager is going to ream you a new one for doing this experiment on his team."

"When he wakes up," said Billy with a wink.

***

Major Billy Blagg knew he wouldn't be getting in much trouble for his experimental prank. Everyone knew he was on a fast-track to the top in the Australian Defence Force.

Billy was the son of the current Australian Ambassador to the USA. He had powerful connections in Australia and his father gave him access to senior people in the US army's senior ranks.

From the discussions they'd had, Willow could tell that Billy's work was highly secretive. It was definitely on the 'plants as weapons' end of the military survival spectrum. Not the 'plants for food or medicine' end.

With his laconic Aussie drawl and easy-going charm, Billy Blagg could always get away with blue murder.

Willow liked to call Billy 'the smiling assassin'.

***

Billy's rotation to Bulgaria ended two weeks before Christmas. He was heading back down to Australia, with a quick stop in Washington DC, to visit his father.

136

Willow and Tezz dropped him off at Bulgaria's Burgas Airport for the long series of flights to DC.

"I won't miss this fucking snow." Billy shouted, to be heard above the powerful gusts of icy wind.

As Tezz lugged Billy's suitcases onto a trolley, Billy whispered to Willow, "If you ever decide to come home, make sure you look me up. We could use someone like you."

He gave them both a quick hug and disappeared into the terminal.

CHAPTER 26

DATE NIGHT IN ZHERAVNA.

It was date night, and the towns around the NSTA looked impossibly romantic. Most villagers already decorated their homes with tinsel, baubles, and Christmas lights.

Willow and Tezz headed off-base to the local town of Sliven. With the horrors of the freezing Toxic Valley exercise behind them, and Christmas just around the corner, they were feeling festive.

They'd done a romantic walk in the snow around the medieval Tuida Fortress. Then, late afternoon, they jumped a taxi and headed twenty miles out of town to a tiny village called Zheravna. It was the home of a rickety old timber restaurant friends had recommended. In the fading sun, it looked like a decrepit shanty, but as the sun set, and lanterns on the verandah were lit, it became a place of magic.

The delicious smell of Lukanka, a cured Bulgarian sausage, wafted into the air as they tucked into a Sirene cheese-topped Shopska Salad and some stuffed grape leaves.

The food was delicious, but the air was tense at their table. Both knew there were some unspoken relationship issues to be digested as they enjoyed their dinner.

During Basic and AIT, Willow and Tezz had no choice but to rely closely on each other, but now they were going their separate ways in their professional lives. Life at the NSTA had become more difficult.

Lab work and SERE training exercises were Willow's focus. Tezz focused on Urban Assault training and frequently received calls to take part in programs back in the USA. The nature of those trips meant that he was forced to be highly secretive about them.

They were now seeing a lot less of each other.

A waitress came over and poured two glasses of the Domaine Boyar Merlot they'd ordered.

"I'll have the Moussaka," said Willow. "And I'll get a side of the Kiselo Mlyako."

Terrence placed his order. "I'll have the Pizza with Lutenica and Lukanka sausage. Thin crust. And a Kamenitza beer."

They clinked glasses and sat back to enjoy the delicious warmth of the restaurant and the occasional sound of a braying donkey outside.

Willow raised her glass and said, "Cheers and congratulations again on your promotion. Here's to First Lieutenant Aguilar. Urban Combat Trainer for the Meat-Eater Group."

The Meat Eaters were the Urban Combat Group that specialized in violent entry rather than the strategic and kumbaya aspects of close urban warfare. Every night, he seemed to come back to the barracks with a new set of bumps and grazes. On a field training days, it was sometimes stitches. His marksmanship was now exceptional.

"There's something we need to talk about," Tezz said.

He put down his wineglass and gave Willow a serious look.

"Next week I have to head back to the US for a while." Willow almost choked on her wine.

"Again?" she protested.

"Crensch has called a meeting," he said, looking down at his glass of wine. "I think there's going to be a small Op to snatch a local Juarez informant. To get some information about Big M and the Sinaloa cartel. Low key, though. It's all happening on the El Paso side of the border. Local El Paso SWAT will do all the heavy lifting."

He sheepishly looked up at her. "I'm only really going to observe. There won't be many more trips like this, I promise. I'm going to stop in Washington on the way back to talk to Crensch about it."

"Will I be able to contact you this time?" She asked.

"You know the drill," he said."In operations like these, mobile devices are too easy for the cartels to track. So there will probably be long periods of time when you can't reach me. It's just too risky. It would be a nightmare if my cover gets blown."

Grey clouds settled over the table for the rest of the evening.

Chapter 27

A Fight Is Brewing.

W illow was in the middle of another hellish Toxic Valley training exercise up on the mountain. The thermometer in her tent had icicles hanging from it.

"I'm done," Willow groaned through chattering teeth. "No job is worth this." It was 4am. She hadn't slept a wink as she slowly froze in her sleeping bag.

At least she was dry. The air was colder than Willow had ever experienced on any survival training bivvie. Four NSTA recruits had called into the main training exercise Command Center in the past two days to quit the course.

Tezz was still over in El Paso, but she was too busy freezing to get depressed about it.

Adrijana Marincovik was fast asleep in the sleeping bag beside hers. Oblivious to the cold. Willow always wondered how the hell Addy could sleep in these conditions. She assumed it resulted from growing up locally in the cold conditions.

Willow kept herself busy in the darkness by clicking on a torch and scanning the lower edges of the tent, checking for leaks. Addy roused beside her and sat up.

Willow moaned, "As soon as it's daylight, I'm handing in my chit. They can cut me from the SERE program if they want. This is like an episode of Survivor on steroids."

Addy whispered, "Hang in there, babe. That wouldn't be a good look for the recruits. It's the last day of the exercise tomorrow. Twenty-four hours and we'll be back down the valley. Back to the warmth of the barracks."

Willow closed her eyes, trying to mask her pain. "We haven't seen sunshine in seven days," she moaned. "Fuck knows how far below zero it is out there right now."

Addy flicked on a torch and looked at her watch. "Only a few hours until the sun is up," she said. "The clouds might break today if we're lucky."

Willow pulled the sleeping bag over her face. "I don't care if I wake up in the tropics. I'm calling 'quits' today. I'm not made for the cold like this," she blubbered.

***

Willow jolted awake.

She was gripping her blanket tightly to her face in the warm bunk in her Barracks Room.

She'd been having the same nightmare for months. Memories of that freezing final night of the last exercise up in the mountains still haunted her. She'd gathered her things later that icy morning to report to Borelli that she was dropping out as a trainer, but the sun suddenly broke through the clouds and saved her.

***

After the last Bulgarian winter training exercise, almost half of the Godzilla Island Survival Training Team had requested returns to their home countries. They were all sick and tired of freezing their asses off.

Jaques Refere, the Lead NSTA Survival Trainer, had also suddenly put in his home return request. He'd endured three years of the winters at the NSTA, but enough was enough.

After a short peer review process, Willow was promoted into his position and awarded the rank of Lieutenant.

She was happy about the promotion. The winters would still be shit, but her new rank would finally see her and Tezz sharing a separate officer's living quarters, as a couple, in the Barracks.

The euphoria of her promotion to Lieutenant was short-lived.

Tezz was often M.I.A. He was spending a lot of his time on briefing and embed trips around El Paso, back the US. Willow was rapidly getting pissed with the whole situation.

To release her anger, she'd turned to the boxing ring.

***

Willow grunted in anger as she bench-pressed a heavily laden bar in the gym. Addy was spotting her behind the benching machine.

"Radio silence. M.I.A." grunted Willow, after taking a deep breath and pressing a heavy barbell into the air, "It's like Tezz has disappeared off the planet. Again."

"Not even a text?" said Addy.

"They said there would be no phones during the Op. I guess they meant it. Who knows?" said Willow, as she caught her breath and prepared for another lift.

Thirty minutes later, she grabbed her gloves and hit the boxing ring.

She built up a sweat, working out her anger in the ring. A group of NATO recruits stood in awe around the edge of the old blood-stained canvas as she annihilated her male sparring partner. Money secretively changed hands beside the ring as the bout continued.

In the corner of the ring Addy shouted, "Slow it down, Wills. It's not the bloody Rumble in the Jungle." The bell rang. Willow leaned against the corner pads, gulping down air and dripping sweat.

Her beaten male opponent used the break to slink away between the ropes. He walked past Sergeant Nickolai Ivanov, a massive brute of a man, who was punching a heavy leather bag. The Sergeant stopped and called out 'pussy', as the guy walked past in shame. Then he turned to Willow and blew her a kiss.

She scowled back at him from the ring.

***

Later in the day, Willow was in sitting in a local bar drinking with Addy and a group of girlfriends.

Sergeant Ivanov entered the room and joined a thuggish group of friends in the corner. Between beers, he looked over at her and blew more kisses. Willow angrily stood to walk over to him, but Addy grabbed her arm and pulled her back onto her barstool.

"Hold your horses," she said, "that guy's about twice your size."

Willow settled back into her seat. Her girlfriends were feeling upbeat because the weather was getting better every week. Spring would soon be upon them.

However, they were all terribly bored, and Willow was sick of the forced silence from Tezz.

Someone suggested they should all hire a car and drive the five hours over to Istanbul to check out the Grand Bazaar there.

A date was quickly set for the trip, but they needed to raise a considerable amount of fast cash to pay for the car hire, accommodation and shopping. Addy had an idea.

CHAPTER 28

FIGHT NIGHT.

Willow figured she just had to land three clean punches. Then the big Serb bruiser would hit the canvas.

In the corner of the boxing ring she leaned back on the thick top rope, flexing her sinewy muscles. Her dark skin glistened in a sheen of sweat. *JAB. JAB. HOOK.* She switched her feet back and forth as she rehearsed her moves.

"You can do this," Willow muttered, in deep concentration. She dropped her head to clear her mind, studying the dried droplets of blood splattered on the canvas from earlier fights.

The old canvas boxing ring at the NSTA sat under an array of rusted tungsten flood-lamps in a decrepit soviet-era bunker. The room still stank of the vinegar smell from the wooden boxes of 125mm M-84 tank shells that were once stored there.

A rowdy crowd of soldiers had gathered around the ring. The soldiers packed themselves in like sardines, adding a heady mix of testosterone and sweat to the sweltering room.

A young Polish recruit with a buzz cut raised his fist in the air.

"I'll take fifty Euros that the black girl won't last a round!" he yelled.

Addy called back to him, "I'll take that bet." A chit of paper exchanged hands to seal the deal. She stuffed the chit into her sweat-stained tank-top and headed over to Willow's corner. Three of Willow's other girlfriends were also working the swelling crowd, taking bets.

While the crowd was distracted, Addy hefted a metal spit bucket from the floor into the corner, then stepped up onto the apron of the boxing ring.

"Give him hell," she said, as she tightened the laces on Willow's boxing gloves.

Addy wiped the sweat from Willow's face, then looked across at Willow's opponent and added, "But play with him a bit first, so we can drive the odds up a bit more."

Willow wasn't sure how to take Addy's advice, given that Addy was sporting a massive, blackened eye from an earlier bout. She'd lost.

"Really Addy? Play with him? said Willow, "He's got to be twice my bloody weight."

She slowly took a few more deep breaths, waiting for the bell to ring for the first round.

"We have an old saying back in Serbia," said Addy, smiling confidently, "Znate šta, dinamit dolazi u malim pakovanjima. It means, dynamite comes in small packages."

Across the ring, her opponent, Sergeant Nickolai Ivanov, paced back and forth like an angry bear in a cage. The massive Serbian, from the 63rd Parachute Brigade, was built like a T-72 Battle Tank. He whipped up the crowd of soldiers around the ring.

Bets exchanged hands like wildfire as he scowled across the ring at Willow.

"Three to one odds here!" shouted Private Sandi Martin. "Three to one. Get it here." Sandi paced around the heaving crowd holding a wad of cash, flirting outrageously in a tight white singlet. She was taking cash bets on the fight hand-over-fist.

Over in Willow's corner Addy reached into the spit bucket and grabbed a four inch long glass laboratory vial. She shook the green liquid inside and then uncorked the top. Addy carefully poured some drops of the liquid onto Willow's gloves. The aroma of eucalyptus and bush pomegranate wafted through the air. Willow quickly shifted her boxing gloves away from her face to avoid the smell.

Curious, Addy took a short sniff from the vial. Her eyes rolled back in her head.

She slumped down to her knees on the canvas.

"Careful babe," Willow said, "where I come from the stuff in that vial will put a bull Crocodile to sleep in no time."

The room went silent as the bell rang to begin the first round.

The referee called Willow and the Serb to the center of the ring. Nikolai towered over Willow. He was a good head and shoulders taller, and at least 100 pounds heavier.

"I will crush you like a sparrow," Nickolai growled.

The betting frenzy started again. Sandi and Addy worked the crowd, taking every bet they could garner.

The bell rang again, and the fight began.

Willow was fast. Weaving back and forth just out of range of Nikolai's mighty fists, waiting for her chance to strike.

"Come on little birdie," Nickolai shouted, as Willow ducked and weaved to avoid another blow.

"It's not really a fight —if you don't fight back," he teased.

The main door to the boxing ring swung open and a uniformed NATO officer, entered the room. The crowd paused nervously for a moment. But he shrugged off the attention as he pulled out a wad of money. The crowd turned back to the fight.

The distraction allowed Nickolai to land a bone-cracking hook into Willow's ribs. She lurched back against the ropes. Winded.

"It looks like the little birdie has a tiny broken wing, perhaps?" Nickolai goaded.

Willow steadied and launched forward. She landed a strong blow on his jaw. Nikolai barely noticed the impact. But he snorted, as the sweet smell of eucalyptus and pomegranate filled his nostrils.

The bell rang and the boxers returned to their corners.

Addy put more drops of the green liquid on Willow's gloves. This time she held the vial at arms length.

"Two more hits –maybe three?" Addy encouraged, "Nice job playing with him. We're making a killing on the bets."

Willow just coughed and cradled her cracked rib cage.

The bell rang, and the fight began again.

"C'mon little birdie. Why don't you show your Uncle Nikki what you've got," Nikolai taunted across the ring, "Maybe after this round you will be my little bitch –Eh?'

He sneered and gyrated his hips in the air. The crowd of soldiers roared.

Willow used the distraction to land another blow on his jaw. He just sniffed and laughed it off.

"Maybe not even a birdie," he goaded. "She hits like a tiny mouse."

Another hit of the pomegranate scent from her boxing gloves entered his nostrils. He sniffed a couple of times and said, "Hmm –a little perfumed mouse."

After dodging more blows, the bell mercifully rang.

Willow returned to her corner.

Addy held up the vial of green liquid and asked, "You sure this stuff is going to work?"

She added a few more drops.

The bell clanged, and the boxers squared off again.

Willow landed a lucky uppercut to his jaw.

Nickolai looked confused. He grew unsteady on his feet.

Willow landed another glancing blow on his face. He sniffed a couple of times. The massive Serb's eyes rolled, then he buckled down onto his knees in front of her.

The crowd of soldiers around the ring went silent.

Willow leaned down, close to his confused, sagging face.

He swayed back and forth, in a daze, on the blood-stained canvas.

'I'm not a birdie!" Willow said triumphantly.

"And I'm not your bitch –!"

"I'm a Botanist!"

She smashed the massive Serb in the face. Nikolai's body twisted and he face-planted into the canvas.

Out cold.

CHAPTER 29

THE AFTERMATH.

Overnight, Willow had become a legend at the NSTA.

Word spread fast about how she'd defeated Sergeant Ivanov in the boxing ring. Photos of her standing over his unconscious body spread like wildfire on every recruit's social feed.

Addy and Willow's other girlfriends had collected a small fortune in winnings after the fight. 'Istanbul, here we come.'

Willow didn't feel so legendary as she lay in her bed the morning after. She moaned as she turned and rolled over in bed. Her right eye had swollen shut, and she had three freshly cracked ribs from the fight. They wracked her with pain whenever she moved.

"Take it slow," said Addy, waking up in a chair beside Willow's bed. "You might have beaten that big Serb bastard, but you really took a beating in the ring last night."

Addy reached over to a side table. She hefted a thick wad of US dollars and said, "But us girls made a killing, thanks to that little green potion you mixed up. Everyone bet big that monster Serb would crush 'the little black chick'. The odds were off-the-planet. You should have seen their faces when he hit the canvas."

There was a sudden knock on the door. Addy walked over and opened it. Dr Ghand walked in angrily.

"I heard you were a mess. What happened?" he asked.

Addy quickly improvised, "She slipped in the snow over at the Base last night. Landed on a big rock in the garden. We got her X-Rayed and they say it's just cracked ribs. She'll be sore for the next couple of weeks."

Ghand just gave Addy a long, blank stare. His bullshit-meter had gone into overload.

He walked over to a chair and picked up Willow's boxing gloves. He gave them a sniff and said, "Fell down some stairs? Hmm. I'd heard something about a big fight in the boxing ring over in the tank hanger last night. You gals weren't over there, I'm assuming."

Ghand looked over at Willow. He gave her a fatherly smile and said, "Take the rest of the week off. Get some rest. Hopefully, Terrence will be back soon. Have you heard anything from him?"

Willow moaned, "Radio silence." Just shaking her head made her torso squeal with pain.

Ghand turned to leave the room. "Try not to take your anger out on the local population," he chided.

Willow spent the morning wrapped up in a blanket in a chair, surrounded by support pillows.

At around 4pm, a text popped up on Willow's phone. She struggled to reach and lift it to read the message. It was a text message from Tezz.

'ANOTHER FEW DAYS. DEF LESS THAN A WEEK. SOME FAMILY ISSUES TO DEAL WITH. SORRY. WILL TRY TO CALL SOON. XXXX TEZZ.'

She moaned and laid back in the chair.

CHAPTER 30

DARREN STARK. SPECIAL AGENT.

Four hours after leaving El Paso, Tezz was jumping into a cab at Ronald Reagan Airport in Washington, DC.

Not long after, he was walking across the giant grey crest of the Central Intelligence Agency inlaid into the marble floor of the lobby of CIA Headquarters. Crensch was waiting for him at the security gates.

"Welcome to Langley. I heard many good things about the last El Paso Op," said Crensch as they stepped into a lift.

"Still not sure why I'm doing this stop in DC on the way back home," said Terrence.

Crensch said, "Lots of people for you to meet today. Not much time. That last Sinaloa cartel informant gave up some good information about Big M, after a little persuasion. We're getting close to him now. Time to step things up. Let's get moving."

As the lift doors opened, he handed Tezz a CIA Security Pass and a large yellow envelope.

"In here you'll find a new passport, under the name of Darren Stark. That will be your new identity for the next phase of the operations," said Crensch. "There's also some documentation for you to memorize and some cash to buy plane tickets from Bulgaria back to the US under your new identity. If we are going to bring you back into the country, we don't want any travel booking information or credit card transactions traceable back to you at the NSTA."

"Big M has eyes and ears everywhere." Crensch added.

Tezz shot him a confused look and said, "I'm coming back to El Paso? Again? I've already had three trips back in the last six months. Willow already wants to kill me."

They awkwardly took seats at Crensch's desk.

Crensch said, "Big Operation coming. Timing not confirmed yet. Lots of red tape to wade through across the agencies. We might be operating on both sides of the border this time, so we'll need to coordinate with the Feds and the local DEA. To avoid stepping on toes. Hmm, –it might even be a good idea to bring you back permanently. Let's make a note to talk about that."

He rose from his desk and beckoned Tezz to follow him. They walked down a hallway to a glass meeting room with eight people sitting around a table. After they entered, Crensch pushed a button on the wall and the glass walls went opaque.

"Ladies and gentlemen, I'd like you to meet Special Agent Darren Stark. Moving forward, he'll be helping us with the recent developments in Juarez," said Crensch.

***

As he'd promised, Tezz returned home to the NSTA a day later, but the joy of nesting in their new couple's quarters on the base disrupted. The new joint DEA/CIA operation in Juarez lead to more trips back to the US.

Willow fought with him each time he left. She felt lost and lonely as Tezz became more and more secretive about his visits back to Langley and El Paso.

As springtime approached in Bulgaria, her anger was boiling over.

BAD NEWS ON GERGYOVDEN.

On May 6 each year Bulgaria springs to life from its winter doldrums. People across the Balkans celebrate Gergyovden, or St George's Day, with street parades, pagan rituals, and lots of drinking.

It's also Bulgarian Armed Forces Day, so the NSTA and the villages around it have huge celebrations, while the Bulgarian government shows off its latest military hardware in street parades. Willow, Addy and a bunch of the latest female recruits had headed over to Mokren, a local village just off the Base, to celebrate.

Tezz, of course, was M.I.A. He was over in the US for more secretive 'meetings'. He'd been in El Paso for the past two weeks. It was radio silence as usual.

Addy had been enjoying St George's Day a little too much.

Massively drunk, she squealed with delight as she joined a circle of local women, some in red tunics and others wearing black dresses and white head-scarves, dancing the traditional Horo, a line dance performed by all ages in the village. They didn't seem to care that she was drunk.

By 4pm on Gergyovden, most of the village of Mokren was smashed.

As the sun slowly set, Addy and Willow chilled out on a seat at the edge of a long, green meadow. It was peaceful and quiet, away from the festivities in the middle of town. The first spray of young spring flowers covered the meadow. They watched the last golden rays of the sun while enjoying a glass of warm mulled wine.

Willow looked wistfully at the sun and said, "I hope this is a better year than the last one, because I'm not sure I can take this much longer." The recent girls' road trip to Istanbul had lifted her spirits, but she was dropping into the doldrums again.

Addie lifted her glass of mulled wine and toasted, "To next year!" They chinked glasses and Willow downed the last of her wine. She said, "We'd better think about getting back soon."

She turned and look down the road as she heard some vehicles approaching.

A convoy of three black SUVs appeared down the road from them. Willow and Addy gawked as the SUVs ground to a halt nearby.

Willow was surprised when Dr Ghand stepped out of one of the vehicles. He usually wore jeans and a tailored shirt under a lab coat, but today he was wearing a formal business suit. Strange.

Two female officers exited another vehicle and waited.

Ghand walked over to Willow. He looked gaunt.

He asked her to join him. They slowly strolled across the meadow.

Once they were out of earshot of everyone else, he turned to her and said, "I have bad news."

Willow said, "Huh?", thinking something terrible had happened back at the Laboratory, or on the base.

"I can't sugarcoat this, so I'll just say it," he said.

"Terrence has been killed in a covert DEA operation in El Paso."

Chapter 32

Every Good Funeral Needs Snipers.

Willow had little time to grieve.

By 2am she was strapped into a jump seat on an Airforce C-17 GlobeMaster lumbering down a runway out of Graf Ignatievo Military Base. She was bound for the United States.

During the journey, she received a briefing about the situation. The CIA had received information that identified Big M's location. He was living in a compound near Luz Alba – not far from the outskirts of Juarez. The CIA assembled a team of five and sent them over to Mexico to arrest him and bring him back to the States.

The CIA and the DEA had been double-crossed. When they arrived at the compound, Big M was nowhere to be found, and a cartel hit squad lay in wait. The gun battle killed all five members of the CIA team.

Tezz had been with the group.

Twenty-three hours later, Willow landed in the blistering heat at Holman Airforce Base, Texas. She felt shattered.

As she walked off the plane, Major Crensch, in full military uniform, stepped out of a black SUV waiting on the tarmac. A gray-haired man in a formal business suit, who'd stepped out of a gray Chevy Tahoe, joined him.

Crensch was expecting Willow to be upset. He wasn't expecting the upper cut that pole-axed him to the ground.

Crensch wiped blood from his split lip as he got back on his feet. He waved away some soldiers who had run over.

"Well –I guess I deserved that," he said.

Crensch turned to the man in the suit.

"Lieutenant Barrant, I'd like to introduce you to Jason Blagg. The Australian Ambassador to the US."

Blagg tentatively put his arm on Willow's shoulder.

"We were shocked to hear the news, Miss Barrant. May I call you Willow?" he said in a comforting Aussie drawl.

She looked him in the eye and said, "You can call me Willow. I know your son, Billy. He was seconded to the NSTA just over a year ago, and I met him there. He was a funny bloke."

The Ambassador smiled and said, "You can join me in my car. It will be a ninety-minute drive from here over to El Paso. We'll have plenty of time to talk on the way."

Blagg walked toward the Tahoe. Willow followed.

"I think you also might have met the traveler we've asked to join us for the ride over to the funeral," he added.

The rear door of the Tahoe cracked open. A walking stick touched the ground, and a man stepped out wearily.

"Dad!" Willow screamed as she dropped her camo duffel bag and rushed over to hug him. She cried, "How did you get here? You don't even have a passport."

The Ambassador said, "Let's just say we pulled some strings. You can thank the Major for last night's jet flight over from RAAF Tindal in the Northern Territory."

***

Two days later, they buried Tezz with full military honors in his hometown of El Paso. Willow was spared the shock of having to identify the body. Gabriela, Tezz's mother, had already done that.

The funeral was bizarre. Gabriella and Tezz's close family joined the funeral at the last minute, protected by a phalanx of armed guards in military vehicles. Willow's keen eyes had noticed at least three US Army snipers, positioned to scan the surrounding parklands, discreetly distanced from the cortege of mourners.

Tezz's coffin was draped in a US flag, which was folded and presented to his mother. She looked shell-shocked.

As soon as the funeral was over, the protection unit whisked away Tezz's family. Willow barely got to speak to them. As the military convoy disappeared from the cemetery, Willow stood next to Ambassador Blagg under a shady tree.

Billy Blagg, in his Australian Army uniform, strolled over to join them.

"Jesus, it's hot here," he said, making small talk, as he edged into the shade with them.

"I heard you made Colonel after you went back." she said. "Congrats."

Billy was smoking a cigarette and offered it to Willow.

She tentatively accepted and took a deep drag, which was followed by a coughing fit. They all burst out laughing.

As she regained her composure, the Ambassador whispered to her, "If you ever need any help. Anything. I mean it. Please don't hesitate to call. Billy –or my office."

Billy Blagg asked, "Willow, what are your plans?"

Willow shook her head and said, "It's all too sudden. I'm not really sure where 'home' is anymore. Tezz was the only reason for staying at the NSTA. I guess all I can do is head back there and see what happens."

Her father, Willy, had slowly hobbled over to join them. She held her elbow out for him to rest against and said, "It looks like there's no use staying here. Gabriela and his family are all deep in hiding from the Sinaloa cartel."

Since the bungled ambush on Big M outside Juarez, the CIA and DEA were both on high alert.

Willow put her arm around her father's shoulders and said, "I think I'll fly back to Weipa first, to make sure Dad gets settled back in. Maybe lick my wounds there for a bit. Ghand told me I could take all the time I need. Then I'll head back over to the NSTA and see how it goes from there."

CHAPTER 33

RADOVAN LIKED TO SMASH THINGS.

Veliko Gradiste. Serbia.

The year of 1979 was a big one for births. The world marveled at the first Sony Walkman. Michael Jackson released the seminal 'Off the Wall'. China introduced their One Child Policy.

In the town of Veliko Gradiste in Serbia, Mrs. Jelena Vukovic gave birth to her son Radovan. The labor took thirty-six hours. Rad was a big, chubby baby. His father was a nightclub bouncer and part time street wrestler, taking on all-comers in grubby back-alleys for cash.

Young Rad grew up on a steady diet of violence and intimidation.

***

It was Rad's fourth birthday, and his little voice cooed from inside his bedroom as his mother, Jelena, walked past.

"Majka. Majka." Rads little voice called, between childish giggles and screams of delight.

Jelena hurried toward the laundry with a tub full of wet clothes and called out to him, "Just a minute, little Rado. Mummy's putting the washing away." She dumped the load of washing on a bench and looked out the window. The rumble of thunder and ominous black clouds filled the sky. It wasn't going to be a good day for drying the clothes.

"Don't worry about getting the car out," she called out to her husband, "I'm going to wait until these clouds clear before I go to the market." Jelena scurried back to little Rad's room. She peeked inside apprehensively.

Little Rad was having a wonderful time in the bedroom. Beheading his sister's much-loved dolls. Tearing up her artwork. Breaking up every toy in the room. Giggling and laughing at the chaos.

Radovan Vukovic liked to smash things. He still does today.

***

Rad's hometown was a basic place.

Veliko Gradiste, roughly translated, means 'large construction site'. Say no more.

The side of the town that fronted the Danube River was nice, but the part of town where the Vukovics lived was populated with brutal soviet-era apartment blocks and smelled like damp blankets. Radovan would grow to become a man with few airs and graces.

Ominous clouds were also approaching every aspect of young Radovan's life. He was born just a few years before the Serb-Croatian war and the rise of Slobodan Milosevic. As a teen he would see the absolute worst of humanity, in a conflict that would introduce the words 'ethnic cleansing' into the human vocabulary.

At fifteen, Radovan killed his first man.

It was a forty-year-old soldier from Kosovo, who'd raped Rad's sixteen-year-old sister during the conflict. Rad hunted him down, dragged him to a cold, dark room behind a butcher's shop and killed him slowly with a paring knife.

By the time he was eighteen, Rad was already a player in the Baltic drug trade. He rose quickly through the ranks, from selling weed and amphetamines in clubs and alleys, to organizing teams of street-urchin dealers and taking a cut of their sales.

Radovan turned twenty the year an organised crime group assassinated that President Zoran Dindic. In the country-wide witch hunt that followed, authorities killed many involved in the narcotics trade. Radovan decided it might be a smart move to get out of the drug trade for a while. So he enlisted in the Serbian Army.

Joining the Army turned out to be the smartest move he ever made.

***

Over the next twenty years, his political skills in the army would place Rad at the center of organized drug trade for most of the Baltic states, as he rose from drug dealer to drug boss.

Today, police and armed soldiers did much of the Baltic drug cartel's bidding. There were rumors that Radovan would run for president one day, but he preferred the solitary life.

Apart from visiting relatives up near Brasov in Romania, he rarely stepped off Serbian soil.

Radovan knew he was high on an Interpol hit list.

CHAPTER 34

THE BLIGHT HITS THE BALTICS.

Radovan Vukovic had aged gracefully over the years, but he still wasn't happy about reaching fifty-years-old.

The extended Vukovic family was enjoying his birthday party on a long private cruise-boat on the Danube River. At the far end of the floating gin-palace, his teen daughters and friends were dancing to a new Taylor Swift song, away from the 'oldies'.

Rad sat at the head of a long table, at the 'parents' end' of the boat. As he looked at the riverbank creeping slowly past, he thought about how much he loved this part of the world. Serbia on one side of the river. Romania on the other riverbank. The river offered easy escape routes from his home in Serbia. He could easily flee into Romania, Bulgaria or Hungary if the shit hit the fan and Interpol came knocking.

Cannabis plants thrived in the local volcanic soil. Thousands of acres were hidden away in a patchwork of crops throughout the surrounding hills and valleys. Most of the local farmers had their plots on the Romanian side of the Danube, where the laws were less severe, and the authorities would happily turn a blind eye in return for hookers and cash. Tending the crops was the only source of income for thousands of local immigrant farmhands.

The revelers at Rad's party had quaffed fine wine as the boat drifted past the crumbling Roman military fortifications along the Danube. They'd sat down at long white linen-draped tables to eat marinated venison as the elegant boat chugged past the lush Derdap National Park. At around 3pm, the boat turned and headed slowly back downstream, toward the quaint border town of Gornji Milanovac.

Rad and his guests started hearing gunfire as his family began singing Happy Birthday.

As they chugged around a bend in the river, they saw a column of black smoke rising from the quaint riverside town. The sound of sporadic gunfire echoed across the river. Rad figured it must be coming from near the Demarch (Mayors) offices.

He was right.

A riot was boiling out-of-control in the town square.

Flames swirled from the municipal building in one corner. A single firetruck was doing its best to quell it. Parked tractors and other huge farm vehicles barricaded one end of the town square. A truckload of limp brown cannabis plants and manure had been unceremoniously dumped and set on fire at the other end of the civic square. It crackled and smoldered, filling the air with choking smoke and the rancid smell of burning weed and cow shit. Protesters, mostly farm workers, chanted slogans on the steps of the old orthodox church. They scattered when the shooting began.

The farm workers found shelter behind tractors and fired potshots at the local police, who cowered behind three large white statues on a manicured green lawn.

The police hadn't started the fracas in the square. It began in the morning, when a fist-fight broke out between two local cannabis farmers and a few of their farmhands who had come into town to demand unpaid wages. The fight escalated to the entire square when additional desperate farmhands arrived in trucks. Guns and spades were inevitably drawn.

Radovan, and his younger Romanian cousin Stanjo, stomped along the deck. They peered from the bow of the boat. The full extent of the fighting slowly came into view as the boat headed toward the shore.

"Fuck. –Again! –This has to stop!" said Radovan.

"These fights with the weed farmers are breaking out everywhere." said Stanjo. "It's not good for the trade. The local police are losing control everywhere."

Another group of males joined them at the bow of the boat.

"What's happening?" asked one of them.

"It's the fucking weed growers and their workers," explained Stanjo. "The cannabis blight has spread across most of the south now. Killing crops everywhere. Greece and Bulgaria got hit two weeks ago. Fuck knows how it's spreading so fast."

An old white-haired man pointed at the hills above the river flats.

"It's killing whole cannabis crops," he said. "It can happen overnight. I've seen it with my very own eyes. Over at my brother's place."

Rad frowned and said, "It's everywhere. It moves like a wildfire. They say it's come in from farms in Latin America. Fucking Colombians –they screw everything up. I'm flying to Miami in a few days to talk to the other cartels about it. We must stop this."

The shots from the square intensified. A siren wailed.

Rad said, "The farmers and their workers have lost their livelihoods right across the valley. In less than a week! They want help from the government, but it's washing its hands of the matter. It's cannabis. If they step in to help, it will be a political nightmare."

Stanjo looked back, dejected, to the fighting onshore.

"If the blight moves north towards our farms in Romania and the Ukraine," he said, "we'll all be fucked. May God help us."

CHAPTER 35

So, I Fucked a F.I.F.O. Worker.

Mine Workers Accomodation Camp. Weipa.

One eye, blurry and tired, fluttered open. Willow stared at the ceiling of a cheap shipping container down near the Weipa bauxite mines. It had been converted into a single workman's bedroom. An old air-conditioner clattered as it strained against the scorching Weipa heat. Six months had passed since she'd moved back into her dad's house in Weipa. Most of the time she was on a bender, desperately trying to put the ghost of Tezz behind her. The last week had been a bad one.

She sat up in bed, her head throbbing from the alcohol haze of the night before. Two empty bottles of Bundaberg rum sat on a bedside table. At the end of the bed, a twenty-something mine worker was pulling on his Hi-Viz miner's jacket.

He stubbed out his cigarette and said, "I'm due to start my shift in fifteen minutes, luv. Gotta go." Then he stood to leave and added, "Just lock the door when you go. Leave the keys on the fridge."

Willow started to respond, but realized she didn't even know his name.

Without a word, or even the shallow promise of a text message, he had gone out the door.

She looked down at the side table and groaned as she saw a used condom on the floor beside it.

Slinking back under the duvet, she moaned, "Oh God –."

Since her arrival back home in Weipa after Tezz's funeral, Willow had spent most of her time drunk or stoned or bored. Often all three at once.

After the funeral, she'd spent a few weeks moping around her father's house. Then she'd sobered up, and flow back to Bulgaria to report back into the lab at the NSTA. She'd already made up her mind she wasn't going to stay long.

Not long after reporting for duty, she discovered it wasn't that easy to get out of the US Army. You couldn't just resign and leave a month later. Like a normal job. The CIA was also more than a little nervous about the details of Tezz's covert operations she might have been privy to.

The US Army gave her a firm 'No'. She would need to stay at the NSTA and serve out the remaining eighteen months of her rotation before they would even discuss it.

The CIA wouldn't even answer her calls. Tezz's death at the hands of Big M's thugs was an operational fuck-up, and no-one wanted that leaking out into the general population.

Thankfully, some phone calls to Ambassador Jason Blagg bought some help from the Australian consulate in Washington. Billy Blagg, now a rising-star Colonel in the Australian Defence Force, could also pull some strings with contacts in the US Army.

Two months later, after the signing of multiple NDA's and an epic send-off party at Godzilla Island, Willow found herself back at Willy's place in Weipa, her US Army days behind her.

CHAPTER 36

THE BACK-FILL OFFER.

"Out of bed sleepyhead. It's 7am," said Willy Barrant, "Breakfast is on the table." Willow slowly crawled out of bed.

Since returning to Weipa, she'd started hitting the booze, but now she was six days into trying to be sober. She still felt like crap. She'd promised Willy she would get her shit together. Over six months had passed since Tezz had been murdered. The last two months were a complete haze. Willy and Willow had a huge bust-up fight on his birthday a few weeks earlier.

Tensions in the Barrant household were high.

Willow trudged into the bathroom and splashed water on her face. Her hair looked like a rat's nest. She headed to the kitchen. Willy sat at the table reading the local paper. The local newspaper headline read; *'RAAF Scherger. Active For Talisman Saber'*. He peered over the paper and said, "There's a kale smoothy in the blender."

Willow poured a glass and grimaced at the green slimy liquid. She popped a Panadol tablet from a blister pack and used the vile liquid to wash it down.

"Eggs?" Willy asked.

"Let's see if I can hold this down first," said Willow.

***

Once every two years, Weipa transforms from a sleepy mining town into a bristling military establishment.

Over two weeks, the combined might of the US and Australian military machines, plus many allied countries, descend on northern Queensland. They hold a massive Joint Forces combat war-gaming exercise called Talisman Saber. This year was no different. For a month before the event Army vehicles filled the local roads around Weipa. Jets and large cargo planes buzzed the skies around Scherger RAAF base. Navy ships from many nations jostled for position in the small seaport at the mouth of the Embley River.

The US and Australian forces spent most of the time arguing. They couldn't even agree on the name of the exercise; the name alternated between Sabre and Saber each time the exercise was held.

American and Australian soldiers inundate the town for the two weeks the military exercises last. Then the town goes back to sleep, as live-fire military exercises are replaced with locals working the bauxite mines and doing their usual fishing and pigging activities on the weekends.

***

The fly-screen door of Willy's kitchen creaked as Willow pushed it open and she stepped out onto the front porch of the house.

She balanced a plate of eggs and toast. She sat in an old chair and looked down the line of old fibro and tin houses along the street, each with a dusty front yard and a decrepit chain-link fence. Most of the houses had rusting car bodies or dusty kids' swings in the front yard.

Willy didn't live in the nice part of Weipa. This was where the Napranum Aboriginals lived.

They made up about 20% of the local population and lived in low-cost fibro-cement houses with unsealed roads, in a community built by the government back in the Seventies. When Centrelink did community studies, the southern part of Weipa that Willy lived in always excelled in *incarceration, unemployment, substance abuse problems and short life expectancy.'* Not a great social services scorecard.

As she ate her breakfast, a khaki green Toyota Landcruiser turned into the street. The vehicle was conspicuously clean and undented. It threw up a massive plume of red bulldust as it drove slowly along the line of houses.

It drew to a stop outside Willy's house. Willow choked as the dust from the car engulfed her on the porch. She covered her nose and eyes.

When the bulldust cleared, Willow saw Billy Blagg, in his full Colonel's uniform, standing beside the car.

He looked up at her and smiled. "God –you look like shit," he said, as he walked toward her.

He paused and looked up and down the row of cheap houses.

"This is a little different to the uber-modern lab over at Novo Selo," he quipped as he walked up onto the porch. He dusted off a chair and sat opposite her.

"So, what's going on, Lieutenant Barrant?" he asked.

"Lieutenant Barrant has left the building," she answered. "It's just plain-old Willow now."

Willy stepped through the fly screen door to join them. Billy rose and shook his hand.

Willy beamed a huge smile and drawled, "You're a long way from home, Billy. I thought you were based down in the big smoke."

Billy said, "Well, if you can call Brisbane 'the big smoke'. I've set up a new unit based down there."

He looked over at Willow and added, "A new Survivalist Unit. With a new specialist section of the Plant Sciences Unit of the University of Queensland."

Willow gave him a look of suspicion.

"We're up here for the Talisaman Saber Joint Forces exercise next week," Billy said, "Just out at the Scherger Air Force Base. My unit is running a SERE course for the participants."

He slowly eyeballed Willow and said, "We'll be running a simulated remote plane crash site –the usual stuff."

He continued eyeballing her. She held his stare. "One of my trainers busted her leg yesterday," he said, "While we were setting up the site. Fell out of the back of a BushMaster truck."

The penny dropped for Willow.

Billy said, "She was my best native vegetation specialist. So, I'm looking for an urgent back-fill for a couple of weeks. I thought you might be interested. Right up your alley."

CHAPTER 37

THANKS —BUT NO THANKS.

Back on Willy's front porch in Napranum, Willow said, "I'm sorry," as she shook Colonel Billy Blagg's hand.

Billy smiled and said, "I understand why you might not want to do it. Worth a try, though."

Willow said, "It's just too early to make a decision like that. When I left the NSTA, I decided the Army wasn't for me anymore. I think I'm going to head back into Civvie Street. I really just don't know anymore."

Billy said, "Well, the offer is still open –and you have my number. I'm out at Scherger for the next few days."

Billy stepped into the waiting car, and it slowly disappeared in a cloud of red dust.

Willow walked back into the house. She stepped into the kitchen and grabbed a cold beer from the fridge.

Willy sat at the kitchen table, frowning.

"So –this is what it's going to look like?" he asked.

"Huh?" said Willow as she twisted the cap off the beer.

Willy chided, "It's barely morning. And your life plan is to knock back a great new opportunity –and to knock back a beer instead?"

Willow slowly lowered the bottle.

"Girl, I was thinking I raised you better than that," said Willy.

She crossed her arms. Annoyed.

Willy dug the knife a bit deeper.

"And I think Terrence would have expected more, too."

Willow exploded. Tears rolled down her face.

"Well, I wasn't expecting much either," she screamed. "I wasn't expecting him to disappear and leave me alone. Definitely wasn't expecting him to be gunned down by a fucking drug cartel. I wasn't expecting to be living back in your shitty house. In your shitty street. In this dirt-bag of a town."

She hurled the beer bottle across the room.

It smashed against the fibro cement wall.

REPORTING FOR DUTY.

That night, over at RAAF Scherger, Colonel Billy Blagg was fast asleep in his room at the end of a long dormitory filled with sleeping servicemen. He awoke to a loud knocking on his door.

The turgid air in the dorm reeked of the sweat and dirty socks of a hundred men, squeezed like sardines into a room designed for sixty. The ancient wheezing air-conditioner made no difference to the stifling humidity.

Billy slowly opened his door. He found Willow standing there. She was wearing a t-shirt and shorts, with a camo duffel bag over her shoulder.

"Lieutenant Willow Barrant, reporting for duty. That is, if you'll have me," she said.

Billy yawned and looked at his watch. It was 2am.

"I'm not even going to ask how you sneaked onto the Base and found me here. Don't you have a phone?" Billy asked.

Willow smirked and said, "I know this base like the back of my hand. Willy and I used to come to Weipa to visit our relatives –when I was a kid. All the local kids used to come out to sneak around the Base. After 4 o'clock each day, there's no-one here at all. Not even the dogs."

"Hmm," said Billy, still half asleep.

Willow said, "Busted my arm once, falling off those rusty old stairs up to the Control Tower."

She folded her arms. Looked him square in the eyes.

"So, does the deal still stand?" she asked.

Several of the sleeping servicemen had awoken and were now sitting up in their bunks.

Billy said, "Yes, the deal still stands. Do you think you're up for it?"

She gave him a wry smile and said, "Me. I'm not so sure. But Dad. He's REALLY sure. So, I'm figuring, let's give it a shot."

Billy pointed to the door at the far end of the dorm room.

"There's no room in this building," said Billy. "But there's space in the female barracks next door. Grab a bunk and I'll pick you up around 8am. If you don't get arrested in the meantime."

Willow gave him a brief salute. "Yes Saaah," she said.

Billy said, "Tell Sergeant Cordo I sent you over. I'm sure she'll appreciate you waking her at this hour."

Then he slowly swung his door shut.

As she walked along the room of sleeping soldiers, she heard one of them snoring loudly. She looked at the sleeping form under the covers on one of the lower bunk beds. She'd heard that distinctive snore before.

Willow muttered, "Nah, couldn't be." She kept walking.

A soldier peeked out from the top bunk and said, "Wills? Is that you?"

It was Caz.

"Caz, what the fuck?" she squealed.

Freddie peeked out from the bottom bunk, rubbing sleep from his eyes, and said, "Bugger me. Willow?"

They both rolled out of bed and tippy-toed down the bunk room until they were outside, standing under a light.

"Hold on a sec," said Freddie. He pulled out his mobile phone and dialed a number. "We're just outside Barracks Room Three," he said. "You need to get down here straight away. Yes, I know it's 2 o'clock, but you need to get down here."

Caz looked her up and down and said, "Jesus, what happened to that mousy little Aboriginal chick we shared a house in Melbourne with?" He took her arm and studied some of the tattoos she'd collected over the last few years. Many had military themes.

"Did you end up signing up? What branch of the ADF did you join?" he asked.

"Long story," she said. "I did join an army, but not the Australian one. I spent some time at the NATO training facility at Novo Selo, in Bulgaria, training to become a SERE and survival operative. I was sponsored by the US Army and, as I discovered later, maybe a bit by the CIA. I was discharged from that about four months ago, and I've been living up here with my dad ever since."

The sound of fast footsteps interrupted her explanation. Shu burst into the pool of light and gave Willow a big hug. "Willow! Fuck me, it really is you," she squealed. "What are you doing here?"

They pulled apart from the hug, and Shu looked at her from head to toe. "Last time I saw you was when we came to Zurich. You were on that fellowship," Shu said, "But you just disappeared off the map after that. I thought you'd gone off and married a Prince, or something like that."

They danced around in the pool of yellow tungsten light.

Caz said, "You two had better be quiet, or we're going to find out ourselves arrested out here at this time of the morning."

Willow said, "If everything goes well in the morning, it looks like I'm going to be here for the next two weeks. I'm working on a special assignment for the SERE training team. One of the trainers busted her leg and I'll be covering for her. We'll have plenty of time to talk."

***

Willow was nervous. It had been almost nine months since she'd last run a SERE training session. That last training exercise had been on top of an icy mountain in Bulgaria, and now she was sweating in a dusty bush clearing at a remote part of the Scherger RAAF base waiting for a group of joint forces soldiers to arrive.

A Bushmaster off-loaded a group of soldiers and she motioned for them to follow her. They dutifully headed toward the end of a long table under a green camouflage tent.

Willow got them to gather around a whiteboard and said, "Today we'll be covering these four things." She pointed to some words on the whiteboard and continued,

"Foraging for food."

"Medicinals."

"Anesthetics ."

"And Antiseptics."

Willow drew a circle around the words and said, "To help you survive if you get stuck in the middle of nowhere."

"My name is Willow Barrant. I'm a Botanist and a NATO-Trained Battlefield Survivalist. Today you'll be learning about surviving in the Australian bush after your plane goes down." She took off her baseball cap and wryly said, "As you can probably tell, I'm a 'local'. Basically, we'll be covering what to eat, what not to eat, how to heal and what will kill you. Got it?"

Willow pointed to the long table in the tent and said, "If you are lost and separated from your squad, some plants on that table will feed you." She picked up a bowl of large purple berries and said, "Some, like these, will help heal an open wound if you get injured."

She picked up another bowl at random and added, "Some will knock a person out. Some will make you itch like you want to rip your skin off. Some will give you a slow, painful death. So, treat them with respect."

Willow spreads her wings.

CHAPTER 39

A Real Job.

The two weeks of SERE training went by in a heartbeat. She loved every minute, but it brought home too many raw memories of her time with Tezz.

Billy Blagg had offered to sponsor her to fast-track into the Australian Defence Force but, after giving it some thought, she declined. The years of back-breaking working on the farm had also taken its toll on her father Willy. He was doing poorly, so she'd decided she needed to hang around in Weipa for a while to look after him.

After the Joint-Forces exercise, Freddy, Caz and Shu hung around in Weipa for a couple of weeks. Over many drunken sessions at the Weipa Bowlo, Willow discovered they were all keen to get out of the army. They'd spent many years serving, and it was time to try something new. They'd also seen lots of jobs on offer at the mines that paid ridiculous amounts of money.

Willow also needed a new challenge, but job opportunities for world-class educated botanists and expert SERE trainers were somewhat 'limited' in a town like Weipa. She really didn't relish the idea of becoming a barmaid or a mine worker.

***

Willow sat on the dusty front steps at her father's house, reading the local newspaper. The local rag wasn't much of a source of news, but it was fantastic for swatting blowflies away.

As she smashed a blowfly, she noticed a tiny classified job ad with a cannabis leaf logo on it. The ad was minuscule. It was the sort of tiny ad that HR departments placed when they needed to make it look like they had attempted to hire a local.

The headline of the ad read; SENIOR BOTANIST. GENETICS SPECIALIST.

It was right up Willow's alley, so she immediately went online and applied for it.

Chapter 40

The Witch Of The North.

Catherine Sneesby worked at Cannacom, a fifty acre medicinal cannabis farm just out near the RAAF base at Weipa.

Sneesby was a trained Botanist, but she hated the smell inside the farm's hothouses and cannabis drying rooms. It reminded her of wet, molding hay. She preferred the crisp, dry air in her spotless, white office. The large brass name plaque on her office door announced to the world that she was 'Chief Science Officer'.

Sneesby's path to running the lab at Cannacom, Australia's largest medicinal cannabis production facility, was hardly stellar. She'd graduated in Botanical Sciences at a second-tier South Australian university. After that, she tried to establish herself in the 'big-end-of-the-street' Botanical Sciences community, but somehow ended up working at a small run-down commercial weed farm in the Adelaide Hills.

On her 50th birthday, Catherine had a meltdown. She quit her middle management job in a huff and headed north to run the lab operations at Cannacom, up near the remote town of Weipa.

Catherine didn't take the job for the experience. She didn't take it for the money. She only did it for the grandiose title it gave her. A fact she relished reminding people of. Sneesby's plan was to hang around at Cannacom for a couple of years. She'd keep a low profile, then she'd get out of Dodge for a 'real' senior management job back in the big smoke.

***

Despite Catherine's complete lack of enthusiasm, Cannacom's cannabis operations grew fast. The laboratory expanded as the farm's acreage grew.

In a move only designed to secure more investor funding, the Cannacom Board had decided to launch a Plant Genetics Research Wing.

She didn't want the new wing, but the Board was insistent. It was another sexy-tech toy to woo and impress their investors.

***

Out of the blue, an email arrived in Sneesby's Inbox. It was the Board's job description for the new hire.

Two days later, Catherine sat glowering in front of her laptop. She was in a heated argument on a TEAMS video call with the Cannacom Board. They were discussing the potential new hire.

"Army?" snorted Catherine, looking at a candidate CV. "You want to employ this fucking Army Survival Trainer? Willow Barrant? To run our Genetics Lab? Over my effing dead body! That would be crazy."

Kip Norman, the Cannacom Chairman, interjected, "But her qualifications are outstanding, Catherine," Kip said. "And she's already located up your way. She can start straight away. She's perfect."

He flicked through his own printed copy of Willow's CV. "Her experience in the genetics of Hops plants is perfect for our needs," he added. "And, of course, she won the Gott Prize at Melbourne University. The investors will lap that up."

"It has to be a lie," Catherine said. "Has someone cross-referenced this CV?" She shook her head in disbelief.

"An indigenous girl? From a farm in Queensland? Wins Australia's premiere Botanical Sciences award. And gets shipped off to Zurich to study with the world's best?" Catherine shook her head again and said, "And now she's living just twenty miles down the road –in sleepy old Weipa. I just don't believe it. Someone's playing a joke on us."

Kip reassured her, "HR has checked it out. It's real." he said. Flummoxed, Catherine couldn't understand.

"Calm down Catherine," Kip responded.

"Just meet with her," he pleaded. "The investors will eat up the Gott Prize thing. She's coming in to see you on Wednesday. Let's talk after that. I'm sure you'll get along like a house on fire."

Kip hung off the video call. Catherine seethed and hung up.

Her house was well and truly on fire.

***

193

Willow easily won the new position at Cannacom, but from the first day, she clashed with Sneesby over everything. Willow came to refer to her as 'the witch of the north.'

Catherine followed the conservative, risk-free rule book for cannabis propagation. *'Cannabis Farming 101'*.

This process involved developing seedlings and then moving them into greenhouses. Temperature and humidity conditions were tightly controlled. Once mature, the flowers went to drying rooms. Then they were packed to send out to customers, who derived the oils and turned them into medications. Exactly like every farm on the planet.

Rinse. Repeat.

Sneesby's lazy "101" approach to the operation drove Willow crazy. The reliance on the massive greenhouses at the farm made the operation cost heavy. Willow figured that the business model could be completely transformed by just growing the maturing plants outside. Particularly in hot and moist tropical areas where mold was an issue.

Willow wanted to devote time to testing new genetic variants that could withstand tough 'open ground' conditions. Like any other farm crop.

So, Willow and The Witch constantly banged heads. Any progressive new ideas Willow had were quickly decapitated. The Witch wasted no time in shoving Willow's 'thinking outside the box' approach right back into its original box. Thankfully, after a few months of working together, Willow and Catherine entered a 'cold war' phase.

Willow had learned how to pick her battles.

CHAPTER 41

WILLOW'S SECRET.

Working at Cannacom was dead boring most of the time. There's not a lot of excitement in watching plants grow. So it's not surprising that most of the staff at Cannacom knocked off at 5-30pm sharp every day.

Except for Willow. She was often alone in the Cannacom lab, working back late. Tonight, the clock on the wall showed it was just after 7pm. She was tired and cranky.

As usual, Willow had waited until after Catherine and the other workers left to go home, so she could conduct some 'off-campus' experiments. She walked over to a bench that was covered in cannabis seedlings. They were all brown and shriveled.

Her white lab-coat had a large green splash across it. The centrifuge on the bench had just spit its slimy, liquefied contents all over her. She picked at chunks of mulched cannabis leaf splattered through her hair.

"Fuck you little guys," said Willow. "Why do you keep on dying on me?"

She frowned and turfed two trays of the dead cannabis seedlings into a big waste bin.

Willow used these secret after-hours lab sessions to conduct her own genetic experiments.

Most commercial cannabis labs around the planet focused on genetically manipulating the plant's THC or CBD content. Their aim was to change the 'buzz', or medicinal benefits of the plant, or to find new ways to resist pests and disease.

Willow's focus was different. She was trying to develop a new strain of plant that could withstand arid conditions. One that could thrive outside a hothouse in any conditions. A plant that could survive the worst that North-Fucking-Queensland's environment could throw at it.

Trays of spindly, dead cannabis plants covered Willow's work-bench in the lab. The success rate of her experiments so far was zero percent.

New genetic strains of cannabis usually came with exotic commercial names; Wedding Cake. Blue Dream. Jet Fuel. Glitter Bomb. Willow was working on a new genetic branch that had a simple name.

She just called her new strain 'The Nug'.

Her new variant would be a nuggety little bastard of a cannabis plant. One that could survive in the middle of a desert if you planted it there. Something that wouldn't need climate-controlled greenhouses to grow to maturity.

Willow wanted to work on the project full time, but the Cannacom Board had denied her request.

They weren't interested in arid survivability. Margins were tight. They'd told Willow, in no uncertain terms, Cannacom was in the business of making money today, not reinventing the weed business model for the future.

So, the development of 'The Nug', on Cannacom company time, was a firm and definite 'NO!'.

The Witch was delighted.

CHAPTER 42

MEET THE NEW SECURITY TEAM.

Willow was enjoying life in Weipa. It was frustrating working with Catherine, but the Cannacom gig was a proper job and it paid really well compared to anything else up that way. She reveled in being back in a lab again.

Within a few months, she could shift herself and Willy into a bigger house in a nicer part of town.

As Christmas approached, things got even better when Freddie, Caz and Shu all turned up in town. In the months after the Joint-Forces exercise, they'd put in applications to get out of the army. Now they were all free to do whatever they wanted.

They'd all moved up to Weipa, taking jobs at the mines, and settled into an idyllic lifestyle involving drinking at the Bowlo, fishing, off-grid camping trips and the occasional Gelsoft gun battle in the scrub.

The work in the mines was boring, but life was good.

'Mexicans.'

That was the name the locals in Weipa called anyone in Australia who lived south of the Tropic of Capricorn. Few Mexicans stayed in Weipa for more than a year.

The remote isolation and boredom had meant that the entire farm security team at Cannacom had resigned just before Christmas. They'd all decided that living in Weipa was a bridge-too-far for them, and walked off.

Willow quickly suggested Freddie, Caz and Shu put their hats into the ring for the jobs, as their army training would make them clear front runners.

Sneesby was pissed. The last thing she wanted was a group of Willow's friends working on the team. However, there was a big issue brewing at the farm because the lack of security personnel would mean that many of the staff would have their Christmas leave cancelled. When she realized that securing people with the necessary security qualifications would be a month-long process, she quickly relented and hired them. They had to start immediately.

***

Willow, in her white lab coat, sat in the back corner of the room during the staff orientation session. She prayed the guys wouldn't put a foot wrong on their first day in a new job.

"The Cannacom facility covers a fifty-acre allotment," Catherine said, as she started the standard Cannacom Employee Orientation presentation. "Most of the acreage is for the mature plants and is protected by a Class 1-certified security fence. This is mainly to keep the townsfolk from pulling over on the side of the road and taking a free sample home with them. The entire facility is designated as bio-secure. Nobody enters or leaves without screening and signing a form that accepts the strict terms of our grower's licence. Your job is to make sure that happens. All clear?"

Her next slide showed a map of the farm.

Catherine said, "As you can see, the facility begins on the main road and extends down to some dense bushland and mudflats to the west. There is no access to that western area for two reasons. First, dense bushland blocks most of the area, and the mudflats along the Embley River are infested with crocodiles. Second, the other part of the fence-line borders a restricted area that belongs to the Scherger RAAF Base. Nobody is allowed to enter that area, us included."

She glared at them for a moment and repeated, "All clear?" Freddie, Caz and Shu just nodded in agreement.

***

The original Air Force base was built in WW2, then left to fall into disrepair.

It had been reactivated in the 1990s with new runways, hangars, and support infrastructure being built, but Scherger lay dormant for most of its life.

It was what the RAAF called a 'Bare Base'. It was full of moth-balled, empty buildings and a Comms Tower that had seen better days. When called into emergency action, the facility could house thousands of servicemen, but, most days, the base was only manned by three bored servicemen and two sleepy German Shepherd dogs.

***

Catherine clicked on her laptop and a picture appeared on the presentation screen behind her.

It showed the inside of one of the farm's hothouses. One of the side walls had been ripped open. Around fifty mature cannabis plants were flattened or eaten.

Catherine said, "Your daily job will be farm security, but your first job today will be to sort out a wild pig problem over on the western fence-line. Several of our farm workers had the crap scared out of them yesterday when they went to check out Hot-House S-22."

She ended the presentation on the screen and said,

"It looks like a small herd of local pigs has broken through the fence and taken a liking to the crop down there. I need you to check out the damage and work out how we can stop them from coming back. You can grab two farm ATVs to get down there. Take a gun if you need it. The last thing I need is one of you in hospital, if the pigs bail you up."

CHAPTER 43

THE BRIAR PATCH.

Unlike Sneesby, Willow loved getting her hands dirty. She'd grown up on a farm, so she never missed a chance to get out of the clinical environment in the lab, out into the fields and hothouses.

The security fence down on the western edge of the farm stretched almost two miles. It marked the boundary between the pristine cannabis planting area of the farm and the wild upper reaches of the Embley River. An impenetrable thicket of sodden mangroves and spiky Karoo Thorn grew on the other side of the fence.

Everyone knew it as the 'Briar Patch'. Its spikes and thorns could rip you to pieces. During the farm's construction, teams of workers had cut and hacked at the Briar for weeks, to run the farm's new security fence down there. They eventually had to admit defeat. The fence builders often reported crocs roaming the swampy side of the fence, like sentries.

Nobody from Cannacom was venturing across the Briar. Ever.

***

The local wild pigs had a different idea. Pigs love the taste of cannabis.

A herd had gathered from across the valley. They'd easily pushed their way through the Briar's sharp thorns. Eventually the smell of the hothouses full of carefully tended green cannabis, growing just on the other side of the fence, was too tempting. After days of digging, and some brute force, they finally tore an entry-hole in the fence, then easily smashed their way into the nearest hothouse.

***

Willow, driving one of Cannacom's ATV four wheelers, pulled up alongside the large hole in the farm fence. The corner of the hothouse had been ripped to pieces, and the pigs had eaten about fifty plants inside.

Another Cannacom ATV arrived shortly after with Freddie, Caz and Shu aboard. The guys inspected the damage while Shu lifted a large drone from the rear tray of the vehicle.

"Fuck me," marveled Freddie. He pulled on a thick piece of bent stainless steel fencing mesh hanging from a post. "That must have taken some strength,"

Caz stood over at the corner of the mangled hothouse, shaking his head. He tried to wiggle one of the upright steel wall posts.

"It's like they ripped the hothouse wall straight off the steel upright," Caz said. "They tore the welds straight off the galv post. These piggies must be big mother fuckers."

Freddie smiled and added, "Big, tasty motherfuckers."

The residents of the northern tip of Australia love wild pigs.

Not in a sustainable 'Greta Thunberg' way.

More in a 'slowly roasting on a Spit BBQ' sort of way.

The surrounding air filled with the whirring sound of a drone lifting into the sky. Shu expertly piloted it using a joystick on a flight pad.

Freddie walked over to the first ATV. He pulled out a long SR 98 rifle with a huge scope mounted on it. Standard 7.62mm Australian army issue. He'd trained on the sniper weapon when he'd served in the ADF. With an accurate range of 800m, it was perfect for pig hunting.

"Hey Shu." Freddie called out. "What can you see from the drone? Are they still nearby?"

Shu studied the video screen on the drone controller.

"From what I can see, they've left the farm area," she said. "They'd stand out like dog's balls if they were still inside the fence. They must be back over in the Briar. Might have heard us coming and bolted." Shu set the drone into a static hover above them. "What do you want to do, Wills?"

Willow was taking pictures of the crop damage. She popped her phone back into the pocket of her white lab technician's coat.

"Let's patch the fence as best we can," she said. "All we can do for now."

She walked back toward the ATVs.

"We'll come back tomorrow. It'll be the weekend, so there won't be anyone around on the farm to get in the way."

She looked at Freddie's rifle.

"Maybe Freddie can work out a more 'permanent' solution to the pig problem. I'm sure I can get the Witch to approve some weekend overtime."

Willow walked over to the wire and looked down the fence line.

"Shu, can you see any way through the Briar?" she asked. "Using the drone camera?"

Shu made the drone tilt and pan sideways.

"Not from here," said Shu.

"And I can't take the drone over the other side of the fence. That's officially the Scherger RAAF military base over there. No drones allowed. Nothing goes in the sky over there."

Freddie said, "We are going to need to find a way through the Briar if we are going to terminate those boars. Hey Shu, you wouldn't need to fly over there very long, would you?"

Shu smirked and said, "I suppose I could 'accidentally' do a sweep over the fence with the drone, and record the vision. That wouldn't take much time. We can look at the video footage later."

Caz walked over and casually bumped into Shu's shoulder.

"Like if I bumped you like that, and you lost control of the unit, you mean?" he said.

Shu nodded. "Yes, something like that."

Shu clicked the Record button on the Controller and set the drone on a slow path high over the Briar. It whizzed way past the end of the Cannacom fence, then along the riverbanks beyond.

She guided the drone a few kilometers over the Air Force base land, then slowly bought it back around to them at the farm fence again.

Shu expertly landed the drone beside one of the ATVs.

"Oops," she said.

"I wouldn't worry too much about getting caught," said Caz. "I've heard the Air Traffic control system at RAAF Scherger is switched off most of the time anyway. It's as old as the hills. They only really use it for annual exercises these days."

CHAPTER 44

A FLY PAST AT THE WEIPA BOWLO.

Later that day.

The Weipa Bowling Club was heaving with patrons, most of them drinking icy cold glasses of Great Northern beer and munching on baskets of hot chips. Most of the patrons were busy watching an amateurish YouTube video of the local Weipa Raiders rugby team match. They were getting beaten, yet again.

In the corner, Willow, Freddie, and Shu gathered around an iPad. They were intently watching Shu's drone footage. Caz joined them with a fresh set of brews.

On the ipad screen, the drone's aerial view swept along the silver razor wire of Cannacom's fence. Then it continued along the edge of the briar thicket as the rows of cannabis plants disappeared from view. The Briar ran all the way to the edge of a muddy tidal mangrove flat.

"Here's where the real footage starts," Shu said.

The drone view tilted and tracked west along the thick mangroves on the shallow water's muddy edge.

"What the fuck is that?" said Caz, as a group of decrepit old concrete buildings swept into view.

The buildings were half hidden by decades of mangrove trees and vines that had grown around them.

"Jesus," added Freddie, "That looks messed up, like the fucking temple scene out of Apocalypse Now."

Shu froze the image on the iPad screen.

"Check that out," said Caz. "That looks like a spillway for a dam to me. These buildings look a lot like a small hydro station, but they've been buried in a landslide. What's that doing way out there?"

Shu hit 'Play' on the drone video again. The mangroves in the video thinned out as the drone left the river's edge.

A grassy clearing came into view.

"Check that out," said Willow. "There's about 2 acres of good flat farmland in that little valley there. And a couple of good creeks. But it's surrounded by the Briar, maybe that's where the herd of pigs are coming from."

The drone view crossed back over the Briar. It headed slowly west again.

Willow shouted, "Stop! Wind that back!"

Shu paused the video and tracked backwards frame-by-frame.

"There!" said Willow, pointing at the left side of the screen.

"That looks like a break in the Briar to me. You could get there using an ATV. Along that dry creek bed. And then through that gap."

Freddie nodded in agreement and said, "Let's try it tomorrow. Nothing to lose."

"What's left on the video?" asked Willow.

Shu looked excited.

"You guys aren't going to believe this," she said. She hit 'Play' again.

The drone view swept back over the two-acre grassy plot and continued along toward the mangrove swamp. Then the drone tracked southwest. The mangrove swamp abruptly ended. A wide patch of glistening, clear blue water swung into view.

"What the?" said Freddie.

"Fuck me –if part of the Embley River doesn't come back above the landslide at the power station –" said Shu.

"See, just above the mangroves and the power station buildings. There's a big stretch of river hidden there. It's on the Air Force base land, but it's not under the Scherger flight path. I can't see road access from anywhere."

"Except from that gap in the Briar." added Willow.

"You could get some off-road vehicles into there."

Shu jabbed the Pause button on the video excitedly.

"And there's this!" she said.

Framed on the iPad screen was a perfect waterhole in the middle of the large circular billabong.

Tall rocky cliffs surrounded it, with a small idyllic yellow sandy beach along one edge.

They had just discovered the perfect bushland paradise that would just become known to them all as 'Ned's Corner'.

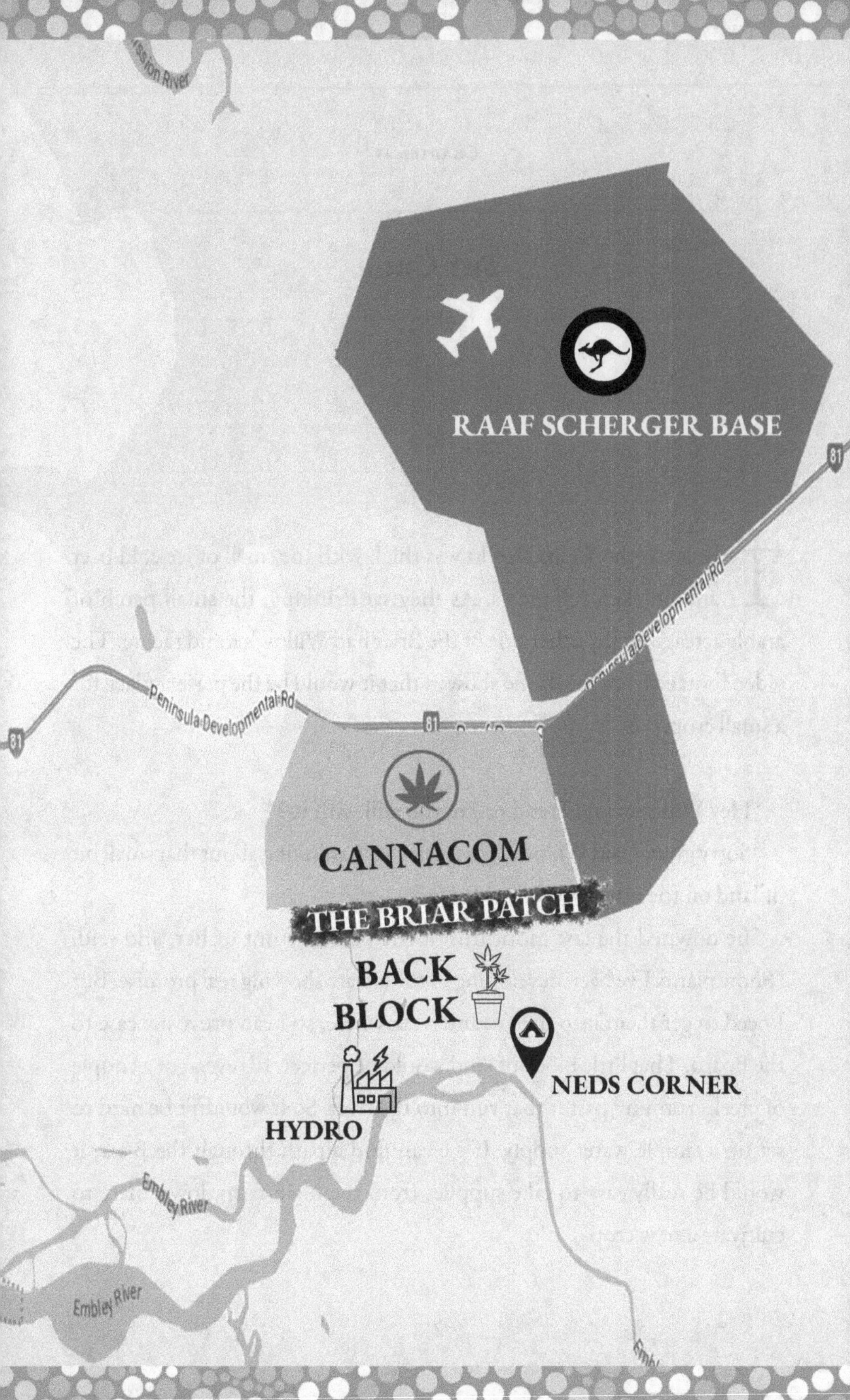

Mission River
Peninsula Developmental Rd
Peninsula Developmental Rd
Peninsula Developmental Rd
81
81
81
RAAF SCHERGER BASE
CANNACOM
THE BRIAR PATCH
BACK BLOCK
HYDRO
NEDS CORNER
Embley River
Embley River
Embl

Chapter 45

The Crop.

The air at the Weipa Bowlo was thick with the smell of ice cold beer and chicken schnitzels. As they sat drinking, the small patch of arable acreage on the other side of the Briar had Willow's mind racing. The video footage from the drone showed that it would be the perfect place for a small crop.

"Hey Willow," said Freddie. Are you still with us?"

"Sorry guys," said Willow, "I just can't stop thinking about that small bit of land on the other side of the Briar."

She downed the last mouthful of the beer in front of her, and said, "Some plants I've been developing in the lab are showing real promise. But I need to get them into the ground somewhere, so I can prove my case to the Board. That little block of land would be perfect. It's even got a couple of creeks running past it that run into the river. So it wouldn't be hard to set up a simple water supply. If we can find a path through the Briar, it would be really easy to take supplies from the main farm down there to cultivate a new crop."

Shu added, "And it's under the no-fly zone for the Air Force base, so we wouldn't have any problems with it being visible from the air."

"I'm getting really close," Willow confided. "I've developed a new cannabis strain that's a tough little bugger. Not soft and coddled like its greenhouse cousins. It won't need drip irrigation, controlled humidity, tight soil PH levels or even artificial light conditions. It will just grow straight in the soil. Tough, just like a weed. All it would need is a cheap ebb-and-flow irrigation system so we could flood it with water every-so-often."

"I'm thinking of taking some of the new specimens over to the other side of the Briar," said Willow. "To see if they can survive in the real world. It would take a few months to get some seedlings up to maturity."

***

When Caz and Freddie fixed the broken fence down near the Briar, they rigged it so there was a section that could be easily opened.

Over the next two weeks, they found a path through the briar to visit the small two-acre clearing.. The soil was friable, so it would be easy to plant a small crop. Two small creeks ran past nearby. One was fed by a spring, so it ran all year round. Perfect.

Using some old PVC pipes, Caz helped her to jerry-rig a flood watering system from the creek. They erected a couple of makeshift sheds to store equipment and provide some shade, plus an old second-hand generator to run the water pumps.

Late one evening, they used one of the ATVs to bring about fifty of Willow's experimental seedlings down to the block and planted them. Her goal was to plant about 250 seedlings, but she got carried away, and within six months, the crop had expanded to a couple of thousand plants at different stages of maturity.

A timer on the watering system flooded the crop once every four days.

Willow's new strain of cannabis thrived. However, this soon became a concern because what had started as an experimental planting of a few seedlings had suddenly become what the police would call 'a commercial quantity of drugs'.

As a backup plan, Willow had bought several butane powered burners they could use to torch the entire crop if things ever got dicey.

***

Freddie needed a good excuse for occasionally venturing past the Briar to the crop. In case they ever got caught out and Catherine asked awkward questions. He'd been using the quest to cull the local pig population to explain why he needed to go over there.

As the crop grew, the pigs created a fresh problem. Willow couldn't fence her secret crop because it would make it too visible from the air as military aircraft flew in and out of the RAAF base. So Freddie had to find a way to scare the pigs as far away as possible. Or capture the ones that were too stupid to get the message and leave.

Caz to the rescue.

The 'Boar Buster' was a crude invention that Caz had bought on-line one night, from an obscure Canadian agricultural retailer. He was extremely drunk at the time.

The boxes arrived three weeks later, so they decided to take a weekend and test it out down at the Back Block.

It worked like a gigantic steel mousetrap, for capturing whole groups of marauding wild pigs at one time. The main part of the Boar Buster was a massive circular, heavy duty wire cage. About twenty feet in diameter and five feet tall. Four tall steel poles suspended the cage high in the air. An inbuilt motion sensor would detect the pigs and drop the cage, trapping them inside.

Shu and Caz had struggled all day to follow the basic instructions to put it together. Finally, they hoisted the massive circular trap high above the ground, ready to suddenly drop on some unsuspecting pigs.

Caz cut up some pears and apples and scattered them on the ground. Shu activated the wireless movement detection device that monitored movement in the area directly under the trap. They both headed up a nearby hill to see what would happen. They drank a few beers while they waited. Two hours passed.

Shu suddenly put down her beer and pointed to the little monitor that showed the view from the Boar Buster's proximity camera. The flashing light on the unit showed the camera detected movement where the fruit was placed.

Shu excitedly clicked the button on the remote, to activate the trap. They both heard a satisfyingly loud 'Whump" from down the hill, as the massive circular steel cage came crashing down to the ground.

They ran back down the hill, like excited school children, but there were no pigs inside the cage.

Trapped inside was a furious Freddie, who'd come out to find out what they were up to.

***

Freddy had been spending a lot of time down near the crop trying to keep the marauding pigs at bay. The terrain was terrible and was taking a toll on his four-wheel drive. He desperately needed something else to use.

His problem was solved when they found an old Ford flatbed truck abandoned opposite the entrance to Scherger Air Force base. It looked like a complete wreck but Caz managed to get it running again.

They nicknamed the truck 'the Banger' because it was mighty noisy. The exhaust manifold was cracked and the exhaust pipes were full of rusty holes. But that actually helped in scaring the pigs away.

One weekend, as a joke, Caz and Freddie brought their welding gear down to the back block, and they built a gun turret and plate metal shield on the back tray. They painted it in camo colors, so the vehicle looked like a militia 'Technical' from one of the war games they played online.

***

The pig hunting excursions took Freddie deep into the upper reaches of the river they'd seen on the video from Shu's drone.

He discovered that the half-buried buildings at the edge of the river were, in fact, the remains of an old power station.

Most of the buildings were rusted-out hulks. A wide concrete slipway blocked the river next to the power station buildings. It held back a pristine area of water that had become a happy home for many crocodiles.

CHAPTER 46

1942: THE FIASCO ON THE EMBLEY.

January 23, 1942.

In the 1940s, a war was raging in the Pacific. Japan's troops stormed into Rabaul in 1942, which meant they were just a stone's throw from the northern tip of Queensland. It looked like the Imperial Japanese Army would soon arrive on Aussie soil.

A month later, bombs fell on Darwin. The Australian government shit its pants.

A hastily gathered committee recommended the Government should build a new forward supply base, way up north. It would consist of a Navy dock and a small-scale hydro-electric power station, to service the escalating war-effort. A group of under-qualified Surveyors chose the aboriginal community of Weipa, on the easily fortified Embley River. It was well hidden from passing Japanese patrols and sub, and just 250 miles from the strategic pinch point between Australia and Papua New Guinea.

The mission to build the base was a screw-up waiting to happen.

Engineers hastily drew up the plans, then awarded the contract to an over-stretched local Queensland builder. They set about designing a large dam across the upper part of the Embley River. Several miles upstream from the coast. A gaggle of supply vessels and workers hastily constructed the dam and the buildings for the power turbines for the small hydro generator. When complete, all they had to do was wait for the empty reservoir behind the dam to fill.

Job done.

The monsoon arrived a few weeks later, but the rains quickly filled the dam to bursting point, mostly with silt and debris from the surrounding creeks. During a massive cyclone, the dam ruptured and flooded the whole Embley River system with millions of tons of thick mud and dead trees.

Before it ever produced a spark of power, the power station was drowned.

In its haste to cover up its military blunder, the government closed off the entire area for public access.

In the years that followed, giant crocodiles decided the newly grown mangroves and the thick mud offered the perfect conditions to make a home. The crocs provided a great incentive for the locals to stay away from the place.

The power station lay buried in mud for the next decade.

***

Decades later, they built Scherger Air Force base to make use of the land nearby. The air above the swamp now buzzed with jets and lumbering heavy transport planes during training exercises at the Base. It's no-fly-zone status kept local prying aerial eyes away too. Weipa, which means "fighting ground" in the local dialect, had finally met its reason for being.

***

In 2018, under pressure to fill its coffers, the government forgot about the secrecy surrounding the upper reaches of the river. They sold off a fifty-acre farm allotment adjacent to Scherger.

Cannacom, the cashed-up darling of the medicinal cannabis revolution, snapped the land up. They conveniently built a massive security fence around the new farm, blocking the last remaining road access to the decrepit power station site and the mud-caked upper reaches of the Embley River.

The embarrassing evidence of Australia's biggest wartime bungle was now completely concealed from prying eyes.

CHAPTER 47

THE OFF-GRID BIVVIE AT NED'S.

Freddy's excursions to hunt the pigs had also taken him across to the pristine billabong above the old power station.

He named the place Ned's Corner, mainly because it felt like somewhere that the bushranger Ned Kelly would hide out at.

The sandy beach area looked like a beer commercial. All that was missing was a catchy TV jingle playing in the background. Two tall red earth cliffs surrounded the large, deep pool of water. The small, sandy beach curved perfectly between them. The same couldn't be said for the mud and stone track into the place. If you made it past the Briar you had to navigate a few miles of tire sucking mudflats, rocky creek beds and basking crocs. The no-fly zone kept aerial guests away. Cell phone and Wi-Fi coverage were non-existent.

They'd all ventured over to Neds for a weekend away. It was perfect. As they were packing up their campsite they hatched the plan to do a much longer stay once they'd all accrued some holiday leave. They decided to bring in enough provisions to stay there for three weeks of off-grid bliss.

Everyone was counting the days!

***

A few months later, the day had arrived. Neds, here we come!

They all clocked-off at Cannacom and headed home to pack a small convoy of 4WDs for their epic three-week bivouac.

***

The sun was setting as they slipped through the main Cannacom farm gates and headed down to the back corner. After slowly crawling through the briar, they made a quick stop to check the crop.

They halted beside two makeshift tin work sheds they'd erected. Caz unloaded a large drum of diesel. Willow started planting some new seedlings into the ground.

Freddie stepped out of the first vehicle and walked over to Willow.

"We've got more fuel for the generator," he said. "How's the irrigation been holding up?"

"Good so far," said Willow. "I've set the timer to flood the place every four days. The water level in the creek is holding up too. I'll come back over here to check it every few days."

She waved at the other vehicles and shouted, "Hey, can you guys give me a hand with the last few seedlings?"

The occupants reluctantly tumbled out into the heat haze.

Freddie looked bemused and said, "Hey Willow, do we really need to add new plants?" He looked out across the crop. There were well over a thousand large, healthy plants swaying in the breeze.

Willow said, "This will be the last of them. I promise. When we get back after the three weeks away I should have enough data to present my case to the Board."

After an hour of planting and a final check of the crop watering system, the convoy rolled out for the short bush-bash over to Ned's Corner.

The rules for the next three weeks of the bivvie were simple;

Live off the land.

Drink beer and rum.

Have fun.

No Internet or contact with the outside world.

They set up their camp under some tall, shady trees near the edge of the natural sandy beach. The clear water of the lagoon was deep and cool, except for the western side, which had recently been blocked by a massive fallen gumtree. A camper's 'wet-dream' of tents, solar panels, and seriously kitted-out four-wheel drives adorned the tree-lined area behind the beach. The delicious smell of a slowly roasting haunch of wild boar wafted from a crackling campfire next to a camp kitchen.

Time to have some fun.

***

Shu perched herself at the top of a tall sandstone cliff overlooking the waterhole. She triggered the rotors on a large DJI Matrice 350 RTK drone. A loud buzz filled the air as she sent it skywards.

She navigated carefully, aware that the night vision camera, gimbal camera mount and six directional sensing systems had cost her almost two months' pay.

The drone zipped effortlessly between the red cliffs surrounding the watering hole. Shu guided it using a large hand-held video controller. She set the drone into a hover, then grabbed a small field radio.

She barked, "I'm in position, guys. Arriving in ten seconds."

Atop the other side of the cliffs Freddie Delgardo, looking part-boofhead and part tanned Statue of David, burst into a sprint toward the cliff's edge. He jumped off the cliff and went airborne. Screaming. Caz quickly followed him.

They were both closely followed off the cliff by Shu's speeding drone.

It lurched down to track them with its camera as they both catapulted forty feet down toward the cool waters below. Their shrill screams of joy were followed by the satisfying sound of their bodies bombing into the refreshing lagoon.

***

Under a shady group of trees behind the main campsite, Willow was entertaining some guests.

Willow sat in a quiet, shade-dappled bush clearing. She looked up and smiled when she heard the screams and splashes from the direction of the campsite.

She stood slowly as she heard the buzz of the drone approaching. It zipped into position above her and went into a hover.

She gave the hovering drone the 'bird' and shouted, "Hey. Fuck you, Shu. We're looking for some zen over here!"

The drone scooted away.

Jenny Tarka and Jeremy Renn sat on a blanket in the middle of the clearing with Willow. They were mid-twenties FIFO (Fly In Fly Out) workers at the bauxite mine in Weipa. After a big night of serious drinking at the Bowlo, they'd both been invited to join the inaugural Ned's bivvie. They maintained the big trucks at the mine, so they were handy to have around. Everyone called them Jen and Jez, or sometimes just "the Jays".

Willow sat back down on a large, traditional woven blanket. It had a colourful motif of eroded puli puli stones decorating it. There were small bundles of native plants, fruits, and seeds laid out in front of her.

She picked up a bundle of light green leaves and said,

"This is Tetragonia Tetragonoides. It's great for basting fish when you soak it in oil. Roll it between your fingertips and taste it."

The Jays dutifully rolled a sprig, and then tentatively tasted it.

"Hmm, it reminds me of spinach," said Jen.

Willow picked up an almost identical bundle of leaves and said, "But this one could slowly kill you if you ate it. So, watch out."

Willow grabbed a shallow tin dish of yellow berries.

"This is called Solanum Centrale. It's a bit like a bush tomato. My dad called them 'desert raisins'. They're yummy when dried."

Jen pointed to a long, thin black aluminum tube on the blanket.

"What's that for?" Jen said.

The sleek black tube had a rubber mouthpiece on one end, and a grey neoprene rubber quiver wrapped around its middle. Five thin orange-tipped arrows, each about nine inches long, rested securely in the locked quiver.

"It's a blow dart gun," said Willow. "I can't stand shooting bullets at the pigs if they attack our camp. I leave that to Caz and Freddie. This blowpipe, and poison, are the deterrent I use instead."

She picked up the pipe and handed it to Jen.

"Don't touch the darts." Willow said. "They're coated with poison from a Stinging Tree. If it gets on your skin, it hurts like hell. Burns like acid. The dart won't kill a pig, but it will send it away howling."

Jen couldn't put the blowpipe down quickly enough.

"Funny story," Willow said, "My ancestors called the leaves from the Stinging Tree 'The Devil's Toilet-paper'. It's got big wide leaves covered in tiny stinging needles. If you wiped your bum with it –" Jen and Jez smiled and laughed out loud.

Willow pointed to a branch that looked a lot like Christmas Holly and said, 'This is Abrus Precatorius.'

Jez grabbed the green branch with red berries and playfully dangled it over Jen's head. "Anyone for a kiss?" he said.

Willow said, "Where I grew up, we called it gidgee gidgee or jumbie beads. See the red berries. Just one of them has almost enough poison to kill you. They smell like lavender when they flower."

Jez quickly threw the branch back down on the blanket, then wiped his fingers on his t-shirt.

Jen asked, "Are they used for anything?"

"Yes," replied Willow. "Sometimes they're dried and used in a percussion instrument for music. Or people can crush them and use them to stun fish in a waterhole."

Jez asked, 'Do they grow around here?'

"Not at Neds," Willow said, "But there's a deep valley, about fifty miles away, where just about everything you can see here grows. The spot's a bit of a freak of nature. Desert for miles and then this deep tropical valley slashed into the earth millions of years ago."

Willow traced a curve into the red sand at her feet.

"We call it 'The Nibulin', which sort-of means 'falling seeds' in the local Wagiman language."

Jen asked, "Can we go there?"

"Yeah." said Willow. 'It's not sacred or anything. I spent a lot of time there when I was researching my thesis on arid species for Uni."

Jen thought for a moment and said, "I'm in. We can split the driving."

Willow stood. She started gathering the plant specimens up and said, "Let's get back to camp. I can almost taste that roast boar from here."

As they stood to pack up. BOOM! A massive explosion rocked the area near the main campsite.

CHAPTER 48

3 —2 —1 BOOM.

A massive fallen tree was floating in the entrance to the lagoon. A line of smoke and fire burned along a shallow gunpowder-filled groove Caz had cut along its length.

The crude 'fuse' slowly burned toward a large explosive charge, strategically rammed into a hole in the middle of a massive fallen tree.

The tree had been annoying the crap out of Freddie and Caz during the first few days of their stay at Ned's. It blocked one of the creeks running out of the lagoon, causing a massive build-up of dead leaves across the otherwise pristine waters. It had to go. One slight problem. The trunk must have weighed two tons.

They had one stick of dynamite stored in one of the sheds over at the crop. It was left over from when they did the initial land clearing.

Nobody wanted to endure the trip over there and back to get it, so, using his experience in the Army's Munitions Corps, Caz improvised. He figured that the crude fuse he'd cut into the top of the floating log would give Freddie at least fifteen seconds after he lit it. Then BOOM.

There was nowhere safe to run after the fuse had been lit, so Freddie would just have to dive off the log to escape the blast. Even then, Freddie wouldn't be far enough away to avoid flying debris. He'd have to dive underwater and swim hard to get to a safe distance. Over near the shoreline, Caz looked at the burning line of gunpowder, then nodded to Freddie.

He yelled, "15 seconds!" then hid behind a large boulder.

The burning line of gunpowder edged closer to a canvas package strapped to the log. It was carefully packed with a mixture of fertilizer, hydrogen peroxide, and ammonium nitrate. Caz had carefully calculated the amount of charge needed to break up the tree.

Freddie leapt from the log and swam hard. Arms threshing the water like a combine harvester. Swimming like he was going for gold in the Olympic 100 metres freestyle. As he swam, he counted down the seconds down in his mind.

"15-14-13-12 –" he counted, as his powerful arms wind-milled through the water.

"Swim!" yelled Shu, as she manipulated the joystick on her drone control handset to capture the action below.

Shu's drone lifted into the sky in a perfect arc, to get the widest possible view of the lagoon. She manipulated drone's gimbal camera, to frame the massive floating log perfectly in the centre of the video screen.

Freddie gulped down deep breaths. Swimming away from the log as fast as he could. He continued the mental countdown. '9-8-7-6 –'

When Freddie's countdown reached 'three' he took a last huge gulp of air –and submerged. At that distance, he was out of the blast zone. He rolled his body under the water to look back toward the log. It should have blown by now. But nada.

Freddie threshed his arms to keep himself safely below the surface.

Thirty seconds passed. His lungs were pleading for air.

He finally decided he'd need to push to the surface to grab a gulp of air, when BOOM, the massive log disintegrated into a million pieces.

Shards of timber filled the sky above the lagoon and chunks of timber smashed into the surrounding water. An airborne piece of flying timber smashed into Shu's drone and sent it spiraling. Shu fought with the joystick to regain control.

"Erm, sorry guys!" Caz shouted. He stepped out from behind a large sandstone rock he'd been hiding behind to avoid the blast.

"May have overdone it on the nitrate."

Shortly after, Willow, Jez and Jen arrived back at the camp. They looked impressed as the huge pile-up of leaves started to drain away from the billabong.

One of the branches from the exploding tree had embedded deeply into the ground just beside their camp kitchen. They dug it out, chopped it up into firewood and then settled the in for the night.

CHAPTER 49

THE PORK WARS.

Several days had passed since the bivvie began.

The mornings were chilly, but the rest of each day was perfect. Everyone had settled into a routine of sleeping, drinking, and preparing food in the camp kitchen. A friend had briefly visited the day prior to drop off a resupply of ice, beer and food. He was itching to let them know what was happening in the outside world, but they weren't interested.

The temperature was chilly the next morning. In an effort to keep warm, the Jays were doing some early morning 'horizontal folk-dancing' in their double sleeping bag in their tent. That's when the earth started to rumble.

Jen and Jez lay there panting and listened as a thundering sound got louder.

Suddenly, the tent door unzipped, and Freddie poked his head inside.

"Sorry folks. Out of the tent," he yelled.

"Pigs incoming."

The feral pigs at Ned's were –well –feral. But more-so than anywhere else on the Cape. Willow had a theory that it was something they were eating. Something hallucinogenic. Mushies?

The attacks, usually around dawn, had become a regular feature of the bivvie. A herd of about forty wild boars would storm through the camp, stealing food, pissing everywhere, and causing chaos. And the chaos wasn't a pleasant sight when it had tusks and weighed almost half a ton.

Caz, ever the jokester, had implemented what he called 'a surefire solution'. He'd been saving up his empty bottles of Sweet Baby Ray's BBQ sauce all year. Everyone fell about laughing as he strategically strung up the empty bottles around the camp to form a 'protective barrier' to keep the pigs at bay.

Jez poked his head outside the tent.

"Oh My god," he yelled back inside, "It's a war zone."

The campsite had changed into a battlefield. Caz was hiding behind his ute, shooting his .308 repeatedly. The Ruger Scout had a massive variable scope, but that was useless in a melee like this, so he was just taking potshots at the biggest boars.

Freddie was taking a more direct approach. He was running around the camp in his undies, just shouting out loud like an angered bear.

Willow walked around, also in undies, banging a pot and pan together.

The boars eventually got the message and thundered back into the bush.

Caz put the Ruger back in his lockbox with some other hunting rifles on the side of his truck.

Willow, still catching her breath, yelled out, 'Everyone OK?'

Voices tentatively called out, "Yes." from the dim pre-dawn light.

She looked a little concerned. "Shu? –Shu?" No answer.

Shu lay on a mattress in the back of her truck, blissfully unaware of the melee outside, with Rammstein's 'Du Hast' blaring through her noise-canceling headphones.

The rear canopy of the truck lifted, and several worried faces looked inside. Jen peered around the LED-lit truck interior. Mouth agape. It looked like a scene out of 'Men In Black'. The side walls and roof were one giant gun rack, with an assortment of high-tech weapons.

On one wall there was a Magpul FMG-9 submachine gun, a TrackingPoint TP sniper rifle, a Chiappa Rhino pistol, A KRISS Vector assault rifle, an XM25 CDTE grenade launcher.

And, just for fun, a prototype PHASR light emitting rifle.

The opposite wall displayed more 'people-friendly' weapons.

AR-15s, camo-covered ATAC rifles, an SRC SR4 Mamba Gen 2, a couple of Remington 870 shotguns, night vision goggles, plate vests and tactical helmets. Even a few flash bang grenades and smoke cannisters.

"Fuck me," said Jen. "Is this stuff legal?"

Caz pointed to the exotic guns on the right-hand side wall and said,

"Everything on that wall is a 'Grade A' 3D printed replica. We made them ourselves. Pretty cool. They look real –but nothing works inside."

He pointed to the weapons on the left-hand wall.

"The guns on that side are all Gelsoft Blasters. Normal stuff you'd find on a public course. They look real, but they only fire pellets."

"We'll be having fun with those this morning. All good," he said.

Caz then pointed directly at Shu lying on the mattress.

"That, in the middle, is a Grade-A nerd."

***

For the next few days, the focus of the activities switched to gun battles.

After donning tactical army gear they'd bought along, they spent endless hours waging war in the scrub with the Gelsoft guns.

CHAPTER 50

THE ROAD TO NIBULIN.

The first two weeks of the bivvie flew past.

As the final day approached, Willow and Jen got bored, so they decided to do a girls' road trip to check out the valley at Nibulin. On the way back, they'd stop in at the gas station at Ghoolie Creek to get some supplies for the final night before everyone headed back to town.

****

Willow stepped out of her tent. She stretched and yawned. Caz, Freddie and Shu were already awake.

Freddie was methodically rearranging the camp kitchen, to get it to be ready to be packed up. Caz was unpacking some of the army tactical gear he'd brought along for their battles.

Willow cooked breakfast. The aroma of sausages and eggs filled the air as the last of the cool morning condensation burned off the countryside.

Jen poked her sleepy head out of her tent and called out to Willow.

"Hey Wills, are we still going over to the valley this morning? Nobulin?"

Willow replied, "It's called Nibulin."

She looked up at the sun and said, "We'd need to leave by 10am if we want to get there and back before sunset. Is Jez still hanging around for the Gelsoft?"

"You bet," Jez shouted from inside the tent.

He pushed past Jen and stood in front of the tent, already kitted out in full tactical battle gear.

"GI Jez. Reporting for duty. Sah!"

He saluted the sky.

Phfftt. Phfftt.

Two tiny plastic Gelsoft rounds struck him in the groin.

They bounced harmlessly to the ground.

Across the campsite Shu, holding a Classic Colt 1911 Gelsoft pistol, yelled out, "My bad. Just checking the guns."

Jen stepped out of the tent wearing cut-off denim shorts, orange rubber sandals and a stringy tank top.

Willow said, "You might need some pants and good shoes today. Getting down into the valley can get a little rough at times. Lots of scrub and rocks. Well worth the effort, though."

After breakfast, Willow checked the 4WD they were going to use for the trip. Fuel. Drinking water. Radiator. Oil. All good. Check.

The surrounding bush reverberated with the sound of shouting, laughter, and the zing of Gelsoft pellets flying. Freddie, Caz, Shu and Jez were waging a pitched gun-battle in the scrub. Two grey canisters thudded onto the ground fifty feet away. Smoke grenades. The bush filled with a massive cloud of blue and yellow smoke.

Jen jumped into the passenger's seat as the colored smoke cloud moved toward them. She'd changed into jeans, t-shirt and boots.

Willow said, "I'll drive out of here until we get to the cattle grid on the main road. You can take it from there."

Willow tooted the horn. The 4WD pulled away as the cloud of smoke enveloped the campsite.

After they hit the main road, they drove past the locked gates to Scherger Airforce base, crossed a shallow river at a wide ford and then drove down a long red dirt road that stretched to the horizon. Lazy kangaroos and dust-devil whirlwinds dotted the dry, red land around them.

Willow brought the vehicle to a halt at a rusted cattle grid cutting across the road.

A barbed wire fence stretched into the distance to the right and left. A single gnarled melaleuca tree stuck out of the dirt. The mid-morning temperature outside was rising fast.

"Ahhh. Civilization." said Willow, breathing out a huge sigh. She turned to Jen and said, "Your turn to drive. Just head thirty miles down this road until you hit a 'T' intersection. You'll see a couple of old farm houses there."

Willow stepped out of the vehicle and checked the tires. She walked around to the passenger's side of the vehicle as Jen walked around and sat in the driver's seat.

Willow continued, "Then turn left. Go for twenty more miles. I might have a kip. I had a crap night's sleep. Wake me up whenever you want."

Jen slammed the driver's door shut. They headed off down the corrugated dirt road. She cracked the driver's side window open to eject some blowflies that had joined during the stop.

Willow settled into the passenger's seat, then cranked the angle back a few notches. She yawned deeply and rolled up an old, roughly knitted blue cardigan to use as a pillow. Despite the bounces, she nodded off as the sun steadily rose in the bright blue sky.

Chapter 51

Welcome to Nibulin.

Willow's slumber was interrupted by a heavy bump as the 4WD drove over a cattle grate.

Jen said, "I think we are around the twenty-mile mark, sleepyhead. You need to wake up so you can show me where the turnoff to Nibulin is."

Willow let out a big yawn and said, "Pull up down near those trees. I can drive for the last bit."

Jen pulled the vehicle over and they both got out to stretch their legs. The landscape was flat red earth with scrubby spinifex all the way to the horizon. Hardly Shangri-La.

"I was expecting to see a mountain range coming up. Hard to imagine a valley around here," said Jen.

Willow nodded and said, "That's the weird thing about Nibulin. It's not above the ground. Looks like some giant dragon creature took a slash out of the flat countryside. It's fed with springs. I think that's why the environment down there is so unique. Not just the plants. The rocks and the wildlife too."

After another thirty minutes driving Willow drove off-road toward a thick copse of trees.

She pulled up and said, "Welcome to Nibulin."

They both got out of the vehicle and walked past the line of trees, arriving at the shoulder of a massive deep ravine.

"Look at the shape," said Willow. "It's got a curve to it, like a giant claw ripped it out of the planet. Always gives me chills when I first get here. We go down into the ravine over there." Jen and Willow headed off down a rocky path through the spinifex and descended into the deep valley.

"Bet you're glad you changed into jeans," said Willow, as the shrubbery thwacked against their legs.

When they descended to the bottom of the deep rift, they felt as if they had been transported to a tropical oasis. A shallow spring-fed creek gurgled its way through the rocks. At points along the valley floor, they had to wade waist deep through the water to get to the next section.

Along the way, Willow pointed out trees and plants that could be used as food, or antiseptic, or glue to hold things together.

Jen marveled at the stories.

Willow scrambled up onto a big flat rock. She looked up at the sun and said, "We can stop down here for about an hour. Then we'll have to head back." Jen filled her bottle with fresh spring water.

"This place is freakin' amazing," she said.

They stripped off their wet clothes and stretched out like lizards on the big flat rock. Basking in the sun.

***

An hour later, they started the climb back out of the valley. Willow stopped and pointed out some plants nearby.

"That tree with the long leaves and red berries is called a Desert Quandong," she said. "I've never seen one this far north. Usually, you only get them down in the Flinders Ranges. When you dry them, they can be stored for years. They make a mean jam."

She walked over to a tall pine tree, leaned down and picked up a green pine cone and said, "This is a Bunya or Araucaria Bidwillii. These cones are full of nuts. I've seen the cones grow as big as your head. My brother Jumu used to put sticks in the dirt and use the biggest ones as bowling balls. They don't roll very straight, though."

Jen laughed.

A few minutes further up the valley, Willow stopped at a low green plant. She picked a few red berries from it, then gave a handful to Jen to taste and said, "This is the Ruby Saltbush or Enchylaena Tomentosa. A tough little bugger of a plant. Almost impossible to kill. Salt. Drought. Sand. It just doesn't care." Jen said, "Sort of sweet and salty all at once."

Willow ate a few too and said, "Let's take some back to the camp at Ned's. They go great with ice cream. We'll get some at the gas station. "

They gathered more saltbush berries and put them in Jen's daypack.

Jen walked over to a tree covered in beautiful pink and white pods and said, "How about these? They look nice too."

Willow shook her head and said, "Not those. That's a Finger Cherry. For years, there's been a problem with kids eating them and then going blind. I did a research paper on them once. The pods themselves aren't that toxic, but they often have a fungus growing on them that causes the problem."

Forty-five minutes later, Jen and Willow were in the 4WD driving toward the gas station at Ghooli Creek. Willow was driving and Jen was singing along to an old Springsteen song.

The Global Meltdown

CHAPTER 52

THE NEWS FROM GHOOLI CREEK.

Benji McEllery really needed to take a dump.

He peered down the endless red dirt road out front of the remote Ghooli BP Roadhouse looking for cars. All clear. Then he strode to the public toilets out the back, newspaper under one arm, without even locking the roadhouse's front door. He wasn't worried, though. At this time of day, you were lucky to see a car passing through Ghooli Creek once an hour. Benji had plenty of time.

Ten minutes later, he was engrossed in the Sport Section of the newspaper. The Weipa Raiders Rugby League team had given Kodal United a good drubbing on Saturday. His joy in recounting the game was broken by the unmistakable sound of a car pulling up to one of the gas pumps.

"Bugger!" Benji said.

He left the cubicle and placed the newspaper on the grimy wash-bench. The headline on the front page shouted; *'Colombian Government Toppled. Martial law declared'*.

As he walked back to the front counter of the Roadhouse, Benji waved to the two young ladies that had pulled up in a 4WD. A small TV hanging off the wall behind him played a TV commercial with an annoying jingle for a sports-betting app.

Willow entered the roadhouse and headed for the back fridges. She grabbed two cold bottles of water and a tub of ice cream from the freezer and took them to the counter.

"These and the petrol," she said.

"Thanks, love," Benji said. "What brings you two lovely ladies all the way out here?"

"Holidays," said Willow. "There's a bunch of us on a bivouac for a few weeks. Camping off-grid."

The TV played a toothpaste commercial with another annoying jingle.

Benji looked at Willow's tattoos. He pointed to a military insignia tattooed on her forearm and asked, "You've served? ADF?"

Willow smiled and said, "Long story. I was in the US Army. I did basic and AIT with them. Then worked as a SERE Trainer."

Benji looked confused as he slid the payment terminal across the counter and said, "You don't sound like a yank. And you look very –err – 'local'."

Willow smiled and said, "It's a long story. I'm not active anymore. I got out a while ago. Best decision ever."

Benji smiled back knowingly and said, "Me too. My rotation in Iraq messed me up. That's why I like it out here at Ghooli. Nice and quiet. No mission. No objectives. No ghosts."

He tore her receipt off the machine, handed it to her, and said, "You have a safe trip back to wherever you're going."

Willow gave him a brief salute and said, "And, hey, you keep those ghosts at bay."

She walked outside and headed for the car. Benji pondered that thought in silence for a moment.

***

After Willow walked out, the TV on the wall behind Benji switched to a news bulletin.

A reporter was shouting live, over a montage of footage of a wild street riot in Colombia.

"The past two weeks of civil unrest continues across Latin America! The breakdown of basic services hit a new peak today in the Colombian capital of Bogota." the Reporter said, "UN peacekeepers have arrived to help authorities restore order and get an election for a new government underway. A spokesperson is reporting that the drug cartels are now running the streets. We are getting similar reports from Guatemala, Peru and Paraguay. The Mexican government has declared martial law."

The TV screen changed to a map of Asia, with a bold headline saying, '*Unrest spreads to Asia*'.

The footage on the screen changed to a gun battle in central Bangkok. Then to a village in Laos where shots were being exchanged between farmers and the police. Tractors and farmers with guns blockaded the street.

A young Thai Chinese reporter yelled over the gunfire, "Meanwhile, we are getting reports of similar unrest in the Bokeo area of Laos, on the border with Myanmar. Police have been trying to quell the riots for the last fortnight, fueled by local warring Golden Triangle drug cartels, as the drug trade goes into an economic free-fall. No comment from the Chinese or Laos government officials. India has sent troops to its eastern provinces."

The news report changed to a piece of stock footage of party revelers in Times Square in New York, then a gay pride street parade in Sydney.

A young, blonde female reporter turned to camera and said, "We are getting reports that the street price of cannabis has quadrupled in the past two weeks in cities worldwide. This is also driving up the cost of harder drugs and the use of meth."

The TV report cut back to the news anchor, who concluded, "The mystery blight is spreading like wildfire, decimating the global cannabis crop in just a matter of weeks. The UN Assembly has been called into an emergency session to debate the issue, but is frozen in a deadlock about doing anything to support the drug trade."

***

Outside, on the dusty road back to the tranquility of the final night at Ned's, Willow and Jen were oblivious to the global storm heading their way.

The War Begins.

CHAPTER 53

THE MIAMI MEETING.

If you mention 'the drug trade' in Miami, the conversation always turns to the city's seedy places, like Liberty City and Little Haiti. However, the middle-class suburb of Coconut Grove was the true epicentre of the trade.

'The Grove', as the locals like to call it, was a convenient car chase straight down the 27th from Little Havana. Or a quick dash down the Don Shula Expressway to Miami Executive Airport, to a drug lord's private jet, waiting with the engines running, for a fast take-off.

The suburb's perfect placement allowed Latin America's drug barons to slip into and out of Miami relatively unnoticed. Which was ironic, as the CIA and DEA also use the same airport as a major base of operations. Strange bedfellows.

***

Aung Win Zin's G650ER private jet was an early arrival at the airport that morning. Win and his entourage had come straight from a massive party weekend in Dubai. They'd done a quick stopover in Cairo to jettison some leggy Nubian girls who had provided the in-flight entertainment. Win's jet had a very plain livery on the outside to keep its origin discreet. The inside of the plane had done away with the corporate walnut walls and cream leather seats and replaced them with an LED-lined airborne bordello.

Win and his small entourage exited the plane dressed in their 'passport-inspection best', carefully covering their tattoos.

An airport border guard approached and asked, "Purpose of visit?"

Win's accountant stepped forward and said, "Delegation from the Myanmar government attending the International Conference on Agricultural and Biological Science." He opened a briefcase and handed over all the necessary Myanmar government paperwork, hotel bookings, and conference passes to prove the point.

"Duration of stay?" said the guard.

"Just two days," said the accountant.

After getting their passports stamped and luggage cleared, they headed over to a waiting black Escalade for the quick trip across to The Grove.

Inside the car, the driver handed Win a small golden box. Win opened it and tipped a small amount of white powder onto the walnut pop-up desktop beside his seat. He smiled and took a quick snort as a line of coconut palms whizzed by the speeding car.

"We're early," Win said, "Let's get a drink before the meeting –Driver? Anywhere good nearby?"

The limo driver said, "I know a place on the way that has good tequila, some putas and makes a great Cubano sandwich. We could kill an hour or two there."

"Va. Let's go!" said Win.

***

Two hours later, a small NetJets Bombardier Global 8000 also touched down at the same Miami airport.

Radovan Vukovic preferred the large jets favored by the Russian oligarchs, but they had started attracting too much heat since many of the wealthy Russian families had begun siphoning assets out of the mother country. Rad's flight had taken a circuitous route from Paris to Toronto to Miami, to hide its origins in Serbia. As usual, Radovan was traveling alone. He trusted few people whenever he stepped outside of the border of Serbia.

After clearing Customs Rad hailed a taxi.

***

Thirty minutes later, another small private jet touched down.

A sleek blue Rolls Royce cruised up to it as Aung U-Chin, Win Zin's gray-haired grandfather, exited the plane. U-Chin waddled down the stairs as fast as his aged legs could carry him. He walked to the Roller. Its door slid open automatically. He was stepping inside when he heard a noise from the plane. A beautiful young Burmese woman in a sharp black business suit struggled to carry a small, cheap-looking suitcase down the stairs.

"Uncle. You almost forgot this," she said, as she placed the heavy suitcase beside him in the Rolls.

He said, "Wait with the plane, my dear. This is going to be a quick visit. I'll be back well before nightfall."

She looked at the suitcase and asked, "So, why do you need that? It's really heavy. What's inside?"

He smiled and raised his bushy white eyebrows.

"Respect!" he said. "This suitcase contains a great deal of 'respect'."

***

Coconut Grove looked like any other middle-American suburb until you ventured over to the old waterfront down near the Rickenbacker Causeway. Hidden away from passing traffic and pleasure boats was a group of derelict dockside buildings.

The locals called the area The Slump. Mostly because of the rotting dumpster smell that emanated from it on boiling hot days. Graffiti covered the long-empty industrial buildings, which were surrounded by cesspools of slimy water. Tall wire fences with No Trespassing signs surrounded the entire area to keep the local kids out. The only road into the place had an armed sentry point that was manned 24/7.

The buildings in The Slump looked like most other defunct industrial estates. The Graffiti-covered walls bordered on 'art installation chic', after decades of teens had added their tags. Many buildings had chimney stacks that looked close to collapse. The mossy canals looked like dream homes for the alligators that strayed in from the nearby glades.

The Smithson Drywall Company building stood out from the other rusting relics of a bygone industrial age.

It had rust covered walls with a patina of fading green paint and two tall ventilation towers, but not a single graffiti tag. The skateboarders and spray-can cowboys that often scaled the fence to get into The Slump had learned not to go near the Smithson factory. If you looked closely, you could see an array of high tech CCTV cameras and thermal detectors surrounding the place. A couple of Starlink dishes were perched on the roof. A smaller fence, topped with razor wire, created a final secure border around the site.

Today, multiple black Escalades and a gunmetal colored G-Wagon occupied a car-parking area across from the old building's entrance.

***

The guard at the main sentry gate of The Slump was roused from his nap by the throaty roar of an approaching car.

A dark black Reventon Veneno Lamborghini cabrio, subtly trimmed in dark red striping, cruised up to the gate, like a scene from a Batman movie. The guard scrambled from the booth and saluted the lone female driver.

"Buenos dias, Miss Munoz", he blurted out nervously.

"Estoy muy bien, have the other guests arrived?" Valeria Munoz replied.

He checked his clipboard and said, "An Escalade arrived about an hour ago, then a taxi –and the usual staff earlier this morning."

Valeria grabbed a small walkie-talkie from the passenger's seat of the Lambo. She whispered into it.

"Alpha One. Spotter One. Any unexpected guests?"

A woman in an army uniform lay under a tree on a hill over-looking the entry gate to The Slump, cradling a sniper rifle on a tripod.

"Alpha One, all clear." She responded into her throat mike.

The Spotter, another female soldier, was perched on a hill opposite. She looked at Valeria through her Nightforce Optics rifle scope.

"Spotter clear," she reported, "I'm liking those shades you're wearing."

Valeria smiled. She pointed at the gate impatiently. It slid open and the grey Lambo roared through. The supercar twisted and turned along the roads between the decrepit old buildings. Birds scattered, fleeing the noise.

Valeria pulled up beside the other cars in the car park in front of the old drywall plant.

Inside the building, a computer technician sat in front of an ultra-modern bank of security camera monitors. He saw Valeria step out of her car.

He zoomed the HD security camera in close on her. Then he took a moment to take in her toned muscles and curves as she walked.

"Hmmm," he muttered to himself. He pressed an intercom button.

"Valeria Munoz has arrived," he said. "She's on her way in. How's the hack going?"

A voice on a speaker on his desk said, "I'm still working on the encryption. Might have to call in a last-minute favor, or two, on this one. Won't be cheap. The Mark I'm talking to is asking for 25 g's this time."

The technician said, "Do whatever you need to do to get through Sentinel's firewall –but get it done –today is important."

CHAPTER 54

HLVd+. The COVID of Cannabis.

Valeria pressed a button, and a retinal scanner appeared from behind a metal faceplate. After a brief scan, the old drywall factory door unlocked.

Once inside, a thick reinforced steel door automatically slid open, revealing a large ultra-modern warehouse area beyond. The only original parts of the warehouse were the heavy steel ceiling beams and the polished concrete floor. Air-conditioning ducting, sleek steel ethernet cable carriers, and long banks of blinking computer servers filled the rest. The air hummed with the sound of whirring computer fans.

A massive array of video monitors were mounted, like a cinema screen, on the far wall. They bathed the main room in blue light. A group of computer technicians sat at long tables filled with laptops, consoles and curved flat screen monitors. NASA Launch Control would be proud.

The right-hand corner of the warehouse looked more like a strip club.

Plush crimson banquette seats and recliners faced the main screen. A nervous latino waiter mixed drinks for guests. A blonde girl in a short skirt was serving canapes and an assortment of drugs on a gold platter. A truce had been declared, as Radovan Vukovic, Win Zin, and his entourage sipped on drinks while they waited for Valeria to arrive.

Valeria walked straight past, ignoring them. She whispered to one of the computer technicians at the end of one long table, "Enrique, do we have our access to Sentinel?"

"We had to send someone out to borrow a working code from a DEA guy we have on the payroll," he replied. "It cost us 25 g's for the access code, but it's good."

Valeria looked relieved and said, "OK, load it up on the big screen. Let's have a look."

She turned to face the gangs from the Baltic and Golden Triangle cartels.

She nodded to Win. The Sinaloa cartel had a poor relationship with the Asians at the best of times. They weren't exactly on speaking terms. He just nodded back.

Radovan stood and hugged Valeria in a way that could best be described as 'diplomatic'.

"How is your brother, Big M, these days?" Rad asked.

Valeria said, "You know Manny. He's always stirring shit. These days I think he spends more time hiding from the Americans than running the West Coast."

"Yes." agreed Rad, "That bombing in El Paso was an extremely –err –inadvisable. Poking the bear, as they say."

Valeria shifted the conversation.

"We all know why we are here," she announced to the group. "The Americas– The Triangle– The Baltics –, everyone has been reporting crop deaths. The blight is spreading fast. Our best scientists are not even close to figuring out how to stop it."

Win sipped a glass of champagne as he heckled, "I don't know what all the fuss is about cropping weed is the past. Let it all fucking die. It makes the market better for my Meth and China Girl and Ket. That's the future."

A door slammed at the far end of the warehouse. Win's grandfather, U-Chin, entered, fuming at what he'd just heard.

"Have you seen the price of Yaba over the past year?" he shouted angrily, "It's tanking bad. And the trade in precursors is getting harder every day. We all need the croppers. It's where the margin is, and it doesn't get the same heat from the Feds. You have a lot to learn, my boy."

"Yes," Radovan agreed, "that's the reason the weed trade is important in Europe too."

Cutting them off, Valeria said, "The reason we are here today is to find out just how bad it is. Our team has gained access to Sentinel, the DEA's new global drug trafficking satellite system. The same system they use to spy on us every day. This system uses thermal and chemical signatures to find illicit cannabis crops anywhere on the planet."

The cartel members looked impressed.

The DEA had spent $200 million to ensure that Sentinel, its most advanced global drug tracking system, was un-hackable. It only took Enrique and his team a morning to smash through its encryption wall.

The interface from the Sentinel system appeared on the massive video wall at the end of the building. Enrique typed in a password and the computer system screen flashed the words; 'GOING LIVE'. A global map appeared on the screen. A pop-up box appeared, and Enrique typed in the word; 'Colombia'.

He grabbed a large joystick and slowly angled it to the left. The Sentinel system map shifted to zoom in on the country of Colombia. Many small patches of bright orange dotted the map.

"The orange color on the map means that HLVd+ has killed the crops there," Enrique said.

"Purple means it's alive."

Radovan asked, "What is this HLVd+?"

Valeria answered, "It's still not that clear. We have scientists looking at it. Hop Latent Viroid Plus is a virus that normally affects beer hops plants, which is bad for the beer industry. But hops are closely related to cannabis. Our guess is that a mutation of the hops virus has leapt across to cannabis plants. It causes severe stunting and brittle stems, then chlorosis rapidly sets in to the leaves. That just means the plants die soon after."

Radovan asked, "How could that happen?"

Valeria said, "It's probably come from the rapid expansion of the medical cannabis trade. They all have genetics programs trying to alter the terpine levels in their plant stock. To deliver more, or sometimes less, of a buzz. Our feeling is that the mutation has come from this. Like when COVID escaped from the labs in Wuhan."

Win shouted, "So you are saying this is the COVID of cannabis?"

"Yes, and no," said Valeria.

She pointed to the map on the Sentinel screen and said, "It spreads like wildfire –just like COVID –but things like farm tools would normally spread something like this. From what you can see on the map, something is spreading it worldwide. Fast. We suspect it may be bird-life or some kind of flying insect."

Radovan asked, "But why is it killing the entire crop?"

Valeria said, "Plant pathogens are like that. In beer Hops, the disease is controllable, but this cannabis variant can spread across plants quickly and easily. Unlike COVID –this virus is 100% fatal."

U-Chin stood and walked slowly over to the Sentinel screen. He studied the patches of orange. "So, what can we do about it?" he asked.

Valeria said, "We tried burning crops down in Panama, thousands of them, but it made no difference. We couldn't burn as fast as the virus was advancing. It also resulted in mass rioting by farm workers on the streets of Panama City. They assassinated three of our major operatives down there."

Enrique stood up from his chair. He pointed to the big screen and said, "Two weeks ago Colombia was at 75% orange –now it's 100% as far as we can tell."

Radovan interjected. "So, what's special about Colombia that's causing this virus to spread?"

Valeria answered him, "There's nothing special about Colombia at all. That's the problem. From what we are seeing, every crop, from the new commercial cannabis growers in Canada, down to tiny farmers in Chile. It's all approaching 100% of the global crop."

Radovan listened. Aghast.

Valeria continued, "Nothing is immune and it can spread across farms, valleys, rivers and mountain ranges."

Radovan interjected again, his face now growing red with anger. He sneered at Valeria, "So, your fucking Colombians started this?"

Valeria shook her head at him and said, "No, the global drug trade started this. It's spread like a pandemic. Coca plants and poppies are unaffected. But Cannabis plants are falling like a plague has hit."

U-Chin asked again, "So, when will it end?"

Valeria waved her finger at Enrique. He shifted the joystick on the desk in front of him.

The big screen zoomed and rotated as Sentinel showed several parts of the world. Brazil. Canada. Russia. South Africa. Spain. Each region was a patchwork of orange colored death.

Valeria continued, "The rate of spread is massive. It looks unstoppable. It could kill every crop on the planet before we find a way to combat it."

She turned to Radovan and Win and added a barb, "And your trawlers and narco-subs off the coast of America, Europe, Australia and Africa have been equally to blame.

We ALL have dirty hands in the spread of this."

CHAPTER 55

SMASHING THE SYSTEM.

Win Zin couldn't help himself. He always liked to stir the pot.

"Same old cropper mentality," he taunted Rad, "you guys need to diversify. It's not 1980 anymore."

Valeria snapped back, "Can you just shut the fuck up, Win? Let's take a look at how your part of the world is affected. Enrique, show us what the Triangle looks like."

Enrique punched some details into his keyboard, and the world-view on the big screen shifted. The DEA's Sentinel system tracked across the planet and hovered over Myanmar, Laos and Thailand on the big screen. Then it slowly zoomed in on the fertile western corner of Myanmar. It had orange patches covering it evenly. No purple to be seen.

U-Chin looked horrified.

Win Zin looked disinterested and took another sip from his margarita.

Valeria barked across to Enrique, "Now take us over to the Baltics."

She looked over to Radovan and said, "Vuko, my friend, you can pick the country."

Her fake warmth did not impress Rad. Cold-faced, he responded, "OK. -err -Romania."

Valeria, showing off, shouted across to Enrique, "I think that data will come from Eurosat-4, from memory." Enrique replied, "That far north would be Eurosat-2 -here we go." He slowly angled the joystick in front of him.

The DEA's Sentinel system tracked across the planet again. It hovered over Romania. The country had no color on it. Radovan breathed an enormous sigh of relief.

"It looks clear -No?" he said.

Enrique said, "Not so fast, the Eurosat's are older tech -they need a bit of time to build their resolution. See that bar on the screen? When it gets to 100% you will know." Radovan looked angry. The color drained from Radovan's face, as patches of orange start appearing all over Romania. "Nooo," he moaned from deep in his gut, "It can't be."

Valeria interjected, "We've been looking at it since it began a few weeks ago. It's everywhere. There isn't a single country unscathed. Russia. Europe. Africa. Asia. North America. Corporate and cartel. Gone."

Radovan didn't believe her.

"Go in close on Brasov. North of Bucharest." he said, "Just to the east of the town. My brother-in-law has a big operation there. I was there only five days ago for a party. It was not affected."

Enrique punched some keys and the view on the big screen. It settled on a rural area near the middle of the country. The view was close enough to make out roads, villages and snow-capped mountains. The resolution bar slowly rose to 100%.

Radovan held his breath.

He exhaled sharply when a bright orange patch appeared over a green valley on the left side of the screen."

Win Zin chirped in sarcastically, "Uh oh –I'm guessing there won't be any partying going on at your bro's place tonight."

Radovan leapt from his chair.

He grabbed Win Zin by the throat and pulled him out of his seat. Win's Margarita smashed on the floor as Rad threw him across the room. Win's group quickly stood up and pulled out their firearms. Valeria's security detail drew more guns in response.

Win broke the brief standoff by smashing into the back of Radovan, catching him by surprise. He sent Rad crashing into one of the banquette seats. Its glass table shattered under Rads' bulk.

Radovan rolled over the banquette and smashed into one of Win's lackeys. It sent him sprawling into the wall. As he lost his balance, a spray of automatic gunfire arced across the room.

The bullets smashed into the screens on the computer technician's tables. Technicians scrambled out of the way, making the main desk sway and the computer monitors topple to the floor.

Enrique's keyboard and joystick clattered across the floor. As it bounced around the concrete floor, the view of the Sentinel feed on the big screen rotated wildly around the planet.

Fights broke out between the Latinos and the Asian contingent. Another spray of bullets blew a server stack apart. Valeria screamed, "Calm the fuck down! All of you!" but the fighting just continued to escalate.

At the back of the room, U-Chin calmly popped his small, cheap airline bag onto a table. He unzipped the bag and hefted out a stubby XM556 rotary microgun. Its heavy 800 round ammunition feed belt dangled back into the suitcase.

U-Chin aimed it at the roof-space. He held his finger on the trigger for just three seconds, sending a billow of smoke and hellfire as 600 NATO 5.6mm rounds tore into the rafters. The room went silent. Shafts of bright Miami sunlight poured through hundreds of holes in the roof.

U-Chin scowled.

"As the young lady said!" he shouted, "Shut the fuck up – and sit down."

He leveled the mini gun at them. "All of you! Now!"

They all nervously took their seats.

Win Zin remained standing. Embarrassed. Defiant.

U-Chin turned his gaze, and the XM556, toward his Win and calmly said, "And you, my boy, will show some respect for your elders!"

Win Zin considered his options, and then dutifully took his seat.

U-Chin turned to Valeria and said, "Young lady. The floor is yours." He smiled and looked up to the bullet-riddled ceiling, "And I guess the bill to fix your roof is mine".

The tech operators righted the long control desk and edged back into their seats.

Enrique picked his keyboard and the joystick up from the concrete floor. He put them back on the desk. His desktop monitor had a massive hole blown through its center.

Radovan stood and glowered around the silent room. He looked up at the huge Sentinel screen on the wall and exclaimed,

"What the fuck is that?"

A Glimmer Of Purple.

Everyone in the room looked at the big screen in awe. The Sentinel system was showing a small green valley, edged by a mangrove swamp, a river, and some sparse red desert. The interface on the big screen read 'Satellite: Austral-1'.

A small pop-up window appeared a moment later, when the resolution reached 100%. It read; *"12.6493° South, 141.8470° East. CANNACOM. FARM. WEIPA. QUEENSLAND.*

The big screen showed an aerial view of a remote road and some farmland. It was cross-hatched in orange –like the rest of the planet. But behind the farm, near the mangroves, there was a small acreage glowing in bright purple.

A living cannabis crop.

Enrique said, "How can that be? The small crop is less than three miles from the main farm. We've seen HLVd+ spread hundreds of miles in a week everywhere else. It's not possible." He used his mouse to zoom in on the small purple-colored crop, while the other technicians worked to replace his blown monitor.

"My team has been looking at the Sentinel data for almost a month," Enrique said. "Nothing escapes this virus. We've seen patches of purple recently when we've hacked into the system. But, a week later, they're all gone. Always."

Another Tech nearby typed on a laptop keyboard. He pulled up a recent Google News story on his screen. The Tech said, "The local paper, The Cape York Weekly, reported that the Cannacom farm crop died off just over two weeks ago. That other crop should be dead as a doornail by now."

Valeria said, "It's got to be an error in the system. How close can Sentinel zoom in? Take us right in on the crop."

Enrique reminded her, "We can zoom in, but remember, Sentinel isn't a camera system. It uses chemical spectrum analysis. That crop is 100% alive, no matter how close we look"

Valeria turned to the other technician and said, "Pull it up on Google Maps, anyway."

Then she added, "Where the fuck is this Weipa place, anyway?"

The Tech typed into his keyboard and then yelled out, "Australia. Queensland. The pointy bit up the top. Near Indonesia. The town is only there because of a local bauxite mine —and an airforce base. Only 4,000 people. Middle of nowhere."

He opened a webpage with a picture of a massive saltwater crocodile, then added, "And fucking big crocodiles. Look at that hombre." Valeria looked at the croc and nonchalantly added, "Just looks like a lot of potential Louis Vuitton handbags and shoes to me."

She turned back to Enrique and said, "OK. You know the data better than anyone else. What are we looking at here?"

He studied his new screen for a moment and said, "Well —Google shows no crop there when it last took images. But that was a year ago. Local aerial mapping shows no crop there just six months ago —so, this crop is new. It appears that someone planted it in the last few months. The crop isn't on the main farm. I've rechecked the data and the Sentinel system is working correctly."

Enrique gathered his thoughts and said, "We could be looking at something remarkable. This could be the only remaining healthy crop of cannabis on earth. It could be resistant to the disease."

A Tech nearby looked up from his laptop and said, "I might have some more information about the local operation. I'll throw this up on the main screen." He clicked through several web pages as he talked. "Cannacom.

Small sized operation. Nothing remarkable. Chief Science Office called Catherine Sneesby. She only has basic creds. Nothing special."

He paused for a moment to open some more web pages on his screen, then continued, "They set up a Genetics lab and hired a new Geneticist just over a year ago –Willow Barrant –young –but good creds." A picture of Willow, in a lab coat, appeared on the big screen at the end of the room.

The tech continued, "She's a maverick. Attended Zurich University on a fellowship. Hops virus specialist there. Botany prize winner."

He paused as he read a new web search page, "Hmmm." he said, "She's also done some unspecified work with NATO, at a training facility called Novo Selo." Radovan raised his eyebrows in surprise.

"She wrote a dissertation on cropping in arid environments," the Tech added, "She was a NATO SERE trainer –in Bulgaria, then suddenly she's back in Australia working for this two-bit medical cannabis grower. No reason why."

He pulled up a page of Cannacom Board meeting notes. "She was recently reprimanded by Cannacom HR for breaching laboratory rules. Nothing else on her."

Radovan looked at Willow's picture on the screen and mused,

"Strange. How does a black Australian girl end up in the US Army –at a NATO base –in Bulgaria? I'll have my people there look into it."

CHAPTER 57

How To Steal A Cannabis Crop.

Willow's picture remained on the big screen in Miami as the three cartel leaders considered their options.

Valeria, Radovan, Win and U-Chin huddled next to Enrique's computer, deep in a private discussion.

"We need to talk to this woman," said Radovan, "between us we have fishing boats and submarines that pass through that area —on the way down to the big cities on the east coast of Australia. We should get a team into that 'Weipa' place to take her and get some living samples from that crop."

They all considered that option for a moment, then U-Chin spoke.

"It makes sense that my operation, Sam Gor, takes the lead on this," he said. "We are the closest to Australia, and we already have many operatives in places just across the Timor Strait. All of our bulk product to the

Australian capital cities travels through there at some time, mostly hidden on fishing trawlers or cargo ships. Sometimes small planes and helicopters. But our boat skippers and crews will know that area well."

U-Chin turned to Enrique and asked, "Pull up the local map again." Enrique pulled up a map of the region on the big Sentinel screen.

U-Chin said, "Within a few days we could gather a small crew out of Shan Province. Probably pulled together from the Kokang Border Guard. Professional soldiers. We'd fly them down to Papua to meet one of our trawlers and then get them straight into Weipa. Then back out on the same boat –before anyone is the wiser."

Win looked pissed off, but not enough to openly disrespect the old man.

U-Chin turned to the group of cartel bosses and said, "The key is to be low profile and fast. Do you agree?" Radovan looked at Win Zin and scowled, "You're going to send HIM –to run a fast, low-profile operation? They'll hear him coming a mile away."

U-Chin dismissed Rad. "He's my grandson. He knows how to follow orders."

Win Zin looked smug. Radovan moved forward, like he was going to thump him. Valeria stepped in before the tension escalated again. Rad slowly took his seat.

"I agree with U-Chin," Valeria said. "The Triangle is closest, and most familiar with the terrain. They should go in. Get a lot of crop samples and take the key scientific staff. We can extract them to somewhere neutral.

Maybe Davao, in the Philippines. We all have friendly contacts there. Then we can all talk again."

She looked at Radovan again and said, "Agreed, Vuki?"

Rad was clearly not happy with the idea of Win Zin taking the lead, but he relented. "OK. Quiet In –Quiet Out. Otherwise, we'll have US Agents all over our asses."

He stared at Win and growled, "Do you understand –fancy boy? You fuck this up and Interpol will be the least of your problems." Rad stood and towered menacingly over Win's seat and growled, "In Serbia we have a saying, 'Za srce si me ujeo'. In English, it means, 'you bit my heart'." He eyeballed Win.

"If you fuck this up and betray this trust, I will bite more than your heart. You understand, pretty-boy? Us 'croppers', as you like to call us, have a healthy trade in cannabis. We make billions from it during the German summer festival season alone. If this crop is somehow resistant, we need to have it. I'll say it again! You understand?"

Through clenched teeth, Win repeated, "Quiet In –Quiet Out."

Valeria took control of the discussion and said, "OK, it's agreed, the Triangle will lead the extraction. We'll all meet again in Davao to discuss next steps."

She looked directly at Win and said, "Quiet in –."

Win sullenly answered back, "Quiet Out –."

U-Chin called Win away from the meeting at the desk and said,

"Let's go. My plane is waiting near yours at the airport. You can start organising on the flight home."

Win, who obviously had plans to do a bit of partying in Miami for the evening, looked torn. He'd been completely embarrassed in front of his entourage.

He started, "But –."

U-Chin gave him a stern look and said, "Bo Aung Win Zin! To the airport! Now!"

Since he was five years old, Win had learned that it was not a good idea to mess with his grandfather when he was calling him by his full formal family name. Repercussions would swiftly follow.

Win turned to his entourage and said, "Gather your things. We are heading for the airport –Now."

THE EYE IN THE SKY.

CIA Headquarters. Langley, Virginia.

A group of DEA, CIA and FBI agents sat around a long desk looking at a bank of computer monitors. One screen was running a mirror of the Sentinel feed. The other showed a recording of a live overhead drone camera view of the Smithson Drywall Company in the Slump.

"We know the cartels are in the Miami warehouse as we speak, and we know that they've accessed Sentinel for the past two hours," said a young CIA Analyst, "Who wants to take a guess at what they're up to?"

"The feed from the Sentinel system says they've been looking at northern Australia. Hell knows why," said one of the DEA Agents, "a lot of the Aussie drug trade goes PAST that point in boats –but there is nothing happening onshore there. Are we missing something?"

The CIA Analyst pointed to the monitor and said, "Someone's coming out of the building."

On the screen, a woman was leaving the building. "That's Valeria Munoz, from the Sinaloa cartel," he said.

Valeria crossed the car park and got into her Lambo. Then cruised away.

"Fuck, I love that car," said the FBI Analyst.

"There are more people coming out of the building now," said the DEA Agent, as a group of Asian men exited the warehouse. "We think this is the group from the Golden Triangle's Sam Gor Cartel. Win Zin for sure." He pointed to the last person on the screen.

"Not sure who the old guy with the carry-on suitcase is. He arrived separately. Let's get eyes on them at the airport. We've traced two jets in from Myanmar this morning. It's got to be them."

Minutes later, a taxi pulled up outside the warehouse. A lone male walked over to it.

"Not sure who this guy is," said the CIA Analyst, "He arrived alone. Looks European. Our closest guess is that it's Radovan Vukovic. From the Baltic cartels. But we've never seen him on American soil."

The group of analysts considered their options for a moment.

"The Golden Triangle. The Latinos and the Baltics. Together at the same time. Something big is cooking," said the CIA Analyst, "but why the fuck are they looking at Australia? Makes no sense."

Another DEA Analyst asked, "Should we let the Aussies know?"

The CIA Analyst said, "Not yet. Let's try to follow this further. We don't have the resources to throw at this right now anyway —with all the riots that are going down across Latin America and Europe, anyway."

He picked up a phone on the table, urgently dialed a number, and said, "Get me, Major Crensch."

The Double-Cross.

CHAPTER 59

BROKEN PROMISES.

The agreement to let Win Zin take the lead in securing the crop was broken in an instant. Before Radovan and Valeria had even stepped out of the building.

Each had decided the mission was too important to let an imbecile be in control. Whoever possessed living samples of the resistant crop, and understood the genetics, would control the global cannabis trade for decades to come.

The crop, and the scientist, were potentially worth trillions of dollars.

***

Valeria Munoz was on the phone the moment her Lambo pulled away from the meeting. "Drop everything. Get my private jet ready to fly down to our submarine base in Colombia," she said, "then, find out what assets we have down near Indonesia and Australia. I'm going to need a vessel that can carry a heavy load but remain undetected. I think we already have a submarine down there somewhere. Set up a call with the captain for tomorrow morning."

As Valeria pulled onto the freeway and sped up towards her father's mansion on Indian Creek Island, she said, "Get a squad of our best operatives to meet me in Panama. Only the best. After Colombia, we'll be heading over to the Philippines to gear-up and make our final plans. Contact our guys in Brisbane. See if they know of anyone we could use as a spotter in a little town north of there called Weipa. –W.E.I.P.A."

***

Valeria had itchy feet. After she'd discussed the Miami cartel meeting with her father, Money Munoz, and the other Latin cartel cadres, they'd decided not to wait and see if Win Zin and U-Chin would deliver on their promise to extract the staff and some crop samples.

Valeria didn't trust Win. She liked to call him; 'that little Burmese bastard'.

Growing impatient, she'd jumped on a plane from Miami down to La Florida Airport in Tumaco, near the location of the cartel's submarine base on the Colombian coast. It was a sleepy shrimp farming town filled with houses built on stilts over the water. Sporadic fighting with the local FARC guerrillas kept the tourists away.

The local Tumaco authorities were well-paid to turn a blind eye to the Sinaloa cartel's secretive narco-submarine base on the Rio Mara, just twenty miles south of the town.

Valeria knew that the only useful asset the cartel had near Australia was a large narco-sub. It took drugs, from different ports in Indonesia, down to a remote inlet near Karumba on the Australian mainland. From there, the drugs went overland to the major Aussie cities.

She talked to the sub's Indonesian skipper, Captain Ismail Gunawan, on an encrypted satellite phone. The ex-Indonesian Navy officer had partially surfaced the submarine near Sumba Island to take the call. The sub was the most sophisticated in the Sinaloa fleet, built with an aluminum hull and long-range diesel motors.

Below decks, it could store ten tons of cargo. For protection, it also had an XM913 50 Caliber turret-mounted gun that could be fixed to the sub's top deck.

"That's right, Ismail," Valeria said. "I want you to dump the cargo you have on board and head toward Weipa in Queensland. I need you to get there as fast as possible. Once you arrive, find somewhere to hide until I contact you again."

Ismail protested, "That's over 1,800 miles! With refueling stops, that will take me four days. I could –maybe –get there by Friday earliest."

Valeria said, "Friday will be fine. But absolutely no later than that!"

***

With the submarine dispatched, Valeria had flown Panama City to meet a private jet that would take her, and several of her best mercenary fighters, to Manila in the Philippines.

They'd then flown down to a remote airstrip on Basilan Island, in the southern Philippines, to meet a local militia crew they'd drawn from the rebel Philippine's New People's Army.

The Basilan Island airport shared its main runway with a small Philippines Air Force Base next door. As Valeria's plane taxied toward the main passenger terminal, she noticed an Australian RAAF plane. It was a C-130 Hercules cargo plane. The fuselage had been jacked up. A team of bored local mechanics were doing repairs on one of the wheel hydraulics.

Valeria cooled her heels for the next few days in the Philippines' backwater town, waiting for news of Win's progress in securing the crop samples. Win was not returning calls from any of the cartels. Prick.

"I need eyes on the ground over there," she said to Mans Buscayno, one of the local Filipino crew.

"I have a cousin who is working in the mines in Weipa as a diesel mechanic," he said. "I could send him over there to be our lookout. It will cost you, though."

Valeria rolled her eyes and said, "I'll send you images and map coordinates for the Australian crop location. Get him camped out over there with a long lens camera and some good binoculars. ASAP. I need photos and live reports if there's any action going on. Pay the guy whatever he wants."

***

Radovan Vukovic also didn't have the slightest intention of living up to the agreement made in Miami.

The Sinaloa and Sam Gor cartels had been steadily eating into his European trade for years. This was his perfect chance to completely remove them from the playing field.

"Fuck them all," muttered Rad, as his taxi left the Miami meeting. He immediately diverted the private jet waiting for him at Miami Airport to a new destination; Brisbane, Australia.

As soon as his jet cleared US airspace after the Miami meeting, he was on the phone. The Baltic Cartels didn't have operations on the ground in Australia, but the Serbians ran most of the motorcycle gangs down-under. Radovan had a few relatives who were key players in the notorious Bandidos bikie gang.

***

Zoran Bojanic's phone rang at 1-30am Brisbane time.

Bojanic was the President of the Bandidos in Brisbane. Radovan was his close cousin.

"Zoran –my brate (brother)," said Rad, "how is life treating you down there? We haven't spoken in ages."

"Very good, Rad," said Zoran. "What can I do for you at this early hour?"

They started with some small talk about family and the local cannabis trade. Zoran's ears pricked up when Radovan talked about Sentinel, the Miami cartel meeting and the surviving crop in Northern Queensland.

Rad said, "With your help, we will gain a massive advantage over the Sinaloa cartel and the Asians." The call fell silent for a moment as they both pondered the gravity of that thought.

Rad said, "I'm on a plane right now. Coming in from Miami. I should arrive in Brisbane late tomorrow. I need your help brother –to secure that crop –and the people who grew it."

Over the next thirty-six hours, Rad flew a circuitous route via several countries to avoid being tracked. He arrived in Brisbane. After clearing Australian Customs, he took a flight to a nearby regional airport called Wellcamp.

Zoran greeted him with a huge bear hug and ushered him into a hangar. A flight attendant arrived shortly afterwards and deposited two suitcases and a large amount of fishing gear inside the hangar door. Rad had told Customs he was heading up to Northern Australia for a wild barramundi fishing trip.

The scent of fresh-cut flowers filled the refrigerated hangar at Queensland's Wellcamp regional airport. A large sign on the hangar doors read: 'Hardies International Flora Group'.

Hundreds of crates of fresh flowers were packed to the ceiling behind a small prefab reception area. They were mainly the types you'd find at a cheesy wedding. Pink and yellow Gerberas, lilies, puffy white bunches of

Gypsophilia and blood red carnations. Forklifts shuttled in and out the large main door, while two armed guards patrolled inside.

Hidden behind the tall wall of wooden flower crates, another group of workers weighed and packaged Ziploc bags of ket, meth, ecstasy and cocaine. The drugs were destined to be smuggled around the country, hidden amongst the large crates of wholesale bunches of flowers.

A crew of five Bandidos had ridden in from Brisbane on thundering Harley Davidsons. They'd pushed all the drug packing tables across to one side of the room. Under cover of darkness, they'd used a forklift to unload several large wooden crates from trucks that came and went.

Just after Radovan arrived, a large chartered CONVAIR CV-580 turbo prop cargo plane landed and then parked close to the flower hanger. It lowered its rear cargo door. Ready for action.

At the back of the Wellcamp hangar, the Zoran Bojanic introduced the small crew of Bandido's members he'd pulled together for Radovan's operation.

Zoran pointed to a tattooed guy sitting at a laptop and said, "Mio, our intelligence guy, has some news for you. He used a dish to intercept the C-band satellite link in the Weipa area. That's the band most satellite phones use. It wasn't that hard to find the phone that Win Zin is using up there. It's remote, so there are hardly any handsets in use up there, and he was the only one using a Chinese knock off of an American model —so it was easy to decrypt his signal. We recorded this last night."

The thug at the laptop played a recent audio file of Win talking to U-Chin, telling him they'd arrived on the trawler and would mount the attack on the crop the next day. U-Chin scolded Win on the call, reminding him it was an extraction –not an attack.

Radovan looked concerned and said, "If he's going to attack soon, we need to get up there in case he fucks things up. How long before we could be ready?"

Zoran opened Google Maps on a laptop and typed in 'Weipa'. The screen showed the town's remote location. He said, "It's only a six-hour flight to Weipa. We'll have to refuel along the way because we have a heavy load. We could be up there late tomorrow afternoon. As a precaution, we sent in a guy on a regional F.I.F.O. worker's flight yesterday. He's checking things out on the ground for us."

Zoran pointed to the map.

"There's only one road into Weipa," he said. "We might have to leave overland via that route. A flight out of the airport might be too risky if it all goes pear-shaped."

Zoran pulled up a picture of Willow on the screen and asked, "How are you planning to get the girl and the crop samples out?"

Radovan smiled and said, "I'm planning to use a submarine."

***

The South American cartels made the best narco-subs in the world, from flimsy fiberglass fast-boats for quick trips up to Mexico, to steel hulled juggernauts with heavy guns and stealth technology.

The Sinaloa cartel submarine base at Playon in Colombia made the best. They'd happily sold many units to the Asian and European Cartels over the years. This also meant that the Sinaloa cartel's Playon submarine base was full of lowlifes and snitches, people who would happily sell valuable information for a few crispy US dollars or a flight to a whorehouse in Bogota for the night. Radovan already had several local workers there on his payroll.

***

Rad's circuitous flight route into Australia had taken him from Miami to Panama City, then to La Paz, French Polynesia and into Brisbane.

On the flight to La Paz, he got a call from a snitch located down near Playon.

"That Munoz bitch turned up here. The hot one," the snitch said.

"Are you sure? Valeria?" Rad said.

"Yes —I've seen her many times before. I was in the room when she was there," the snitch added.

"Why was she there?" Rad asked,

"I heard her on the radio, talking to the skipper of one of our subs located down in Indonesia," he said. "Something is going down in Northern Australia. Must be big. She asked the guy to dump his load and hightail it down there. She's meeting him there at the end of the week, at a place called Weipa."

Two years earlier, Rad had flown into a remote island in Indonesia. He'd gone to there take a test ride on a long distance, steel-hulled submarine he was buying from the Sinaloans. It was the same model as the one he was planning to buy for use in the Mediterranean. It wasn't cheap, so he decided he needed to see it for himself.

During the trip, he'd struck up a good relationship with the sub's captain, Ismail Gunawan. He thought the captain might make a good future employee if they expanded their Mediterranean fleet, so Rad had wined and dined him and taken down his mobile number.

Rad placed a call to the captain over in Indonesia.

After making a bank transfer of $1,200,000 USD to the captain's personal bank account in Malta, Radovan knew exactly what Valeria's plans were in Weipa.

He'd also just made a down-payment to 'buy' Valerias narco-sub. The one she'd ordered over to Weipa to use for her ex-fil operation.

WIN ZIN GETS HOT AND HEAVY.

Taung-ywa, Myanmar.

The remote island called Taung-ywa sat off the coast of Myanmar. On one side of the island, the local Burmese farmers eked a bare existence from the rugged basalt cliffs. On the other side, a secret aerodrome bristled with billionaire military play toys.

The Golden Triangle's Sam Gor drug cartel, which operated the base, was funded by decades of illicit sales of heroin, synthetic drugs like yaba and meth, and cannabis.

A Shaanxi Y-9, the Chinese knock-off of a C-130 military cargo plane, gingerly landed on the short runway that had been carved into the island's only piece of flat land. Its brakes squealed and smoked, finally bringing the big plane to a halt. It pulled up at a hangar and lowered its rear cargo door.

The Shaanxi was transporting a heavy load of weapons, including a massive ZBD-03 airborne combat vehicle. The eight-ton Chinese amphibious assault vehicle was tethered to a Russian-built parachute system, which could drop it from the plane mid-air. It looked like a tank and was fitted with a powerful dual-axis stabilized ZPT-99A 30mm auto-cannon and six smoke grenade dischargers.

A squad of twelve elite mercenaries from the rebel Shan State Army (SSA) filed off the plane.

Hawk and Win walked inside to check the weaponry that had been delivered. Hawk was wearing the standard uniform of an Officer in the Tatmataw, Myanmar's main military force. Win wore the latest tactical gear, which had been imported straight from the USA.

Hawk studied the combat vehicle, raised his eyebrows and said, "Bro –a little bit of overkill –isn't it? You need all THIS to extract some hick Aussie farmers armed with single-action rifles?"

Win said, "I always like to carry a big stick."

Hawk reminded him, "You promised your father a quiet and quick extraction down in Australia."

Win picked up a khaki green PF-89 Chinese army rocket launcher, China's latest lightweight RPG system. He hefted it onto his right shoulder and looked through its optical sight.

"I changed my mind," said Win, "I'm thinking hot and heavy."

****

Hawk and Win exited the plane to brief the mercenaries about the operation ahead of them in Australia. They gathered them around a table and handed each a target package containing details about the mission, the local geography and a recent photo of Willow.

They weren't concerned about taking out the people on the farm when they got there, but flying a big Chinese military plane into Australia, fully laden with a foreign combat force, wouldn't be an easy task. Landing the Shaanxi directly on Australian soil wasn't an option. You had to fly past the CIA's massive array of monitoring systems at Pine Gap in the Northern Territory and the Australians' own radar.

Fortunately, the Sam Gor cartel's narcotics operation had a network of fishing trawlers that regularly passed through the Timor Sea with loads of illicit drugs. The Indonesian skippers knew the coastline like the back of their hands.

Win and Hawk devised a plan to fly the Shaanxi to Komoran Island, a flat sandy river delta on the southern tip of Timor, safely across from the PNG border. This would keep them off the Northern Australian radar network.

Once above Komoran, they'd air-drop the ZBD-03, and the SSA mercenary force, onto the sandy beaches of the island from the plane, then they'd overland across the island to meet a trawler big enough to carry it.

This would be followed by a twenty-four-hour overnight trip over to the mouth of the Embley River at Weipa.

After the mission, they'd exfiltrate Willow Barrant and the sample plants back up to Indonesia on the same trawler.

***

After a bumpy flight and a hair-raising nightime para-jump down to Komoran, Win and Hawk sat in a grimy room in one of the cartel's Indonesian fishing trawlers. They huddled around a laptop with several of the mercenaries.

It was 4am. The boat lurched in the waves as it cut its way through the Timor Sea. The ZBD-03 tank was covered in camo net and safely lashed to its rear roll-on-roll-off deck.

Hawk traced a line on the screen and said, "We'll head straight up the Embley River, past the town while it's still dark. It looks like we can navigate about fifteen miles up the river. Which should bring us out right behind the cannabis farm." The mercenaries listened intently.

Hawk pointed to a position on the river about two miles from Willow's Back Block and added, "We'll offload the amphibious vehicle here. Then we can overland to the crop location."

Win pulled opened a manila folder. He pulled out a photo of Willow and a photo of Catherine Sneesby. He pointed to the picture of Willow.

"As you know from your target package, this is Willow Barrant. We want her alive," he said.

He pointed to Sneesby. "This one is a hack. No need to exfil. Kill her if she gets in the way. Anyone else on the ground is expendable. Kill on sight."

Tong Lo, one of the SSA team members, pointed to an airport runway on the map and asked, "What's that?"

Hawk replied, "That is a local RAAF Base. Our intel says it's only manned by three servicemen and maybe a couple of dogs. We'll be twenty miles out of Weipa, so we don't expect the local police to be a big problem."

Hawk zoomed-out the map to show an aerial view of Australia.

"The nearest main bases are RAAF Townsville and Tindal," he said. "The No. 75 squadron at Tindal is probably the biggest threat to the operation. About 1,000 miles away. They have a few F35 fighters. If they scrambled a jet, it could be above us in about sixty minutes. But, at that point, the jet would be starting to run low on fuel. So it couldn't hang around very long."

Hawk pointed back to the map.

"The main issue will be noise," he said. "We will only be five miles from Scherger Air Force base. They shouldn't be able to hear light weapons from that distance, but the sound of the 30mm gun on our tank would be heard. We need to avoid firing it unless absolutely necessary."

The voice of the trawler's skipper crackled over a speaker. "I can see the lights from the main port of Weipa coming up ahead. Let's kill all of the lights on the ship until we are safely past."

Just after sunrise, the ZBD-03 lumbered off the rear deck of the trawler onto a mud flat. A stone's throw from the Back Block.

Its tank treads made easy work of the mushy terrain, as giant saltwater crocs lumbered out of its way.

CHAPTER 61

BACK TO THE REAL WORLD.

It was the final day of the Bivvie.

There was an air of sadness at Ned's Corner. Soon they'd all be heading back onto the grid, after three weeks of remote bliss.

Tonight, they'd be having one final bender, to end the bivvie on a high note. They sat around the campfire for the final time. Everyone was knackered from a final monster Gelsoft battle they'd had earlier in the day.

At the edge of the campsite, Shu, wearing a green and yellow Weipa Raiders football jersey, was rummaging around in the back of her 4WD. She pulled out a big brown cardboard box. She walked over and placed it near the campfire, then she plugged a long power extension cable into a socket on the back of the vehicle. Tonight was a big night on the Queensland Rugby League's Far North League calendar. The Weipa Raiders were playing their arch enemies to see who would make the cut for the finals.

It was time to plug back into the grid.

Shu opened the box and pulled out a brand new Starlink Satellite Internet kit.

"I've been itching to try this out ever since we got here," she said excitedly. Freddie and Jez helped her assemble the router and laptop connections. Caz took the dish and moved it to a place that had the best access to the open night sky. In fifteen minutes, they had a laptop connected to the web.

Shu opened up a Sports TV app on her laptop and they all huddled around the screen in the campfire light. The rugby game was a close one. The Raiders snatched the win when the opposition halfback fumbled a ball with a minute to go.

After the game, everyone hit their beds, knowing that they had a big job packing up the camp in the morning.

***

The next morning Willow was shaken awake by Shu.

"Wills," she said, "you've gotta come and have a look at this, something big is happening on the TV."

Willow shook herself awake, got dressed, and headed outside. The fresh morning air was filled with the smell of eggs and sausages cooking on the campfire. Shu, Jen and Jezz were huddled around the laptop, intently watching the local morning TV news broadcast. Shu handed Willow a strong coffee as she took a seat next to them.

"You're going to need this," Shu said.

On the screen, an American TV reporter was talking over a montage of images of street riots in Mexico. A line of bloodied, naked bodies hung from a bridge. Troopers fired bullets and launched gas cannisters into crowds of protesters. A government building was on fire.

The TV reporter said, "Civil unrest and riots continue to engulf more than forty major cities around the world."

The reporter continued, as the TV broadcast cut to an image of a large commercial jet taking off down a runway, "We are getting reports that the President of Nicaragua has fled the country to Brazil, as a junta lead by the Norte del Valle drug cartel seems to have toppled the government."

The TV coverage switched to a Weed shop burning on a trendy street corner in Brooklyn, New York, then it cut to a boarded up weed shop in San Francisco. The TV reporter continued, "And widespread looting continues to occur in many cities, as cannabis supplies dry up."

The coverage switched to an emergency session at the UN. Several members shouted at each other as a vote was taking place. "While the UN still seems to be locked into inaction as the cannabis virus kills crops globally," said the reporter. The TV report cut to an interview with the UN Ambassador from New Zealand. She said, "We just can't condone any action by the UN to support the international narcotics trade –it finances terrorism, human trafficking and harder drugs."

The news story cut back to a reporter standing in the middle of a massive greenhouse, filled with withered, dead cannabis plants.

"The virus, identified as HLVd+, is a new variant of a Hops virus," said the reporter. A graphic of an RNA helix appeared on the TV screen. "The pathogen has quickly decimated cannabis crops worldwide. At commercial facilities like this –and in illegal crops hidden in the jungles around the world. Scientists are unsure how it's spreading so fast. They suspect that wild birds, or insects, are carrying the spores."

"Fuuuuck," said Willow.

The TV news story cut back to a local Queensland TV reporter. She was standing in a large hothouse, surrounded by thousands of dead cannabis plants.

"Tania Hardy, reporting from Cannacom," the reporter said, "I'm here at Australia's largest medicinal cannabis operation, based near the town of Weipa, up in the northern part of the Top End." The camera panned around the greenthouse.

"As you can see, the devastation is total. Five days ago, these were all healthy plants. Kip Norman, the CEO of Cannacom, says they have no idea what is causing the spread."

The report cut to Kip, talking on a Zoom call.

Kip said, "We are getting the same reports from every commercial operator in Australia. Everyone has dead crops. The government is offering zero support. The police are also reporting crop deaths from illegal cannabis growing operations. So, it looks like nobody has been spared."

The story cut back to the reporter in the greenhouse.

"ABC News has contacted the Inspector-General of Biosecurity for comment, but none is forthcoming from the Department of Agriculture, Fisheries and Forestry."

She finished the report. "Tania Hardy –reporting from Weipa, Northern Queensland.

Willow and the group, seated around the laptop, stared at each other, open-mouthed.

Shu eventually spoke up,

"Well –I guess we'll all be out of work on Monday."

CHAPTER 62

PRAISE THE LORD!

After watching the TV news report –twice, they'd packed up the camp at Ned's in record time.

By 11am they were slowly bashing through the bush toward the crop at the Back Block. Jez and Jen were in one of the 4WDs with Willow.

Willow was despondent. "All my fucking work. A year of testing. All down the drain," she moaned, "I guess we'll all be on the chopping block when we get back."

Jen lamented, "All that work you all did down on the Back Block. Hard yakka from the look of it."

As the 4WD crested the hill overlooking the valley, Willow braced herself for a shock, but in the valley below stood two acres of lush green cannabis plants.

All in perfect health. Praise the fucking lord!

It was a miracle.

***

After checking out the crop and the watering system, Willow and the guys decided to camp at the Back Block overnight. They already had all the supplies they needed.

Willow was in a bind about what to do about the crop.

Just before sunset Freddie had taken one of the ATVs and driven back through the Briar, to check out the main Cannacom farm. Every single plant in the hothouses there was wilted and dead. Fifty fucking acres!

He spoke into a field radio as he drove past the greenhouses. "Dead as a doornail –all the greenhouses –just like the news report." He swiped his security pass at the main gate and parked in the Cannacom car park. He stepped out of the ATV and lifted the radio again.

"It's like a ghost town here. Everyone's gone home," he said.

Shu chipped in over the radio, "The Weipa Running Festival is on this weekend. Not surprising that nobody is around. Everyone's going to be at the Bowlo, over at The Alby or down at the Showgrounds Oval all this weekend."

CHAPTER 63

WILLOW HATCHES A PLAN.

Willow and Caz had driven the Banger to the far side of the Back Block crop.

"Buggered if I know what to do," Willow said, as she checked a spigot on the watering system.

"We can't go to the cops and just tell them we have a crop that's resistant to the disease. This crop is WAY outside Cannacom's commercial license."

Caz agreed. "With two acres like this, we'd all end up in jail for a long time."

They walked until they had completed a full circuit of the crop. Every plant was alive and healthy.

By the time they joined the others, Freddie had returned from the main farm, and Willow had hatched a plan.

As they all sat around the campfire, she explained the plan to them.

They'd spend the morning making sure there was no evidence that it was them that had planted the crop. Then they'd take some samples of seedlings –and a few full sized plants –so they could tell the cops they'd stumbled across the crop on the way back from Ned's, if they ever had to.

She knew they'd be in trouble for trespassing on Scherger's side of the fence, but that would probably be a lot less trouble than being caught growing tons of illegal weed.

Jez and Jen busied themselves by checking the makeshift sheds, destroying any evidence. They wiped down surfaces to get rid of fingerprints.

Caz figured they'd have to drive the Banger out and park it somewhere.

Back at the crop Willow, Caz, Freddie and Shu parked an ATV.

They got out and started gathering plant samples. Shu grabbed a shovel and started digging out a mature plant.

***

On a hilltop nearby Tong Lo, a Shan State Army sniper, whispered into his field radio.

"She looks like Willow Barrant, the Aboriginal woman in my target package. I could take an easy head-shot from here."

CHAPTER 64

WIN ZIN ATTACKS.

Caz, Freddie, Shu and Willow had potted some plants and were loading them into their ATV.

Caz saw a flash of light from the hill above the crop. It looked oddly familiar. He squinted and focussed on it, then his spidey senses went on high alert as years of infantry training kicked in. That was a reflection off a snipers gun-sights.

"Shooter! Everyone down!" he shouted.

The four of them hit the ground as bullets started flying around them. They scurried along the ground on their bellies, then they bolted into the safety of the tall cannabis plants. Bullets whizzed by as they crashed through the foliage.

"What the fuck was that? Spread out." Freddie shouted.

Shu cried out and stumbled as a bullet grazed her shoulder. Willow pulled Shu to her feet and dragged her forward.

"Lets get back over to the sheds!" shouted Willow as the hail of bullets continued.

Up on the hill, Tong Lo pressed a button on his throat mic and reported, "They are heading toward some sheds. At the edge of the crop. To the left of your current position."

Hawk and Win signalled for the squad to gather in a huddle.

***

Win, brandishing his prized new M16 US Army assault rifle, felt this would be an easy fight. He decided to take the long and lazy route down toward the sheds. Hawk looked at Win's rifle and reminded him, "Your grandfather wants the Aboriginal woman alive –remember –I don't want you getting trigger-happy with that new toy."

The squad started walking around the perimeter of the crop. There was no rush. These Aussie farmers wouldn't offer much resistance.

***

Freddie got back to the sheds first.

He knew he had to buy them some time, so they could figure out who was shooting at them, and why?

He ran to Shu's 4WD and flipped open the tailgate. He rummaged around in the back and grabbed some of the smoke canisters left over from their Gelsoft battles. Then he ran back through the crop, straight toward the approaching SSA attackers. He stopped and hunkered down when he heard them walking along the track. He hurled three smoke cannisters toward them. Moments later, a dense cloud of blue and yellow smoke started spewing out.

The others arrived at the sheds and hid inside, catching their breath.

Freddie arrived shortly after. "That smoke will slow them," he shouted, "but it won't work for long. What are we going to do? If they all have guns, we don't stand a chance."

Shu sat on the tailgate of the Banger. Willow was treating the small tear in her shoulder from the sniper's bullet. She carefully covered it in gauze and a clear plastic medical patch from their First Aid kit.

Caz jumped into the back of the Banger and shouted, "I've got an idea! Freddie, get me your gun. Jez, I need you to drive."

***

The blue and yellow smoke had enveloped the Win Zin and the SSA squad.

Surprised and confused, they hunkered down. *What the fuck were Aussie farmers doing with smoke grenades?*

Win shouted, "Go. Go. Let's keep moving!"

Hawk called back, "No, let's wait until this smoke clears. In case they have any other tricks up their sleeves."

"Fuck –No," shouted Win.

"Fuck –Yes," Hawk shouted back, waving cautiously to the SSA squad to hold their positions.

After several minutes, the smoke partially cleared. Hawk signaled to the Squad to edge forward, as their view of the path around the edge of the crop was clearing up.

"See?" said Win angrily. "We could have had them already. These guys have nothing but some pig shooting guns and shovels."

Hawk calmly replied, "Quick and Quiet –Remember?"

The reminder of the promise to U-Chin just made Win even more enraged. He stomped down the path ahead of them.

The smoke eventually cleared completely to reveal a clear path down toward the sheds.

"See!" yelled Win, "There's nothing to stop us. Let's go."

He raced ahead alongside the crop. They lost sight of him as he rounded a corner. Hawk and the SSA Squad picked up their pace to follow the fool.

The SSA squad slowed when they heard a loud vehicle coming directly toward them. As they reached the corner of the crop, they saw Win. He was running toward them, waving his arms.

Just behind Win, the Banger was hurtling down the track, with Jez at the wheel. Caz stood behind the home-made machine gun turret mounted on the back. He was firing Freddies pig shooting rifle. One shot blew the $47,000 set of L3Harris Ground Panoramic Night Vision Goggles right off Win's tactical helmet.

"What the –!" shouted Hawk, as he and the whole squad dove for cover in the bush. The Banger hurtled past in a blur, coming inches from running Win over. The SSA opened fire, but their shots bounced off the steel plate Caz was standing behind. Jez took a hard left and disappeared back into the into the safety of the crop. Out of view.

"What the fuck are they doing with a Technical out here?" shouted Hawk. "How –?"

Win pulled the mangled night vision goggles from his tactical helmet. Now he was seething. Embarrassed. The SSA Squad members tried not to make eye contact with him. None of them was wearing NODs. This was a daytime operation.

Hawk suggested they reconsider their approach to attacking the sheds. They went into another huddle under a tree.

Win, still pissed, sent two of the squad members back to their weapons cache up the hill.

He'd asked them to grab two of the PF-89 rocket launchers.

SURVIVAL OF THE FAKEST.

Back at the sheds, Shu had activated Quiet Mode on her DJI Matrice 350 drone.

She sent it skyward. On the flight pad, she could see Jez smashing his way back to them in the Banger. She turned the drone to look at the track beside the crop. She saw ten armed soldiers huddled under a large tree. Two more were moving up the hill behind them.

The Banger arrived. Caz stepped off the back.

Shu said, "Fuck –there are at least twelve of them."

Caz said, "Yes, and they looked like the real deal to me. Army from the look of their uniforms. I nearly ran one dude over. Why the fuck would they be out here, in bloody Weipa?"

Shu shifted the position drone, following the two soldiers up the hill. She zoomed in.

"Jesus!" she said. "They've got a big cache of weapons back up the hill. Enough for a small army."

Shu took a deep gulp of air and said, "Holy crap! "You are not going to believe this –there's a tank –parked up at the top of the hill!"

Jez said, "A tank. It can't be." They all moved over and stared at the screen on the flight-pad in awe.

Jen was freaking out. She said, "We can't fight back against soldiers with guns. Let alone a tank. We're so fucked."

"The two guys up on the hill are on the move again." Shu said.

She moaned deeply, and said, "They've just picked up two RPG cases."

"We need a plan. Fast." said Willow, "I don't think we can outrun them through the Briar. It will slow us down too much."

Caz started doing a mental inventory.

"We have three real rifles," he said, "One with a decent scope."

"And we have six Gelsoft guns," he added, "Useless as tits on a bull."

Jen said, "You're forgetting something." She pointed to the gun rack in the back of Shu's 4WD. "You have six of Shu's 3D printed guns in there, and they look real-as-hell to me. From a distance, they'd make anyone have second thoughts."

Freddie scratched his chin, deep in thought.

Jen continued, "And you guys have your tactical uniforms. Helmets. Webbing. Comms. Patches. Most of which are made up of your old standard-issue Australian Army uniforms."

Jen mused, "We may not be able to out-gun those guys –but we might be able to out-fake them."

Freddie looked at the 3D printed guns and said, "If we could bog those guys down somewhere, and then ambush them? Use the element of surprise? We might stand a chance."

"Yeah. Nah." said Jez. "That wouldn't work in a million years."

"Hold on a sec," said Willow. "I know how we could bog them down." She pointed to the center of the crop.

"If we can get them to head through the crop, instead of around it. We could turn on the watering system. That would flood the paddocks and they'd be standing in the middle of a quagmire before they realized what was happening. They'd need to backtrack out of there. We could stage an ambush –of sorts –when they come back out. Anyone got a better idea?"

Jen said, "I don't know one end of a gun from another. I'd be useless in an ambush. Maybe I could be the one that creates a diversion –while you guys set up an ambush. I'd just need something loud to get their attention. To get them to come across the crop, instead of going around it."

Caz fired up the Banger and revved it loud. Flames and smoke leapt from its broken exhaust manifold. "This should do the trick," he said.

Shu went over to the back of her 4WD and fetched two plastic cannisters. They looked like old WW2 hand grenades. Shu said, "I still have two of these M84 Gel Ball Grenades left. These might help create the diversion, but they aren't very loud."

Freddie came out of the closest shed, clasping a stick of dynamite in his hand. He said, "And we still have this, from when we blasted the watering trench down at the creek."

"Let's do it," said Jen, "We're fucked otherwise." She planted a kiss on Jez's check and stepped into the driver's seat of the Banger.

Freddie pushed a long fuse into the stick of dynamite and carefully handed it to her. "This fuse will burn for twenty seconds," he said. "Light the fuse, throw it, and then run away as fast as you can. Do not pass Go. Do not stop to collect $200."

Caz said, "Let the two Gelsoft flash-bangers off first. That will get them looking over your way and draw them over to your side of the crop. If you stand in the back of the Banger's tray, you should be able to see them moving through the field toward you. Wait a few minutes, until they're in the middle of the field, then hurl the dynamite towards them."

Jen nervously packed the dynamite on the passenger's seat and then drove off toward the far side of the crop.

Caz, Freddie, Willow, Shu and Jez changed into their tactical uniforms. Shu handed out the fake guns. They were light and flimsy, but they looked very real.

Caz took a fake Magpul FMG-9 submachine gun. He tucked the fake Chiappa Rhino pistol into a holster for good measure.

Willow took the fake KRISS Vector assault rifle.

Jez took the fake AR-15 assault rifle. It felt as light as a kid's toy, but Shu had made every detail perfect.

Shu took the SRC SR4 Mamba Gen 2. It was a Gelsoft rifle, but it looked plain evil. The large patch of drying blood on the shoulder of her shirt added to the menacing look.

Freddie took the only real gun. The trusty .308 Ruger Scout. It had a polymer five shot magazine for pig hunting. This only gave them five shots against a group of twelve trained professionals who were armed to the teeth.

Willow went inside one of the sheds and turned on several valves. This fully opened the crop's watering system. The generator and pump kicked in. At the far end of the field, water gushed from ten different points along the creek. She rejoined the others.

Their years of army training kicked in, and they instinctively formed-up as an Ambush Squad. Freddie made a silent hand signal, and lead them down the track toward the right-hand side of the crop.

This battle would be won, or lost, in a heartbeat.

THE SHORTEST BATTLE IN HISTORY.

The two SSA squad members arrived back from the weapons cache up the hill next to the tank. They were holding two of the PF-89 rocket launchers.

Hawk shook his head in dismay, but Win was technically the Squad Leader, so he deferred. They set off alongside the tall cannabis crop again, in classic Ranger File; single file, about six feet apart. Now wary and prepped. Hawk took the lead point position. Win took the rear.

A few hundred yards away, Willow and the guys were walking along the same side of the crop. Straight toward them, on a collision course.

Caz cradled the Magpul FMG-9 submachine gun in his hands. Shu had done a good job on the replica. She'd even made it look old and battle-scarred. It looked the part, but it felt light and flimsy.

He shook his head and said, "If Jen's distraction doesn't work, this will be the world's shortest battle."

Jen arrived at the other side of the crop in the Banger. She revved it loudly as she drove along the track. The Ford's V8 motor boomed across the field. She pull to a halt, then stepped up into the rear tray.

Following her instructions from Caz, Jen pulled the pins on the two Gelsoft grenades and hefted them far into the middle of the crop. They both exploded with a loud pop, more than a bang. Win and the SSA squad froze in place as the sound of the two small explosions echoed across the field.

Win said, "It sounds like they might have moved away from the sheds. Let's cut across the field."

Win signaled for them to enter the field. The soldiers looked over at Hawk for guidance, but he gestured for them to follow the order. They pushed their way into the field of tall cannabis plants.

A few minutes later, Willow, Caz, Freddie, Shu and Jez came upon a part of the crop where many of the plants had recently been flattened.

Willow said, "It looks like they've taken the bait and cut across from here. If they are going to come back out, it will be from this position, so let's set up here and wait for them."

They quietly took ambush positions around the edge of the crop.

In the middle of the cannabis field, the SSA squad continued pushing their way through the tall cannabis plants.

They barely noticed the first slow trickle of water below their feet as the watering system flooded the surrounding crop. Within minutes, the hard ground turned into boot-sucking mud. They were already close to the other side of the crop. They came to a halt as they saw the Banger through a gap in the rows of plants. Jen was standing on the tray of the truck looking out over the field.

They silently hunkered down, as Tong Lo silently mounted the PF-89 on his shoulder and took aim.

Jen had heard them approaching across the field. They were a lot closer than she was planning, so she switched to Plan B.

She lit the fuse on the dynamite and started counting down from twenty, hoping desperately that Freddie's calculations were right. When her countdown reached five, she hurled the stick of dynamite. The burning stick arced through the air and traveled a surprising distance. Six months playing outfield for the local Weipa softball team had paid off!

The dynamite landed with a silent thunk in the mud beside Tong Lo as his finger pulled the trigger.

BOOM!

Most of the SSA mercenaries were ripped apart by the massive explosion. The only thing remaining of Tong Lo was a pair of smoking boots sticking out from the mud. The others turned and ran. Stumbling as they retreated across the dense field, their ears ringing from the concussion from the massive blast.

Willow heard the explosion, followed by the sound of the mercenaries crashing through the tall plants toward them.

"Party time," Shu whispered through her Comms, "Good one Jen."

A few minutes later, Win, Hawk and the only two remaining SSA soldiers crashed through the edge of the crop.

They stopped and stared at the ambush party that immediately stepped out from behind a group of trees. They weren't expecting a group of Australian Army soldiers with sophisticated weapons.

One of the SSA mercenaries instinctively raised his weapon to fire, but a single shot rang out from Freddie's Ruger. The bullet sent the guy falling to the ground, clutching his leg.

Willow, brandishing her KRISS assault rifle, yelled, "Drop your weapons." Caz stepped forward, about to 'unleash' his fake Magpul FMG-9 submachine gun.

Hawk, Win and the remaining mercenaries dropped their weapons to the ground. Willow quickly stepped in and kicked them out of reach.

They were surprised when she lifted one of their rifles off the ground and then tossed her own assault rifle away. The rifle landed on the trail with no sound at all. It should have hit the ground with a heavy thud.

Shu stepped in and took another SSA rifle off the ground. She expertly checked the magazine and breach. Then she aimed her SRC SR4 Mamba Gen 2 squarely at Win. She pulled the trigger and a spray of Gelsoft rounds splattered against his expensive new Militech NIJ ballistic vest.

"Par tal ma!" (whore) he shouted at her in disbelief.

Jez and Caz had used cable ties to bind their hands and feet. Win Zin squirmed in a fury. He glared at Willow.

"Nea nga yea lee thwa sout liet," (You can go suck my dick.) he sneered. She didn't understand what he said, but she understood what he meant. Willow smashed her fist into his mouth. Win Zin spat out his two expensive and orthodontically-perfect front teeth.

History's shortest war was over. Just one shot fired.

CHAPTER 67

THERE WAS A LOUD BANG.

A few miles away, at the Scherger RAAF base, Corporal Mandy Eyesen was on duty. She pricked up her ears when she thought she heard a couple of small bangs in the distance. She assumed it was pig hunters out for a beer-fuelled weekend.

The Corporal locked the door of Scherger's ancient Control Tower and headed down its rusty old stairs. It was a familiar ritual for the Scherger Radio Operator, as the tower often went on the fritz.

Mandy had wanted to stretch her legs. They were sore from training for the annual Weipa Running Festival. So, she'd walked, rather than driven, over to the tower. The two canines on the base, Rex and Fatso, had ambled along behind her. After switching a Circuit Breaker inside the ancient Control Tower, she'd booted the system up. Then she'd checked it was operating correctly. Finally, she'd set it to power-down again.

Maintenance was always an issue at Scherger.

The three staff that manned the bare base struggled to keep it mothballed and ready to be called into action if an emergency arose. These days, the base was only staffed from 07-30am until 4-30pm. A sign advised visitors that mobile phone coverage was unreliable at best.

While the system powered down, she thought she heard rapid gunshots in the distance. The dogs below started barking. She noted the sound of the gunshots in the Control Tower Log on her iPad. When she reached the bottom of the stairs, she conducted a final system test.

She clicked on her field radio and said, "Hey –Terry –can you tell Jackie I'm about to test the siren warning system."

"Roger. Mandy." said Terry, the base commander.

She pressed a large red button and the Scherger Base warning system came to life. Large speakers on poles squealed a series of loud beeps, followed by a deafening robotic voice bellowing, "Alert –Alert –Alert."

It was just loud enough to smother the sound of the dynamite blast over at the Back Block.

Mandy walked back to the main base Caretaker's Office unaware that a gun battle was taking place just a few miles away. As she entered the office, her iPad auto-connected to the Wi-Fi. The Tower Log app automatically did an update to the RAAF Command Centre in Brisbane.

Back down in Brisbane, the report of the shooting nearby went unnoticed.

LATE NIGHT IN WASHINGTON.

It was bedtime at Major Crensch's house in the leafy Washington, DC suburb of Chesterbrook Gardens.

His house was just an eleven-minute drive down Kirby Road to the CIA Headquarters Building. It had been a week since he received advice about the mysterious Miami cartel meeting.

Crensch was packing the dishwasher when his phone bleeped. He clicked on the screen and listened intently to an audio recording.

It was a recording of the satellite phone call they'd intercepted between Win Zin and his grandfather U-Chin, as they had a heated argument about taking Willow Barrant captive rather than shooting her.

"What the?" muttered Crensch. "Willow Barrant?" Last time he saw her, she had nearly broken his jaw.

He quickly dialed a number.

When the person picked up, he said, "Sylvia, why am I listening to a recording of a couple of Asian Sam Gor cartel members talking about the girlfriend of one of our operatives?"

Sylvia, a CIA analyst, replied, "Your guess is good as ours. We just intercepted the call. The two people on the line are the head of the cartel, and his grandson. They were both at that Miami cartel meeting we're investigating. That's why we had the tap on the grandson's phone. We tracked the call, and it came from a location near a commercial cannabis farm, just outside of a little town called Weipa in Australia. It sounds to me like the woman they are talking about is at risk of getting killed."

Crensch was deep in thought as she continued.

"We don't really know what's going on, but Weipa was also the place that the DEA's Sentinel system was looking at before it went offline. So that place in Australia is, somehow, connected to this unprecedented meeting of all the cartels."

Crensch listened some more and then said, "Overnight, can you get the team to run a full scan on the location, the phone call, the son's movements? Pull together a briefing document on what they can find. I'll send you some details about Miss Barrant. Just in case, get them to do a spot check on the current movements of the other cartel members that were at the Miami meeting, too."

Before he hung off the call, he added, "And get an urgent message to the Australian Ambassador. Yes. Jason Blagg. We may need to brief him on this —but keep it off the local radar for now."

Crensch said, "See you at 06-00." He disconnected.

***

Over the next eight hours, the gaze of the CIA fixed squarely on Far Northern Queensland. Trouble was brewing.

By the end of the following day, both Major Crensch and Ambassador Jason Blagg would be sleeping on a CIA jet on an urgent flight from the USA over to Tindal Airforce Base in Australia's Northern Territory.

TRUTH SERUM.

The sun had set quickly after the battle around the crop.

Win Zin squirmed and twisted angrily against the cable ties binding his wrists and feet. Willow had learned more than a few Burmese swear words in the last couple of hours as he hurled a torrent of abuse at her.

"What the fuck?" said Willow, picking up one of the PF-89 rocket launchers. "Who are these guys? All of their gear shouts 'Chinese Army', but they definitely aren't from the P.L.A."

Freddie pointed to the SSA prisoners and said, "Those uniforms are definitely Chinese." He pointed to Win.

"Except that guy. He looks like he got his uniform at 'Soldiers R Us'. I reckon his gear cost more than my car. He's not talking –but I'd swear he understands every word we're saying."

Willow had spent a frustrating couple of hours trying to get Win to talk, but he wasn't saying anything. She decided she needed to step the interrogation up a notch.

She was considering her options when they all heard a dull rumble in the darkness alongside the crop. A set of headlights slowly appeared as the ZBD-03 tank lumbered toward them.

Freddie said, "Don't worry, it's only Caz. He went up the hill to see if he could figure out how to get that tank-thing working."

Caz pulled up. He killed the motor and said, "I got it working, but the gauges are all in Chinese. It's a Chinese Army amphibious assault vehicle, but what's it doing out here –in the middle of nowhere? And why would you need a tank to capture a group of little hokies like us?"

Hawk shook his heading in dismay. Win scowled at Caz.

Willow said, "It's time to get the truth out of these guys. Let's stay out here for another night while we figure out what to do. It's bad enough that we've got an illegal weed crop, but now we've also got a Chinese tank and a bunch of dead bodies scattered across the field. We need to find out exactly why these guys are here."

She grabbed a torch and walked into the bush.

She returned twenty minutes later with a small bag filled with berries and mushroom. She also had some branches covered in small white flowers.

"Huh?" said Freddie. "What have you got there?"

Willow showed him the branches.

"This is Pituri," she said. "It's related to the tobacco family of plants. Elders chew it. They say it lets them communicate with the spirits of our ancestors."

Willow held up a branch of Acacia and said. "When you mix it with this, it increases the potency,"

She poured an assortment of colored berries and the mushrooms into a steel bowl.

"And these have a high concentration of a natural barbiturate. Just what we are going to need to get these guys talking."

She poured a nip of rum into the bowl and crushed the ingredients into a wet, green pulp. She wrapped the pulp in a piece of linen tea towel and squeezed out a slimy green liquid.

She pointed to Win and said, "Hey soldier-boy, time to have a little talk."

It took two hours for the crude truth serum to build up in Win's body. By late evening, the potion had reduced him to a blathering idiot. He told them everything they needed to know. Sentinel. The Miami meeting. The cartels. His mission to kidnap her and take the samples.

Willow looked out toward the tall crop of cannabis plants waving in the pale Queensland moonlight.

She marveled, "Faaark –the last cannabis crop on earth."

CHAPTER 70

VALERIA FLYS SOUTH.

Valeria Munoz had spent the last few days hunkered down in a private hanger at Basilan Airport in the Philippines.

The spotter they'd hired to monitor what was happening at the location of Willow's crop had been sending back a series of phone reports and images.

It had become clear that Win Zin had fucked up big time. The spotter reported that most of the team that went in with him were dead.

Valeria paced around the aircraft hanger. She was shouting angrily into her phone to her father back in Miami, "We have a lookout at the crop. That little fucker, Win, he air-dropped a Chinese tank in there, and a squad of goons. And he still got beaten!"

"Calm down Val," said Money. "We can't fix that. But this creates a big problem for us. They must have alerted everyone at the RAAF Base –and the local town. The police will be all over the place before we know it. Then nobody is getting that crop."

Valeria replied, "The spotter says there's been no police or military activity so far. He's been monitoring the police radio channel for us. I think we still have some time up our sleeve to do something ourselves. But we'll need to move fast."

"How far away from you is it?" her father asked.

"Too far," she answered. "I'm still up in the Philippines."

Valeria looked across the airport runways.

The RAAF C-130 Hercules still sat outside over at the Air Force base hangar.

The mechanics had worked into the night, finishing the repair job. It was 11-30 pm, and the airport was deserted. The plane's aircrew were playing poker around a large oil drum under a wing as the mechanics were packing their van to leave.

Valeria shouted to one of the mercenaries from her team, "Bring me the briefing notes on the crop location. And my laptop."

She spent the next hour learning everything she could about the operating procedures at Scherger RAAF Base.

***

Beneath the wing of the RAAF C-130, Flight Lieutenant John Cooper was on a winning streak.

The Aussie RAAF pilot reckoned he was $800 up from the game of poker. The two Flight Officers he was playing with grimaced at their cards. Cooper looked at his watch. "Time to wrap this up. Wheels up in six hours." As he scooped up his winnings, he said, "It's been a pleasure, gentlemen." He stood to stretch his back and stuffed the wad of cash into his pocket.

A beautiful, dark-haired woman stepped out of the shadows under the military plane.

She was wearing summer-weight army greens. The RAAF guys assumed she must be one of the Filipino 'local girls' who hung around the base, flirting with anyone that looked like a marriage prospect.

She was hot as hell.

Valeria sashayed over to Cooper and said, "You look like you are having a good night, Officer."

He looked at the thick wad of cash he'd won and teased, "I could be interested in a better one." She walked up close to him. Looked him in the eye and smiled demurely.

In a blur, she pulled a pistol from behind her back and placed it hard against his temple.

Valeria said, "I'm sorry, honey. We won't have time for that. You see, all of us will be taking a little flight down to Australia tonight."

Her Sinaloa cartel mercenaries stepped from the shadows. They pointed assault rifles at the two shocked Flight Officers.

"Everyone on the plane!" she shouted.

***

After paying a massive bribe to the late-shift Air Traffic Controller, the RAAF C-130 was airborne and on a direct flight-path to Scherger.

Lt Cooper, with a gun held to his head, had logged a flight plan straight down to the RAAF base at Townsville.

The route would take them directly over the top of Scherger, just before sunrise.

It suited Valeria's plans perfectly.

CHAPTER 71

THE WAKE-UP CALL.

Sgt Terry Delaney, the base commander at Scherger, was fast asleep at his home in Weipa when his mobile phone started ringing. It was around 3am.

He sleepily fumbled for the phone. The voice on the phone said, "Is this the Base Operations Manager for the Scherger RAAF base?" Delaney answered, "Yes, I'm Sergeant Terry Delaney. What do you want at this god-forsaken hour?"

The voice on the phone said, "I'm Flight Lieutenant John Cooper, I'm flying a C-130 from the Phils down to RAAF Townsville. We may have a problem with the hydraulic system on our landing gear. I'm requesting an emergency clearance to land at Scherger."

"How bad is it?" Delaney asked.

"We're not sure. We had mechanics working on it earlier today. Looks like we are leaking fluid. I'd rather get the plane on the ground before it becomes a big issue."

"How far out are you?" asked Delaney.

"About sixty minutes," replied Cooper.

Delaney did some mental arithmetic and then said, "OK –slow your approach if you can –I can be out at the base and have the runway activated in about forty-five minutes."

"Roger," said Cooper, "it will probably turn out to be a false alarm –but better safe than sorry."

Sgt Delaney jumped out of bed and pulled on his work clothes, then he raced out the front door into the night. He called Corporal Mandy Eysen once he got into his car.

"Mandy –I need you out at the base –pronto," he said. "We've got a RAAF C-130 inbound with an hydraulic problem. I'll need you to activate Air Traffic Control and the runway lights."

Minutes later, Eyesen was also driving toward the base.

Forty-five minutes later, the massive light array at Scherger switched on, flooding the main runway with lights. Eyesen bolted up the stairs to the Control Tower. She unlocked the door, stepped inside and started the sequence to activate the Air Traffic Control System. It slowly booted up.

Rex and Fatso barked at the bottom of the stairs.

Fifteen minutes later, the blinking lights of a RAAF C-130 came into view in the night sky.

The plane did a perfect touchdown and taxied toward the main apron. Sgt. Delaney breathed a sigh of relief.

***

About 1800 miles to the south, a warning panel activated on the screen of the main RAAF Air Traffic Control system at Amberley Air Force Base. It showed that the Air Traffic Control system at Scherger had just gone fully active.

The Duty Controller hit a button on his radio and said, "Mandy? Are you there?"

Mandy replied, "Hi Joe. We had an emergency access request from a Flight Lieutenant named John Cooper. A C-130 en route from the Phil's down to Townsville. Hydraulic issue. The plane just landed –and it's fine."

The Amberley Duty Controller checked his flight logs.

"Cooper –Yes," he confirmed, "Been held up in the Phils getting a repair done –oil seal. That's strange –we had them logged to leave the airport at Basilan at 6-30am. When you see the pilot, ask him to file a report."

"Heading over there now," said Mandy.

Back at in the Control Tower at Amberley, the Duty Controller logged the emergency landing issue into the system. This automatically generated a message and texted it to the Command Centre at the base.

The RAAF Junior Duty Officer at the Command Centre got the message. He turned to his Senior Officer and said, "Scherger's gone active. Emergency access request. C-130 with hydraulic issues. Landed OK. Should we wake anyone up?"

"Are you kidding?" he said, "It's 3am. I'm not waking anyone up unless World War Three has begun. It can wait until the morning shift."

Sergeant Delaney and Corporal Eyesen yawned as they walked over to the parked C-130. Its engines slowly wound down. Rex and Fatso followed behind, their tails wagging excitedly.

Delaney waited patiently as the rear cargo ramp of the plane slowly lowered to the ground.

As the ramp hit the red dust, the interior lights of the plane flickered on, and they found themselves staring at a squad of Sinaloa cartel mercenaries holding assault rifles.

Valeria's elite unit took control of Scherger in no time at all.

Before heading over toward the crop, they forced Cooper to park the C-130 in the middle of the runway, then they shot out all of its tires, so it completely blocked the tarmac.

Valeria knew they would be leaving on the submarine that would be now waiting in the river near the crop. She didn't want the RAAF landing any troops at the base to chase them as they escaped in the narco-sub.

After tying up the airmen and the base staff, Valeria locked them into a storage container, she took a jeep and a massive BushMaster and headed toward the base exit.

CHAPTER 72

VALERIA ATTACKS.

Valeria knew she was running out of time. She crashed straight through the front gates at Cannacom and drove straight down towards the back fence.

The massive BushMaster rolled straight through the perimeter fence and easily crashed through the thick Briar. The jeep followed its path of destruction. They made a beeline toward the GPS location for the crop. She halted about a mile from the crop site to launch the final assault. Her team rolled out of the stolen BushMaster and prepared to move towards the crop on foot.

Valeria pulled out her satellite phone and placed a call to Captain Gunawan on the narco-sub. She was relieved to find that he had arrived.

"We are beginning the extraction operation now," she said. She looked at the GPS map on her laptop and added, "You should move up the Embley

River to its furthest navigable point. Then send me the coordinates to meet up with you."

Valeria and her small team exited the vehicles, formed up, and moved off through the trees as the first rays of sunlight appeared in the morning sky.

She was completely unaware that the captain of the sub had sold her out.

***

Willow and the guys were sleeping in their tents beside the sheds at the crop when Valeria's attack began.

Fortunately, Caz had remained awake near the Win and the SSA prisoners. He has just walked to a bush clearing nearby to take a piss when he saw the gunmen approaching. He ran back toward the sheds and let out a shout. Then all hell broke loose.

Bullets and flashes of tracer rounds came from every direction. Everyone scrambled out and ran for cover, as the shots ripped through the walls of the makeshift sheds like tissue paper.

Freddie yelled, "There's nowhere safe. Get to the tank. I can't even see where the shots are coming from. It feels like they're all around us."

They all ran for the Chinese tank and threw themselves inside. Caz fired up the beast's engines.

Freddie took control of the tank's mounted gun and fired randomly, back in the direction the shots were coming from. The attackers stopped shooting for a moment.

Willow shouted, "We can't stay here! Let's head down to the river. To the old power station. We might get out that way."

The amphibious tank lurched off toward the river, rifle shots clanking off its steel-plated exterior.

BOOM!

An RPG round fired from the direction of the sheds. Caz veered the tank to the right, taking out several trees.

The round whizzed past, missing them by inches. It smashed into the parked Banger and blew it into tiny pieces.

***

Back in the sheds, Valeria pressed the button on her throat mic.

She whispered, "Hold up. It looks like they are heading for the river. Just where we want them to go. Let's push them toward the sub. We'll come back for the plant samples after we capture the woman."

Valeria was leaving when she heard muffled voices at the rear of one of the sheds. She found Win's squad cable-tied to the support posts.

Win was rolling around in the dirt near a campfire, still off-his-face on the psychedelic truth serum Willow had force-fed him. His eyes rolled back in his head as Valeria approached. She pulled him to his feet. Dazed, Win tried to focus on her face.

"What's down near the river?" she asked Win.

"The moooooon in the sky–" he garbled incoherently, lisping through his missing front teeth.

"What's down near the river?" she asked again.

"The biiiiig crocodiles–" he garbled again, then laughed out of control.

She threw Win to the ground, "Useless –as always," she said.

Valaria took out her satellite phone and took a short video of Win rolling around in the dirt and talking gibberish.

She attached the video to an email to her father, back in Miami, reading; "The adults are taking over this mission. Exfil via sub as planned."

In an act of sheer spite, she also forwarded a copy of the video to Radovan and U-Chin.

Following a silent hand-signal, Valeria's kill squad formed up and moved forward toward the river.

CHAPTER 73

A Political Nightmare.

Crensch's jet had just arrived at RAAF Tindal Air Force base, about 1,000 miles to the west of Weipa.

His phone chirped. A message on his phone screen read:

'SORRY FOR LATENESS. THIS WAS JUST INTERCEPTED FROM U-CHIN's PHONE.'

The video of Win Zin that Valeria had sent to her father was attached. He watched the video of Win Zin rolling around in the dirt next to the cannabis crop. It was followed by a shot of Valeria laughing. Crensch could see several well-armed Latino mercenaries standing around her.

He passed his phone to the Ambassador Blagg and said, "The Sinaloa cartel has arrived at the crop location. I think this problem just went global. The woman you can see in the video is Valeria Munoz, their leading military operative."

***

A few hours later, Crensch convened a meeting at Tindal.

Colonel Billy Blagg had flown in from Amberley overnight to join his father and a small group of military specialists.

Crensch showed them all the video of Valeria and Win, then the message she'd sent to her father.

Billy rubbed his eyes in dismay and said, "So this means that we have a Burmese SSA squad, and a Sinaloa cartel kill team, active on Australian soil? Right now? Right next to one of our bases?"

"Yes," replied Crensch. "We've received some new satellite images from yesterday afternoon, and it looks like a battle has taken place. There are several bodies in the fields. We have no idea why this action has taken place or what their motives are. Currently, we can only link it to a secret meeting that took place in my Miami that was attended by the heads of the biggest global drug cartels."

He paused and pulled up a picture of Willow on the screen in the room. Then he continued,

"And we know that, for some reason, one of their objectives is to kidnap a scientist from the local commercial cannabis farm. If you look closely at the satellite images, the other thing you'll notice is that this crop is alive. And there aren't many living crops of cannabis on the planet today."

The Ambassador said, "It's a bloody political nightmare."

"Well –it's your local jurisdiction," said Crensch. "How do you want to proceed from here?"

The Ambassador thought for a while and then said, "I think all three of us have to spend today kicking this up the tree with our respective governments for feedback, before we can do anything. I can cover Defence and the PM. Crensch –you'll need to cover your US counterparts."

He looked over at Billy and said, "And there's the bigger question of how two drug cartels got mercenary forces and equipment on the ground here without anyone knowing."

Crensch pondered that thought.

"The message I'm getting from the US government is clear. They want the crop, and the scientist, as much as the cartels do. The death of the cannabis crops is destabilizing global economies and friendly governments. This crop will play an essential role in getting things back under control. That's my priority, Jason."

Ambassador Blagg said, "I think the Australian Government would concur with that. But the drug trade is a hot topic locally right now. I'd need to clear it with several departments and get a formal PR response ready."

Crensch looked over at Billy and said, "You have a base near the crop location. What assets, or intel, can you provide to go after Valeria on the ground?"

Billy said, "It's a remote bare base. We only use it for training exercises. The last time I looked it was staffed by three servicemen and a couple of dogs. We've tried to raise the base, but its hours of operation are limited, so the base servicemen aren't an option for us."

Billy stood and poured himself another coffee and said, "I've checked with Command at Amberley and there are no local incident reports yet. This isn't in the media. Yet. The area around the crop is completely hemmed in by the Air Force base, the cannabis farm, and a river full of massive crocodiles. That should keep the locals out of the area."

Crensch said, "We need to get some local eyes on the crop location. We can't just send a response force straight into town. The media would be all over it."

The three of them pondered for a minute.

"Maybe we could arrange for someone from Tindal to do a fly-past in a jet tomorrow?" the Ambassador suggested, "To do a simple recce for us. Something low key?"

Billy said, "We could send a single F35 over for a recce. Scherger is around 1,000 miles away. It would take an hour of flying time, but that would put an F35 jet at the limit of its combat radius. You'd get about fifteen minutes over the location, then it would have to head back home, or land and refuel at Scherger."

Crensch and the Ambassador nodded. Options were scarce right now.

"Let's do it," they agreed.

CHAPTER 74

McVee.

There was a section of river above the wide concrete spillway at the old Embley River hydro station. It was 'Crocodile Central'.

Over the decades, the waterway spawned a new sanctuary for fish, crabs, pigs and bird life. All perfect 'snacks' for the saltwater crocodiles that had moved in.

'McVee' was born in 1942, the same year the Embley Power Station was buried in mud.

He was a tiny baby croc with distinctive dark V-shaped scales along his spine. It made him stand out from the rest. Over the next seventy-five years, McVee grew into a 2,000 lb, twenty-foot-long killing machine. A fine example of the world's largest living reptile.

Freddie had given the ancient croc his nickname, after McVee had almost made him shit his pants.

He'd been walking across the lip of the wide concrete spillway that ran beside the main hydro buildings, holding the water back from the river above. A thin veneer of water constantly ran down over its wide, slimy surface. Freddie was halfway across when the massive croc, looking for an easy lunch, silently launched itself from beneath the water.

Rather than latching onto one of Freddie's legs, McVee missed.

The aging leviathan had smashed into him with its stubby nose, sending Freddie on a terrifying slide down three hundred feet of wet, moss-covered concrete and into a shallow pool filled with jagged rocks.

As the aging McVee sank back into the water, his 'wife', a diminutive Salty just seven feet long, growled and chirped at him.

CHAPTER 75

BALLET AT THE POWER STATION.

C az maneuvered the Chinese-built tank, as best he could, down toward the old power station on the river.

In his panic, he wasn't really steering the beast. He was just smashing through trees and crashing over rocks. It was slow-going at times, resulting in a hail of bullets from behind whenever Valeria's team got back within firing distance of them.

"We're going to need to do the last bit on foot," Caz shouted. "They'll catch up to us at this rate!"

Caz killed the engine and said, "Everyone out. Follow me! Maybe we can get some cover down at the old power station. It's going to be too dangerous if we just stay on the riverbank."

They all leapt from the tank, grabbing the assault rifles and ammo clips they'd taken from Win's squad. Jen opted not to take a gun. She'd never shot one before. Instead, she shouldered the remaining Chinese rocket launcher. It was surprisingly light.

The massive sloping slipway of the old Embley River Hydro Station loomed into view.

As they arrived at the Hydro main buildings, they heard five or six shots from down the hill. Valeria must have found the tank. This meant that she wouldn't be far behind.

It was easy to get inside the power station.

The brackish water from the river had rusted out the metal windows and doors decades earlier. A couple of giant mangrove trees had taken root inside the main building, pushing thick branches out of the upper windows and punching massive holes through the rusty corrugated tin roof. As they stepped inside the cavernous concrete pumping room, birds scattered from around the giant sets of rusting turbines.

"We need to get right up to the back of the room," shouted Willow. "Maybe there will be somewhere we can hide."

Freddie pointed to a set of rusting stairs and metal gantries leading up to a Control Room. "Up there might be good," he said. "Let's try to take some high ground."

They all scampered past the rustic turbines and up the creaking stairs. Shu moved slowly, trying not to aggravate her painful shoulder wound.

As they crossed the lowest gantry, the rusted mesh floor gave way. Jen screamed as she crashed down onto a machine below. Jez grabbed her arm and pulled her back up to safety. The rusted metal ripped a gash in her leg.

After climbing four sets of stairs, they collapsed, panting, into the safety of a small upper room.

Jez pulled a First Aid kit out of his webbing. Jen bit her lip as he cleaned her bleeding leg.

Caz and Freddie crouched by a window, looking down into the cavernous hydro pumping room below. Willow joined them, swatting a bee away from her face.

They watched as Valeria's team prepared to enter the room. Her team were true professionals. It was like watching a masterclass in urban assault.

A hail of percussion grenades came in through the windows, followed by a series of deafening explosions that echoed around the cavernous building.

Valeria's team expertly entered and 'sliced the pie', making small, well-practiced moves as they cleared the shallow and deep angles between the massive power turbines in the room, ready to fire at any resistance. The squad of trained Latino killers progressed, like a well-rehearsed troop of ballet dancers, methodically moving closer and closer toward the stairs at the back of the room.

Caz turned to Freddie and said, "Mate. We are going to die in here."

THE GRATE ESCAPE.

Caz and Freddie quietly backed away from the Control Room window. They searched around in the dim light in the back of the room. There were no exit doors.

On one side of the Control Room there was a large metal grate securing the entry to a long dark cave. Two massive water pipes, each ten feet across, snaked into the cave and disappeared into the blackness. There was a tiny crawl space between the pipes.

"These must be the main water pipes coming down from the top of the dam," said Freddie.

Caz called out from the other corner of the dark room.

"There's another grate over here. Much smaller. Looks like it covers a rubbish chute. It's dark inside. I can't see much –but it might go outside."

He pulled on the rusted grate and it easily lifted free of the bolts that once held it in place.

Freddie started looking around the room for something to jimmy open the lock on the grate to the big tunnel holding the water pipes.

Caz went back over to join Willow at the Control Room window.

Jen stifled a squeal as Jez pulled a shard of rusted metal from her wound. Shu grabbed a sachet of antiseptic powder from her first aid kit and sprinkled it on the cuts. Across the room from them, Freddie had found an old crowbar and was forcing open the heavy access grate over the large water pipe tunnel.

Caz and Willow peered down into the pumping room, deep in thought.

Valeria's squad had almost reached the stairs. Caz pulled out his rifle and took aim below.

He turned to Willow and said, "This isn't going to last long –is it?"

Willow turned back to him and smiled.

"I have an idea that might buy us some time," she whispered, "but you all need to move right to the back of the room. As far back as you can get."

Caz crept back over to Jez and Jen and said, "Follow me." He edged over toward the rubbish chute he'd opened. Jez helped Jen limp over to it. Caz called out to Freddie, "Oy –there might be an exit here. Let's go."

Freddie called back, "Nah, I might try going up this way, toward the top of the dam. Might give you some over-watch if you manage to get back outside from here."

Caz looked at the black, gaping mouth of the pipe tunnel and said, "You're a braver man than I am, Gunga-Din. See you outside."

Freddie flicked on a torch, then grabbed the remaining Chinese rocket launcher and his rifle. He disappeared into the pitch blackness between the massive water pipes.

Back at the Control Room window, Willow checked the rifle she'd taken from one of the SSA soldiers. She silently pushed the barrel of the rifle out of the window opening, then braced against the window frame to steady her body. She peered through the large sight mounted on the gun and slowly exhaled.

A massive wasp nest hung from one of the mangrove tree branches growing inside the room. A large cloud of busy wasps swirled around the sunlit hole in the roof next to the nest. Willow centred a red laser dot on the limb it was hanging from.

Willow took two quick shots, then quickly pulled herself back inside the window frame.

Valeria's team instantly looked up, and their guns rained fire on the window. Willow hit the floor as ricochets bounced around the walls of the room. Below, she could hear the sound of feet running toward the bottom of the stairs.

The dark brown wasp nest swung back and forth like a pendulum, with only a thin string of bark securing it to the branch. Gravity gradually took hold. The heavy nest plummeted toward the floor of the pumping room, releasing thousands of angry wasps.

Valeria's squad beat a hasty retreat from the lower floor as the angry swarm spread across the room.

Willow joined Caz and the others at the back of the Control Room.

They stood at the rubbish chute leading out of the room. It was about six feet wide and very steep. They had no idea where the chute went, it just disappeared into pitch blackness. They considered their options. Shu tried to contact Freddie on her radio, but the concrete walls had killed any chance of a signal getting through to him.

Two minutes later, a swarm of bats flew out of the tunnel Freddie had disappeared into.

"Jesus!" said Caz. "It looks like he might have found some friends in there." A storm of tiny black bats swirled in a panic as the angry cloud of wasps rose from the pumping room and slowly crept through the Control Room windows and door.

Time to go.

Caz jumped into the rubbish chute first. Then Willow. Then Shu, grasping her bloody shoulder.

Finally, Jen and Jez slid down the chute in tandem. They screamed as they slid through the darkness for about thirty feet, before spilling out the side of the building onto an old heap of coal and debris.

They were back outside, halfway up one side of the spillway.

Next to the heap of debris, there was a derelict wooden platform. It held a rickety old miners trolley cart with small metal wheels.

The trolley was sitting on a steep set of thin, warped iron rails running back down the hill next to the main building. During the construction, the long-abandoned rail line had been used to remove waste. The trolley car hadn't moved an inch in more than seventy years.

Jen winced as a bullet ricocheted off the concrete wall beside her. They instinctively ducked down. Caz and Willow crept to the edge of the heap.

They saw Valeria and her squad working their way up a long set of narrow concrete stairs along the outside edge of the dam's steeply sloping spillway. One member of Valeria's unit had separated from the others. He'd taken a higher sniper position nearby, to take potshots at them if they moved.

They were pinned down by the sniper as Valeria's kill squad climbed closer.

Valeria's sniper suddenly ducked down. Several shots rang out from a higher position on the opposite side of the spillway. Freddie was returning fire from on top of the dam. He peered through the sight on his rifle, patiently waiting for the sniper below to make a move.

He saw the guy move out from behind a wall and took his shot.

CLICK. Nothing happened. Freddie pulled the magazine from his rifle. It was empty.

He pulled out his field radio, "Shu –you guys OK down there?"

"We're pinned down," said Shu. "it's only a matter of time before they get all the way up to us."

Freddie looked across the skinny top edge of the dam spillway wall. He remembered what happened with the crocodile the last time he tried to walk across it. McVee and his crocodile friends hung out in the still water just on the edge of the lip.

Freddie wasn't keen to try crossing that again.

He only had one option left.

Freddie took the Chinese rocket launcher out of its canvas carry bag. He figured he could take out the sniper with it. Crude but effective. However, that would only delay the inevitable as Valeria's team climbed up the spillway stairs. *Fuck!*

He looked across at the giant spillway gear mechanism. It was held in place by a massive steel cable that moved the top section of the dam up and down. Freddie figured that the dam was currently in the 'Up' position.

He picked up the field radio and said, "Shu –is there any way you can get off that dam wall? Pronto!"

On the opposite side of the dam, Shu looked at the trolley.

"It would take us ages to pick our way through the rubbish up here. Jen can hardly walk. There is a trolley, and an old busted up railway line. It leads down –away from the spillway," she replied, "but it looks like a suicide mission to me. I'm not sure it will even move."

Freddie said, "Well, from my position here, they'll reach you in a few minutes, and you're going to be dead then, anyway. You need to get out of there. I'm out of ammo. I have trick up my sleeve –but you need to get right away from the spillway."

Shu said, "OK mate –we'll make the move. Can you create a distraction to get that sniper off our asses?"

"Don't worry Shuey," Freddie said, "In a couple of moments, there's going to be more distractions than you can imagine. Get that trolley moving now."

Freddie raised the Chinese rocket launcher and took aim at the steel cable connecting the spillway mechanism to the dam wall.

BOOM.

He scored a direct hit. The thick, rusted steel cable at the top of the dam frayed and the cogs on the spillway mechanism shuddered. But it held in place.

"Damn!" said Freddie. He looked down at Valeria's kill squad. They'd paused when the explosion rang out, but they were now moving again.

He looked at the thin edge of the slipway and considered the risk of being attacked by a lurking crocodile.

The top of the spillway groaned. The massive cogs securing the top of the spillway juddered and slipped again.

A cloud of rust billowed from the ruptured cable, and then it snapped with a loud BANG. The giant cogs slowly rotated, and the spillway top slowly began to lower.

A cascade of water tumbled over the edge and grew larger by the second, quickly becoming a deadly waterfall.

***

When the explosion rumbled out from the top of the dam, Willow and the guys made their move.

They ran over to the trolley and jumped onboard. Shu disengaged the brake lever. Nothing happened. It was rusted in place.

Willow, Freddie and Jez leapt back out to see what was stopping it. The old trolley creaked as they pushed hard, trying to get it moving. Jen was standing inside holding a bandage on her bloody leg. She ducked down as new shots from the sniper peppered the roof.

The trolley slowly edged forward as more shots dug into its thick wooden sides. As it gained momentum, they all jumped back inside and held on for dear life.

The relief of moving away from the spillway turned into horror as Shu shouted, "The brakes aren't working!"

The trolley careened down the steep slope out of control, jumping and bouncing along the old, warped rails.

Above them, the top of the spillway had only dropped a little, but that was enough to send millions of gallons of water and floating logs crashing down, as the billabong behind it rapidly drained. The powerful wall of water from the dam took out the rubbish heap they had been standing on. It obliterated the wooden platform at the top of the trolley car line. Then it slowly ripped the rail tracks off the side of the hill.

The wooden trolley ground to a halt on an incline at the end of the old rail line. Just in time.

They leaped out and scrambled up a hill.

Moments later, the massive wall of water and debris smashed past them, missing them by a few feet, destroying everything in its path.

CHAPTER 77

CROCODILE TEARS.

Valeria's team weren't so lucky when the massive wall of water cascaded over the spillway.

Her elite team was smashed by the initial rush of water, debris and massive logs, killing most of them instantly and eventually drowning the rest.

Just as the wall of water hit, Valeria managed to swing up above the waterline. She desperately clung onto an old piece of railing bolted above the stairway, her rifle hanging from her shoulder.

The rushing water tried to suck her down the slope, but Valeria was strong. She managed to dangle from the railing for several minutes. The rusty old pipework cut deeply into her hands. As the initial rush of water slowed, gravity took its toll on her. She had to let go of the rail and take her chances in the flood below.

She was pulled, flailing, down the spillway. As she rolled and slid downwards, the wall of water became more shallow. It was fast, but now only inches deep. Large fish and mud crabs flailed around her when she reached the bottom.

Valeria staggered to her feet, steadied herself, and checked her rifle. She was bruised and battered and she could barely walk on her left ankle.

She limped her way through the water and tree branches at the bottom of the slipway, amazed that she'd survived. She was halfway across when she noticed some movement up at the top of the dam. Several long dark shapes bobbed up and down at the edge of the wall of water overflowing the top of the dam. Some slowly started to roll over the edge. Tumbling down toward her. She braced for falling logs.

But the long dark shapes weren't logs.

It was an avalanche of angry, threshing saltwater crocodiles, sliding out-of-control down toward her.

***

McVee and his crocodile brethren had been slowly dragged toward the edge of the spillway wall, as the water from their billabong home had rushed over it.

They swam hard against the force, but their stubby legs were no help. The crocs were built for fast attacks, not endurance swimming. As the flood of water was drawn over the lip of the spillway, the crocs in the water behind it were pulled inextricably forward. They kicked and threshed, fighting the steady drag of the water's flow. Gravity eventually won, and they tumbled over the concrete lip.

McVee's 2,000 lb mass slid down the slimy concrete spillway slope, taking a beating as it rolled over and over down the hard, wet concrete slope.

Mrs. McVee followed close behind him.

At the bottom of the steep spillway, the water leveled out and slowed. The massive crocodiles both came to a slow halt as their legs finally gained traction.

Mrs. McVee surfaced next to Valeria, who was standing knee-deep in the slow-moving water, holding her rifle.

McVee roared in horror as the woman took a shot. The skull of his seventy-year-old wife exploded.

He lashed his tail to move forward to strike Valeria, but the flow of the slow-moving water was too strong. It pressed against McVee's aging bulk, inevitably dragging him slowly downstream.

The giant croc eyeballed the woman holding the rifle as he helplessly floated away.

INACTION.

Over at RAAF Tindal Base, Crensch and the Ambassador were desperate to get boots on the ground over at Weipa. Things weren't moving as fast as everyone wanted. Politics were getting in the way of progress.

Crensch and Billy had agreed that the recce flight was the best immediate course of action, given the potential for a political backlash. They'd also agreed to keep the events unfolding away from the local police and Weipa Airport. They'd logged the F35 recce flight as an 'engine test'. A fighter pilot had been briefed. Her jet was waiting on the runway, ready to scramble for the sixty-minute flight over to Scherger. It was fully loaded with fuel, but with weapons kept to the minimum to reduce weight.

***

Colonel Billy Blagg walked out on the tarmac and joined the pilot for her pre-flight walk-around.

Billy said, "It's important we keep a lid on the real purpose of this flight. At least for now. There are only four people on this base who know what's going down near Scherger right now."

The pilot said, "My fuel load will allow me to fly over to Scherger –do a quick recce –and return. Only fifteen to thirty minutes above the location. If I need to stay longer, I will have to drop into Scherger to refuel –or Weipa Airport if that's a problem."

Billy said, "We'll have to cross that bridge when we come to it. We still don't have any communication with Scherger. An unannounced call into Weipa Airport by an F35 would set off a PR shit-storm."

***

Back in Tindal's Situation Room, Ambassador Jason Blagg was stalling for time.

"We can't make a quick call on this," he said. "My request has to be pushed all the way up to the PM for sign off, and I have counterparts in the US I have to inform. We have two foreign aggressors on Australian soil. That's the first time in our history. The potential for this story to blow up is huge."

Crensch said, "We need to find out the situation over there. If the local media or police get wind of what's happening, it could get really ugly. These cartels won't mess around, they'll just kill any local responders that get in the way."

Eventually, they were forced to accept that nothing was likely to happen immediately.

They sent a message to the pilot to stand down for now.

Billy contacted the Superintendent of the Weipa Police District. He asked him to send a police car out to Scherger.

The Cop told him they had their hands full manning the road closures for the annual Weipa Running Festival. After talking to Weipa's mayor, the Cop politely told him to push the matter upstairs in Brisbane. It was his subtle way of telling Billy to 'fuck off'.

Communications with Scherger were still non-existent.

CHAPTER 79

WILLOW'S BURNING ISSUE.

Down near the hydro station, Willow lay exhausted on the back deck of the Chinese tank. They were waiting for Freddie. If he was still alive.

After surviving the spillway flood, it took hours to make it back. They'd had to pick their way through thick bush and a jumble of muddy flood debris. Jen was limping badly from the gash on her leg by the time they arrived.

Freddie arrived an hour later. He'd worked his way across the top dam when the flood subsided and then followed them down.

Shu was relieved to see him. Her field radio had been smashed on the wild trolley ride down the side of the hill.

Caz fired up the tank to return to the crop.

"I hope that was the last of them." Caz said, "We lost all of our weapons in the flood. If there's any more of them, all we have is this tank's 50 cal gun and its smoke grenades. We don't even have a bog standard rifle left."

The tank clanked slowly back up the hill. They were all beaten and tired from the past two days' ordeals.

Jez said, "I need to take Jen to Weipa hospital once we get back. The wound's not too deep but there was a lot of rusty metal in it. She's going to need a tetanus shot at the least –maybe stitches."

Willow said, "Take one of the ATVs. That will get you back through the Briar the quickest. Then take my car. It's parked up in the farm carpark."

Jen asked, "Should we say anything at all about what's been going on out here?" Willow thought for a moment.

"Say nothing for now," she said. "I'm sure you can come up with ten good reasons for the cut on your leg."

When they got back to the crop, Jen and Jez left for the hospital.

It was quiet around the sheds. They found that Win Zin and his surviving mercenaries had managed to cut their ties and had disappeared like ghosts.

Everyone was too tired to do any packing that afternoon, so they double-checked to make sure Win was gone and then re-lit the campfire. Caz cooked some of the canned food they had left. Freddie cracked open their last remaining bottle of the rum.

***

Willow sat alone, well into her second big glass of rum. She leaned back in a log and gazed up at the star-filled night sky.

The events of the last 24 hours had been insane. They'd come so close to being killed. Several times. All over a stupid crop. All because of her vanity. She thought about Tezz. What would he want her to do? Then she started to cry.

How had her life become so fucked up?

Freddie, Caz and Shu walked over and sat next to her.

"I think I've made a decision about something important," Willow said. "Tomorrow morning, we are going to burn the whole crop."

CHAPTER 80

THE NIGHT OF THE BANDIDOS.

Kip Norman, the CEO of Cannacom, tossed and turned on the cheap mattress at Weipa's three star Albatross Bay Resort.

The place was crap, but it was also the best place money could buy in town. It was 10pm in Weipa and Kip was missing his luxury home on the waterfront in Sydney's Double Bay.

Kip had flown up to Weipa to handle the 'media optics' of the situation. Out at the Cannacom farm, fifty acres of prime cannabis plants lay wilted and dead from HLVd+. The shareholders were screaming as the share price tanked, and then Cannacom ceased trading.

The business was, in a word, 'fucked'.

He'd just managed to get back to sleep when the noise of a large low-flying plane woke him up. *'Who the fuck is landing a plane at this hour of the night,'* Kip thought.

***

Radovan's heavily laden CONVAIR CV-580 cargo plane landed at the Weipa Airport on the other side of town. It was just before 11pm. The flight had taken seven hours. Longer than expected.

It was an uncomfortable flight. Rad and the Bandido bikies could barely fit around the large wooden crates that had been crammed onto the plane. Weipa Airport operated around the clock, but the last passenger flight arrival was late afternoon. Hours earlier, the airport's security personnel had packed up and gone home for the day.

The airport was quiet as the cargo plane came to a halt. The pilot had logged the flight as a private hire for a luxury fishing trip, so it raised no suspicion.

The streets of Weipa were quiet. Most of the townsfolk were either at home, or in the pubs, preparing for the Weipa Running Festival the next morning; the biggest social event on the town's annual calendar. The mines had declared an unofficial public holiday for both days of the weekend.

The pilot had parked the cargo plane near a small rent-by-the-day hangar in a dimly lit part of the airport's commercial operations area. Two forklifts were waiting by the hangar's doors. The cargo plane lowered its small rear deck.

"OK," yelled Zoran, "let's get the big crates off first. They need to be inside in case someone decides to get nosey." Two of the gang members started the forklifts and headed for the plane.

Radovan walked over to the hangar. The small side door was unlocked, as expected. He walked in and flicked on the lights. Several large tungsten bulbs lit up its stark concrete and steel interior. Zoran slid one of the main hangar doors open and the forklifts began to unload the gear from the plane.

"Hurry!" Zoran yelled. The heavy boxes from the plane were crammed with weapons, tools and ammunition.

There were four large crates already sitting in the hangar. They'd been delivered the day prior. Zoran and Dragan jimmied the four big wooden crates open. Inside, they found four sleek, black Polaris General XP 1000 Sport AWD ATVs. A 44-gallon drum of petrol stood beside them. Dragan filled each of them with fuel.

Rad walked over to some large blue boxes from the plane.

"Is this the boat?" he asked.

"Yes," Zoran said, "It's an inflatable, with an electric motor. To keep the noise down. We'll drop it down near McKenzie's Dock before dawn, then use it to rendezvous with the sub in the estuary."

"Perfect," Rad said.

"You sure the guy on the sub isn't going to fuck you over?" Zoran asked.

"He's got more than a million reasons not to," Rad replied.

Everything was ready in the hangar by 2am.

They'd unpacked and prepared four black ATVs, the small boat and an array of exotic weapons.

They drank coffee and played Ulcer Rummy, a Serbian card game, to kill some time as sunrise approached.

CHAPTER 81

X Marks The Spot.

The first glimmer of light appeared in the sky at the airport hangar. Radovan had enjoyed wiping the floor with Zoran and his bikie mates playing the games of Ulcer. They had been away from the home country too long, Rad hoped their fighting skills weren't as rusty as their game playing.

They lifted the inflatable boat onto a small trailer attached to one of the ATVs, then the convoy of four ATVs headed for the river in the darkness. Their destination was McKenzie's Dock, a small pier and boat-ramp miles up the Embley estuary. Soon after, Rad and Zoran were heading up the river in the inflatable boat.

Rad was nervous. He was about to find out if Ismail Gunawan, the narco-sub's captain, was true to his word, or if he had taken the $1,200,000 and done a runner with it.

It was still dark when they took a left branch in the river. Rad breathed a sigh of relief when the sub came into view out of the morning fog on the river. The captain stood on the deck brandishing a machine gun. They tethered the boat to the deck of the sub and Rad stepped onboard.

"Morning –," said the captain. "This fog will be helpful, but it will burn off over the next few hours."

Rad cut through the small-talk. Time was short. "Have you been up to the crop location?"

The captain nodded and said, "Yes. We spent some time finding a way to get up there along the riverside, rather than using the main roads. There was a lot of gunfire up there yesterday. Not from the crop, but from some old buildings down near to the river. At an old power station. Valeria was there."

Rad looked surprised.

"Did she secure the crop and the people?" Rad said.

"No. There was a lot of shooting, then the spillway of the power station collapsed. Valeria and her team must have been on it. There was a big flood. I think they're all dead. We found several Latino bodies in military uniforms floating in the river," the captain said.

Rad looked confused.

"What happened to the others? The Aboriginal scientist?" Rad asked, "Were they killed too?"

Ismail shrugged and said, "We don't know. The guy we sent up there to observe said they were on the other side of the buildings. I think the flood hit them too. Who knows?"

The captain handed Rad a hand-drawn map and said, "Follow this path beside the river for three miles. That will get you to the crop location."

He pointed to an 'X' on the map and said, "We will meet you at this point when you radio us for the extraction. At a dock called McKenzie's. We can moor there but the water is very shallow. We will need to go a long way back up toward the town before we can get the sub underwater and up to full speed."

Rad said, "We've just come from that dock. We know it well." He shook the captain's hand and stepped back onto the small boat.

"If all goes well, we should be back at the jetty with the woman and the plants –in about two hours," Rad said.

Ismail looked at his watch and said, "Be quick. It's the weekend, so the main docks in the town will be deserted. But I'd like to get out of here before the town really wakes up. We don't want to end up with a Navy patrol boat on our tail as we head back up to Indonesia."

Rad cast off from the sub and waved farewell. Zoran drove the inflatable boat back downriver to the waiting bikies. They hid the inflatable amongst some rocks, then the four black ATVs rumbled alongside the river banks and back roads, their powerful headlights lighting the skinny tracks ahead. Zoran took the lead. His ATVs' fat, knobby tires made easy work of the dirt and mud.

Zoran suddenly pulled to a halt. The others stopped behind him. He pointed ahead, up through the trees. A thin column of smoke was visible in the pre-dawn light. It rose through the tree line about a mile ahead.

"Campfire," he said, "that must be them."

Rad said, "The Captain said there were five or six of them."

Zoran suggested, "Let's head up to higher ground so we can see what we have to deal with." They killed the headlights on the ATVs and slowly headed up hill. They parked when they reached a small rise that overlooked the crop.

Radovan used some binoculars to get a closer view.

To his horror, he saw four people standing next to a campfire. In the twilight, he could just make out that each was holding a long, flaming butane burner.

"Fuck!" Rad yelled, "Move out! They're going to burn the crop."

CHAPTER 82

THE BOTANIST WHO KILLED CANNABIS.

Willow had woken up just before the first glimmer of light appeared in the dawn sky.

She got the campfire started and put on a blackened kettle to boil some water for coffee. In the twilight, she gazed out over several thousand healthy cannabis plants. Willow almost felt that they were staring back at her. Accusingly. They were all about to burn.

The rest of the camp was slow to rise. They were all beaten and sore from the battle over at the Hydro Station.

Shu was the first to appear. She poured herself a coffee and then walked over to the first row of potted seedlings. She picked one up. It was a baby. Only ten inches tall.

"So – Wills – " Shu said, "Are you still going to do it?"

Willow just answered, "Hmmmm."

Shu lifted the seedling close to her face and coo'ed,

"Hey baby –you going to die today –how do you feel about that?"

She tickled the lower leaves of the tiny plant.

Willow said, "Oh –lay off it Shu –this is hard enough already." Shu sat down beside her. She blew the steam from her hot coffee mug.

They both stared deep into the glowing fire.

Willow said, "I keep wondering what Tezz would do. He was always good at helping me make the hard decisions. I miss him so much."

"Let's flip for it!" said Shu, trying to ease the pressure, "Heads, we burn it and get out of here –Tails, we keep it –and we all get arrested and spend a lot of time in jail."

Willow laughed and said, "The funny thing is I'm not so worried about the legal aspects. I'm more worried about the 'genocide' I might be committing. If I kill this last crop. I'd probably be causing the extinction of a whole plant species."

Shu furrowed her brow. Confused.

Willow rubbed her brow and said, "I'm a Botanist. From everything we've seen in the news reports, this could be the last living cannabis crop in earth. And I'm talking about potentially making a whole plant species extinct. That's not what I trained to do."

She rubbed her forehead and said, "If us Botanists had an Hippocratic Oath, I'm sure it wouldn't be; *I swear I will kill entire plant species.*"

Willow picked up a stick. She threw it into the campfire and said, "And there are millions of people who actually use this stuff for pain relief –Epilepsy –MS. That could all end today."

She gave Shu a guilty look and said, "I'm not sure I'm ready to go down in history as the Botanist who killed cannabis."

Freddie and Caz crawled out of their tents. They joined them beside the warmth of the fire. Freddie started dabbing antiseptic ointment on the many cuts he had on his legs and arms. They listened silently while Willow wrestled with her conscience.

Willow mused out loud, "Then –there's the other side of the coin. The global drug trade. Murder. Executions. Addiction. Gateway drugs. They killed my Tezz. I could help end all of that misery."

Caz added, "Yeah Wills –but that just leaves a world full of heroin, coke and pills. Not exactly nicey-nicey options. Give me plain old weed any day."

Willow had to concede he had a good point.

Willow walked over to one of the sheds. She came back holding four long butane-powered burners.

"I've always kept these here, in case of an emergency, just like this," she said. She lit each burner and handed them out.

They stopped and looked toward the Briar when they heard the rumble of vehicles approaching.

Headlights cross-crossed through the twilight in the scrub. Visitors!

Willow's decision was about to be taken out of her hands.

Chapter 83

Burn Baby Burn.

Freddie yelled, "Cops!"

Shu said, "No. I've been monitoring the local police radio band and there's been nothing other than chat about blocking the roads on the other side of town for the Running Festival."

Willow said, "We can't take any chances. Let's set the crop on fire and get the hell out of here." She pointed to the crop. "Spread out," she said. "Take a corner each and then work your way back along the edges until your are back here."

They were about to walk to the crop when the noise from the approaching vehicles suddenly stopped. A few moments later the headlights disappeared. They stood in silence as they heard the vehicles start again and drive up toward the top of the valley.

Willow shouted, "You three head toward the far corners of the crop! I'm going to set both of the sheds on fire down here first. Then I'll start on this corner myself."

Caz, Freddie and Shu raced off along the edges of the crop.

Willow emptied a can of petrol over the two makeshift sheds and set fire to them. Fire and smoke snaked into the dim morning sky.

She jumped into her 4WD to move it a safer distance away from the burning sheds.

One of the Bandidos came thundering alongside the crop on his ATV. He slowed to a crawl when he saw two sheds burning ahead, then pulled a shotgun from a gun rack on the vehicle.

He saw Willow sitting in her 4WD, took aim, and quickly fired two shots at her. Her passenger side window shattered. Willow gasped as several shotgun pellets tore into her shoulder.

The bikie reloaded and slowly rolled ahead along the track again, shotgun at the ready.

It didn't take the thug long to reach the burning sheds. He carefully exited the ATV and edged toward Willow's 4WD, pumping another couple of blasts into it for good measure.

Willow had jumped from her 4WD as soon as the window exploded. Her shirt was soaked red with a growing patch of blood. She edged along the far side of the vehicle, holding her bleeding shoulder, trying to see where the shot came from. She immediately saw the bikie on the ATV.

BOOM. Another window blew out beside her. She desperately looked around, trying to figure out what she could do.

Inside the vehicle, she saw her blowpipe in its carry case. She reached through a smashed window and grabbed it. Then she backed into the safety of the nearest trees. She hid behind a large gumtree, where she silently unpacked the blowpipe and assembled it.

PHHT. She sent a silent blow dart toward him. It missed by a mile. She moaned as the pain in her shoulder intensified. She pulled out a second blow dart and then steadied her shaking body for another shot.

BOOM. BOOM. The guy blasted two more shots into her 4WD as he carefully circled around it. He was very close now. He paused to reload.

PHHT. The second of Willow's darts hit him in the neck. He swatted the short, thin dart away, then fired two blasts randomly into the trees surrounding her. One shot narrowly missed her, ripping into some branches beside her. The second shotgun blast ripped through her heavy cotton pants and into her thigh.

The bikie crouched into a low defensive position as he reloaded again.

PFFT. The third of Willow's blow darts bounced harmlessly off one of his hard tactical knee pads.

PFFT. The next stuck into his thigh. He wiped the dart away, then edged forward toward her again. He rounded a tree and saw her crouching down, just feet away. He raised his shotgun to fire, but suddenly growled a low moan. He clutched at the tiny wound in his neck, as the poison from the Stinging Tree dart suddenly hit his bloodstream.

PFFT. Willow hobbled onto her knees and slammed her last dart into his shoulder. The bikie groaned deeply as the poison from the earlier dart in his leg took hold. He dropped to all fours, groaning in pain as the poison from the darts spread throughout his body.

He blindly fired two more blasts from the shotgun as he writhed in burning pain. Then he dropped his gun. He grabbed for his field radio, but it was too late. It fell out of his hand. He fell flat on the ground, convulsing uncontrollably.

Willow fell back to the ground and dropped the blowpipe. She grimaced from the pain in her shoulder and leg.

CHAPTER 84

SHITSVILLE.

Freddie clutched his burning butane torch as he walked toward the furthest corner of the crop.

Suddenly, a black ATV rounded a corner ahead of him. A Bandido gang member was at the wheel, driving fast. He steered the vehicle straight at Freddie, trying to run him down. Freddie jumped off the track. The vehicle missed him by inches.

He watched as the ATV continued for about 200 feet down the track, then slowly turned around. It sped back down the track toward him again. Freddie looked at the burner he was holding, then threw it aside. It would be useless against a ton of speeding metal.

"Shitsville," he muttered.

As the ATV thundered back toward him, he wrenched a tall wooden fencing post out of the sodden ground. He rammed the long post under his arm like a lance and raced straight toward the approaching vehicle. As the ATV bore down on him, he rammed the long pole into its open roll cage. It glanced off the Bandido's shoulder, forcing him to wrench the wheel sideways, sending the vehicle careening into the bush.

The driver braced for the impact as the ATV speared into a tree. It rolled onto its side, spilling weapons and several four-gallon plastic fuel containers across the ground. One container smashed into a rock and split open. The air quickly filled with the stench of petrol fumes.

The Bandido unclipped his harness and rolled out of the overturned vehicle. He caught his breath and grabbed a weapon from the rear of the carry tray.

The weapon looked like a scythe. It was about six-feet long, with a long wooden handle and a razor-sharp curved blade.

He walked back toward Freddie.

FREDDIES LAST STAND.

When the ATV crashed, Freddie hid, as best he could, amongst the cannabis plants. He saw the bikie angrily striding back down the path toward him.

The weapon the guy was carrying looked like something out of Game of Thrones. Freddie desperately looked around for something to fight with. The only thing that resembled a weapon was the thin steel butane burner he'd brought to set fire to the crop. He picked up the steel rod and turned the flame up as high as it would go. The ten-inch flame was far from intimidating.

The Bandido finally found him and they faced off like warriors, albeit in a very one-sided battle.

As Freddie sized up his chances against his opponent, he noticed the guy was wearing ornate heeled cowboy boots. Not exactly the best footwear for a day on the farm. Using this to his advantage, Freddie side-stepped, and entered deeper into the cannabis field. It was still thick with mud from the flooding the day prior. His feet sunk into the mud, but his work boots gave him a firm footing.

"Come and get it –!" Freddie goaded.

His opponent saw through the trick immediately. One by one, he kicked off his cowboy boots as he waved his weapon. Then he stepped into the mud barefoot.

Freddie used the chance to rush him. He bounded forward, slipping and sliding for traction. The Bandido flipped his weapon and slammed the long wooden handle into Freddie's gut. Freddie fell backwards into the mud. Winded. The bikie flipped the weapon back again and swung the razor sharp curved blade down toward Freddie's chest.

Freddie lifted the long steel rod of the burner to protect himself. The scythe-like blade glanced away, but the tip ripped a gash in his shoulder. He squirmed around in the mud in pain, but got back on his feet. He edged slowly back toward the track, waving the burner back and forth.

The Bandido bikie walked slowly toward him. Freddie edged further backwards down the track, holding the burner's thin rod between him and his attacker. Then he edged into the trees, to limit the amount that the guy could swing the long weapon. They 'danced' through the scrub, with the bikie taking swings and pokes with the curved blade.

Freddie parried back with the burner rod and stepped gingerly around trees and rocks to protect himself.

He almost tripped over when he stepped on one of the fuel containers at the ATV crash site. The smell of the recently spilled petrol filled his nostrils. The bikie swung the weapon again. It deflected off the steel rod but swung downward and the tip of the blade made a deep cut into Freddie's thigh. He dropped to his knees.

The Bandido moved in for the kill.

Freddie, sensing it was his last chance, threw the burner toward the spilled fuel around the crashed ATV. The scrub around both of them ignited into a rolling ball of blue flame. Freddie, being lower to the ground, took less of the blast.

The explosion knocked the Bandido off his feet. He desperately rolled around in a ball of flames as the explosion subsided. Disoriented, he stood and beat the flames off his leather jacket.

Freddie looked around, desperately searching for something to use as a weapon, but it was too late. The Bandido thrust his weapon forward. The point of the razor-sharp blade stopped inches from Freddie's throat.

He slowly raised his hands above his head.

The bikie pointed down the path toward the sheds, then jabbed Freddie hard in the shoulder.

"Get moving," he snarled, "Back down toward the sheds. Time to pay your friends a visit."

Freddie was out of options. He turned and walked.

CHAPTER 86

A GREEN LIGHT FOR THE RECCE.

The jet pilot finished her pre-flight walk-around of the gleaming F35A Lightning.

She did a last check of her flight suit and helmet, then walked toward the telescopic ladder, reaching up to the cockpit.

Major Crensch and Colonel Billy Blagg were waiting for her.

Blagg said, "Keep it cool and steady on the way over. The situation in Weipa is still being kept away from the media and local police. We've logged this flight as a simple engine test."

Crensch added, "All we want is a low-level reconnaissance flight over Scherger, and then over the crop location you have in your Nav system. Just report back what you see, then get back here."

Minutes later, the F35A stealth jet was racing toward Scherger, cruising at just over 1000 miles per hour.

Chapter 87

Big M Está Muerto.

After the encounter with McVee on the dam spillway, Valeria had struggled. She painfully made her way through the murky floodwaters below the dam all evening.

Her progress was slow because her ankle was twisted, maybe broken. After dragging her wounded leg over rocks and fallen trees for hours, she'd only travelled about a mile downriver.

Valeria had been trying to contact Captain Gunawan on the sub, but her cell phone had no signal. She'd lost her satellite phone during the flood.

Just before dawn, she'd decided she was never going to make it right down to the river. Exhausted, she lay in the mud under a mangrove tree and considered her options.

Valeria looked at her cell phone. She'd traveled far enough that it was now showing two bars of signal. She tried to call Gunawan, but the call was unanswered.

She checked her email. There was an urgent message from her father;

Valo. I have terrible news. Manny was killed in a raid on his home outside of Juarez. The DEA finally caught up with him. Come home.

Money's email had a link to a news story about the killing.

She clicked on the link. It showed a YouTube video of a group of DEA agents walking toward an ambulance. Manny's body was on a gurney, covered by a blood-stained sheet. They'd blurred out the faces of the DEA agents walking beside the body.

After several dark web internet searches, she found a local Mexican news report on the killing. The video footage remained the same, but they did not blur the faces of the DEA Agents.

Valeria scowled as she studied each of the Agent's faces closely, committing each to memory.

Fueled with anger, she rose and started walking again.

THE MOUSETRAP.

Caz and Shu had been walking around the western edge of the crop with their burners when they heard an ATV rapidly approaching.

One of the Bandido gang members was at the wheel. He drove with one hand on the steering wheel and a sub-machine gun, at the ready, in the other.

He slowed as soon as he saw them. Then he started spraying bullets at them through the open rollbars of the ATV.

Caz yelled, "Head for the trees!"

It was now broad daylight, so all Caz and Shu could do was bolt into the scrub next to the track and hide. There were few places to hide, so they just kept running back and forth between the trees and boulders as fast as they could. A constant hail of bullets smashed into the trees all around them.

The ATV played a game of Cat and Mouse through the dense bushland.

The driver would catch up to them, get out of the vehicle, and spray the area randomly with bullets. Caz and Shu would run and hide until they were out of view again. Then the driver would jump back into the ATV to resume the chase.

As they caught their breath behind a large boulder, Shu hatched a plan. She pointed to a grass clearing up ahead.

***

The bikie was bouncing along through the scrub and rocks on the ATV when he spotted Caz. He slowed.

Caz was sitting on the ground, right out in the open, in a grassy clearing. He waved at the ATV and shouted, "Hey bozo! Over here!"

The Bandido was suspicious, so he brought the ATV to a crawl. Caz just continued sitting cross-legged out in the open. "I wave my private parts at your Aunty," Caz taunted.

The ATV sped up, and the driver aimed the vehicle directly at Caz, who just continued to sit on the open ground waving at him.

The vehicle was about to mow him down when Caz suddenly rolled a few feet sideways.

Shu, hiding behind a tree nearby, pressed the button on a remote. A micro-second later, the Boar Buster dropped its large circular cage.

WHUMP!

The falling steel cage narrowly missed Caz as he rolled out of the way.

391

It caught the speeding ATV inside. With a savage force, the ATV crashed into the circle of steel mesh and bars. It dragged the steel structure across the ground. The heavy mesh cage tore and bent from the impact, wrapping itself around the vehicle like a ball of yarn.

The driver found himself trapped inside. Dazed.

Caz walked over to the ATV, reached in, and picked up the machine gun.

Caz whooped, "Looks like we caught ourselves a piggie!"

The driver slowly extracted himself from the mangled wreck and crawled over to a tree.

"Yes!" shouted Shu, as she stepped out from behind a tree.

Her joy was short-lived, as she heard the 'click' of a Glock pistol being cocked behind her.

Radovan Vukovic stood about ten feet behind her. He had his gun drawn. Point blank.

He shouted across to Caz, "You'd better drop that gun. Or I'll drop your little friend here."

Caz considered his chances, then reluctantly dropped the machine gun.

CHAPTER 89

KIDNAP AND KILL.

Radovan and the bikie roughly secured Caz and Shu's hands with cable ties. Shu gasped in pain as her old shoulder wound ripped open.

He turned to the injured bikie and ordered, "Let's walk back down to the location where their cars were parked. Near those sheds. I don't want to start another gun battle if we can avoid it. So, keep a close eye on these two. If they try anything stupid, kill them."

Radovan pointed his gun down the track toward the sheds and said, "Let's go."

Shu and Caz started walking, hands secured tightly behind their backs. Rad and the ATV driver hung back about fifty feet behind them, far enough to remain out of sight, but close enough to shoot them if needed.

***

Willow had spent ten minutes trying to stop the bleeding from the shotgun pellets that had winged her.

Thankfully, her thick clothing had stopped them from going too deep. The bloodstains made the wounds look far worse than they were. She forced down several painkillers from the first aid kit she'd found in the wreckage of her vehicle. Although she was in pain, she dragged the guy who she had poisoned with her blow darts and propped him up against a rock, so he didn't end up choking on his own vomit. He was in far worse shape than she was.

She heard footsteps approaching, then felt relief when she looked up and saw Freddie walking down the track toward her. Mud covered his face and most of his hair was badly singed. That relief turned to shock when she saw the bikie walking behind him, holding a staff with a menacing silver blade.

She desperately searched around for something to use as a weapon.

No luck.

The bikie kicked Freddie hard in the back, making him tumble to the ground. He pointed the weapon at Willow, making her back away toward the smoldering sheds. He pulled two cable-ties from his pocket and said, "Tie his hands behind his back. Don't try anything funny!"

Willow took the ties and secured Freddie's hands. The bikie leaned down to check that the bindings were tight.

Willow used the distraction to disarm him. She kicked at the staff and sent it flying into the first row of cannabis seedlings.

He stood and faced her.

Willow squared off into a boxing stance.

He looked confused for a moment, then burst out laughing. "What do you think you are going to do? Duke it out with me?" he said.

Willow nodded back confidently, which made him laugh even more.

"I have a policy," he sneered. "I don't fight women. The results are not usually, erm, good for them. Girlie, why don't you just sit the fuck down and join your friend?"

Willow took two quick steps forward and delivered a quick uppercut to his chin. He instinctively raised his arms, exposing his ribs. She drew back, rotated her torso and transferred her full bodyweight into a right cross that smashed into his ribcage. He slumped sideways as three of his ribs cracked, then steadied himself as he let out a low moan. Willow was far from finished.

She grabbed the back of his head and lifted her knee hard into his face, splitting his nose open. The momentum made him topple backwards as his head spun and his eyes rolled back. Then his legs gave out. As he fell to the ground, she kicked him hard, breaking more ribs as the blow reverberated right through to his liver.

"Those the results you were expecting?" She asked sarcastically.

He moaned in pain as she used some rope to bind his hands.

Willow untied Freddie and checked his wounds. Apart from a couple of deep cuts, he was mostly unscathed.

She cleaned the cuts and used a couple of butterfly closures to help stop the bleeding. He'd need stitches, but that could wait for now.

Willow was finishing bandaging Freddie when she saw Shu and Caz approaching along the edge of the crop.

"Thank god," said Willow. "I was worried. I heard lots of shooting over your side of the crop."

Her smile turned to a frown when she realized they had their hands tied.

Radovan stepped out from behind them. He leveled an assault rifle at Willow and Freddie and said, "Come and join your friends."

Rad pulled Freddie roughly over to Caz and Shu. He cable-tied them all together, then made them kneel on the ground beside the crop.

Rad turned when he heard someone moaning. One Bandido lay propped up against a rock near one of the burned out sheds. He was shivering as the poison from the blow darts wracked his body. He wasn't going anywhere.

Another was lying on his back nearby. Rad untied him. The guy stood painfully, nursing his cracked ribs.

Radovan barked. "Let's get samples from the crop. A mix of the large and small plants. As many as we can ram into the vehicles. I'll take the woman and the plants back over to the sub."

Over the next half an hour, Rad and the Bandidos loaded up a trailer on one of the two remaining ATVs with about fifty potted seedlings and mature plants. It was slow work for the two injured bikies. Then they tied

Willow into one of the rear seats of the vehicle. Rad forced a gag around her mouth.

Rad stepped up into the driver's seat of the first ATV and said, "You two check around here. Make sure we've left no evidence behind."

He pointed to the crop and said, "Grab as many seedlings and plants as you can fit into your vehicle. Then set fire to the rest of the crop. I'll see you back at the sub."

Rad pointed to Freddie, Caz and Shu and said, "You know what to do with these three. As I said. No evidence."

THE FLY-OVER.

The F35 jet arrived at Scherger exactly fifty-seven minutes after it flew out of RAAF Tindal. The pilot had faked several radio calls back to the Control Tower about how her 'engine test' was going.

Billy and Crensch paced nervously in front of an array of large monitors that covered one wall of Tindal's Situation Room. The F35 pilot's voice came over the sound system in the room.

"OK." the pilot said, "You won't believe what I'm seeing here. I'm going to share the imagery from the FCAM on the plane with you." Billy turned to Crensch and said, "That's the daylight camera view from her helmet's heads-up system."

The large screens in the room lit up with the pilot's view of RAAF Scherger's runway.

"We have a RAAF C-130 blocking the center of the runway," she reported. "It's tires look blown out. Definitely not a landing accident."

The FCAM view from the F35 shifted to Scherger's Control Tower, as she continued her report,

"Someone must have burned out the Control Tower. There are no flames or smoke, so it must have happened a while ago."

The jet's aerial view shifted to the Admin Buildings. Two German Shepherds were running around barking at the noise from the plane.

"No sign of people about. Just two canines. That C-130 is totally blocking the runway. Right in the middle," the pilot continued, "I can't land here. I'm going to head over to the second location. The crop. I'm already low on fuel."

Billy and Crensch watched the camera view as the jet tracked along the main road out of the base and across the Cannacom farm.

"I'm going to slow this the aircraft as much as I can go, without risking a stall," the pilot said.

Suddenly, the pilot gasped. "Are you seeing what I'm seeing here?"

"What the fuck is that?" Billy said, as he walked over the one of the large monitors on the wall.

Crensch asked the pilot, "Can you do another slow pass to get another angle?"

"Give me a minute. I can't go much slower than this, though. This aircraft is a racehorse –not a donkey," the pilot replied.

The camera vision next fly-past confirmed what they thought they saw. Three people were on their knees beside a green field. Arms tied behind their backs. Two men with rifles were standing behind them. It looked like an execution was about to take place. The men on the ground looked up at the jet as it flew low in the sky above them. One of them fired his rifle at the slow flying plane.

Billy asked, "Can you do anything to help with the situation on the ground? To take those guys out?"

"Not much," said the pilot. "I only have a 25mm GAU-22 rotary cannon and two JDAM guided bombs on board. But the rotary gun can't pick off those two guys on the ground. You'd risk killing all of them. The gun will fire off all of my rounds in no time at all. It's designed for bigger targets."

They all fell silent for a minute as they pondered the risk.

The pilot mused, "Look. Those guys don't know what I can do from up here. I can't shoot them, but maybe I can scare the crap out of them. If I unload all my rounds nearby, it will feel like Dante's Inferno down there on the ground."

The pilot paused and said, "Is that worth a try?"

More silence.

Crensch finally spoke up. "I think it's worth the risk." Billy nodded his agreement and said, "You have approval to fire."

The pilot sent the F35 into a slow, wide arc, bringing the jet around to the ideal course to strafe the ground nearby. Low and slow. As the jet flew past, the pilot pressed the 'FIRE' button. Hundreds of rounds spat out of the plane.

The ground around the crop shook like an earthquake as the large caliber rounds punched into the ground just fifty feet away from Caz, Freddie and Shu.

The pilot brought the jet around to get another view from the FCAM. The Bandido shooters were still standing their ground.

"Shit. Tough mothers. They aren't moving," the pilot said.

"Fuck!" Billy shouted at the monitors in frustration.

"I have one last party trick we can try," said the pilot. "I'm really low on fuel, so this will be our last shot." The jet did another slow loop. As it approached the crop, the pilot put the jet into a steep incline, the nose lifted, exposing its belly to the people below. The two inboard weapons doors slid open on the jet, revealing the two massive bombs inside.

It had the desired effect.

The two Bandidos watched as the approaching jet's bomb doors open, then sprinted to their ATV. They drove over to the remaining parked 4WDs and shot out their tires, then sped away from the crop.

***

As the ATV raced away, the pilot said, "I'm going to follow these guys, to make sure they don't have second thoughts and come back. Then I need to bug out back to Tindal. Unless you want me to refuel at the commercial airport in Weipa."

"That's a hard 'No'," Billy said. "If we land an F35 unannounced at the local airport, the media and the aviation authorities will be all over us."

The pilot said, "OK. I'm going to harass the shit out of these guys on the ground for another five minutes, then I'll return to Tindal."

The pilot switched off the FCAM feed. The large monitors in the Tindal Situation Room went blank.

Billy picked up a phone and barked, "Get me a long-range chopper. One of the new Blackhawks. We need to get over to Scherger. Fast. And find me a route with a couple of refueling points along the way −no −it will need to be a chopper. We won't be landing any sort of plane at Scherger today."

Billy turned to Crensch and said, "Get your stuff together. It will take Air Traffic a while to work out a route to get us that distance in a helo. Blackhawks aren't designed to fly such a long distance. We'll need to do one or two refueling stops."

***

They were leaving the room when the large screens on the walls suddenly lit up with the view from the F35's FCAM again. They both stopped and looked. The view was from above the river.

There was a strange-looking vessel moored next to an island on a bend in the river.

The pilot reported, "I was about to bug out −and I saw where these guys are heading. If I'm not mistaken, that's an 'effing submarine waiting out the back of that island."

Crensch looked at the screen. He pressed a button to freeze-frame the FCAM image. He saw Radovan dragging a black woman along a short dock toward the submarine. Three other men were unloading tall green plants from an ATV trailer onto a trolley.

Crensch said, "That's got to be Willow." Billy peered at the blurry image and agreed. Crensch moved closer to the screen. He peered at the guy dragging Willow. "Fuck me. It can't be! The last time I saw that guy, he was walking out of the cartel meeting in Miami. We think it's Radovan Vukovic. A Serbian national who's the head of the biggest cartel in Europe."

Billy spoke to the pilot. "The situation has changed. Can you send us the exact coordinates for that sub? Then I want you to do anything you can to stop it from departing –short of blowing it up. There's a hostage onboard."

The pilot replied, "No can do. I'm at the limit of my combat range. I'll already be running on vapor to get back to Tindal. I'll need to refuel if I need to hang around here."

Billy was torn, but he relented and said, "OK. Request an emergency landing and refuel at Weipa Airport. Just tell them that the runway at Scherger is down for maintenance."

"OK. Contacting local Air Traffic Control," replied the pilot, "The turnaround should take about forty minutes."

Billy turned to Crensch and grimaced. "This is about to go very public –and there's nothing we can do about it."

Crensch said, "If it's going to blow up into a political shit-storm, I think your father should come over with us on the chopper. We might need some political muscle over there when the press get a hold of this."

Billy said, "I'll track him down."

***

Down on the dock, Radovan didn't even notice the jet pass by. He was too busy supervising the loading of Willow and all the cannabis plants onto the sub.

He yelled at the Indonesian workers, asking them to move faster. Time was running out.

He dragged Willow along the short dock. The cable ties cut into her hands as he forced her down a short ladder into the narco-sub's cargo hold.

The cramped hold was dimly lit and stunk of body odor and burnt cooking oil. Willow kicked him hard. Rad punched her hard in the mouth and she fell limp. Once inside, he used more ties to secure Willow to a large water pipe sticking out of the hull wall.

The crew began lowering the plants from the crop into the hold. They started with the tallest and heaviest plants, carefully placing them to keep the vessel balanced.

Back at Tindal, Billy called his father's cellphone. It rang for a long time. The Ambassador was occupied elsewhere on the airfield.

When he finally answered, Billy said, "Things are blowing up over near Scherger. This is about to go very public. We're going to take a helicopter out there. There's a plane blocking the runway at Scherger. We should be airborne in the next hour. You'll need to join us to help deal with the local fallout."

"OK," said his father. "I'll need thirty minutes, anyway. I'll be bringing two extra passengers. Can you fit them?"

"Yes," said Billy. "I'll call up a second chopper."

Tindal RAAF base shared a runway with the public airport in the tourist town of Katherine.

A sleek black private jet, chartered by the CIA, had just touched down from the USA.

It taxied to a halt close to the RAAF perimeter fence. After a few minutes, the door of the plane slowly dropped open.

The Ambassador's vehicle pulled up next to the jet.

Two men in black suits and dark sunglasses stepped off the plane.

The Ambassador shook their hands, then the staff ushered them straight into the waiting vehicle.

The vehicle turned and sped off toward the RAAF base, where two Blackhawks stood waiting for an immediate take-off.

CHAPTER 91

McKenzie's Dock.

After the two Bandido executioners jumped into their ATV and fled, Freddie, Caz, and Shu remained sprawled on the ground, shaking in shock,

Their ears were still ringing from the deafening roar of the F35's payload of machine-gun fire.

Freddie yelled, "You guys, OK?" They could hardly hear him.

Shu twisted her arms behind her back and said, "I can't get these ties to budge." The three of them slowly got to their feet and staggered over to the smoldering remains of the sheds. They rummaged amongst the cold ashes, trying to find something sharp. Freddie found a broken bottle and used it to hack at the thick cable ties.

As he hacked at the bindings, a walkie-talkie sprang to life with chatter. One of the Bandidos had dropped it. The one that had been writhing in pain from Willow's blow-darts. They listened as they overheard the guy driving the ATV talking to Radovan.

"We are on our way back to the sub," the thug said, "Along the riverbank. Maybe twenty minutes away from the McKenzie's Dock."

Radovan asked, "Did you get the job done?"

The Bandido didn't want to answer. He just repeated, "We are –maybe –twenty minutes away from the sub." Then he threw the walkie-talkie into the scrub.

Back at the crop, Freddie finally cut the ties that were binding them. They considered their options.

Freddie said, "We don't have any working vehicles left. So we can't follow them. I doubt we could catch up to them, anyway."

Caz said, "We still have the tank. It's slow, but it's amphibious, so we could travel directly upstream. Much quicker than land. They said they were going to McKenzie's Dock. That must be where they've taken Willow. There's a chance we could catch up to them that way."

Shu paused and said, "Did that guy on the radio just say something about a submarine? A bloody submarine? Here?"

Caz fired up the Chinese tank again. He figured the trip to McKenzie's Dock would take about thirty minutes if they really thrashed the unit's 350 horsepower Dongfeng diesel engine.

They jumped onboard and headed down toward the riverbank.

At the river's edge, Caz experimented with the Chinese controls and finally got it into amphibious mode.

Shortly after, they were ploughing through the water back toward Weipa, zig-zagging wildly at first, as Caz wrestled with the foreign controls.

Driving the amphibious beast was nothing like driving a boat.

***

At McKenzie's Dock, the narco-sub sat low in the water, its deck just inches about the water level of the river.

The vessel wasn't really fully submersible. It traveled just a few feet below the surface when it was at full cruising speed, deploying a short floating snorkel to suck down air for the engines and passengers. Once it slipped below the waves, it was almost impossible to detect.

The Captain was impatient. The sub was exposed in the shallow waters of the estuary. He wanted to get out of there as quickly as possible. Once they were in the open sea, it would be impossible to follow them. He stood on the deck, shouting at the deckhands to load the plants faster. Loading the living plants was proving to be a slow task, compared to the bricks of cannabis, cocaine and heroin they usually carried.

The Captain grew even more angry when Rad asked him to wait until the remaining Bandidos arrived with more plants to load into the hold.

Inside the sub's dimly lit hold, Willow squirmed and pulled on the ties holding her to the back wall. It was stiflingly hot. Sweat made her ties slippery, but she was bound too tightly to pull her wrists free. The shotgun pellet wounds in her leg and shoulder hurt like hell.

The deck hands had loaded all of all the plants from Radovan's ATV, filling half of the sub's cargo space. After they stopped loading the plants, they'd all headed up on deck for a welcome breath of fresh air. The only noise from the deck above her was Rad and the Captain, constantly shouting at each other.

The hold of the sub was rammed with pots filled with plants, ranging from tiny seedlings to mature plants a few feet tall.

Willow had lugged plenty of the larger pots during the past year of planting. She knew that the bigger pots had a tendency to become brittle after too much exposure to the scorching Queensland sun. She'd cut her hands on the sharp plastic edges many times.

Willow used her feet to sort through the pots nearby until she came across one that was sun-bleached to a dull gray color. She gave the pot a mighty kick, and the plastic shattered. She dragged a large plastic shard over with her toe, then used it to hack away at the cables behind her back.

The shouting on deck stopped when the other Bandidos finally arrived.

A few minutes later, the deckhands came back below deck to load more pots into the cargo hold. Willow continued to quietly hack away at her bindings while she backed up against the wall in the shadows.

She was getting close to cutting through her ties when the Captain climbed down in the hold with two crew members.

They opened a large metal lockbox near the base of the ladder and pulled out a menacing, dark-gray machine gun. They hauled out a heavy belt of fifty caliber ammunition. Then they struggled to lift it up the ladder to the deck.

She could hear metal clanking as they mounted the gun on a turret welded onto the deck. The heavy duty machine-gun was the Captain's insurance policy if things ever went pear-shaped.

Back on the dock, Radovan shook hands with the two remaining Bandidos. They made a quick exit on the two ATVs. He walked back to the submarine and stood on the deck next to the machine gun. The captain signalled they were ready to leave.

Radovan loaded the belt of massive bullets into the gun, then checked its firing mechanism. The crew members started to remove the ropes tethering the sub to the dock.

Below deck, Willow was still having a hard time cutting through her bindings. She felt dismay as the diesel engines of the sub kicked over and she could hear the crew on deck casting off the final ropes.

Soon the sub would be out to sea, and she'd be lost forever.

THE ESCAPE.

Over at Weipa Airport, the F35 pilot had to play a delicate game with the local re-fuelers. She had an air of 'business as usual', but her gut was busting to get airborne over the river again.

To save time, she didn't take on a full load of fuel. There were annoying delays while the airport staff double-checked the fuel grade for the jet. There was a longer delay while they worked out who would pay the tab for the fuel. For an F35, a half of a tank of aviation fuel cost around $10,000.

After checking into Tindal, someone patched the pilot through to the Blackhawks that were racing towards Scherger. She reported in.

"The police radio band has lots of chatter about the jet landing. I heard a report of smoke in the sky out near Scherger. There's talk about sending a firetruck out that way to have a look because the police are too tied up with the Fun Run. I don't think the media has the story yet."

***

By the time the F35 got airborne again, the narco-sub had cast off and was speeding toward the river's deep-water channel.

The pilot reported in to the Blackhawks again.

"I'm airborne. Over the river again. The sub is heading for deep water. What do you want me to do?"

Billy said, "You can't blow it up. There's a civilian hostage on board. Can you slow it down?"

The pilot said, "Roger. I can. But I don't think it will stop them. The estuary gets too wide and deep up ahead."

Billy replied, "Do whatever you can. I don't think we can keep the lid on this anymore."

Inside the cockpit, the pilot set the targeting computer to a point about 500 feet ahead of the moving sub. She released a precision-guided 2,000-lb JDAM bomb. Lasers guided it to the spot.

BOOM!

Over at the Weipa Fun Run site, the whole town turned and looked west towards the docks as the sound of a massive explosion rang out.

The JDAM explosion created a massive crater in the shallow riverbed of the estuary, generating a huge wave of water that smashed into the side of the submarine.

Radovan gripped the machine gun to avoid getting washed off the deck. The captain steered the submarine violently to the right, trying to avoid the blast area.

Below decks, the floor of the cargo hold tilted wildly. A wall of large, heavy potted cannabis plants broke free and slid wildly across floor crushing one of the crew members.

The force of the turn pulled Willow violently away from the side wall of the cargo hold. Her ties cut deep into her wrists as the floor tilted to a forty-five-degree angle. The captain executed another wild change of direction. The sub's floor slanted wildly in the opposite direction.

The force of the turn pulled Willow away from the side wall of the hold, then she slammed straight back into the wall as the vessel levelled. A sliding wall of heavy pot plants smashed into her, pinning her to the wall.

A deckhand, near the ladder, rolled around in pain, his left leg crushed by a flying pot. Another lay unconscious at the other end of the hold, blood seeping from a gash on his head.

The force of the wild movement winded Willow, but it finally broke her hands free. More blood seeped from her deeply cut wrists.

As the submarine plowed through the waves, the remaining crew in the cargo hold scurried about in a desperate panic. They tried to use more ropes to secure the larger plants.

Willow slowly edged along the side wall of the hold, keeping to the shadowed areas. She waited until the crew was at the far end of the hold, then she scurried toward the short ladder, and up to the deck above. She moaned from the pain in her wrists, leg and shoulder as she climbed its rungs.

When she reached the open hatch to the deck, the bright sunlight blinded her for a moment.

As her eyesight adjusted, she could see Radovan at the front of the sub's deck clutching onto the machine gun turret. The wild machinations of the sub drenched him in sea spray.

He scowled as Willow pulled herself up onto the deck. Taking hold of the machine gun's stock, he swiftly rotated it in her direction. Willow limped across the deck and hid behind the snorkel unit housing. A spray of bullets smashed into the snorkel housing, ripping it away from the deck. She was exposed.

Radovan pointed the gun straight at her. He steadied to take another shot, but the sub's deck tilted wildly again.

The sub was now plowing straight toward a mangrove lined mud flat next to one of the town's main docks. The captain swerved sharply to the left, to move back toward the deep-water channel.

The second spray of Radovan's bullets missed Willow as Radovan struggled to keep his footing next to the gun turret.

Willow didn't want to risk a third round.

She crawled to the edge of the deck, gulped down a deep breath, and rolled into the water.

She swam underwater until her lungs were bursting. Bullets peppered the water around her as Radovan continued firing. Her injured body screamed in pain. She surfaced and gulped another lung full of air and then continued swimming underwater.

Thankfully, the water became shallow. Her hands felt the murky bottom of a mudflat on the edge of the river. She lifted her head above water and quickly sucked in some more air.

Willow got to her feet. She tried running, but the mud just sucked her feet down. She could barely move at a crawling pace. Back on the submarine, Radovan was scanning the river looking for her.

***

All the docks in Weipa had gigantic signs reading; 'BEWARE. CROCODILES'.

Several large saltwater crocodiles were basking in the morning sun alongside the mudflat. They slowly raised their sleepy heads as they heard the noise of Willow's frantic threshing and slow footsteps nearby. The sweet scent of her bleeding wrists washed toward them.

Willow gasped as, with a strong swish of their tails, they all propelled themselves across the mudflat toward her. She stopped and braced.

The crocs scattered as more of of Radovan's bullets smashed into the surrounding mudflat. The rounds ripped apart two of the smaller crocs, then the bigger ones beat a quick retreat.

As the sub lurched and rolled in the waves of the estuary, Radovan stood on the deck, angrily spraying shots in Willow's direction. The shots slowly worked their way closer to her as he improved his aim. A line of the bullets was heading directly toward her. She was firmly stuck in the mud, unable to move.

***

Radovan stopped firing when he heard shots ringing out across from the opposite side of the river.

Bullets ricochetted off the hull of the sub as the amphibious Chinese tank rounded a bend nearby.

Caz was in the driver's seat, struggling with the controls. The big diesel engine was screaming.

Freddie was manning the tank's main gun, firing at Radovan. His aim was terrible. The rise and fall of the waves sent most of the bullets in random directions, but he still got Rad's attention. Radovan shifted his aim from Willow to the amphibious vehicle, now approaching the sub fast from across the river.

Freddie and Caz dropped to the safety of the tank's rear crew deck as bullets smashed into the front of it. Caz wrestled with the steering as the tank ploughed through the waves, but he couldn't really see where they were heading.

***

At a remote airfield hundreds of miles away, the Blackhawk choppers were parked for refuelling. It was the first stop on its way as they raced the 1,000 miles over to Weipa.

Inside the chopper, Billy, Crensch and the Ambassador stared at a small monitor with a feed from the FCAM on the F35. They were looking at an aerial view of the main Weipa docks area. The narco-sub was maneuvering back toward the river's deep central channel. Billy gasped as the ZBD-03 tank appeared from down the river.

"Is that what I think it is?" Billy said.

"Yes," said Crensch, "from its markings –it looks –no it can't be –Chinese Army. Huh?"

The Ambassador rubbed his temples and said, "God Almighty. When are the Russians going to arrive?"

The F35 pilot said, "From what I can see up here, the amphibious vehicle is firing at the sub, not defending it. I have one JDAM bomb left to use. What do you want me to do?"

"Hold your fire," Billy said. "Let's see what's happening here first."

The FCAM view showed the amphibious tank steadily pushing across the river on a collision course with the sub. It was being slowly ripped apart by a barrage of fire from Radovan's gun.

***

Freddie, Caz, and Shu huddled on the tank's rear deck. Caz had his foot pressed down hard on the throttle, but didn't dare look up to see where they were heading.

Bullets ripped shards of metal off the front of the tank. Freddie popped up to fire back at the sub, but nearly got his head blown off.

Caz was madly scanning the Chinese controls on the tank. Pushing buttons at random. He pushed one button and all six smoke cannister launchers fired.

"Erm, slight problem," Caz said. "I got this thing into Amphibious Mode when we hit the river –and I can just about steer it –but I haven't quite figured out how to make it stop on the water. On the land, it was easy. I just used the brakes. This thing is a bit of a runaway train right now."

The tank ploughed across the river, still on a collision course with the narco-sub.

Over on the mudflat, Willow wasn't making much progress. Her feet were stuck in the mud like an insect on flypaper. Taking a cue from the crocs, she got onto her belly and snaked across the top of the mud. It was slow going, but at least she was finally moving toward dry land.

Every few minutes Radovan would swing his gun toward her and take potshots at her. Thankfully, the explosions in the mud around her kept the crocs at bay.

The F35 did another slow fly past along the river.

The jet's FCAM showed the Chinese tank surging straight toward the sub, which was now starting to turn to avoid a collision.

A few hundred miles to the west, the Blackhawk was airborne again. Billy, watching the FCAM feed, yelled to the F35 pilot, "Can you shift your camera view closer to that mudflat – over to the east? Next to the town's main dock."

The pilot looped the jet around and did a low run closer to the town's shoreline. As the mudflat came into view, she paused the video image on the screen. It showed the body of a black woman, snaking prone across the surface of the mud like a Commando.

Crensch said, "That's got to be Willow. She must have got off the sub."
Billy sighed in relief. "That changes the ballgame."

Back on the deck of the sub, Radovan stopped shooting. The Chinese tank was now only fifty feet from the sub, churning through the water at top speed. Realizing the inevitable, he grabbed the gun turret and braced for an imminent collision.

On the tank, Caz yelled, "Hold on to something –this isn't going to be pretty." Freddie and Shu grabbed onto their seats and braced themselves for the impact.

KERAASCH!

They plowed into the side of the narco-sub.

The F35's FCAM caught the impact. The sub's captain had made some progress on his turn, so the tank hit at an angle. The sub's hull buckled, but held together. Like a ping-pong ball, the tank bounced off the sub. It veered toward the trees on the Weipa township side of the river.

Caz was still frantically trying to sort out how to slow it down. No luck.

Willow finally made it to dry land. She winced as she watched the collision back in the middle of the river. Two giant crocodiles snaked toward her, so she climbed up onto some large concrete sea-wall blocks and desperately caught her breath.

The main town pier and the seawall were connected. From her vantage point, she saw the tank was now ploughing out-of-control across the river. Straight toward her. She scrambled higher up the blocks, now frantically waving at Caz.

***

Back on the sub, the crew were detaching the gun and taking it below deck. It was time to leave.

Rad had grabbed an automatic assault rifle and was still sending angry sprays of bullets toward the tank as it careened toward the shoreline. Freddie and Shu ducked low as more bullets ricocheted around in the rear deck.

Caz frantically punched buttons, trying to work out how to stop the tank, but most of the controls had been blown to pieces.

The main town dock loomed into view as the out-of-control tank surged through the waves. Speeding straight toward it.

CHAPTER 93

THAT SINKING FEELING.

When the controls on the dashboard of the tank started smoking, Caz yelled, "Sorry guys –I think it's time for a swim."

The tank was making a beeline straight for Weipa's main public dock. Radovan was still pumping a stream of bullets into the tank's rear deck.

"We're heading toward the dock's refueling station –and I can't stop this thing." Freddie and Shu popped up and had a look. They didn't need convincing. The three of them plunged into the river.

BOOM!

A massive explosion rocked the dock as the tank slammed into some bowsers and a large gasoline storage tank down near the waterline.

Caz, Freddie and Shu dragged themselves onto the seawall beside the burning dock. Willow clambered down to join them, panting. They hugged and then fell exhausted onto the concrete blocks.

***

When the dock exploded, Radovan had given up on shooting. He'd thrown his gun overboard, then climbed inside the sub and closed the main hatch to the deck.

The sub was speeding up toward the safety of the river's deep-water channel.

The F35 was on another low-level run. Billy, still watching on the Blackhawk's FCAM screen, gave the pilot an order.

"Take that sub out before we lose them," he said.

"Roger Wilco!" the pilot said.

The pilot switched to infra-red mode and locked her targeting computer onto the heat signature from the sub's engines. She pressed a button on her joystick and said, "Bomb gone."

Seconds later, the narco-sub exploded into a cloud of tiny pieces. The pungent smell of burning cannabis and diesel drifted across most of Weipa as the plants onboard were vaporized.

***

Willow, Caz, Freddie and Shu watched from the seawall as a mighty explosion ripped the narco-sub apart. Willow was covered from head to toe in murky slime from the crawl across mudflat.

"You look a mess," said Shu, as she tended to Willow's bleeding wrists.

Willow looked at herself and laughed. Yes, she resembled a strange alien mud monster.

Smoke was billowing skyward from the explosion at the main dock. They heard loud sirens wailing as a firetruck and police squad cars rolled up in the carpark.

Moments later, the local Police Superintendent poked his head over the side of the dock.

He boomed down to them on the seawall, "OK –you four hooligans –get up here NOW!"

Busted.

CHAPTER 94

A LONG ARREST SHEET.

An hour later, the police formally arrested Willow, Caz, Freddie, and Shu at the docks.

The police Superintendent wasn't really sure what the charges would be. He thought the wreckage of the tank that smashed into the dock was a good starting point for a very long arrest sheet.

Before taking them to the lock-up, the local police took them to the medical center to get their injuries treated. A couple of burly policemen hovered at the door as an ER nurse stitched and wrapped their wounds.

Caz was miraculously unscathed. Freddie and Willow sat in the corner while the nurse finished working on Shu. Willow's wrists were a mess, but had been carefully bandaged to allow some space for handcuffs.

The Superintendent entered the treatment room and asked the nurse, "Are these guys OK to travel yet?"

The nurse asked, "What the hell happened to them? They look like they've come from a war-zone."

The nurse pointed to Willow and said, "I pulled some shotgun pellets from her shoulder and her leg. They weren't deep, though. Her clothing slowed them a lot. She'll be fine. We gave her some clean clothes."

The nurse pointed to Freddie and said, "That one looks like he's been in a cat fight. Maybe several cat fights. More scratches than skin on him. Stitched up his shoulder and a deep leg wound. They looked like knife injuries to me."

She turned to Shu and said, "This one has a nasty graze from a bullet on her shoulder. I stitched her up and gave her an antibiotic shot, too."

The nurse stood, hand on hips, and looked at the four of them. "Hmm —I guess they could go. I'll pack you up a box of painkillers. They are going to need more of them soon."

The Superintendent eye-balled the four of them and said, "Good! You guys need to come with me. We've had a radio report from a car we sent out to Cannacom. We sent them out to investigate a fire. They found a lot more than that. I have so many questions I need to get answered out there!"

He motioned to a couple of cops standing outside the door and said, "Cuff these four and get them into a car."

***

A flotilla of Weipa police vehicles and Cannacom 4WDs had descended on the Back Block.

The Superintendent was on a rampage. Every few minutes, his 'crime scene' expanded dramatically. When the police arrived from town, the scene around the crop looked like a standard drug bust. An illegal crop of weed. The crime scene grew as they discovered discarded high-tech military weapons and several wrecked ATVs.

The Superintendent went apoplectic when his detectives found the bodies of several dead SSA soldiers, all wearing Chinese Army uniforms, and a dead bikie wearing Bandido leathers.

Wide-eyed, the police had collected weapons from around the crop. Assault rifles. Machine guns. Used military smoke cannisters. Night vision goggles. A mud-covered Chinese RPG case.

Willow, Freddie, Caz and Shu stood handcuffed and helpless next to a police 4WD.

The irate police Superintendent stomped over to them and announced, "You guys are going away for a long time. There must be 2,000 plants in this crop. Illegal weapons. Potential murder charges. And I haven't even got started yet. What the fuck were you thinking?"

Catherine Sneesby walked over, holding several potted seedlings. She reveled in Willow's problems as she dropped the plants unceremoniously at Willow's feet.

"So many breaches of company policy." Sneesby sneered, "You'll never work as a Botanist again."

Kip Norman, the Cannacom CEO, stood in wonderment at the edge of the crop. He was thinking, *"How the hell are all these plants still alive?"*

***

They all looked west as the rumbling sound of two approaching military helicopters filled the sky.

Two sleek RAAF Blackhawks came to a halt above the crop. They hovered for a minute, looking for clear spaces to land.

One Blackhawk landed in a grassy clearing beside the crop. The other continued to maneuver, looking for another space to set down further away. It gingerly descended nearby, trying to avoid the wreckage of the ATV that had smashed into the badly mangled Boar Buster.

As the rotors on the first Blackhawk wound down, the side door slid open. Three Australian soldiers, holding assault rifles, alighted and immediately moved to take up protective perimeter positions around the chopper.

Major Thomas Crensch and Colonel Billy Blagg stepped down to the ground. Ambassador Blagg, in a black business suit, stepped down and joined them. They marveled at the cannabis crop, and the surrounding destruction, for a few moments.

Three Chinook helicopters appeared in the sky. They criss-crossed the site for a moment, then they peeled off toward Scherger base.

430

Crensch and Billy walked over to police Superintendent.

"Colonel William Blagg. ADF." Billy said, introducing himself.

The police officer apprehensively shook hands. "Superintendent Ronnie O'Tuku, Weipa District Police." he said.

Billy turned to introduce Crensch.

"This is Major Thomas Crensch representing –erm."

Crensch stepped forward and cut in, "The US Army. Pleased to meet you, Superintendent O'Tuku."

Billy turned to Jason and said, "And this is Jason Blagg. The Australian Ambassador to the USA."

The Superintendent turned defensive. This was more top brass than he'd met in his entire life.

He asked, "So what gives you the right to land military choppers directly into my active crime scene? Under which authority do you think you are acting?"

The Ambassador stepped forward and said, "This might be a good time to make a call to your boss down in Brisbane. Commissioner Jeff Matushka –if I'm not mistaken." He handed the cop a satellite phone.

"I've already keyed in his direct number," the Ambassador said.

They waited while the Superintendent pressed the Send button and made the call. He had to shout over the sound of the second chopper, still slowly landing beside the Boar Buster.

After less than a minute on the line, the cop handed the phone back to Jason. The Superintendent signaled to his local detectives to head back to their 4WD police vehicles.

"You have the crime scene until nine am tomorrow morning," he said angrily, "then this will revert to a local police matter."

The Superintendent walked over to one of the Police 4WDs nearby. He grabbed Willow, still in cuffs, and pulled her toward the back door. He shouted, "Round the others up –and let's get out of here."

The Ambassador stepped forward and said, "Not so fast. We will need to have them remain here for questioning."

The Superintendent replied, "The drug charges are a local jurisdictional matter. This crop is the biggest illegal cannabis bust in Queensland Police history. I'm taking them with me. They'll still be in the lock-up in town in the morning, if you need them. I doubt they'll get bail for a bust this size."

Kip Norman stepped forward and introduced himself. "Kip Norman. CEO of Cannacom."

"I see this differently," Kip said, "I think you are arresting four of my employees for growing a crop on land –if I know my farm survey –and I can assure you I do –that is covered by Cannacom's Medicinal Growers license with the Australian Government."

Kip pointed toward the river.

"Our farm allotment goes all the way down to the river. We just never extended the farm all the way down there. The terrain was way too rough," he said.

Billy added, "And, at that point, the farm joins the border fence of RAAF Base Scherger. I guess that technically means this acreage is far from any form of public land."

The Ambassador held up the satellite phone again and said, "You want to check that with your boss?"

The Superintendent relented. He signaled to a detective to remove the cuffs from Willow, Caz, Freddie and Shu, then he angrily slammed the door on his 4WD, and the convoy of police vehicles drove away.

Willow walked over to Billy, Jason and Crensch. She gave Billy and Jason each a huge hug. She turned to Crensch. He rubbed his jaw and said, "You going to sock me in the mouth again?" She smiled and shook his hand.

Willow asked, "So –what happens to us from here? Are we all going to do time in a jail somewhere?"

The Ambassador grinned, and said, "Far from it. We agreed a working plan on the chopper flight over. And we've cleared it with the Australian and US Governments."

Crensch added, "The turmoil in the drug trade is causing too much unrest globally. Friendly Governments are under fire. What remains of the cartels is out of control and they're shifting their focus to synthetic drugs. All of which are way more dangerous. We need to restore some order. Fast."

The Ambassador said, "So, we've decided we are going to reintroduce cannabis to the world. Slowly. Using your resistant strain of plants. The better of two evils, I suppose."

He turned to Kip Norman and said, "It looks like you, and your shareholders, are about to become very wealthy people." Then he added, "But it will be a joint effort, that will be highly coordinated by the Australian Government, the US DEA and, I suppose, eventually the UN."

Crensch turned to Willow and said, "As we move forward, you'll be working with a Specialist DEA technical team. Headed by one of our best qualified operatives. You may have met him before."

He looked across to the second Blackhawk as its rotors whirred to a stop. The side door slid open.

Tezz stepped out.

CHAPTER 95

TEZZ.

Willow's knees buckled when she recognized Tezz walking from the chopper. She gasped and dropped to the grass. Crensch reached down and lifted her up.

She turned to him and said, "Wha –?"

Then she turned and limped toward Tezz, fighting against the pain of her wounded leg.

They met at the edge of the crop and just looked at each other in silence. Tezz said, "I'm SO sorry, babe. I know what all of this has meant to you."

Willow tensed up. She slapped him hard in the face.

Tears welled up in her eyes as she stammered, "How. Could. You. Do. That. To. Me?

Tezz looked her hard in the eyes and said, "Someone completely exposed my DEA cover. All the way back to you in Bulgaria and your family here. Big M and the cartels –it was only a matter of time before they'd come for you too. Like they did with my mother. I just couldn't risk it. If I was 'dead', you were no longer a threat to them. I had no other options."

Willow asked, "Why couldn't you tell me?"

"You know it doesn't work that way," Tezz said. "My only chance was finally to bring down Big M in Juarez. Otherwise, we would have spent our whole lives together looking over our shoulders. Wondering if some hit-man would be sent to kill us, or our families."

He wrapped his arms around her neck and moved her face close to his.

Tezz said, "But I got him Wills. All the fighting amongst the cartels finally brought him out into the open. Big M died when we arrested him at a safe-house outside Juarez. He's gone –forever. We found computers at the scene, with lots of information, so the DEA are going after his father in Miami, and his sister Valeria, too."

He lightly kissed her on the forehead and said, "We're free, Wills. Free. And I've had enough of all this law enforcement crap. I just want my 'Meredith' back. The girl I fell in love with. The wide-eyed girl in Zurich in the white lab coat."

He stared deeply into her eyes and said, "If you'll have me."

They held each other's gaze silently for a full minute. Then she reached around his waist and slowly pulled him close to her.

She kissed him gently and whispered,

"You always had a way with the girls, McDreamy."

EPILOGUE.

Tezz and Willow were inseparable for the rest of the day, while the military team poured over the evidence around the crop and down at the Hydro Station. A female medic from one chopper gave her a spare clean t-shirt and shot of powerful painkiller to help with the increasing pain in her leg and shoulder.

After a couple of hours, they slowly made their way down to the river to get away from everyone. Willow limped with an arm around Tezz's shoulder for support.

Crensch and the Blaggs were focused on quelling the media and political shit-storm. Kip Norman took Caz, Freddie and Shu back up to the main Cannacom farm to talk to them about their new roles in the business. He'd fired Catherine Sneesby, effective immediately, down by Willow's crop. She had to walk all the way back up to the farm, through the Briar, to collect her belongings.

Willow and Tezz lay in the grass by the Embley riverbank as the sun set.

Tezz picked a tiny yellow and red wildflower and placed it behind her ear. The sounds of birds and insects preparing for the night to arrive filled the air.

He gently kissed her on the cheek and looked at the little yellow flower, "Yellow Bush Pea –from the Fabaceae Family, if I'm not mistaken," he said.

She smiled and teased, "Good guess. We might make a Blackfella out of you one day."

Tezz looked at the river and trees and laid back on the grass, looking up at the clear blue Australian sky.

"I could get used to living here," he mused.

The peaceful silence around them was broken by the sharp sound of a bullet being chambered into a rifle.

Willow and Tezz looked across and saw Valeria.

She was caked in mud, with cuts and scratches all over her body. Her ankle gave out as she stepped toward them. At the water's edge, she painfully propped herself up against a gum tree. She slowly raised her rifle at them.

Valeria looked at Willow and sneered, "You –bitch."

Then she shifted her gaze across to Tezz.

Valeria slowly studied his face, then stammered, "I know you. I saw you in the video. You were in Juarez."

She frowned and said, "You –you –killed my brother."

Tezz instinctively moved his body in front of Willow to protect her.

Valeria aimed the gun squarely at Tezz's chest.

There was a stirring in the water behind her.

A small ripple spread out across the river. The water's surface exploded, as 2,000 lbs of angry saltwater crocodile launched onto the shore.

Its giant jaws latched onto Valeria's leg.

Valeria dropped the rifle and let out a blood-curdling scream, as McVee dragged her back into the river.

Her screams continued as she slowly disappeared beneath the surface.

Before becoming an author, Tony Sharples spent decades working in global marketing and content creation for brands like Coca-Cola, Pepsi, Heineken and IBM. He also likes to dabble in screenwriting.

The genesis of this book is when he sat down and created a list of impossible scenarios to write a new book about. The list included things like: What would happen if the oceans dried up? What would happen if the moon disappeared? What would the world be like if GPS suddenly stopped functioning?

This book came from the topic: What would happen if the global crop of cannabis suddenly died?

His next two book projects, co-written with his sister Julie, will focus on Australia's bushranging past, in an epic series of stories he describes as "Yellowstone meets Ned Kelly". The multi-part story centers on Australia's biggest ever gold bullion robbery in the 1860s, then follows the exploits of the bushranger Ben Hall during his final year alive.

www.tonysharples.com

www.ingramcontent.com/pod-product-compliance
Lightning Source LLC
Chambersburg PA
CBHW011026190726
48290CB00011B/2716